A *Tyranny of Petticoats*

A Tyranny of Petticoats

15 Stories of
BELLES, BANK ROBBERS
& OTHER BADASS GIRLS

EDITED BY

Jessica Spotswood

CANDLEWICK PRESS

Compilation and introduction copyright © 2016 by Jessica Spotswood
"Mother Carey's Table" copyright © 2016 by J. Anderson Coats
"The Journey" copyright © 2016 by Marie Lu
"Madeleine's Choice" copyright © 2016 by Jessica Spotswood
"Los Destinos" copyright © 2016 by Leslye Walton
"High Stakes" copyright © 2016 by Andrea Cremer
"The Red Raven Ball" copyright © 2016 by Caroline Tung Richmond
"Pearls" copyright © 2016 by Beth Revis
"Gold in the Roots of the Grass" copyright © 2016 by Marissa Meyer
"The Legendary Garrett Girls" copyright © 2016 by Y. S. Lee
"The Color of the Sky" copyright © 2016 by Elizabeth Gatland
"Bonnie *and* Clyde" copyright © 2016 by Saundra Mitchell
"Hard Times" copyright © 2016 by Katherine Longshore
"City of Angels" copyright © 2016 by Lindsay Smith
"Pulse of the Panthers" copyright © 2016 by Kekla Magoon
"The Whole World Is Watching" copyright © 2016 by Robin Talley

First paperback edition 2018

Library of Congress Catalog Card Number 2015942989
ISBN 978-0-7636-7848-7 (hardcover)
ISBN 978-1-5362-0025-6 (paperback)

17 18 19 20 21 22 BVG 10 9 8 7 6 5 4 3 2 1

Printed in Berryville, VA, U.S.A.

This book was typeset in Adobe Caslon Pro and Caslon 540.

Candlewick Press
99 Dover Street
Somerville, Massachusetts 02144

visit us at www.candlewick.com

Contents

_____

Introduction

———

I grew up right outside Gettysburg, Pennsylvania, site of perhaps the most decisive battle in the Civil War. My family and I picnicked on the battlefield and went for hikes there, pausing to read the historical placards. Later, in high school, my friends would play their guitars and we'd watch the sunset at Devil's Den and try to take pictures of ghosts in Triangular Field. History wasn't just a collection of dates I memorized from textbooks; it was tactile and ever present.

When I was twelve, I read *Gone with the Wind* and fell in love with historical fiction. As an adult I can see the many ways in which the novel is problematic, but at twelve I was utterly enchanted by Scarlett O'Hara and Rhett Butler. My grandparents took me on a trip to Louisiana that summer, and we toured plantation museums and walked the streets of New Orleans. I came home and began writing a series of thinly veiled *Gone with the Wind* knockoffs about headstrong Southern girls, all set in Louisiana instead of Georgia. Those novels live in my closet at my parents' house—deservedly so, because they're terrible. But I still love reading and writing historical fiction. My first trilogy, the Cahill Witch Chronicles, is set in an alternate version of 1890s New England.

One of the reasons I sought out historical fiction rather than reading straight-up history, the way my Civil War–buff father did, was because I wanted to read about girls. But their stories were mostly missing from textbooks and historical sites. Despite their many important contributions, women — especially queer women, women of color, and women with disabilities — have too often been erased from history.

While on a writing retreat with my friends Andrea Cremer, Marie Lu, and Beth Revis, I mentioned that another friend had suggested I edit an anthology. I loved the idea of creating a collection of YA historical fiction; I couldn't imagine any theme that would intrigue me more.

"You should do it," my friends said. "We'd all write stories for you."

How could I say no, with three terrifically talented *New York Times* best-selling authors on board? I am forever grateful for their encouragement and enthusiasm.

"You need more of a theme than historical fiction," my agent said. And I realized that what I really wanted was to edit an anthology of stories about clever, interesting American girls throughout history, written by clever, interesting (though not necessarily all American) women.

Some of the authors I approached are dear friends and critique partners. Others I haven't yet had the chance to meet but have long admired their work. Some of our contributors — Katherine Longshore, Kekla Magoon, Robin Talley, and Elizabeth Wein — are known for bringing real history — of the doomed wives of Henry VIII, the Black Panthers, 1950s Virginia during school desegregation, or female pilots during World War II — richly to life. Others — Marie Lu, Marissa Meyer, and Beth Revis — are trying their hands at historical fiction for the first time.

It's been such a joy to work with all of them.

When I asked them to come up with premises, I suggested that we think diversely in terms of geography, historical eras, and our heroines' races, sexualities, religions, and opinions on all manner of things. America is a melting pot. I hoped our fifteen stories could, in some small way, reflect that reality.

And so our heroines are monsters and pirates and screenwriters and schoolteachers. They are brave and scared, uncertain and sure. They are white and Chinese American and black and Native American. They dress as boys if that's what's needed to get the job done, whether it's robbing banks to feed their families or sinking a Spanish ship off the coast of the Carolinas. They kiss girls or boys or no one at all because they've got more important things on their minds, like catching spies. They debate marriage proposals, murder, and politics with equal aplomb. They are mediums and assassins, heiresses and hobos, bartenders and bank robbers. Their friends are faithless, their heroines die—perhaps some die themselves—but they carry on because there is a spark inside them that refuses to be extinguished. They are naive and world-weary, optimistic and sad, beautiful and terrible.

Most of all, I hope you will find them interesting.

From corsets to cutlasses and petticoats to pistols, we want to bring American history to life—from the viewpoints of strong, clever, resourceful American girls.

Thank you so much for reading.

Jessica Spotswood

Mother Carey's Table

J. Anderson Coats

M Y FATHER SAYS HE'S SAVED MY LIFE nine times. Once at my birth, once when we fled master and overseer through rows of struggling tobacco beneath a sky choked with stars, and the other seven paid out over all our years before the masts of ten different ships.

The oldest two I must take at his word, as I have no memory of either. The first of the seven was the time Pop shut me below when I thought to skip up the rigging to the topmost yard of the *Barbry Allen* in a near gale off Barbados, the decks awash and the sea yawning up before us. Six years into life and already I was full of the piss and vinegar he taught me to walk with. The kind he said would serve me well no matter what the tide.

"Boys are all piss and vinegar," he would say as he scraped his grimy razor over my scalp till I was bald as an egg. "It's what keeps them alive, pet. On the sea or off."

Mostly I think I've saved my own life. I knew enough to listen to Pop from the first moment we stepped on shipboard and learn the ropes from anyone with something to teach. When we came upon the *Golden Vanity* a few months ago, the bosun handed me the ledger without so much as a look toward Pop, and I signed the articles on my own for the first time.

I grinned at Pop hard enough to blind the sun. He smiled back, but when he thought I wasn't looking he shook his head, slow and sad.

Pop still thinks we chose poorly, joining the *Vanity*'s crew. "It's a brig, pet. Moves slow, like an ox in molasses. We'll never catch anything faster than a merchantman. We'll never be able to *outrun* anything faster either."

I've given up trying to convince Pop that sloops and schooners might be quick but they can't bring as many guns to bear. Besides, the *Vanity*'s old man has an eye for ships loaded down with plunder and swears the wind tells him things. And if you're bold enough to ask what things, he'll merely wink and say, "Things about things, lad."

Which is no answer at all, but when you're the captain and your name is Half-Hanged Henry, it's an answer you can give a bold sailor who's a little too curvy amidships to be an actual boy.

We're flying a Union Jack we stole from our last prize and lying in wait for the next behind a barrier island off the coast of Carolina. I'll be on watch in another turn of the glass, but for now I'm up on the mainmast yard, my bare legs swinging, the salt-wind curling through my jacket and over my windburned face.

A flurry of seabirds circle the topgallant yard, then dip and glide down to the waterline. But when they gather just above the spray, I flinch hard and grip the mast.

Mother Carey's chickens.

They're not proper chickens, not the kind you'd eat. They're little seabirds, black at the wing with a white stripe across their tails. There are four, and they dance eerily over the surface of the water without ever landing.

I wonder if I knew them. They were once men, and I've seen my share of floating corpses since I was a cabin boy. These birds are the souls of drowned sailors who've escaped the wife of Davy Jones and returned to warn seamen of storms. Even crews like us who use captured flags to lure prizes close.

I shinny up the mainmast till I reach the topmost yard and can go no higher without becoming a bird myself. The sky is clear and gray. Not blue, but no angry clouds mount. The air doesn't smell like a storm, and the wind promises naught but a good chase once the prey comes in sight.

"Ha! Almost got that one!"

Hanging over the rail near the bowsprit are Johnny and Black Tom. They signed the articles in Port Royal, no older than me and full of showy false swagger that lasted a single turn of the glass. Pop took pity on them and now they're our messmates, two sons closer to the big family he always wanted.

Black Tom flings a stone and it misses one of Mother Carey's chickens by a handswidth.

I'm down the mainmast in a trice and I haul those two coves collar and scruff away from the rail. They go stumbling and fall into fighting stance before seeing it's me. Then they straighten and eye me warily.

"What gives, Joe?" Black Tom has squinty pig-eyes and a constant white-boy sunburn. Johnny's the one who's blacker than me and Pop put together, with ritual scars like Pop remembers on his granddad.

"Don't you make Mother Carey angry, harming those birds."
I stab a finger at the feathery shadows tiptoeing across the water
below. "Or else she'll call up a storm so she can serve our drowned
guts to Davy Jones for tea."

"You really believe that old yarn?" Johnny asks. "Them's just
birds. Souls go to heaven or they go to hell."

Eight bells rings, four sets of two peals, short and pert.

These lads must stop. Killing even one of the little harbingers
could bring us all to a bad end, and Pop's grown attached to both
Johnny and Black Tom, orphans like him, like he's terrified I'll
end up. I want to smile at them, to use honey instead of vinegar,
but Pop says nothing makes me look less like a boy than when I
smile.

"I do." I say it over my shoulder as I head toward the mainmast. "And you'll do best to believe it too, 'cause if you let them,
they'll save your life."

Still no sign of a storm. And we've been watching every bearing.

Just after three bells, we weigh anchor. The old man's got wind
of a massive treasure ship limping her way up the coast of Spanish
Florida, blown off course and separated from her warship escort.

Prizes don't get any more tempting than that, and Johnny and
Black Tom lead the whooping and speculating.

I'm trimming the staysail when the old man strolls past.

"Joe, you'll be in the boarding party, got that?"

"Ah . . . beg pardon, sir, but I'm a topman."

Pop puts down a bucket and edges closer. I hate that I'm glad
for it, but I am.

The old man squints at me. "A big strong lad like you? How
old are you, Joe?"

I frown, reckoning, and Pop hisses, "Sixteen."

"Sixteen, sir."

"And you've never boarded a prize?"

"No, sir. I was a runner and a surgeon's boy when I was little, then a powder monkey and now a topman."

The old man scoffs cheerfully. "Nah, you're wasted up in the rigging, moving sails. See Davis after your watch. He'll give you a blade."

"But I . . ."

I can splice a line and take a sounding and play a passable hornpipe. I can fight like a bag of wet cats, but I know I can't kill. Just the thought turns my stomach.

But boys my age are well scarred like Johnny, like Black Tom. Boys of any age are full of piss and vinegar, and they'd be spoiling for a chance like this.

"What is it, sailor?" The old man isn't smiling anymore.

I signed the articles. I took the ledger from the bosun and balanced it on my left forearm while inking a big shaky *J* beneath all the other names and marks. I could have handed it over to Pop, let him make a mark for us both and taken my half share like always.

My father puts a hand on my shoulder. His voice is quiet but steady when he says, "Nothing, sir. Right, Joe?"

"Yes, sir," I mutter, and it's to both of them, to the old man and Pop too.

The bosun sends me aloft and I'm glad for it, but now I see Mother Carey's chickens everywhere and I shouldn't be seeing any when there are still no storms off any bearing. All I can do is wonder what the little souls are trying to warn us of, since birds of this kind never just appear.

When eight bells ring out once more and I'm off watch, I head down to my rack below, snug among the guns. The canvas is still warm from when Pop slept in it earlier, and there's a little packet of rock-hard ship's bread waiting for me wrapped in his kerchief.

Pop hasn't given me his rations since I was nine and laid up sick and sweating with cowpox.

The *Golden Vanity* runs on bells a lot tighter than most other ships Pop and I have sailed with, but Pop says the old man was in the Royal Navy before he turned pirate, and bells are what he knows.

Pop says it in that voice he uses when he's hopeful for something but doesn't want to be. He's hopeful for one thing, mostly — to crew a vessel that takes a prize big enough that he can retire on an able seaman's share.

Whenever he talks about it, I smile and nod like I'm eager to put on shoes and petticoats and sip tea in a drawing room, but I already know there's no way I can follow him. I stopped being a girl that day on the Charleston dock when Pop signed the articles that first time, when he put his hand on my newly shaved head and told the old man of the *Veracruz* his *son* would make a fine cabin boy. Pop had no way to keep me unless I spit and swaggered and pissed through the curved metal funnel he made for me out of an old drinking cup.

So even if we do hit a once-in-a-lifetime treasure ship — maybe like the one we're sneaking toward now — even if Pop does land enough silver and gold to buy that little farm or the tall Boston townhouse he's always on about, now that I'm old enough to sign articles for myself, I have no desire at all to leave the sea.

But I can't tell Pop that. Not after everything he's done to keep me, starting with swinging me on his back that night he fled his future and mine — days beneath the sun and years beneath the lash.

I must have drifted to sleep, for I'm jolted almost out of my rack by an insistent thudding that sets the bulkheads trembling.

Black Tom's at the head of the gun deck, pale beneath his sunburn, and he bangs on the bulkhead with a stick of kindling to the same wild clang as the ship's bell.

They're beating us to quarters.

We've come upon our prize.

I'm awake in an instant, and I'm clearing hammocks and sea chests from the guns before I remember the old man wants to see me out on deck, blade in hand and ready to board and subdue the enemy ship. I shouldn't like how the dagger Davis gave me feels in my hand—sturdy, heavy, menacing—but I do.

As I step out on deck, Pop nods me near. He's breathing in sharp little bursts as he grips his blade. Pop's been in boarding parties before, but I've never seen this look about him.

If I didn't know better, I'd say Pop was afraid.

"That's not a treasure ship," Pop says in a low voice. "She's riding too high. Look at the waterline."

I step to the rail and peer out. And pull in a sharp breath of my own. If the ship were loaded down with treasure, the deck would be only a fathom or so above the waves. Instead all the gunports are clear.

Two whole rows of them.

"She's a warship, isn't she?" I whisper.

Pop nods.

"And we're trapped against the coastline, aren't we?"

This time Pop doesn't reply because questions I know the answers to I shouldn't have to ask.

All she's got to do is come broadside to us and fire. Two volleys and we're sunk.

We've hauled down the Union Jack, since England and Spain are still at war the last anyone's heard, but flying no flag at all will draw every captain's eye.

His grapeshot as well.

The bosun's whistle cuts the clamor, and we fall silent as the old man swings onto the quarterdeck and waves his arms for attention.

"She's Spanish, all right," the old man says, "but there's not a single coin aboard her. We'll never be able to outrun her, and we're all dead men if we try to fight."

A rumble moves through the crew. Unease and discontent and more than a little raw terror. The wind has led Half-Hanged Henry astray.

Pop steps closer so our shoulders are touching. Signing pirate articles means you're always with a crew that'll overwhelm an enemy, and any captain worth a damn never starts a fight he can't easily win.

But that vessel is a forty-gun frigate, and there's no way we're sailing past without being sunk or boarded.

Pop and me and Johnny and others like us—we're done for either way. Half-Hanged Henry and his lawless lot treat us like sailors so long as we act like it, and every seaman brown or white is the same to Davy Jones. But if we're caught, we're part of the plunder and hauled in chains to the auction block. We won't get a show trial or even hang on the harborside gallows like the white pirates.

I can't speak for Pop or Johnny or the others, but I'd rather be a guest at some underwater table with Davy and his missus. There's no way I could crouch between rows of tobacco now that I've felt the foredeck swaying beneath my feet, tasted salt on my lips, and run before the wind in a little sloop under a sky blue enough to make me forget every storm I ever sailed through.

Mother Carey's chickens usually warn of a storm she's busy stirring. At least a storm would take both us and the Spanish warship down to the bottom, where Mother Carey herself would dice up our flesh onto dishes made of shells and use our bones to comb her long green hair.

"We cannot fight her." The old man is pacing, toying with the spyglass. "If we cripple her, we might be able to run past."

"Her mainsails are dropping!" shouts Black Tom from the rigging. "She's coming about!"

The old man snaps the spyglass closed. "Can any man among you swim?"

Pop fidgets with his blade, and at his other elbow Johnny looks utterly greensick.

"C'mon, lads, speak up! There must be one of you who can sink that ship sneakylike, with auger and drill."

No one says anything. Like as not because none of them can swim.

But I can.

There's only so much a child can do in squalid ports with ten grogshops per man and not a church in sight. While Pop drank his ghosts to whispers, I whiled away long afternoons in quiet inlets, splashing and collecting shells—and paddling about the shallows and deeps till I could swim like a fish, even in a wind-whipped ocean current.

"There'll be silver in it for you," the old man says with an edge of terror I've never yet heard from any man who's turned pirate. "My gold watch too." He rakes a look over us, shouts, "My daughter's hand in marriage! What the devil will it take?"

My father has saved my life nine times. He wanted no part of the *Vanity*, and I was the one who finally wore him down.

"I'll do it." I step before the old man. "I'll sink that frigate if you'll trade your shares for mine when we find and take the treasure galleon."

Pop stiffens. That treasure ship is still out there, and a captain's haul is always seven shares. Seven, when a single share from a prize like that would grant Pop's hopes thrice over.

The old man shuts his mouth. Narrows his eyes. Looks to the warship. Then he says, "It's yours, Joe. It's yours if you sink that ship."

Everything feels oddly quiet but for the creak of wood and the rattlesnap of damp canvas. I can hear every last one of my father's indrawn breaths somewhere behind me.

The first mate takes off his belt and Johnny holds out a leather sheath, wide-eyed and solemn. I thread the sheath through the belt and cinch it tight under my jacket. When the bosun hands me an auger, I brandish it like a pistol with more piss and vinegar than I feel before tying it into the sheath.

Johnny laughs nervously, then paws my shoulder in an awkward sort of half-hug.

"Back to your labor," the old man calls. "If they see us crowded at the rail, they'll know something's amiss."

With both auger and dagger about my waist, I feel a full stone heavier. I can swim well, but I've never tried it weighted. I climb up to the rail and peer over. The water below is not a sparkling sky-blue lagoon where little waves lapped around my baby feet, where I dipped and surged with naught on my back but my smallclothes. It's green-black and choppy, and at the bottom are the bones of sailors who did not have a care for its will.

The wind is sharp from the starboard beam. It won't be a turn of the glass before we're pushed close enough to the frigate to force a reckoning.

Pop is drawn tight like a mainstay line. He badly wants to say something but he's not going to. I'm not even sure what there is to say.

I can't take my offer back. And I can't let us be taken.

I face the water. I slip out of my jacket and dive in.

The water is bonechill-cold and the shock of it hits me like a cudgel. I kick my feet and force myself upward and forward, but my shirt and trousers splay out like a jellyfish, clinging and dragging and slowing every limb I thrash.

So I choke and gasp and struggle, fighting out of my clothes. I break the surface and the cold hits me again, rakes over my stubbly head, but I suck in a mighty breath and tread water long enough to steady myself.

Cold. Oh, Father Neptune but it is cold in nothing but small-clothes and the linen I keep wrapped about my chest.

Black Tom's in the rigging. The old man has the spyglass. One of them's bound to notice.

I'll reap that whirlwind once I'm back on board. For now, I've got a ship to sink.

I tighten the mate's belt and make sure I still have both auger and dagger, then I slice my arms through the water in a nice steady rhythm. I start to feel warmer. Every twenty strokes I look up and mark the warship just to be sure I'm on course.

At first it feels like I'll never get there.

Then she's within a stone's throw.

Then I'm right beneath her.

I tread water once I reach the warship, fighting to catch my breath. It's been a while since I've swum this much, and my arms are weak and melty, my eyes burning from the salt. The ship is moving only with the tide, and I unfasten the auger from my waist and feel along till I find a spongy, worm-eaten patch below the waterline.

There's no way to auger without a grip to hold me steady, and there's nothing to grip but barnacles. They cake the whole ship-bottom like drifted sand, and each is a tiny razor.

I'm too tired to hesitate. I grab a clump of barnacles, and they slice me open clean and thoughtless. And those cuts burn. They burn and burn and I whimper, not an ounce of piss and vinegar left to fight it.

But my right hand is free, and I set to work with the auger. I crank it round and round, round and round. It's all I do. It's all I think about.

Before long I've bored half a dozen holes clear through the hull. The barnacles have already done the job halfway, quietly eating the wood till it all but ripples beneath my palms. Already I can hear the slurpsuck of water punching through my holes and the panicky shouts of men inside, the clomp and clatter as they flee, the futile clang of the ship's bell ringing the general alarm.

My arms throb and my whole left hand is numb from scores of tiny half-moon cuts across my fingers. When I fumble the auger against the hull to start a new hole, it wheels out of my hand and drops like an anchor down and down and gone.

I watch it disappear. The job is only half done. All I have left is my dagger.

I force my stiff fingers around another clump of barnacles. New cuts crosshatch the old ones. I pull the dagger from my belt and stab at the pulpy wood like a murderer.

A raw, violent hole appears beneath my blade. Then two, then many.

The warship is taking on water. The shift in pitch is sobering.

I'm killing these men. They can swim no better than the lads on the *Vanity*.

I've lost count of the holes I've put in, but I'm spent. The warship's list is bad enough that she's in no position to fight us or give chase. And if she goes down, I want to be nowhere near.

I've earned my prize. Pop's prize. And half the rum ration of every man on the *Vanity* whose life I saved sinking this Spanish tub.

I cram my dagger into its sheath, push off the side of the listing warship—the barnacles open up my toes like meat—and thrash through the waves toward home. Each stroke takes all my effort, and halfway there I start to crawl-paddle and sputter out seawater hard enough to set my vitals throbbing.

I won't make it if I think how bad I hurt.

So I think how to explain to Half-Hanged Henry that I don't want his daughter's hand in marriage.

I think of the first time I made it all the way up to the topgallant yard on the *Sally Dearest*, how I felt light enough to spread my arms and take wing like a bird.

And I think of Pop, who only ever wanted a place of his own and a houseful of babies.

My blind, splashing hands clatter against something hard and wet and splintery. The *Golden Vanity*. I grab and scrabble for a barnacle handhold, but Captain Royal Navy actually careens them off proper on occasion, and I must weakly tread water.

Up on the foredeck I see faces of the crew peering over, tiny ovals of color against a flat gray sky and sprawls of dingy canvas and a tangle of rigging.

I dredge an arm out of the water in salute. Any moment now a rope will fall over the side. Somewhere in me is the strength to hold that rope, and I will find it.

One by one, the faces at the rail disappear.

Only the old man is left.

"She's sunk!" I shout. "I sank her. Pull me up!"

The old man doesn't reply. He doesn't throw a rope either. He merely shakes his head.

Over my shoulder, the Spanish warship is tilting like driftwood and the whole quarterdeck is in chaos as men push and fight for dry ground. Seeing her on her way down reminds me how hot and weak my arms are, how much of a struggle it is to keep my head above the waves.

"Captain!" I howl, but it's a mistake because I choke on a sudden harsh mouthful of water.

"Can't do it, Joe," he says, and disappears from the rail.

I'm gasping with every flailed stroke and kick, but I manage to free my dagger from its sheath. I punch it out of the water and shout, "I know well how to sink a ship, Cap! If this is how you'll serve me, I'll take you to the bottom with me. We'll all be on Mother Carey's table together!"

And that's when Pop appears at the rail, fighting the first mate and the bosun, who have him by either arm. There's a length of ratline in his hand and he almost gets it over the gunwale before they haul him away, out of sight.

He'll go to the bottom too.

I open my hand and let the dagger fall, down and down, to Davy Jones.

Pop is roaring like a madman and cursing every Goddamn one of them and shouting at me to stay strong, his last little baby, the only one he could save.

I flail one final stroke and go under.

I'm colder than I've ever been, but nothing hurts anymore—not my arms, not my feet, not my eyes, not my guts.

Above me is a dull shadow set against shades of rippling, glinting motion. It's the size of my thumb, oval but pointed at both ends.

Like the bottom of a ship.

I'm standing before a table on the quarterdeck of an ancient, rotted merchantman. Her mast is a ragged stump and stray chain shot is lodged in the gunwales. At the head of the table is a woman whose face is hidden by shadow and wavered by the movement of the currents around us.

"Jocasta," she says, and all at once I know who she is. I know it even though I have only a whisper of a memory of her. This is the voice that would lilt through fire-warmed, comfortable darkness when I was small enough to be tucked into a willow basket. Then would come her gentle hand, rubbing my back, smoothing hair from my eyes, pushing away the dim of the room and the grit of the floor and the gnaw in my belly.

I have to swallow twice before I can answer, and it's no more than a whisper. "Mama."

"That's right." She swims one long graceful arm at an empty chair before a bare, waiting dinner plate. "Come, sit down. I've been expecting you. Supper's ready."

Pop would never say much about Mama. One day she was there before the fire in our cabin, the next she wasn't. He's always saying I was too little to remember her anyway, but he's wrong.

I remember her voice. I remember her warmth. I remember crying quietly because she hadn't taken me with her, wherever she went.

And here she is before me.

She leans to set a dish on the table, nudging several others to make room. The table is overflowing with platters, all covered with domed abalone shells.

I reach for the chair and pull it out. It glides through the water like my arm, like my backside as I start to sit down.

Then she smiles at me.

Her teeth are all pointy like a cat's.

I freeze, my rump hovering above the seat. "Y-you're not my mother."

"Mama. Or Madre. Or Mater. All of you with salt for blood are mine." She slides her lips over her teeth, her voice all Mama once more. "Come now, Jocasta. Sit down. I've missed you."

Out of the darkness, out of everything cold and miserable would come that voice. And somehow things would grow lighter, starting with her and ending with me.

She's back at her work, carving meat and dicing seaweed and piling everything onto platters made of shells all lined up along the table. This table on the deck of a dead ship.

"Sit." Her voice goes sharp and she aims her knife at me.

The same knife I buried to the hilt in weak, barnacled patches of a Spanish warship, sending her and her crew to the bottom of the sea.

To Mother Carey's table.

I flip over one of the shells covering a platter. It's heaped with severed fingers and slabs of flesh and the odd swimming length of bowel.

I struggle backward, but it's a maddening swish of water and my arms churn, trying to push away, trying to get clear. Mother Carey grins with her pointy cat-teeth as she lifts a goggle-eyed, limp-swaying Spanish sailor from his seat and cleaves his arm from his torso while he burbles *Mamita*.

"You will sit," Mother Carey says as she slits the sailor from neck to navel, "and you will stay. It would be a pity if you didn't enjoy the fine feast you've provided me."

Spanish sailors with empty, slack faces are taking seats one after the other in chairs that hold them fast as Mother Carey prepares a feast of the dead for herself and Davy Jones.

"You wouldn't leave me, would you? Sit down, Jocasta. Sit down and be with your mother."

Mama's voice keeps coming out of Mother Carey's mouth as she stands at the head of her table and pulls helpless Spaniards out of chairs much like the vacant one before me. As she cleaves the poor bastards bone from bone and piles their guts on abalone dishes.

I learned to stop asking about Mama. Pop said it was easier that way. That we love people when they're here, but when they go, they're gone.

Pop. Who never once thought to leave me behind, whatever the cost.

I don't sit down. I kick my feet. I start to rise.

Water moves around me and over me and through me, through my hair and my skin, and flutters the scraps of linen that still cling to me. I wing out my arms and glide.

I am growing lighter.

The wind changes shades. The sunlight changes color.

Most of us huddle up close in the sand. But five of us, we feel it. We know what to do.

I become light. I catch the updraft, sway over the waves. The nests on the dunes are distant but safe for now. Out we go, and out.

A storm builds to the north. A storm my mother is stirring, for she and her man grow hungry once more.

Sails beyond the barrier island, rigged for pursuit. When the sky is this color we are drawn to ships, to those who are as we once were.

I angle my wings, slide along the ship's waterline, pluck up some tiny-shelled creatures to crunch. Dabble my toes against the water, then glide up on a wick of wind.

I am up and into the rigging, toward a brown man with graying hair who sits all alone on the foremast yard, swinging his legs while the wind catches his jacket.

Soon they will go. Capstan chanty, anchor up, ship in sight, beat to quarters. He will be among them. He will grip his blade, swing over harsh water. He is still waiting for his prize. He waits for her even as he curses her.

Around the edge of the sail. Up, and toward him.

The water sings and beckons. The wind wants to nudge me toward the dunes and my nest, and soon enough I will return there, but right now I need to be on this yard with this man. I need to see him.

I need him to look north so he'll stay on this side of the water and not below, where my mother would put his bones on her table.

He holds out a hand and I cannot help but take wing. Too sudden for the shell of me, too much, even though the soul of me would curl up in his pocket, feel the warm beat of his heart one last time.

I make a pass through the rigging, then sweep down to the waterline. I arc over the quarterdeck, where dark clouds are beginning to mount.

I hover there until he sees.

🜂 *Author's Note* 🜂

The late seventeenth and early eighteenth centuries are sometimes called the Golden Age of Piracy, although if you were trying to live through it, you probably called it something less rosy. The New World at that time was dynamic and its culture in flux, and issues of freedom, order, and loyalty were anything but settled.

The Mother Carey legend is part of a vast body of nautical lore. Her name is a corruption of *mater cara* (Latin for *dear mother*), which was one way early Spanish and Portuguese explorers referred to the Virgin Mary. Folk music fans will recognize elements of "The Sweet Trinity" (Child Ballad 286), but the bones of the story developed as a result of my discovery that about 25 percent of sailors on pirate or privateer vessels during the Golden Age of Piracy were people of color. We know of several notable female pirates, and considering that we know the most about pirates who were caught and tried, there's a strong possibility someone like Joe existed without being known to history.

The Journey

Marie Lu

MY MOTHER NAMED ME YAKONE, after the red aurora.

Some said the red aurora was bad luck, the image of blood painting the sky. But my mother believed it meant good fortune, that the spirits dancing in the sky were pleased. She told me she had only seen the red aurora twice in her life. The first was on the night after my father, still barely a man, killed his first whale. The second was fifteen years ago, on the longest night of the year, when the sun did not rise at all. I was born that night.

So I suppose my mother was both wrong and right: wrong, because she could never bear children again after me, and right, because our seer said the fire in me burned strongly enough for all the sons in the world.

My mother carried me on her back and went around our hut for many circles, following the path the sun would travel. She kissed me often and said I would bring my father successful hunts. And I did.

I have many memories of those winter hunts. My father would come back with the other hunters, hauling the bleeding bodies of whales and seals to shore. I would join my mother and the other women to carve *maktak*: rich, glistening chunks of blubber with the thick skin still attached. We would dry them on pokes, split the shares between each family in our village, then load the rest of the *maktak* onto sleds and take the dogs out to deliver the food to relatives in another village. I would watch as we piled the animals' bones high and waited for the lights to glow from the south. Then we would burn the bones, sending their souls back to the ocean.

"There are no boundaries between the great whale's spirit and ours," my father would tell me as we stood together by the fire, watching the aurora wash across the sky. "We all belong to the same life force."

I would listen, kiss my hand, and touch it to the ground near the fire.

The delivery of *maktak* was something I yearned to do with my father. I wanted to see the tundra beyond the light of our fires, cling to the back of a wind-whipped dogsled, witness the seals at sea and the foxes prowling through the snow. I wanted to be the proud bearer of life, giving food to others at the end of a long, dangerous journey.

The next time we gathered before the bones, I asked my father, "Please, take me with you on the next run."

My father gave me a raised brow and a stern look. "Your place is here," he replied, "with your mother. Who will help her when I'm not around?"

"The other women in the village," I argued. "Do you remember the seer's words? I have no brothers — you can teach me about the dogs and the sled. Right?" I looked up at him so earnestly that he threw his head back and laughed.

A winter later, my father started to teach me. How to snare, to make a harpoon, to harness our dogs, to read the stars. He walked with me down the line of our dogs as they whined and quivered in excitement, teaching me to know each—Ataneq, Chinook, Kaya—so well that I could read their moods as well as my own. My mother taught me how to find fireweed and cloudberries, how to store them in the snow to keep them fresh, how to gather bird eggs, how to feed the fire with caribou droppings and dried moss. Father told me stories about the Seal King and Nanuk, the Lonely Roamer, the Great White Bear. "The spirits will guide you," he said, "if you take only what you need and respect them in their domain. Even in the darkest night. Remember that, Yakone, and you will never be lost."

"I'll remember," I replied.

Finally, one early-winter evening, my father smiled as we fed our dogs. "I'll take you with me after our hunt," he said. "To deliver *maktak*." He glanced up at the sky, where sheets of stars had blinked into bright existence after months of light. He raised one hand and traced a rough line between constellations, connecting the diamond of the First Ones to the Caribou. "That is the path we will follow."

The red aurora danced that night, obscuring the stars, and my heart danced with it in anticipation. It was the first time I'd ever seen it for myself. I stayed outside, my eyes fixed on the scarlet sheets, until I couldn't stand the numbness in my fingers anymore. The next morning, my father set out with the hunters.

When they returned, I knew immediately that something was wrong. The hunters shouted among themselves as they dragged their kayaks to shore. Loud and angry. In the dim light, I wrapped my arms around my body and trembled as I waited with my mother. My eyes darted among the men and the bodies of whales, searching, as always, for my father. *Not here.* I scanned the horizon, looking for another kayak behind the others. The water stayed still, vanishing into the dim haze of morning snow.

"He is not dead," my mother said quietly beside me. I looked up at her, but her eyes stayed fixed on the horizon, hard and unblinking. Other villagers ran to the hunters, and their voices all mixed into one loud storm.

It took me a long time to understand what the hunters were shouting.

A strange, monstrous creature—something with enormous white wings and a body as big as a glacier—had struck my father's kayak. It had come upon them in the mist so suddenly that my father could not steer out of the way. "We circled and searched for hours," one of the hunters cried, "but we never found his body."

I drifted in the midst of their shouts, numb. The world blurred around me. I realized through the fog of my thoughts that I was helping the women hack away at the whale carcasses, my limbs going through the rote motions of carving the *maktak*. An ominous hush of whispers hung over our village. The hunters gathered in the *qargi* to make sense of what they'd seen. I stayed outside with my mother long after the low sun set, searching the waves.

"He is still here," my mother murmured again beside me, as we packaged the *maktak* and loaded it onto our sled. "He has not died. We must keep waiting." She said it in a feverish, fierce voice that frightened me.

I couldn't understand. My father had said that the spirits

would guide you, if you took only what you needed and respected them in their domain. Did he somehow anger the Seal King? Had he insulted the great Nanuk?

Finally, the next morning, we saw the monster for ourselves.

Several children saw it first. Their shouts woke the rest of us, and we all gathered near the edge of the land. It floated out of the morning haze, a great contraption of wood and cloth. I had never seen so much wood in all my life, and all on one structure. As we looked on, several small boats left the larger and sailed toward us.

Our elders had always told stories of strangers—*gusaks*—from across the sea and ice, men with an insatiable hunger for furs. Some of these men traded us kettles and needles and warm blankets in exchange for beaver pelts. Others were not so friendly. I'd never thought much of those tales . . . until now.

I stared at the men who stepped out of these unfamiliar boats. They were very tall, with eyes and skin pale as water, their faces sharp and angular. *Gusaks.* Somehow, the word no longer sounded so funny to me. Were these the men who would smile and give us blankets? Several hunters went out to greet them on the ice. I looked on. My eyes darted to the strangers' belts. Odd devices hung from them, cylindrical pipes and leather pouches heavy with a shining rock.

The strangers talked to our hunters in a language I did not understand. Their voices grew louder. I looked up to meet my mother's gaze and stepped forward, but my mother seized my wrist and pulled me back.

"Don't," she whispered, her eyes still focused on the hunters and the pale men.

One of the hunters held his arms out to both sides. He shouted at the white men's leader. "It was your ship that killed Nunviaq!"

The white man pulled the strange cylindrical pipe from his belt. I looked on as he held it up to the hunter's chest.

A loud noise. I jumped.

A cloud of smoke rose from the pipe. The hunter staggered back a step, clutched his chest, and then fell. Shouts of confusion and alarm rose from the others. I stood frozen in place as they bent over the fallen hunter. *Siluk.* His name came to me. My father laughed often with him. I played with his sons. "Dead!" one of the others shouted. Siluk's wife let out a wail.

Then, chaos.

The leader pointed the pipe at others. They fled. The strangers spread out, and in their hands they all held pipes. I could smell smoke in the air.

"Mother!" I shouted.

My mother held my hand tight. "The dogs," she cried. "Quickly!" Together, we hurried toward our hut.

Then something struck my mother. She continued to run, but her gait was uneven, her steps staggering forward instead of moving on an even keel.

"Mother?" I said.

My mother's footsteps began to slow. "Keep going," she said. Her voice came out raspy. I smelled the sharp tang of blood.

By the time we reached the dogs, the animals were already restless and howling, wild-eyed with the knowledge that something terrible was happening. I ran to them and started to work on tightening the half-finished harnesses. Lessons from my father rushed through my mind. "Mother," I called out over my shoulder, "the lead!"

When she didn't respond, I paused to look back. She knelt in the snow, her hands clutched over her stomach. Dark red drops of blood were scattered in a trail behind her, tainting the snow.

I dropped the harnesses and ran back to my mother's side. I pulled her hand. "We have to go!" I cried. The dogs were ready, the *maktak* loaded along with our furs and supplies, the neat little packages we had worked so hard to prepare. *We were so close.*

My mother just shook her head. Already, her eyes seemed more glazed than before. "We'll go," she whispered. And even as she clutched my hand, she collapsed in the snow.

The buzzing in my ears turned deafening. It was as if a storm had come, and the snow blew my thoughts away. I refused to leave. I clung there, shaking my mother's shoulders, even as the sounds of screaming and the crackle of fire roared behind me. The crunch of boots in the snow drew near. Then a hand gripped my shoulder. I let out a yelp, shrank away, and looked up into the face of a young bearded man. He was one of them.

He glanced at the others as they set fire to the village, then looked back at me. I couldn't understand his words, but his urgent hand gestures were obvious.

Get out of here, child, he was trying to tell me. Then he left my side and ran back to the others.

The world rushed forward again, and I scrambled to my feet and ran for the dogs. I leaned down to secure the harness of the lead dog, Ataneq. He was already panting heavily, and I could see the whites of his eyes. *He wants to go,* my father would say if he were here. I made sure the harness was set, tugged on the shoulder strap, and stood up on shaking legs.

As the first huts began to go up in flames, I gripped the handlebar and stepped onto the toeboard. I snapped the reins. The dogs lurched forward. Behind us, a couple of men shouted at us in the *gusak* tongue.

Don't look back. Still, as the dogs kicked up snow and we fled, I turned one last time. The body of my mother looked like a small, crumpled heap. Flames engulfed the village. Men held torches, going from home to home.

I turned back around on the sled, put my head down, and wept.

We traveled for a long time, until the sounds of destruction faded into the background and the silence of the open ice took over. The sled cut through the snow, and the panting and baying of the dogs echoed ahead of me. I felt numb. Just a few nights ago, I had sat around a fire and laughed with my mother and father. Now they were gone.

We'll need to stop soon. My first coherent thought since we had fled. Father would have scolded me to keep my wits about me. I pulled back on the reins and whistled—Ataneq slowed to a trot, and the other dogs followed his lead.

The sun was dropping fast, and with it, the temperature. I pulled out heavy furs and set about pitching a tent. I searched for dry moss and branches to build a fire. Frozen droppings clustered here and there. I gathered them together with my mittens, then brought them back to my tent and let them thaw. By the time the sun disappeared completely, I had managed to get a small fire going. I settled, surrounded by my dogs.

Father's dogs. I glanced up at the sled, where the *maktak* sat, stacked and neatly bound. We were supposed to make this delivery together. Father would have charted our course, and I would have helped him guide the dogs. We would have hunted and fished together. He would be sitting here with me, telling stories around the fire.

Mother would still be alive.

The memory returned: drops of blood, scarlet against the snow.

I would have washed Mother's body and braided her hair. I

would have wrapped her and Father in sealskins and laid them to rest out in the tundra, buried beneath a mound of stones, so that their spirits could join the lights in the sky.

But Father's body sank beneath the waves. Mother perished with the village.

My eyes blurred until the fire was a glowing, shapeless mass of gold. The fire's crackle hid the sounds of my sniffling. Tears ran down my face, freezing at the edges of my cheeks and chin, so that when I reached up to brush them away, I instead found myself flaking away salty ice crystals. Ataneq's eyes glowed in the night. He pressed his muzzle gently against the side of my leg and uttered a low, mournful whine.

"Why did they come?" I whispered, burying my hand in Ataneq's thick fur. My words disappeared into the void of the tundra.

Father had never taught me how to get to the next village. Without his guidance, how could I possibly complete the delivery route? How could I find my way there? What if I was caught in a storm?

My dogs and I would die alone out here, buried in snow, never to be found again.

Stop trembling. I pulled my knees up to my chin and wrapped my arms around my legs. Ataneq's warm muzzle left my leg, letting the cold seep in. I paused in my thoughts to look at him. He tilted his head and let out a series of low barks. The other dogs stirred.

I turned my head up to see what had caught his attention.

It was the red aurora—sheets upon glittering sheets of crimson and scarlet that painted the night sky and hid swaths of stars. *Blood,* some in my village called it. *Good fortune,* my mother insisted. *Perhaps it wasn't. Perhaps I'm not.* All I could think about was the feeling in my stomach as the hunters returned without my father, and the memory of my mother lying in the snow, red spilling across her furs.

I would not find the village. I would not deliver this *maktak,* and those villagers would be left wondering what had happened. I would join my parents' spirits in the sky.

Perhaps I am cursed.

A flicker of light in the sky drew my attention. There. In the midst of the red aurora, a bright, searing line sliced its way across the sky. It streaked past us, then disappeared beyond the horizon in a glittering trail.

My heart caught in my throat. My hand buried deeper in Ataneq's fur, and a dot of excitement lit up my sorrow. *A falling star.*

Never in my life had I seen one as bright as this, like a white-gold fire against the night. I searched the sky, half-expecting another to come. But the rest of the stars stayed where they were, and the tundra fell back into stillness. Wind gusted past me, and I huddled against the thickness of my furs. My eyes lingered on the horizon where the falling star had disappeared.

Slowly, my thoughts began to flow into a river of calm, and the calm brought me focus. My mother's voice came to me.

When hunters are lost at sea, the Seal King turns them into seals. When sledders are lost in the tundra, Nanuk the Great White Bear takes them in and turns them into her cubs. Their spirits stay protected in the animals' bodies until the night a falling star comes to take them away into the sky.

Then, my father's voice.

The spirits will guide you, if you take only what you need and respect them in their domain. Even in the darkest night. Remember that, Yakone, and you will never be lost.

I remembered. I raised one hand and traced the line that my father had traced that evening, connecting the stars of the First Ones to the Caribou. It was the same path that the falling star had followed, as surely as if my father had drawn it himself.

It would not be an easy journey. Following the coastline would take far too long, so we would have to head into the tundra and rely on the constellations. This was a risk in itself. If a blizzard caught us, it would bury us. With nothing but the same white expanse in all directions and a sky shrouded by clouds, even the greatest tracker could lose himself and freeze to death.

But Father had taught me what he would have taught a son, and Mother had taught me what a daughter should know. The thought kept me warm, even as I looked to the bleak trek ahead.

I looked down at Ataneq. "We will follow the falling star and find the village," I murmured. His ears flicked forward at my voice. "And when we complete the star's path, my parents' spirits will be free to rest."

I jerked awake, not because of the weak light but because the dogs were barking.

I scrambled out from the warmth of my furs to see Ataneq facing the way we'd come, his hackles up and his bark punctuated by growls. The other dogs, restless because of their leader, did the same. I saw what unsettled them. Far along the horizon, a band of dark clouds crouched . . . and as I looked on, they crept forward, bit by bit, headed in our direction.

Fear jabbed at me. A winter storm, just as I'd feared. If we couldn't outrace it, it would blot out what little sun we had, it would hide the stars, and it would freeze us where we stood. It would kill us. I whirled to face Ataneq.

"Let's go," I murmured.

The sun moved, and we moved. Afternoon lengthened into an early evening, and the sun set a little earlier than it had the day before. We ran through the lengthening darkness, following the stars, until I stopped us in exhaustion. Hurriedly, I gathered what little dried moss I could, then started a fire. The warmth reassured me somewhat as I wiggled my frozen fingers and toes before it. Behind us, the band of dark clouds loomed, closer now than it had been this morning. A part of me wanted to jump up and force the dogs onward—force us on through the entire night. But that was impossible. We needed to rest. I untied one of the *maktak* packages from the sled, thawed it out before the fire, and sliced it up for the dogs. I kept a piece for myself. My eyes closed as I savored the rich fat. I would have to be careful with our portions. I finished mine, then crawled into my furs. The clouds loomed in the back of my thoughts, haunting me. If we couldn't beat the storm, all the food supplies in the world wouldn't save us.

A strange noise woke me this time. It was the sound of a splash.

I opened my eyes and looked over at the dogs, but they did not stir. The fire had burned low, and the embers glowed red in the night. Ice crystals flaked from my lashes. I shivered. Perhaps I had been dreaming.

Then the splash came again, some distance into the tundra. I glanced behind me. Water? But we'd left the coast behind yesterday. Were we headed in the wrong direction?

I crawled out of my furs. I listened a moment longer, then started to head toward the splashing sound. Behind me, Ataneq woke and watched me go with a curious tilt of his head. He whined, but I held a hand up, reassuring him that I was all right. I cut the strings from last night's *maktak* package into short pieces. I tied these to tiny patches of dry grass and lichen as I went, so that I would remember my path back. The splashing grew louder. Finally, something appeared ahead, a black patch that stood out solidly against the snow. I furrowed my brows. It was a hole in the ground, and the darkness was water.

I swallowed hard, then backtracked a few steps. It was hard to tell, but I had made my way onto the edge of an enormous frozen lake, hidden under the snow. The ice trembled slightly under my weight. A death trap. We would have headed this way come morning. We could have ended up in the water.

Another splash came from the hole in the ice. When I looked closer, I saw a faint white cloud of mist floating in the air. I squinted at the source of the spray.

The largest seal I had ever seen poked its head out of the water.

I gasped. The beast turned its head toward me, its huge eyes gleaming gold in the night. The water around it glowed a faint sapphire, as if lit by something from the depths, and the surface of the water glittered with a thousand tiny lights, as if the stars had shattered into the sea. They lit the seal, outlining its dark silhouette beneath the waves and adding a blue hue to its stormy-gray hide.

"The Seal King rose from the depths," I whispered, "to claim the hearts of drowning hunters." And now it seemed as if it had woken me to tell me about the lake.

The seal did not swim away. Instead, it stared back at me with unblinking eyes. I felt, for a moment, as if I looked into the face of my father. There was something wise there, something *human*. My lips trembled.

"Thank you," I whispered. "For the warning."

The seal only blinked once at me. Then it submerged, and

when it did not come up again, I shook my head and followed my trail of strings back to camp.

I dreamed of fish. I dreamed that the Seal King came to bless us, that he turned into my father, and that when I woke and headed to the lake, the waters were teeming with fish. I grabbed at them as they leaped out of the water, their scales glittering in the sun. They piled along the shore in rows.

I woke with a start. The sun was very low today. A new chill in the wind reminded me of the approaching blizzard, and I looked to the horizon. The clouds were close enough this morning for me to see their bumps and bruises, their angry curves. Overhead, a lone tern glided, separated from its flock.

We had to move faster.

I rode my dogs hard, even as the sky turned darker and the clouds grew thicker behind us. Only when Ataneq slowed in protest, his panting heavy, did I finally snap out of my stupor and let the team rest. I inspected their bright eyes, their frosty noses, and their ice-crusted coats; I watched them chew snow off of their paws. *There are no boundaries between the animals' spirits and ours,* my father had told me. I had no right to treat them so.

Still, we had no choice. I pushed them on.

The second day ended, and the third day began. I set snares in the snow. They caught a few fat lemmings, and I divided the fresh meat among the dogs, saving only a little for myself. Our *maktak* had to last, and the dogs were ravenous. The third day bled into the fourth. The days turned darker, and the nearing storm promised snow. The dogs ran more slowly.

That night, I watched the dogs shift uneasily in their sleep.

Ataneq looked exhausted, but we could rest only a few hours before I had to force the team onward again. I stared up at the night sky, followed the line of the constellations, and tried to believe that I could find our way if the stars disappeared behind the storm.

I didn't sleep that night.

An hour before dawn, I looked up into a gray sky. The sun was gone, hidden behind the clouds. A few fat flurries drifted onto my face. The storm had arrived, shrouding the guiding sky, and the snow was already starting to come fast. I jumped up and started folding my furs away.

My eyes paused on giant paw prints circling our camp.

They were enormous, a dozen times larger than Ataneq's prints, larger than any wolf's, pushed deeply into the snow and frozen in sculpture. I stared, startled, into the darkness of the open tundra.

The Great White Bear? Nanuk has come to warn us about the storm. I squinted and tried to imagine my mother's spirit looking back, but all I saw was emptiness. I shook my head. Believing in old folktales. I was deluding myself, trying to take comfort in anything. I walked over to Ataneq, who did not want to rise.

"*Aahali*, poor thing," I whispered, stroking his head. "We have to keep going." He looked at me but did not uncurl himself. The other dogs did not want to stir either. I went down the line, checking each of them with a sinking heart. They were exhausted. Even though I knew that they would run if I commanded it of them, they would not be able to go much farther. They would run themselves to death out of loyalty.

Suddenly, Ataneq's ears pricked up. He lifted his head and pointed it in the direction of the bleak tundra, and the hackles on his neck rose. A low growl rumbled from his throat.

"Ataneq?" I whispered.

Then he leaped to his feet. He began to bark. The other dogs lifted their heads too.

My eyes followed Ataneq's line of sight. There, from the mist of falling snowflakes, came a flash of light. Then the howling of other dogs.

A faint shout drifted over to us.

It was a language I did not know.

The memory of the *gusaks* came back to me. *They have come to finish me off.*

I rushed to the sled and grabbed the handlebar. The dogs were already restless, anxious to be on the move. I called out a command and the entire line lurched forward, the dogs throwing all their strength into the run. My head jerked back. As icy snow flew in my face, I glanced over the back of the sled to see our pursuers.

The light gleamed again.

We charged on. But my dogs were traveling across the frozen tundra at a slower pace than yesterday. The snow turned thicker, so that the light behind us was shrouded now and then from view. But the storm slowed us down too, painting the entire landscape an eerie white. My breaths came in ragged gasps. I hoped Ataneq could sense where he was leading us.

Behind us, the light suddenly grew brighter. Our pursuers were gaining on us. Now I could hear more faint shouts floating from somewhere behind us. I caught a few clear words.

The *gusak* tongue. "We must go faster!" I shouted to Ataneq, but the wind drowned out my words. There was little we could do. Ataneq could not push the other dogs any faster.

The ground beneath us suddenly changed from soft snow to hard ice. *We shouldn't be on the ice,* I thought frantically, remembering the Seal King's warning. At the same time, Ataneq seemed to realize the sudden shift beneath his paws, and he tried immediately to turn us.

When I looked back again, I could see our pursuers' dogs, dark specks against the fury of falling snow, their sledder wearing a thick fur hat. A strange sense of calm washed over me at the sight. Perhaps this would be where they caught me and killed me as they had killed Mother. Or perhaps this would be where I stood my ground. If I died here, I would die fighting.

The *gusak* sledder shouted something at me, but I couldn't understand what he said. Instead, I gritted my teeth and braced myself.

Abruptly, Ataneq slid to a halt. The other dogs stumbled in their haste to stop, and the team slid across the icy surface. The sled's runners cracked the ice. I only had time to shout before the ice gave way with a thunderous series of cracks. Then the world swallowed me whole. The icy water knocked all the breath from my lungs. Panic clogged my mind. I floundered blindly. The world flashed in and out—the water stabbed at me. I reached out, hoping for something to hang on to. I called for my dogs.

Ataneq! Ataneq!

Through the cold and darkness, I saw a shape curve through the water, its black eyes gleaming bright, tail carving a trail behind it. *The Seal King.*

I broke to the surface with a terrible gasp into the middle of a blizzard. Ataneq and the other dogs barked furiously. Someone had cut their sled leads to keep them from going into the water. Where were the *gusaks*? I tried to grab at the edge of the ice, but my limbs were too numb to pull myself out.

I will die here, I thought.

As I clung desperately to the ice, I saw a hulking figure lumbering toward me. It was enormous, oblivious to the wind and snow that blew against its hide, and its white fur blended in with the storm until I could not tell where one ended and the other began. The creature stopped before me. I lifted my frozen lashes higher until I met the beast's brown eyes.

They were my mother's eyes. Human.

Nanuk. I reached out a hand. The Great White Bear lowered its head so that I could touch its muzzle. I opened my cracked lips, wanting to say something, not knowing what.

"I'm sorry," I finally whispered. Tears rolled down my cheeks. The grief that I had kept bottled since the destruction of my village now came spilling out. "I don't even—even have a token I can keep."

The Great White Bear said nothing in return. Instead, she closed her eyes and leaned against my hand. And I, dying, tried to understand what she wanted to tell me.

I felt something pushing me from underneath. *Father,* I called, but my word came out silent. The Seal King lifted me out of the icy waters into the cold blast of the storm's winds. I crawled forward. I heard shouting, but I couldn't tell where it came from. Ahead, Nanuk turned away from me and walked away across the glittering snow. I called after her, begging her to come back, but she did not listen.

I cried. The blizzard howled, threatening to devour me. The shouting returned, and as I tried in vain to find its source, I saw a pair of hands dragging at my hood. I tried to reach for them, to push them away, but my limbs were too numb. The world sharpened and blurred and sharpened again. As it faded away, a pair of faces appeared above me. They were pale, with thick beards and blue eyes.

Then the world turned dark, and I remembered no more.

A dim light. Footsteps and fire. Bubbling water. Most of all, warmth—a deep, soaking warmth that wrapped its way around my icy insides.

My eyes opened.

Wooden beams lined the ceiling. The glow from a fire lit the walls. I blinked, clearing my eyes, and looked around. A harpoon hung on the wall, and a deerskin covered an old wooden bench. Something bubbled in a pot by the fire, filling the air with rich aromas. It did not smell like anything I was familiar with. A stew, perhaps? Caribou? My eyes went to a wooden wall sculpture that looked like a bare tree with three lines through it.

I tentatively wriggled my toes and fingers. To my surprise, I could feel all of them. The bed beneath me crunched as I struggled to a sitting position and looked around the tiny room. I saw no sign of my dogs. Instead, a woman stirred a pot in one corner while a *gusak* man in a simple robe sat by a table with his head down.

The woman saw me stir first. The man at the table was a *gusak*, but this woman looked like me.

"I'm glad you're awake, child," she said. She spoke flawlessly in the Inupiat tongue. "I am Olga." She nodded to the *gusak* man, who looked up long enough to give her a kindly nod. "My husband, Peter. You're safe here. Your dogs are resting outside."

I could only stare. This woman married a *gusak*?

When I did not respond, Olga went on. "We are missionaries, from across the sea. We found you on the ice."

My pursuers were not the same as the men who came to my village.

Olga wiped her hands on her apron and came to sit beside me. She put a warm hand against my cheek. I trembled, unsure if I wanted to pull away or linger. "We are a part of a larger community," she said, nodding at the window, where snow blanketed the world. "We have taken in many orphaned by the traders. My husband and his men heard of what happened to the village farther north. You must be from there."

Mother, lying in the snow. Father, lost in the ocean. I closed my eyes and felt the Seal King lift me out of the water, the muzzle of the great Nanuk against my palm. I had followed the falling star, just as the tales said, and the star had led me *here*.

"Why did they burn our village?" I whispered.

Olga was quiet for a moment. "The world grows smaller," she finally said. "And small worlds cultivate greed. It is a grievous sin."

A great weight pressed against my chest, and I wanted to cry again. I didn't understand.

Olga gave me a sad look. "We are not all like them. I am sorry, child, for your loss, and I am sorry for them, for seeing such a small world."

Such a small world. When I was a child, I would spend hours looking out at the sea, asking Father what lay on the other side. I used to think that the ocean went on forever, until it became the sky and entered another realm. My thoughts wavered, confused and lost.

How did the world become so small?

Olga nodded at me. "You can stay for as long as you like," she said kindly. Then she told me to rest, and went back to her pot.

I lay back down, thinking.

Olga offered me a rich stew, swimming with chunks of caribou and fat roots. She watched as I ate. Then she and her husband, Peter, turned their backs on me in the night, extinguishing their candles.

I lay awake for a long time. I still had my harpoon. These

gusaks did not protect themselves. They were just like my village. Helpless.

But I continued to lie in bed and did not move. In my mind, Nanuk came to me and spoke. She spoke words so ancient that I could not repeat them. But I understood. The grief in my heart lightened, turning fainter like a dying star until it flickered out of existence, leaving only a feeling of peace.

The promise of the next village, of a place I understood in this small world, lingered in my thoughts. I had to continue on.

I left early the next morning, before anyone woke. It was so early that I could still see the thick band of stars across the sky. Ataneq waited for me in the snow, tail wagging, and with him were the rest of my dogs, sheltered from the last of the passing snow by the wall of the *gusak* missionaries' home. I threw my arms around Ataneq's neck and buried my face in his fur. *"Aahali,"* I whispered. "Good dog." I checked the others, fixed their harnesses, and turned my sled away from the *gusak* village. I thought I saw the cloth at the window stir, and wondered if Olga was watching me. But I did not look back, and she did not come out to stop me.

I took a deep breath, glanced up at the sky, and bid farewell to my parents. Then I whistled, and Ataneq guided us forward. The *gusak* village disappeared behind us. Empty tundra and open sky became my surroundings again.

As evening arrived, I found myself looking down upon an Inupiat village, its lights glittering against the snow. I wanted to laugh, to cry. Already, a few of the village's women had looked up from their work in my direction, and their arms waved in the air. A hunter headed toward us.

As I stood there, I turned my face up to the sky and saw ribbons of a red aurora trailing behind the scattered clouds.

❧ *Author's Note* ❧

Jean Craighead George's *Julie of the Wolves* was one of my
favorite childhood books; the copy I had was completely falling
apart from overuse. Miyax's harsh, bleak, yet awe-inspiring and
very much alive Alaskan wilderness haunted me. So, in picking
a time and setting for an American historical short story, I knew
fairly quickly that I had to set mine in the Great Land.

Researching Alaska, I loved the blurred line between
history and Inuit folklore. This is an old land where the sun
permanently sets for months on end, where dogs pull sleds
across hundreds of miles of snow and ice, and where colorful
sheets of light dance in the sky — the facts already *feel* magical.
I loved reading about the Inuit culture and the connections
between man and beast, as well as the clash of this world with
the modern age, and the end of an era. I hope readers enjoy
Yakone's journey.

{ 1826: New Orleans, Louisiana }

Madeleine's Choice

Jessica Spotswood

I HAVE A SECRET.

It tastes like the sweet lemonade they served at last night's ball and smells of pipe tobacco. It sounds like the waltz we danced to and feels like the press of his hand against mine through my white satin glove.

We can't—won't—touch skin to skin. Not unless—*until*—Papa accepts his offer.

I dream of Antoine's bare skin against mine. Of him bending, his honey-colored eyes drifting closed (people close their eyes when they kiss, don't they? My best friend, Eugenie, says they do), his nose and cheeks sunburned from riding through his family's sugarcane fields, his brown beard with that hint of red in it scratchy against my cheek. I feel certain his beard would be scratchy, and his lips—thin though they are—soft. Gentle. I'd close my eyes too, and melt against him, and—

"Maddie!" Eugenie catches my elbow to keep me from running into old Madame Augustin. Madame purses her lips, her rheumy eyes narrowing in disapproval, face scrunching up till she looks like a pecan—but though I'm the one who was woolgathering and almost knocked her into the street, it's Eugenie she frowns at.

If Papa accepts, will Madame Augustin look at me like that?

"Sorry, Madame!" I squeak.

"Mademoiselle Madeleine." She gives me a quick nod and then sniffs at Eugenie. "Mademoiselle Dalcour."

Eugenie waits until we've turned the corner before muttering, "Snooty old bat."

I giggle and we stroll down the wooden banquette. Above us, the spring sky is a cloudless blue against the lacy wrought-iron galleries. In another month the heat will be unbearable, but just now the sunshine is warm and reassuring against my face. Eugenie links her arm through mine, and my confidence soars. I will talk to Maman this afternoon and tell her about Antoine. *Monsieur Guerin,* I correct myself. There's no need to make things worse with a lack of propriety.

It can't get much worse, my conscience needles me. Maman's going to be so angry.

Four weeks in a row, I've gone to Eugenie's house on the pretext of keeping her company while her mother was at a ladies' aid meeting. Four weeks in a row, I've gone with Eugenie and Madame Dalcour to a quadroon ball instead.

That first time, it was just a lark. I knew Maman would never approve; she thinks the dances are little better than slave auctions, a disgrace to the *gens de couleur libres,* and she doesn't consider Madame Dalcour a proper chaperone because Madame is not truly married to Eugenie's father. It's a *mariage de la main gauche;*

Madame is mulatto and Monsieur Reynaud is white, and under the laws of Louisiana, they cannot marry. My parents raised me for better—to marry a good colored man from one of the good colored families in the Quarter. I thought I'd have some fun, then go home and never think anything else of it. I certainly didn't set out to find a protector.

But Antoine asked me to dance—and then asked for a second dance. And when he inquired if he'd see me the following week—me, not Eugenie!—I said yes. One falsehood turned into two, turned into three, turned into four, and now . . .

Now it's been four weeks. Eight dances, two each night. More would be improper without an understanding between us.

Eugenie elbows me. "At least Monsieur Guerin isn't an *American*." She waltzed with an American last night, and Madame Dalcour nearly had an attack of apoplexy over it. Madame is fiercely proud of her French ancestry. She expects Eugenie to find a protector, but he'd better be a Creole like Eugenie's father—a white man of good French stock.

"There is that," I agree, though I'm not sure it will make much difference to my mother that Antoine comes from a good Creole family with a sugar plantation up in St. James Parish, a family that's been in Louisiana since it was a French colony. She won't care how dashing and romantic he is, or what pretty compliments he pays me, or that my pulse flutters when I spot him across the crowded ballroom.

Maman will only care that Antoine is white, and that it's not marriage he's offering.

But I need her to listen. I need her to intercede with Papa for me and persuade him to accept Antoine.

We stop in front of Papa's livery. Papa's family has been in

Louisiana as long as Antoine's, but they were slaves back then. His great-grandfather was freed after he fought the Indians for the French.

Eugenie wrinkles her nose at the pile of dung in the street and the flies buzzing around. I grew up next to the stables, so the stench doesn't even register until I see her look of distaste. Then I swallow a surge of shame. Madame Dalcour's cottage on the Rue des Remparts always smells of fresh flowers and the Valencia orange trees out front. Eugenie has one older brother, and he lives in France now; she doesn't have to endure the twins tussling and baby Marie Therese shrieking and the horses clomping in and out below. At Eugenie's home, everything is quiet and orderly and beautiful.

I dream of having my own elegant cottage and idle, leisurely afternoons.

Maman tolerates Eugenie, but she's never approved of our friendship. She says Eugenie fills my head with romantic nonsense and uses me to increase her standing in the Quarter. But I don't care what anyone says. Eugenie isn't like that; she's good to me. She's let me rattle on for weeks about how torn I feel between what I want and what my parents want for me.

I bite my lip. Truth is, in the quiet of Eugenie's parlor, an arrangement with Antoine felt possible. Almost respectable, even.

Running into Madame Augustin in the street—well, it's reminded me that people see Eugenie and me differently. Expectations are different.

They expect Eugenie, with her wild curls and smart mouth, to follow in her mother's footsteps. To know about things like kissing. They expect me to be an innocent—a demure, respectable girl who'll grow up to be a staid, respectable wife.

Only I can't stop thinking what it would be like to kiss Antoine, to have him pull me close — closer than a waltz, even, and —

"I'm going to talk to Maman this afternoon," I announce.

Eugenie raises her eyebrows. "That's what you said last week, Maddie. You'd better do it soon or Monsieur Guerin will find another girl."

I clutch the fringed shawl draped over her elbow. "Do you think he would?" It wouldn't be difficult. I saw the way the other girls looked at me when we danced — even Eugenie. She's the one looking for a protector, but I caught the eye of the most eligible man in the room.

"I wouldn't keep a man like that waiting, is all. Why would he keep courting you when he's got dozens of girls ready to fall at his feet? Girls whose parents aren't so — *particular*?" My stomach twists, but Eugenie's right.

"Maman will listen to me. I know she will," I say, a trifle desperately.

"You're such a child." Eugenie adjusts her shawl over the sloping shoulders of her red plaid dress and gives me a little wave. "*Bonne chance*, Maddie. You're going to need it."

"Madeleine! You're late," Maman says the moment I hurry through the door. Marie Therese is squalling in her arms. The twins are playing in the courtyard under our maid Nanette's watchful eye, fencing with sticks. We'll be lucky if they don't poke each other's eyes out.

"Maman, I — I need to speak with you," I say in a breathless rush. "It's important."

I hate the way my voice trembles and makes it into a question.

"Later, *chère*." Maman pulls the blue tignon off my head. I protest as she pats my hair back into place. "You have a caller." She motions toward the parlor, where the door stands ajar. "Etienne Decoudreaux is here to see you."

"To see *me*?" Our families are the best of friends; our papas served together in one of the colored regiments during the Battle of New Orleans. As children, Etienne and I chased each other through the courtyards and played hide-and-seek and begged his mother for her famous lemon pie. Since I turned sixteen and started going to balls — the ones my family approves of, with the best of the *gens de couleur libres* — Etienne and I have danced together, even eaten supper together at dances a few times. But he's never called on me. "What does he want?"

Maman gives me a little push. "Go in and talk to the boy and let him tell you himself."

Etienne is silhouetted against the window, watching the horses in the paddock below. He turns when I come in, giving me a restrained smile that doesn't show his teeth. It's nothing like Antoine's mischievous grin, which lights up his whole face and makes his eyes crinkle at the corners. Etienne is nicely turned out, in a dark, high-collared waistcoat, his cravat a snowy white against the smooth brown skin of his throat. Last night Antoine's cravat was fine blue silk fastened with a gold pin. It's the difference between a cabinetmaker and a planter.

I perch on the blue chintz settee. Etienne sits in a high-backed chair, trailing his fingers along the arm, inspecting the craftsmanship.

We exchange the usual pleasantries about the fine spring weather and business at the Decoudreauxes' shop. I give him short replies, preoccupied with trying to find the right words, the perfect combination that will persuade Maman to at least hear me out about Antoine. I'm being rude, hardly paying attention to Etienne, until I catch something about our families' long friendship and the high regard he holds me in. Then my eyes snap to his. He looks so—earnest.

My fingers turn to ice in my lap.

"I have the utmost admiration for you—the utmost respect," he says. "I'd be a good husband to you. A good provider. Will you do me the honor of becoming my wife, Maddie?"

I suppose if I'd been paying attention, I would have known this was coming.

"I—I'm very honored," I start. My gaze drops to the wooden floor. I don't want to hurt him. I like Etienne. When I'm not being such a scatterbrain, we talk easily enough; he makes me laugh. But my heart doesn't pound, my stomach doesn't tumble, my skin doesn't *thrill* at his touch. Now that I know how love feels, how can I give it up for something so—comfortable?

"This is all very sudden," I lie.

Etienne nods, tapping long, elegant fingers against his fawn-colored trousers. "Of course. You need time to think."

I can't bear the polite fiction of it, the notion that I'm a silly, fragile mademoiselle too shocked by this turn of events to know her own mind. "I'm in love with someone else," I blurt.

He winces. "Who?" And for a moment, it's like we're children again. Honest. Then: "Forgive me. That's none of my concern. I thought—your father led me to believe you were unattached."

I bite my lip, clenching a fistful of my yellow cotton skirt. There's a little tear in the hem; I'll have to sew it later.

"Papa doesn't know."

Etienne's eyes widen. "You've betrothed yourself without your father's permission?"

"No. Not—not officially," I stammer. How did I get myself into this muddle? I can't tell Etienne that it isn't marriage I'm considering.

What would he think of me?

Etienne is a kind man, a good man, and he would think less of me for it.

It slices into me, the sudden surety that my parents will too. Why else have I been hiding it from them? You don't need to hide something unless it's shameful. Maman will look at me the same way she looks at Madame Dalcour, at Eugenie. As a girl who would sell her own virtue.

But it isn't about the money to me, or the position. It's about the way I feel when I'm with Antoine.

What I have done is disgraceful. I have been deceitful and disobedient.

But I'd do it again for the chance to have him hold me in his arms like I'm something precious, like the porcelain dolls Eugenie's father brought her back from France. Antoine makes me feel beautiful. Desired. He could have his pick of any of the girls in that ballroom, and he chose me.

Is it love I feel, or pride? That he chose me — tall, dark, voluptuous — rather than pretty little light-skinned Eugenie?

I fidget, tugging at one of my puffed sleeves. Now that I've told Etienne, it feels even more real — not just something I've dreamed up. "Please don't say anything to my father. I need to talk to Maman first."

"Of course. It's none of my —" Etienne interrupts himself with a shake of his curly head. He stands, lean and graceful. "That isn't true. What happens to you *does* concern me. We've been friends since we were children. I want you to be happy, Maddie."

I remember my mother's smile, the way she shoved me toward the parlor. Etienne is what my parents want for me.

"I don't know what to say," I manage, finally, stupidly.

"Then don't say no. Think about it," he urges.

I nod — because I'm a coward, because it's easier — and then he's gone. The door creaks shut behind him. Maman comes in a moment later.

"Etienne left with such a scowl. What happened?" she asks.

I avoid her gaze. "I told him I couldn't marry him."

"What? Why not?" She plants her hands on her wide hips. "Etienne is a good man. The Decoudreauxes are a good family. He would be a good husband to you."

My heart falls. "I—I know, Maman. But I'm in love with someone else."

"With who?" she demands. "Francois?"

"Francois Meilleur? *Mon Dieu!*" I gape at her. Francois has a rabbity smile and tromps on my toes when we dance. "No!"

"Then who?" She sits in the chair Etienne just vacated, leaning forward, waiting for my answer.

I take a deep breath, summoning up my courage. "Antoine Guerin."

"Guerin?" She tilts her head thoughtfully. "I don't know the family."

I close my eyes. I can't bear to see her face when I confess. "I didn't stay with Eugenie while Madame Dalcour went to a ladies' aid meeting last night, Maman. I went with them to a ball. At the Ursulines Ballroom."

"I see." I can tell from the knife's edge in her voice that she does. "This man—Monsieur Guerin—he is white?"

I nod. "He's from a very respectable family. Madame Dalcour says—"

"Madame Dalcour!" My mother snorts in a very unladylike fashion. "Lisette Dalcour would not know respectable if it slapped her across the face. Which I've half a mind to do. Taking my daughter to make a spectacle of herself in—"

"I didn't make a spectacle of myself!" I protest, stung. "We only danced twice each time. And he made an offer for me! Madame said it's —"

She holds up a hand, forestalling me. "I do not want to hear one more word about what Madame Dalcour says!" She stands, her slippers whispering against the wooden floor as she paces. "Did she ever suggest that you consider what this man has to offer you, besides money? Perhaps for a few years he'll devote himself to you, and then what? He'll marry someone of his own class, his own race, to provide a proper heir, and you'll be left raising his children. He'll give you a nice settlement — or perhaps he'll come visit you a few times a year, and you'll have to live for that. Use your head, Maddie."

Tears spring into my eyes at her tone. "How can you judge? Grand-père was white. He and Grand-mère never married."

Maman draws herself up. She is a tall woman, voluptuously built, not bird boned like Madame Dalcour and Eugenie. I take after her in that and in my straight hair, though not her alabaster skin — the twins and I favor Papa, with his walnut complexion. Some say Maman married down, a liveryman with dark skin; but then some say Papa married down, an illegitimate quadroon girl, no matter how fair.

How many times have my parents told me that our good name is all we have? That we may be free, but we are still judged by the color of our skin and the curl in our hair and the broadness of our features?

Anger sweeps over me. Truth is, part of the reason Maman is so delighted by Etienne's offer is because he has lighter skin than me and more delicate features, and our children would be beautiful. Every colored mother in the Quarter thinks about such things.

An arrangement with Antoine would give Maman even lighter grandbabies. But they'd be illegitimate.

"I am well aware that I am not legitimate myself," she says, her voice low. "But things were different then. Grand-père never took a wife. He lived with us, not in some house out in the country. He and Maman may not have married, but they loved each other."

"Antoine said he loves me and wants the privilege of taking care of me," I argue. "He said I am the most beautiful girl he's ever seen, and—"

"You are beautiful," Maman agrees. "But a future husband should know more about you than that. This man is a stranger. Your father and I have never even met him! You must see how impossible this is."

"Won't you even consider it?" I plead, slumping in my chair. Then I think of Maman's oft-chided *Don't slouch, Maddie,* and straighten. I want her to think of me as a grown woman who knows my own mind, not a child needing her permission.

"Your father and I will not entertain less than a proper offer of marriage. You will not go back to that ballroom. You will not see this man again. Do you understand?" She kneels next to me, grasping my chin with pinching fingers, forcing me to meet her gaze. "Madeleine. Promise me."

"I promise," I mumble.

"Your father and I will not force you to marry Etienne, but I hope you will think about his proposal." Maman stares me right in the eyes. "Lisette Dalcour's life may look pretty from the outside. And perhaps she is happy. Who am I to say? But it seems to me a lonely life. She came from Saint-Domingue with only her mother, and she and Eugenie have no other family now that Charles has gone to France. I want more for you than that. Etienne would be your partner in all things. Like your father and I."

I stare back at my mother, at the shadows beneath her eyes and the gray twining through her silky hair. She's given birth to eight children and buried four before their first birthdays. Even with Nanette's help, she is forever harried, exhausted from sewing, washing, cooking, and chasing after the little ones. By contrast, Madame Dalcour's days seem full of leisure. She calls upon her friends or her dressmaker, she does fine embroidery, and she waits for Eugenie's father to visit.

"I won't even mention this to your father," Maman says.

I scowl at her. "If you are partners in all things, how can you keep secrets?"

Sadness, not anger, flickers across her face. "Because he would be disappointed in you," she says simply, rising to her feet.

"I have no choice?" I ask. "I can never see Antoine—Monsieur Guerin—again, no matter what I feel for him?"

Maman puts her hand on my shoulder. "Think of what you feel for your family instead, Madeleine. You cannot have us both."

It should be easy, shouldn't it? To choose my family and everything I've ever known?

But I keep hearing Eugenie's voice in my head: *You're such a child.* A child still scared of her parents' disapproval. When Madame Dalcour forbids Eugenie something, Eugenie laughs and does it anyway. She's bold. It's always been what I liked best about her.

"I don't want you seeing Eugenie again," Maman tells me before bed. "I knew no good would come from you spending time with that girl. Your father said I was being too harsh, but look what's come of it."

I nod, eyes downcast, guilt pricking my heart because I've no intention of giving up my best friend too. I can't disappear without giving Antoine an answer. Eugenie has to help me get word to him. Perhaps he'll wait for me. Perhaps, in time, I can convince my mother.

The following afternoon, I seize my chance. Maman packs a basket of food and goes to call on a friend whose baby has been stillborn. She gives me extra chores and tells Nanette to make certain I don't leave the house, though I insist that I hardly need a nursemaid. I hate that I am breaking Maman's trust again, but I watch out the window until I see her red tignon disappear around the corner, and then set out.

"I'll be back before Maman. Don't you dare breathe a word to her," I order Nanette. I pay for her silence with the money I get selling eggs at the market. Nanette is married to one of Papa's stableboys, and I know they hope to purchase their freedom someday.

I hurry to Eugenie's home at the back of the Quarter. I hammer on the door of the yellow stucco cottage, shifting from foot to foot, hoping no one will see me and mention it to Maman.

Eugenie opens the door herself, and I barely cross the threshold before I'm pouring out the story—how Maman refused to even consider Antoine's suit, how Etienne proposed, how I hope in time I can make Maman see reason . . .

"In time? You expect a man like that to wait for *you*?" Eugenie shakes her head. By this time we're sitting together on the cream-colored silk settee in the parlor. "I thought you had more sense than that, Maddie, I really did."

"She's my mother," I protest. "Even if I don't agree with her, I have to respect—"

"Do you? I thought you were in love—like something out of one of your novels, you said!" Eugenie's voice is laced with lemons.

"And now you're willing to give him up to please your mother? I thought you had more *spine* than that too."

"I—I do," I stutter, curling into myself. I suppose I deserve for her to talk to me this way. "But Maman loves me. She wants better for me."

Eugenie stiffens, her hand flying to her tight, fuzzy curls, which have gone every which way in the sticky heat. She is light skinned and fine featured, but that hair is the bane of her existence.

Her brother, Charles, with his fine, straight hair and light eyes, could pass for white. Monsieur Reynard sent him to Paris years ago, and Eugenie and Madame Dalcour seldom hear from him. Eugenie says he married a white woman and doesn't want his wife to know about his colored mother and sister.

I think it broke Eugenie's heart a little.

I could cut out my careless tongue.

"Do you think you're better than me?" she demands.

"Of course not! You could marry if you wanted."

She crosses her arms over her chest. "And then what? I'd have a carpenter for a husband. Or a liveryman." She gives me a sideways look.

Anger simmers in my stomach—and guilt, because haven't I thought the same thing? "There's nothing wrong with good, honest work."

"Not if you don't mind your man coming home smelling of sweat and shit," Eugenie says, and I gasp at her crude language. "No. I want more for myself than that. I want a fine gentleman like Antoine, a man who will provide for me and give me a beautiful life."

She looks pointedly around the parlor, and my eyes follow hers to the pink roses in the crystal vase, the fine china on the tea table, the thick patterned rug on the floor. Our rug at home is worn thin from the twins playing on it and stained from food they've dropped and mud they've tracked in. We can't have pretty knick-knacks anywhere within reach lest the little ones break them. And last time Papa brought Maman flowers, we found Marie Therese chewing on a magnolia.

But our house is full of laughter too. Of the twins' rambling, silly stories and Marie Therese's babbling baby talk and Nanette humming songs. Of Papa reading stories from the Bible at night and Maman telling him the neighborhood gossip while she does her mending. The cottage around me now is silent as Saint Louis Cemetery. I remember my mother's claim that Madame Dalcour is lonely. For all that I've envied her—well, it occurs to me for the first time that perhaps Eugenie is too.

I lay a hand on her forearm. "If a fine gentleman like Antoine is what you want, then that's what you'll have. Nothing ever stands in your way, Eugenie."

"Because I *know* what I want," Eugenie mutters. "And I chase after it."

I shrink back against the settee. This all seemed so simple at the ball, when Antoine and I were dancing. Maybe I am just as spineless and easily swayed as Eugenie says.

Or maybe I just need one more opinion. A sign. From some-one who has no stake in this.

I shoot to my feet. "I have an idea," I announce.

The Widow Paris is known throughout the Quarter as a voodoo queen, a healer and conjurer. Women go to her for good-luck charms, husband-holding charms, money-making charms . . . and for darker purposes too. Maman says it's all nonsense, but some of the girls at school swore by her.

I get as far as her front door and then my bout of confidence fails me.

"Are you going to knock or not?" Eugenie demands, tapping her boot impatiently.

The way she looks at me—as if she's expecting me to run home like a scared little mouse—gives me new determination. I reach up and rap on the door of the small one-story cottage.

A tall dark woman in a simple pale-blue frock opens the door. "How can I help you?" she asks.

"We're looking for the Widow Paris? Marie Laveau?" I ask.

The woman nods, her lips twitching in what might be a faint smile. "I am she." She glances from me to Eugenie. "Are you here for a love charm?"

I shake my head. Eugenie has gone uncharacteristically silent, staring at the pomegranate and banana trees in the front yard. It's up to me to speak. "No. But I—I do hope you might be able to help me," I say. "I'm at a—crossroads of sorts, and I don't know which way to turn. My family says one thing, my friend advises another."

The young widow's eyes fasten on mine. I assumed she was older, but she can't be more than twenty-five. Her brown face is smooth, save for a few lines at the corners of her mouth.

"Her parents are trying to force her into marriage with a man she doesn't love," Eugenie spits. "Out of some misguided notion of *propriety*."

"They wouldn't force me," I correct her. "They want what's best for me."

Eugenie rolls her eyes. "And I don't?"

Marie looks sharply at Eugenie. The moment stretches out like a frayed hair ribbon. "I see," she says finally. "Come inside."

Marie leads us into the front room. Dozens of candles are lit and incense burns; the room is small and close with the sweet, heady scent of it. There is an altar with fresh flowers and statues of three saints: Saint Anthony, patron saint of lost things; Saint Peter, who is said to open the door to the spirit world and remove barriers to success; and Saint Marron, the patron saint of runaway slaves. Marie turns the big statue of Saint Anthony on its head, and I stifle a gasp at the irreverence.

"I need something of yours for the *gris-gris,* chère," she says. "Hair, or a fingernail, or . . ."

The girls at school talked about this part, but a tremor of fear still runs up my spine. What if she uses this talisman to curse me or for some other dark purpose?

Eugenie doesn't give me time to think. She leans close, plucks a hair right out of my head, and hands it to Marie. I glare at her and adjust my tignon.

"This will do," Marie says. She opens a small wooden cabinet next to her altar. It's lined with jars full of all manner of strange things: bundles of roots, herbs, hot peppers, sugar or salt, dirt, pins and needles, nails, and Lord knows what else. Some of them look to be animal parts. She mixes items from different jars into a little cloth bag, then chants some unfamiliar words, her hands reaching out toward her altar, supplicating the saints. The candles flicker. Eugenie is watching with wide-eyed fascination, but I bow my head because whether I believe in this or not—and truth be told, I'm not certain—it is clearly sacred to Marie.

When she finishes chanting, I raise my eyes. Marie sprinkles holy water over the little bag and then hands it to me. "Keep the *gris-gris* on your person," she instructs. "It will ward off those who do not have your best interests at heart. Without their false counsel, you will find your own way."

"Thank you." I fumble in my reticule for coins. "I—I don't know how much—"

"Fifteen cents," Marie says, and I hand her the appropriate amount. Between this and bribing Nanette, today has made quite a dent in my egg money. Marie studies my face. "Good luck to you, Madeleine."

The hair on the back of my neck prickles, and gooseflesh rises across my skin. I nod, unsettled, and flee with Eugenie back out into the hot May sun.

A week passes, but I am no closer to understanding my own heart. I spend my days helping Maman and Nanette with a spring cleaning, beating the quilts and rugs, hanging linens on the drying line in the courtyard. I am quiet, withdrawn. Maman eyes me and scoops extra helpings of gumbo into my bowl. I feign a headache to avoid attending a ball with my family; I cannot bear to face Etienne. He asked me to think more on his offer of marriage, and I do. I can't stop thinking of it.

I watch Maman and Papa.

He works late sometimes, and he does come home smelling of sweat and dung and horse. But she doesn't seem to mind. She smiles at him across the dinner table while she relates the little details of our days. They beam at each other when Marie Therese takes her first wobbly steps. Maman cooks liver for him even though she hates the smell. Papa pours her a steaming cup of coffee every morning before he goes to work, and she always thanks him for it, even as she's wrestling the boys into their clothes or nursing Marie Therese.

Am I wrong about love? Is it founded on mutual respect,

on like meeting like, not on heart-pounding, stomach-churning nervousness and pretty compliments?

On the seventh day, Maman looks at the plummy circles beneath my eyes and sighs. "Why don't you go visit Eugenie?"

"Truly?" I ask, and she gives me a pained smile. I jump up and leave a smacking kiss on her cheek. "Thank you!"

I change into a high-waisted petal-pink visiting gown, slip the *gris-gris* into the pocket of my skirts, and leave immediately, though gray clouds are threatening an afternoon storm. I've missed Eugenie's gossip, her bossiness, her big, booming laugh—so unexpected in such a small girl. And last night was the quadroon ball. Did Madame Dalcour tell Antoine that my parents refused his offer? Was he terribly heartbroken? I've imagined all sorts of scenarios; now I'm desperate to know the truth of it.

I'm striding down the Rue des Remparts when I notice the fine horse tied to the hitching post. I hesitate. Monsieur Reynard, perhaps? But he usually rides a black gelding. I notice horses, thanks to Papa. This one has white fetlocks and a gleaming chestnut coat, and it twitches its blond tail drowsily to ward off flies.

I'm still standing there when the front door of Eugenie's cottage opens and a man steps out.

I blink, disbelieving.

It's Antoine Guerin.

My Antoine.

Calling on Eugenie and Madame Dalcour.

My first, foolish thought is that he's come to beg Madame to intercede on his behalf, to plead his suit to my parents.

Then I remember that spark of envy in Eugenie's eyes when Antoine first asked me to dance. Her words play over in my mind. *I want a fine gentleman like Antoine, a man who will provide for me and give me a beautiful life. . . . I know what I want. And I chase after it.*

And I know with a sudden, terrible certainty that she hasn't been pleading my case at all.

I stand there, frozen despite the thick, sultry air of the coming storm. Antoine looks in my direction and—oh, no—his brown eyes meet mine. They don't crinkle now; his lips don't tilt into his charming, flirtatious smile. He doesn't even nod. He just looks away, mounts his horse, and rides off down the street.

Tears fill my eyes.

I can't pretend he didn't recognize me.

He looked me right in the face and cut me dead.

Eight days ago, he held me close while we waltzed. He pressed my hand and told me I was the most beautiful girl he'd ever seen and that he would speak to Madame Dalcour about our future. He said he *loved* me. And now—

Unless I am much mistaken—and I truly don't think I am— he's become my best friend's protector.

I stare at the yellow stucco cottage, at the orange tree in front.

Then I pick up my pink skirts and hurry away as fast as decorum will allow. Marie Laveau's *gris-gris,* tucked into my skirts, brushes against my thigh with every step. She showed me who I could trust, all right.

The rain starts when I'm halfway home. I duck down the Rue Burgundy. It's the shortest route home, and the galleries over the banquettes will protect me from the downpour. But the Decoudreauxes' shop is here. I keep my face turned away from the shop windows, but a familiar voice calls my name.

"Monsieur Decoudreaux, good afternoon." My smile comes out more a grimace.

Etienne's father stands at the open door of their shop. "Mademoiselle Madeleine, please, come inside until the storm passes. How is your family?"

I cannot refuse without being rude, so I follow him. "They're all very well, thank you." The store smells of freshly cut wood and the lemon juice they mix into the furniture wax. Etienne stands behind the counter.

"I'll let the two of you visit a bit," Monsieur Decoudreaux says, grinning as he abandons us for the workshop in back. He leaves the door ajar for propriety.

Etienne comes out, running his hands along a dressing table. "Did you make that?" I ask, and he nods without meeting my eyes. "It's beautiful."

I daydreamed about sitting before a dressing table like that, fixing my hair just so in front of the looking glass, readying myself for Antoine's arrival.

My skin goes hot with embarrassment, and angry tears prick at my eyes.

Etienne steps closer, lowering his voice. "Maddie, you look— not quite yourself. Are you unwell?"

"I'm *furious*, is what I am." The words come out before I can think them through.

He takes a wary step backward. "Not with me, I trust?"

"No. With myself, for being a fool." He gestures for me to sit, and I plop down in a rocking chair, heedless of my posture. My hems are muddy, bedraggled strands of hair are escaping from my tignon, and I'm sure I look a mess.

Etienne props his hip against a handsome desk opposite me. "I doubt you're a fool. At least, you never have been before."

I look up at him. He's a good man. He didn't feed me extravagant compliments, didn't flatter and flirt, but I've no doubt that he *meant* what he said. And if I'm to consider marrying him—well, he ought to know what I am, for better or for worse.

"I almost entangled myself in a—an arrangement. Like

Madame Dalcour. Maman told me she and Papa wouldn't even consider it. And today—today I found out that the man I thought was in love with me has made Eugenie Dalcour an offer. I thought I was special, but it wasn't me he wanted at all—any girl would do."

I bury my face in my hands.

Etienne reaches out and pries my fingers away from my face. "He's the fool," he says softly. "You are special, Maddie."

He doesn't let go of my hands. His bare fingers are big and warm and callused from his carpentry work.

"That's kind of you. Kinder than I deserve," I say. My eyes meet his and then skitter away. "I—I didn't even *know* him. Whether he has brothers or sisters. What his favorite food is. What games he played growing up."

"Are those things you think you should know about a future husband?" Etienne asks, and I nod. "Well. You know my brothers, and you know the games I played growing up because you were there. My favorite food is—"

"Your mother's lemon pie," I interrupt.

He grins. This one shows his teeth. "You remember that?"

"How could I forget? You'd eat the whole thing in a trice if she let you." I laugh, thinking of the way Etienne used to scale the trees in the Decoudreauxes' courtyard to get at the lemons and then beg his mother to make him a pie.

Etienne laughs too, then looks out the front window. The rain has stopped, in the way of spring storms. He stands, letting go of my hands, searching my face with his dark eyes. "May I walk you home?"

"Yes," I say, taking his arm. "I'd like that."

🌼 *Author's Note* 🌼

When I was twelve, I went on a road trip with my grandparents through the South. One of our stops was New Orleans. We took a steamboat ride down the Mississippi, ate beignets at Café Du Monde, and walked through the colorful streets of the French Quarter. I was immediately smitten. Over the years, I've returned to the city half a dozen times, drawn by the fascinating history and the sense that there is no other place quite like it. When I had to pick a place and subject for my story, I knew immediately that I wanted to write about New Orleans and the *gens de couleur libres.*

New Orleans in the early nineteenth century had three distinct castes: white, slave, and the *gens de couleur libres,* the free people of color. While the last are often remembered for the infamous quadroon balls and the arrangements between white men and free women of color, many were respected middle-class tradesmen and business owners. One very mythologized free woman of color was the voodoo priestess Marie Laveau. To read more about her, I recommend Carolyn Morrow Long's *A New Orleans Voudou Priestess: The Legend and Reality of Marie Laveau,* and to learn more about the *femmes de couleur libres,* I recommend Emily Clark's *The Strange History of the American Quadroon: Free Women of Color in the Revolutionary Atlantic World.*

Los Destinos

Leslye Walton

F OLKS AROUND HERE LIKE TO SAY WE came from the stars. Perhaps it's simpler to think of us not as human but as creatures made of stardust—that if you cut us, not blood but constellations will pour from our wounds. And though I've never admitted to having such a thought to my sisters, when I stand under the night sky, with the infinite heavens stretched out above me like a shroud—it's hard to imagine we came from anywhere else.

Many years ago, when creatures made of rock and fire roamed the earth, both gods and mortals trembled in our presence. In the southern lands of Europe, they appeased us with figs and olives plucked from low drooping branches, and we licked the juices off our fingers with delight. A season passed, or perhaps it was a life-time, and we closed our weary eyes and awoke to a world of snow and ice. In the north we were giants, dark and stoic. We sat at the foot of the Tree of the World as the frost turned our limbs black with cold.

But even in our most formidable forms, we couldn't compare to the vastness of the desert sky. It is a sacred thing even on the most ordinary of nights, with Mamá huddled over her *colcha* embroidery and the vaqueros singing Spanish love songs around the fire.

On first sight, that sky was where fear came to rest. It was a sleeping beast we tried not to wake as we stumbled alone in the darkness, catching cactus spines in the heels of our naked feet as the coyotes screamed in the moonlight. My sister Maria Elena was screaming too, only I didn't know her as Maria Elena then, and I didn't know why she was screaming. I hadn't yet seen the damage, the way her foot was turned in on itself.

I'm not sure where we would be now had Papá not found us that night. At first glance, we must have looked like a creature with three heads huddled together under a mesquite tree, all fixated on what were once the hands of old women and were now those of young girls.

Of course, he knew who we were. *What* we were. Everyone always does. There has rarely been a time when our appearance hasn't been preceded by our reputation; our arrival comes with a change in the air, a scent on the breeze that brings both peace and desolation. But Papá had a young wife with a baby she'd just buried in his baptism gown, so when he found three monsters disguised as little girls, he took us home to his morose wife, who didn't seem to mind that the stench of death still lingered in our hair long after she bathed us with yucca root. After all, death was something she'd seen her fair share of, and besides, we have just as much to do with life as we do with death. Or so she reminds herself when she thinks we aren't listening.

But that's the thing about monsters; we're often in places you don't expect. Or want.

We've always been depicted as old women, as if we'd sprung from the depths of hell as hideous spinster crones with hunched backs and clawed fingers crippled with arthritis. Mamá says that's just an interpretation and we shouldn't pay no mind to silly stories folks got in their heads; no one can dispute that my sister Rosa is the prettiest girl this side of El Paso. And Maria Elena's leg might cause her trouble, but I dare you to look at that sweet face and tell me there isn't beauty there. If I'm honest, though, I think I preferred our previous form to this one. At least then the mortals knew to leave us well enough alone.

It's late now. I can feel my eyelids getting heavy, and I know I need to start making my way back home if I don't want one of my father's *peónes* finding me tomorrow morning when they bring the cattle out to pasture. The thought of them finding me asleep in the desert like some lost lamb, with dust gathered in the folds of my serape and my dark hair unraveling from its plait, makes me cringe. I was never much one for the nighttime; that's Rosa's time. When the moon is full and the village asleep, my sister roams the plains with her hair flying loose in the warm desert wind. My time is day, with the *cocina* alive with heat and noise and the smell of bread baking in the *horno* lingering in the air. And Maria Elena, the youngest of us all, her time is the morning, when the sun is just a whisper in the sky. That's what Mamá calls us: *mañana, día y noche*. Morning, day, and night.

From where I sit I can barely make out the ranch in the dark. The flickering light of a solitary oil lamp burning in a window is the only indication that the house stands there at all. I glance down and examine the thread I hold protectively in my hand. Right now, it's a deep carmine color, dyed such by Maria Elena's careful hands. But according to those stars burning high above my head, that color is soon to fade. With that thought, I shiver in the dark, and even I'm unsure whether it's because I'm cold or afraid.

I start down the hill, zigzagging past the puffs of white yucca flowers that stand out against the night like floating apparitions. As I approach our adobe home, I can just make out Rosa's pretty hair in the moonlight. At first, I think perhaps she is waiting for me, as if our roles are a torch we have to pass off, as if day has to hand the sun over to the night. Then I see James. I freeze, and my wool skirt catches in the spines of a lechuguilla plant.

It's been a few years since Texas won its independence, and though Papá still doesn't trust the *Americanos,* with their harsh dialect and strange trading wares, James is different. James has been here all his life — even before my sisters and I were found wandering in the desert. He is as much *Tejano* as we are. That is, if we are *Tejano* at all.

James gently tilts Rosa's chin and leans his face toward hers, and I look up again at the stars, embarrassed by the intimacy of it. The sky makes even the desert look small; though it was the desert that could have killed our mortal forms on that first night, it was the sky, so black in its infinity, that we feared.

I wake the next day to the sounds of Maria Elena hard at work on her loom. As usual, I have slept through most of the morning. I stretch and then rise to roll up my bed to put it away for the day. We sleep on sheepskins covered with wool blankets. They make for soft and pliable beds.

Walking into Maria Elena's weaving room is like pushing into a spiderweb; a catacomb of interwoven strands of yarn hangs from the ceiling and across the smooth adobe walls in brilliant shades of red, yellow, and green. In the center of it all stands the loom, stretching high over Maria Elena's small head.

Maria Elena insists that this lifetime is her favorite. It's true that she says that about every place we've been, but Maria Elena lives for beginnings. New place. New people. New day. She's often awake far before the crow of *el gallo* echoes across the rancho, setting to work on her loom before the sun has peeked up over the horizon.

I make my way into the room and find the loom has stopped. Maria Elena's head is bent and she has a tiny thread cupped in her hands. Hearing my footsteps, she looks up. Her expression is one of hope and sanguinity. "One of the villagers gave birth this morning," she says, holding the thread up for my inspection.

I gently pluck the thread from Maria Elena's dainty grip, but I don't have to look very closely to see that it isn't going to last very long. The thread's intended green hue has already faded, the color slowly being replaced by a shimmering silver with which I am all too familiar. Even if I hadn't already read it in the stars last night, I would know. The child's only fate is death.

Maria Elena's face falls when I shake my head. If we wait any longer, the mother's thread will begin to turn as well. If nothing else, lifetimes of experience have taught me this. "Go wake up Rosa," I say. "They won't last until tonight."

Maria Elena sighs. I watch as she makes her way through the labyrinth of threads that fill the room and block the door. I have to admire her agility; she somehow manages not to catch that leg of hers on even one loose thread.

I open my hand and peer at the thread Maria Elena just gave me. It sits curled in my palm, quiet and complacent, like a docile garter snake. Most of Maria Elena's threads are thick like ropes and just as sturdy. But this one is feeble at best. A weak little wisp of a thread that is growing more iridescent with every passing minute. It is so fragile, its color so faint that I fear if I drop it, I'll never be able to find it again. And neither of my sisters has the capability to help me either. Maria Elena weaves the threads. That's her role. It is my job to decipher which ones need to be cut.

It is Rosa who must cut them.

The uneven thumping sound of my younger sister's steps draws my eyes to the door. Maria Elena's face emerges from the web of threads, quickly followed by our elder sister, Rosa, though she certainly doesn't look much like herself. I stifle a laugh and she glares at me, shaking her foot free from a tangle of threads and rubbing her hands sloppily over her tired eyes. Rosa is typically the epitome of refinement; that she resembles such a disaster in the morning is the only reason I can bear to love her.

Rosa stretches her arms over her head and yawns noisily. "Well, where is it, then?"

Maria Elena points at me before shuffling to her loom and sitting down heavily. She runs her hands up and down the length of her impaired leg, kneading the sore muscles there, and I feel a twinge of guilt at having asked her to wake Rosa.

My older sister peers at the frail thread I hold out to her. "It's ready, then?" she asks me. I nod and then I hear it. We all do. It starts as a low thrumming sound, as if someone has reached over and plucked the string of a harp or a mandolin. The thread has begun its death song.

Rosa gives an irked nod, and a pair of large shears appears in her outstretched hand. She leans over and plucks the thread with the glinting edge of one of the shears' sharp blades. I want her to examine it, as if she can check the thread's *vitalidad* as well as I can, but that isn't Rosa's role. And it isn't her way, either. With barely a sigh of hesitancy, Rosa instructs me to pull the tiny thread taut. She cuts it in half with a quick snip of those mighty shears. I let them go, and the two pieces flutter to the ground like wounded birds, the silver sheen fading to a dull, lifeless brown. The task now complete, Rosa turns on her heel and ducks through the labyrinth, swinging her shears in time with her steps.

There is something that I find particularly frightening about those shears. Perhaps it is simply the rigid way she wields them. They once called her She Who Cannot Be Turned, and it was a proper moniker if there ever was one. There is no compromising with Rosa. Things are black or white with her; it is life or death. There is no in-between. Folks around here are swayed by the silk slippers on her dainty feet, the tortoiseshell comb that rises from the back of her elegant head like a crown, but they shouldn't be. Rosa is as empathetic as a wild animal. As benevolent as a disease. If she is a queen, she is one to be feared more than beloved. And the mortals used to know this. They used to fear her. They used to fear *us*. But, as I've learned, it is quite difficult to fear three young girls, especially ones that come in such beautiful and fragile forms as my sisters.

I glance over at Maria Elena. Now crouched on the ground, she is running her hands over the threads that carpet the floor, as if she can find the tiny thread by mere touch. "You read the stars last night, didn't you?" she murmurs.

I hesitate, considering my answer before I speak it aloud. My younger sister is all heart. She makes up for the sympathy that Rosa lacks. Perhaps it comes with the territory. It is, after all, by her small hands that the threads of life are spun. She needn't burden herself with the responsibility of determining the fate of another living soul. That is my job. And she certainly doesn't need to know the real reason I was out there, that it had very little to do with the brief life whose thread we just cut. So instead, I merely nod and allow my sensitive sister to grieve the short life as she pleases.

I still find it strange to look at my sister and see the face of a twelve-year-old girl staring back. And yet, despite the freckles that splash across her turned-up nose and the perfect ringlets that spill down her back, I can still see every lifetime we shared circling her brown irises like the rings of an ancient tree. Maria Elena has the eyes of an old soul, eyes that are, at the moment, brimming with tears.

I pat my sister's head, waiting for her sorrow to pass. I can tell by the patch of sunshine moving across the floor that the morning has faded into day and it is time for Maria Elena to pass the torch to me.

"Maybe I'll go see if Mamá needs help preparing for the fiesta," she says, wiping her eyes before winding her way out of the room. My heart, in all its wretched glory, stops at the mention of tonight's celebration.

"Or you could see about the *ristras*," I call. Maria Elena's callused fingers make her particularly gifted at stringing the chili peppers we hang to dry in the sun. Mamá says they have healing powers, but I usually can only finish a few before my fingers burn from the peppers' caustic bite.

I move through the room methodically, filling a willow basket with the threads that are fated to be cut tonight. They are easy to find, those flashes of silver amid a sea of color. My sister's threads haven't always been so brightly hued. I assume that it's a consequence of our surroundings. Colors exist here that can't be found anywhere else. Things aren't just *yellow* in the desert; they are saffron flowers on the top of a prickly pear cactus, golden sands encircling a sole mesquite tree. And red isn't just red; red is the carmine dye made from crushed cochineal insects and chili peppers warm from the sun. Blue is the heart-shaped blossoms on the indigo plant and black the pitch of the piñon tree and that frighteningly dark desert sky.

I don't think about the lives that are attached to the threads I'm collecting. It is a method I perfected lifetimes ago, but it seemed easier then, when we damned the gods to fates befitting their sins. Tucked into the band of my skirt is the thread I've carried since yesterday, when its strands began to shimmer. Try as I might, I can't ignore the life that is attached to this one. I wind one end of the thread around my finger and watch as another red strand fades to silver.

By midday, our pueblo ranch is a bustle of movement and noise. Maria Elena sits among a gaggle of old women basking in the sun in the *placita*. The women's cheeks are as withered as the blistered skins of the chili peppers resting in their laps.

"Come, sister," Maria Elena calls joyfully, setting her *ristras* to the side. "You've finished in time to help Rosa with her dress." My head suddenly rushes with a vision of my older sister in her bridal gown, a Spanish lace mantilla cascading down her back. It aches, the weight of it all: knowing the stars gave me no such image. It came solely from my own head.

My sisters were more than happy to let Mamá turn them into her good little *hijas*.

I watched as Rosa's face became beautiful under Mamá's proud gaze, as Maria Elena became strong. Even the names she gave them were telling. Maria Elena's name means "beloved shining light," and Rosa was named for the pink flush of her cheeks. Their tongues easily adapted to the cadence of Mamá's language; their hands lent themselves to menial tasks like cooking and cleaning. Every morning Maria Elena fetched water from the nearby river; every evening Rosa swept the earthen floors. Under Mamá's gentle guidance, my sisters weren't monsters anymore. But me? My hands were clumsy, my tortillas misshapen, my *torrejas* either doughy or burned. My monster, it seemed, would not be so easily tamed.

I follow Maria Elena's tottering steps, listening to the sound of the vaqueros driving the cattle farther down along the riverbed. They say only the promise of dancing with a pretty girl can persuade one of those wild cowboys to dismount from his horse, which perhaps explains the menfolk's unusually jovial tones. The whole ranch has been bewitched by the possibilities surrounding tonight's celebration, and all the while, my thoughts are consumed with the thread I hold clenched in my fist.

We escape into the cool retreat of Mamá's bedroom only to find it filled with many of the other women with whom we share a home—women who insist we call them *tía* and *abuela*, though they share no kinship with either Mamá or Papá. I catch a glimpse of Rosa in the center of the room, but she is too busy being doted on to pay much attention to me. The women greet Maria Elena warmly, pressing sweets into her hands. There isn't a soul in the village who doesn't love Maria Elena. And who could blame them? My softhearted sister with her tottering gait gives them life. And though death flows through Rosa's fingers like river water, she also brings them peace. She eases their suffering and puts an end to their pain. Besides, Rosa is so beautiful it is easy to overlook the scent of death that lingers on her skin.

But me? I'm not beautiful and I'm not broken, and as a result, my wickedness isn't quite as easily forgiven. After all, if Maria Elena is birth, and Rosa death, then I must be everything in between. I am turmoil and loss. I am drought and starvation. I am lost love and lost chances and lost hope. It is my hands that tie knots into their lives. And for this sin, the women choose to celebrate my sister's *boda* around me, avoiding my eyes as if I am the monster their children fear at night.

Rosa's bridal gown lies across the wooden bed where Mamá and Papá sleep. It is one of the only real pieces of furniture we own, and that alone makes it opulent and grand.

"Is the dress not beautiful?" Mamá says in that soft voice of hers. I nod, running my hands over the heavy silk brocade; even my crooked stitches marring the hem can't diminish its beauty. There is something about Mamá's voice that makes me ache for my younger sister's pleasant disposition or my older sister's striking beauty. It is a voice I know I will yearn for throughout the many lifetimes that follow this one. Mamá strokes my hair until her hand gets caught in the tangles along the back of my head. It hurts when she pulls her hand free, taking some of my unruly hair with it, but I don't say anything. Mamá named me Valeria, which means brave. Because what else could I be?

Later, when the church has been draped in flowers fashioned out of corn husks, and the feast is ready for tonight's celebration, I am finally allowed a reprieve from the revelry. I am given strict instructions to change into the dress Mamá made for the occasion, but instead I escape through the front gate, my steps startling the chickens clucking nervously in the yard.

When I see James, his hat is tipped low on his head, and all I can see is the back of his sun-kissed neck. In his hands he holds a baby rattlesnake, its tiny head clasped gently between his thumb and forefinger.

"Spooked the *vacas* a bit," James says cordially when he finally notices me. The snake is beautiful, its long muscled back patterned in dark octagonal splotches in a multitude of browns.

"I should probably kill it, but that seems a bit cruel, don't you think?" He holds it out to me, cradling it in his hands in a way that is far too reminiscent of the way Maria Elena held out that thread to me this morning. I run my finger down its head, and the snake darts out its tongue.

I glance at James's boots. They are covered in dust and mud from last week's rare desert rains. "You don't quite look the part of the groom, do you?" My attempt at gentle teasing falls short. My voice sounds flat and lifeless, as if it derives from a place of sorrow and bitterness. I take a breath, nostalgic for a time when the cold burned my lungs, and even the simple act of breathing was painful.

"Your sister's beauty will have to make up for us all." He smiles and then sets the snake down on the ground. A clangor of church bells fills the air as we watch the snake slink off into the desert. *"Adiós, monstruo,"* James calls, and for a moment, I am unsure as to whether he is talking to the snake or to me.

I met him first. Few folks remember it this way, or if they do, they've realized it's a truth that's hardly worth mentioning. Perhaps that's irony for you; the only love story I've ever played any part in, and my role has been reduced to nothing but an afterthought. Back then we were newly young, newly formed, my sisters and I still uncomfortable in our skin. I've never understood the claim that folks make around here, that young people act as if they're impervious to death; I've never felt more mortal than when I woke up to that dark sky and the looks of wonderment across my sisters' now youthful faces.

I remember the *cocina* was bathed in a gentle quietness, the kind that only comes in the early afternoon when everyone else is taking their daily siestas. The kitchen fire popped and crackled in the hearth, and I could smell the heady, pungent odor of the dried garlic that hung on the walls. A handful of peppers, large and bright green and still warm from the sun, lay splayed on the wooden table in front of me.

And then there he was. This tall lanky boy barely seventeen years of age, strolling into the kitchen like he had as much a right to be there as I did. But then again, his *papá* might have been as *Americano* as they come, but his *mamá* shared the same bloodlines as our *mamá*. So, by all fairness, he did belong there. Far more than I did. Because what blood could have possibly run through my veins? Maybe folks around here were right. Maybe we were made of stardust. And it was with this thought rolling through my head that I took hold of the knife in front of me and sliced a thin line in the tender skin of my palm.

I'd split open what mortals from lifetimes ago called the fate line. That was the funny thing about people. Didn't matter when or where my sisters and I landed, whether we were giants who sat at the Tree of the World or three young girls abandoned in the desert, the people around us always liked to act as if their destinies could be found in the palms of their hands. I looked down, mesmerized by the line of red that bloomed in mine, a welcome reminder that I was as much human as I was immortal. Not one or the other, but both.

The boy strode across the kitchen and wordlessly inspected my injury for a moment. I admired the pleasant variance of his pale complexion against the rich terra cotta that was mine. Then, before I could even gasp in surprise, he lifted my hand to his mouth and sucked away the blood.

It was all so intimate. The quick touch of his tongue against my skin, his body so close I could see his blond eyelashes reflecting the sunlight. It was *too* intimate, far too human for my monstrous heart to bear, and before I knew it, I had fallen in love with him.

Then he met Rosa, who was eager to hide her monster behind perfectly plaited hair. Of course he would choose her over me. My monster wouldn't be stifled; my unruly hair was forever unkempt. Plus, everyone knew she'd make a beautiful bride.

Our friends and family celebrate my sister's happy union with a feast and, when one of the vaqueros brings out his guitar, an impromptu fandango that continues long into the night. Mamá sits along the side, looking the part of the contented mother of the bride, with sweet Maria Elena perched at her side, happily nibbling on a piece of caramelized *cajeta* candy. As our neighbors dance, I can smell the sweet scent of mint leaves and freshly picked wildflowers that sprinkle the ground at her feet.

I watch it all with a feigned detachment that I've perfected over so many lifetimes. The voices painted with joy and elation. The skirts arching high into the air like fans in multitudes of colors. James makes a show of asking Maria Elena to dance. He swings her easily onto his shoulder and she is all laughter and mirth. For a moment, my sisters have everyone fooled, perhaps even themselves. For a moment, Maria Elena is simply an ordinary young girl, and Rosa the quintessential blushing bride. James leans down in passing and kisses me drily on the cheek. It is brotherly and fleeting and utterly heartbreaking, and I hide my hands behind my back and wish I had claws.

Hours later, when I sneak off into the shadows, I can still hear the mellifluous notes of a solitary *guitarra*. For reasons of which even I'm unsure, I persuade Maria Elena to come with me, coaxing her out of the bed Mamá just tucked her into moments before. I carry her on my back, and though her grip remains tight around my neck, I can tell she's half asleep. With each of my burdened steps, her head bounces heavily on my shoulder. I hoist her higher as I make the ascent up a neighboring hill. My skirt snags in the spines of a nearby cactus and I yank it free, leaving a piece of the fabric trapped among the prickles. Trudging upward, I feel as if I'm walking straight into the night, as if I'm climbing into a bucket of dark water.

When we reach the top, I swing Maria Elena to the ground as gently as I can, and as we settle into the dirt, the dust becomes a cloud of grit and sand that irritates our eyes and gets stuck in our teeth. We look down at the ongoing party. The distance makes the lights appear dim and opaque, and suddenly it all seems so inconsequential and I am yet again nostalgic for the days of isolation and seclusion. When my sisters were my only companions. Up here, it seems we have only the stars, but even they seem small in the midst of that terrifying night sky, and it is then that I realize the reason I brought Maria Elena with me. I suppose even monsters can be afraid of the dark.

We wait there for a long while, with Maria Elena shivering against me, until a familiar form makes its way up the hill.

Rosa, still dressed in her bridal gown, is running late for her evening duties, but it is her wedding night. Perhaps she deserves this one luxury.

"Sisters," she says upon recognizing Maria Elena and me, the monsters hiding in the shadows. Her voice is a lilting song against the harsh garble I use in my reply. It is the tongue of a past life, one that we spoke long ago when we looked like the horrors we are. As I speak, I hold out my hand, where a thread lies curled in my palm like the discarded skin of the rattlesnake James saved only hours before. The thread is a withered, transparent thing that resembles nothing of the virile man whose life it embodies. Maria Elena gasps at the sight of it.

Lifetimes ago, when our place was at the foot of the Tree of the World, the mortals believed that a snake encircled the earth, its teeth clamped down at the end of its tail. They believed that if it let go, the world would end.

Rosa's eyes widen and she backs away from me, stumbling over her silk-clad feet in her haste to get away, as if it is truly a snake that I hold cupped in my hand. As if it is that snake whose appetite for its own tail controlled the fate of the world.

"No." It is a simple answer. One said in a voice not of fear or defiance but of resolution. I don't know how to respond; suddenly I know what it feels like when a small pebble collides with a mountain.

Maria Elena takes the thread from me. She strokes it lightly with her finger, and when she begins to hum, her voice is as sweet as a lullaby.

"We have no choice," I say, but my reply is weak, and my resolve even more so.

"And who is it that dictates that?" Rosa screeches. This time her words are formed by that ancient jargon, and it sounds like gravel, grating and rough, and for a moment I feel as though I have my sister back. That it is She Who Cannot Be Turned standing in front of me and not the good girl Mamá turned her into. The heavy pounding in my chest is slowed. But She Who Cannot Be Turned has never refused to cut before. No matter to whom the life was attached. She raises her arms to that sky. "Who's out there? Do you know, sister? Because as far as I know, there is only us. For lifetimes, we have been both the judge and the jury, the creator and the executioner." Rosa's face contorts oddly, and then

I realize: she is crying. She is crying, this merciless sister of mine, and I cannot think how to react. She is ugly when she cries, and for a moment, I am pleased to see her like this. To see there is a crack in the alabaster, a flaw in the perfection. To see the mask of humanity begin to slip and the monster begin to emerge.

A lamenting cry fills the air. The thread begins to sing, and it's a mournful, heartrending elegy, full of regret and remorse and an unfinished life. And with it those shears, all glinting and huge and terrifying, appear in Rosa's outstretched palm. She screams, wrenching her hand out from under them. And they fall, tumbling through the air until they land with the blades wedged in the ground a few feet away.

She falls to her knees in front of me. "Who says there will be repercussions, sister?" she pleads. "What could be the harm in sparing this one life?"

Strands of her hair, now loose and tangled, cling to her cheeks and underneath her nose, plastered there by tears and snot. "It is by our hands that the scales are balanced, sister," I say, brushing Rosa's hair off her face and smoothing it back into place as best I can. "And it is a power that cannot be abused. One that is too large for any one of us to try to manipulate. It is a beast that can never be tamed."

I take a deep breath and say the words I've been rehearsing in my head since last night. "It is a duty that surpasses everything. Even love."

I need her to say that I'm right, but instead she turns her back on me and cradles her knees with her arms. "I won't do it," she says petulantly.

I glance toward those shears so mercilessly stabbed into the earth. My whole body trembles as I pick them up, but my hands are hesitant and unsure and I drop them twice before I have a steady grasp on them. They are so heavy I need both hands to manage them.

I don't know how I'm going to hold the thread in order to cut it until Maria Elena slides toward me. She leans her head down to the thread in her hand and whispers something. Perhaps it's good-bye. Then she holds it out, one tiny hand on each side of that thread. Its mournful cry is so loud I want to cover my ears. I catch Maria Elena's eye. She nods her head. And with trembling hands I raise those shears and cut the thread.

The world is suddenly silent. In the distance, a lone coyote howls, and his forlorn cry echoes across the valley. Hours later, when I finally allow myself to cry, I know I will sound as desperate and lonely as that coyote separated from his pack.

Behind me, Rosa whimpers quietly. Her cheek is pressed against the dirt and her tearstained face smeared with the deep-red clay that covers the ground. I crawl toward her, marking my skirt with the same red that stains her face. Grabbing her hand, I tie one end of the cut thread around her ring finger.

Maria Elena settles herself in my lap, and I consider wrapping the other end of the thread around my own finger. Instead, I hold it out to the wind and we watch as it flutters away and disappears into the dark night sky.

Folks around here call us *los destinos*. They like to say we came from the stars. And when I stare up at the infinite heavens stretched out above us like a shroud, it's hard to imagine we came from anywhere else.

I place my hand over Rosa's trembling one, and after a moment, she intertwines her fingers with mine. And it is like this, while sitting on the hill, that my sisters and I wait for the day to blossom like a flower over the desert plateau.

❧ *Author's Note* ❧

I've always been fascinated by mythology, a fascination that started when I was in middle school and hasn't yet been forced aside by other, more pertinent topics. I always found mythology to be a delicious combination of magic and humanity.

The Three Fates—immortal goddesses that appear in Greek, Roman, and Norse mythology—were once believed to control the destiny of each mortal from birth to death. It was while thinking of these three powerful deities that I also began to wonder what it might be like to live as a young teenage girl during a time of upheaval and change in American history. I thought of all those times when one's cultural and national identity seemed at odds, and I wondered, what might it be like to be divine and yet, at the same time, utterly human? I suppose all these thoughts wove themselves together, because suddenly I had Valeria, Rosa, and Maria Elena, three immortals sent down to live as Mexican American sisters during the years after the Texas annexation.

High Stakes

Andrea Cremer

THE BLOOD SPATTERED ACROSS KLIO'S cheek and jaw had yet to dry. She drew a clean, delicately embroidered kerchief from her pocket and wiped her face, staining the white square scarlet. She tucked the kerchief away and surveyed the room.

This job had been too messy for her taste. For the most part, Klio fulfilled contracts in a quick, tidy manner. She went in, did her work, and left the target with little more than a startled expression forever written across his or her face.

The man sprawled half on the foot of the bed and half on the floor did not look startled. His face had gone slack, his eyes glassy. But the dark splotch just below the left breast pocket of his waistcoat piqued Klio's annoyance. She rarely fell back on her dagger to finish a job.

The room bespoke of a haphazard kill: chairs overturned, papers strewn from the desk onto the floor, an overturned ink-well rolling along the desktop while its contents dripped over the edge to a widening black pool below, and feathers floating in the air above the pillows from which they'd erupted. Jagged shards of glass were scattered across the room.

So many still believe mirrors will make a difference. Klio wondered how such misinformation managed to stay in circulation despite all the evidence to the contrary.

With one last disapproving look about the room, she pulled on her gloves and exited into the hall. The other doors in the boardinghouse remained shut. No curious eyes peeked out. No cries of alarm roused the house matron.

Some of Klio's jobs would have necessitated finding another way out of the room, an escape by which she would not be seen. This boardinghouse, however, was home to those who were doing their best to remain unnoticed, and becoming curious about a neighbor's business was a sure way to ruin their own anonymity ... and possibly lead to their own demise.

Klio fluffed her heavy silk skirts, making sure they lay smooth over her crinoline. In the dim light of the hall, her garments appeared black from prim veiled hat to polished, buttoned boot. Only when she moved directly into the gleam of a lamp did the silk's deep amethyst shade reveal itself.

At this late hour the streets of Boston were quiet but for the occasional clip-clop of shod horse hooves, a sound so banal by day as to be unnoticeable, now harsh as it cut through the heavy silence. Whitby stood alongside Klio's cabriolet, holding the carriage horse's reins. His eyes flashed silver against his ebony face. While his expression otherwise gave nothing away, Klio knew that her coachman was troubled.

When she glanced at the cab again, Klio noticed that despite the clear, warm night, its curtain was drawn to shield the passenger compartment. Klio looked to Whitby, who gave the briefest of nods. Whatever had perturbed her associate didn't present a true threat.

The horse gave a snort and tossed its head as Klio drew near. Whitby tightened his grip on the reins. They had yet to find a horse that grew accustomed to Klio's scent. Most would bolt should she come too close; if they didn't try to run, they shied and reared.

Bothersome animals, Klio thought.

Before she could draw back the curtain, the slender tip of a mahogany cane snagged the edge of the thick fabric and lifted it. Klio nearly jumped back in surprise at the visage peering out at her.

"I pray your forgiveness for calling upon you in this uncustomary manner, Miss Vesper." Hamilton Stuart tipped his tall hat. "May I have a few minutes of your time?"

"Of course, Mr. Stuart." Klio signaled Whitby to take them through the streets. She accepted Stuart's hand and climbed into the cab.

"Ah," Stuart said as she settled beside him. "You do know who I am, then."

"That surprises you?" Klio asked. With the curtain back in place, shadows flooded the interior. The lack of light did little to obscure Klio's vision, if that had been her visitor's intention. Still, Klio tugged on the fingertips of her gloves, loosening them just enough that she'd be able to strip them off in a moment should the need arise.

Stuart laughed, quiet but throaty. "I suppose it should not. But tell me, Miss Vesper, did it not surprise you to see me here?"

"It surprises me to see anyone other than myself in my cab," Klio replied, then decided against being coy. "Nonetheless, your faction hasn't sought my services in the past, so yes, your appearance is unexpected."

"It's an appropriate time for unexpected actions," Stuart murmured. "You're aware of the Game?"

Klio peered through the darkness to study Stuart's features. He looked to be a young man, with dark hair curling at the nape of his neck and an unlined face like porcelain, but Klio knew better. His kind bore the semblance of youth well past the age that death took most mortals. Stuart was likely a century older than she, if not more.

Rather than speak, Klio nodded. A test to reveal whether the warlock had cast a spell that aided his sight in this dark enclosure.

The corners of his mouth turned up in approval. "I'm sure you'll understand the Coven's interest in the outcome of the Game."

"As all the factions are," Klio said. "Whoever wins the Game determines the course of this nation."

"This fractured nation." The pleased note in Stuart's voice faded. "We have thrown our lot in with the Union and a future of free enterprise in the West, while our adversaries hope to expand their plantations beyond Texas and Missouri. We are particularly concerned that this war does not cost us the significant investments we've made. We want to ensure that none thwart our victory."

Klio leveled a sharp gaze at Stuart. "The Game prohibits any attempts upon the lives of the players."

"I'm aware of that, Miss Vesper."

"You do know what kind of work I do, do you not, Mr. Stuart?" Klio was beginning to lose patience. The night's job, while not executed perfectly, was complete, and this pompous warlock was wasting time that she could have spent toasting success with Whitby, then indulging herself in a warm bath.

"Very aware," Stuart replied. "And you are the best at what you do. That is why I'm here."

"Mr. Stuart—"

Hearing the edge in Klio's voice, Stuart dipped a hand inside his jacket and pulled out an envelope. "My superior would like to hire you as a means of protection."

Klio took the envelope, curiosity winning out over her reservations. "There are others who specialize in that service."

"Mr. Cromwell believes you are more suited to the task than a simple guardian," Stuart said. "If a threat to our player arises, you will be able to recognize it more ably than anyone. Killing a player is forbidden, as you've said, but sadly our less honorable peers have proven in the past that they have no qualms about disabling a player."

Klio had no doubts that, honor or no, the Coven had done its share of disabling in the past.

"You'll find all the details of our proposal in that envelope." Stuart leaned toward her with an easy smile. "Mr. Cromwell humbly requests a reply by the week's end." When Klio failed to respond immediately, he sighed, sitting up. "If the generous compensation doesn't prove enough, then perhaps I should appeal to your sense of justice."

"What do you mean?" Klio asked.

"Your man." Stuart nodded toward the front of the cab, to Whitby. "He's a freedman, is he not?"

"Of course he is." Klio bristled. "This is Massachusetts, not Mississippi. And Whitby is not 'my man,' he's a dear friend."

When Stuart showed obvious pleasure at having provoked her, Klio regretted her quick words.

"I would never suggest a lady such as yourself could tolerate the barbarism they so quaintly refer to as the 'peculiar institution,'" Stuart said. "The Coven forbade slaveholding before the colonists decided to declare their independence, you know."

"Yes." Klio also knew that the Coven's power had always been concentrated in the North, making its involvement in plantation farming and the slave trade limited from the first. For her own part, Klio found the "peculiar institution" abhorrent, and not simply because of her friendship with Whitby. She did not, however, respond well to Stuart's attempt to leverage his position by exploiting her moral convictions. She turned the envelope over in her hands. It was weighty for a contract. Perhaps Mr. Cromwell had included part of the promised payment as a show of good faith. She'd be a fool to turn away good money. With the war escalating, the world could easily devolve into chaos.

"Good." Stuart gave two smart raps on the roof of the cab, and it slowed to a stop. "Mr. Cromwell looks forward to receiving your reply."

"One question before you go, Mr. Stuart," Klio said as Stuart drew back the curtain.

"Please." Stuart's smile was as icy as the blue of his eyes.

It took far more than a cool gaze to ruffle Klio. "Who is your player?"

"That very gentleman who has just enjoyed the privilege of your company, Miss Vesper." Stuart flashed his teeth. "And he now bids you a good night."

The air in Natchez was stifling, an unpleasant contrast to the mild spring weather in Boston. Klio suspected the tense, near-choking atmosphere was as much a result of the stresses of the ongoing war as the lack of a breeze. While the action thus far remained in the East, Klio observed men—many of whom might still be called boys—dressed in Confederate gray, congregating before they went to join their compatriots on the battlefield. Her gaze shifted constantly, her body stiff as she moved with the traffic of pedestrians and carriages alongside the Mississippi. As usual, her garb drew curious gazes. Though her sapphire-blue silk gown and matching short cape fit the style of the moment, her small hat with its veil that fell just past the tip of her nose was custom-made and nothing like the bonnets favored by fashionable ladies. Accustomed to stares, Klio ignored them and walked on at a confident pace. She ran her gloved palm over the silk fabric of her skirt and felt the stiff folded papers tucked inside her pocket.

The documents had been inside the envelope Hamilton Stuart gave her, along with a contract and an impressive stack of banknotes. But the princely sum did nothing to relieve the sickness Klio had felt when she'd looked over the papers that would allow Whitby to accompany her on the journey; they named Whitby her slave.

Klio understood the necessity of the documents, but despite their artifice she could barely contain her disgust at having to carry them, and from the wrath she caught whenever her eyes met Whitby's she knew he detested their forced role-playing even more than she did, and understandably. If Klio had had her way, Whitby would never have set foot in any slave state. But Whitby had ignored her pleas that he stay behind, so the ruse was necessary. So long as the Fugitive Slave Act protected them, slave traders could abduct freedmen with impunity.

Whitby carried her bags up the gangplank while Klio strolled behind. Boston was a city of ships, but Klio had never seen the likes of the *Fortuna*. Swan-white save for the great red wheel at its stern, the *Fortuna* looked every bit the debutante awaiting her admirers. Klio appreciated the elegance of the steamboat, but she surveyed its decks with a critical gaze. Ships were designed to hold as many provisions as possible within a confined space. That meant the *Fortuna* would be full of closets, nooks, and compartments—the sort of spaces that lent themselves as easily to staging an ambush as to storing ropes and life jackets.

"Welcome aboard, Miss Vesper." A man in livery greeted Klio when she alighted upon the deck. "Mr. Stuart has asked me to see you to your cabin."

"How kind." Klio spared the man a brief smile. Her attention was on the other passengers.

The Game's importance meant it attracted a throng of spectators, and each faction boasted its own entourage. Most of Klio's shipmates would pose no threat. It was even possible that Hamilton Stuart would be in no danger whatsoever. If all the factions adhered to the rules of the Game, this boat was sacrosanct, neutral ground. But given what was at stake, Klio had to agree with Stuart that his adversaries would exploit any loopholes in the rules to gain an advantage. Something as simple as a charm to draw luck or an amulet to ward off malicious spells could prove a deciding factor.

Stuart's man opened the door to Klio's cabin. The rooms were surprisingly spacious for shipboard quarters. Silk- and velvet-upholstered chairs and settees graced the sitting room, and sumptuous linens and overstuffed pillows decorated the bedroom.

"Are the rooms to your satisfaction, Miss Vesper?" the valet asked.

"They are." Beautiful as the cabin was, Klio doubted she'd spend much time enjoying its luxuries.

The valet nodded at Whitby. "While your man unpacks your bags, Mr. Stuart has requested your presence in his cabin."

"Has he?" Klio's eyebrow lifted. "Would you be so kind to show me to his cabin?"

Stuart's rooms were adjacent to Klio's cabin. Klio tolerated the ritual of being announced to Stuart and offered an assortment of refreshments, but she had little patience for meaningless niceties. Her life was one of relative solitude, her only companion being Whitby, whose nature was as reclusive as her own.

Stuart lounged in a high-backed chair. He wore a crisp shirt and a waistcoat of sapphire jacquard, but no jacket. He had one leg thrown over a chair arm as he sipped amber liquid from a crystal tumbler. His dark hair was rumpled and his face wanted a shave.

"You may leave us, Talbot," Stuart told his valet with a dismissive wave.

Klio relaxed a bit, taking the seat opposite him, pleased that Stuart didn't cling so tightly to convention that he would prolong mindless chatter in the presence of his servant rather than proceed directly to the business at hand. She required no chaperone to preserve her reputation and much preferred dealing with men alone and on her terms.

"What do you make of the *Fortuna*?" Stuart asked. "Does she meet your expectations?"

"I had no expectations, Mr. Stuart," Klio said.

Stuart swung his leg down from the chair arm so he was sitting rather than sprawling. "Hamilton, please."

"If you wish." Klio felt a tremor of unease with Stuart's casual air. For a man only hours away from playing a game that would determine the nation's future, he appeared much too comfortable. His arrogance was evidence, but Klio wondered what schemes he'd set in motion to thwart his opponents.

He leaned forward, eyeing her. "Are you always this stiff? We're alone, you know. Keeping up appearances isn't required."

"I'm here on a contract, Mr.—Hamilton," Klio replied. "This isn't about appearances."

"Yes, the contract." Stuart sipped his drink. "You'll accompany me whenever I'm outside my cabin. Once the Game begins, I give you leave to situate yourself wherever you deem the most suitable."

"Thank you for your confidence," Klio said. "Have the other players arrived?"

"The wolves and goblins are here. The sidhe are expected within the hour. But the necromancers and vampires won't board until after sunset . . . for obvious reasons."

Klio nodded. "Are there any particular animosities between the Coven and the other factions that I should know about?"

Stuart's lips curled in amusement. "What an interesting question."

Klio bristled, lifting her chin. "Mr. Stuart—"

"Hamilton."

"Hamilton." The man was setting Klio's teeth on edge. "You hired me because you may be in danger. It would be helpful if you identified potential threats."

"Identifying threats is supposed to be your job, Klio." Stuart swirled the liquid in his glass, watching it flash amber when it caught the light.

"Very well." Klio stood up. "If that's all you have to tell me, I'll be off to begin *doing* my job."

"Sit down, Miss Vesper." Any hint of mirth in Stuart's tone had vanished. He finished his drink in one swallow and set the glass aside.

Klio didn't balk. He clearly expected her to cower at the first sign of his disapproval. Klio cowered for no one. She expected him to erupt into some sort of tyrannical tantrum, but instead he began to laugh. "I don't frighten you at all, do I?" He shook his head, smiling. "How refreshing."

He gestured to the sofa. "Please, Miss Vesper, it wasn't my intent to offend you. I only wish to know a bit more about you. Your reputation is . . . unrivaled. Yet all of my information about you has been secondhand."

Klio returned to her seat but remained wary. "What would you like to know?"

"A great deal." Stuart's brow furrowed. "But I don't expect you to indulge all of my curiosities." When Klio didn't take to his teasing comment, he rested his elbows on his knees and steepled his fingers. "Let me show you my good will by answering your question. The Coven and the sidhe have been on good terms for the last three centuries. The goblins are brutes and they hate the Coven, but they despise secret plots and assassination and have only disdain for human wars. They're a savage lot, but they couldn't care less about who wins the Game. If the goblins want me, or anyone for that matter, dead, they'd prefer to attack at high noon and stick heads on pikes for all to see. If it wasn't against the Old Laws, they wouldn't bother showing up at the Game."

"I understand." Of all the factions, Klio viewed the goblins as the least threatening—if only in this particular venue. They wouldn't break the rules of the Game, and they would spit at the suggestion of loopholes.

"The necromancers are not unlike the goblins," Stuart continued. "They'll have bodies enough from the carnage while it's being waged."

"So the vampires and the wolves." Klio had already arrived at that conclusion before she boarded the ship, but she appreciated Stuart's confirmation.

"The vampires have ties with Southern planters that go back to the first colonial settlements," Stuart said. "And the wolves haven't made it known whether they support the Union or the Confederacy. The stubborn beasts refuse to ally or confer with any other faction. Since they made their support of the British known before all the other factions declared for the Americans in the War of Independence, they've gotten it into their furry heads that the rest of us colluded against them. If they win the Game this time, we won't know on whose behalf we're fighting until they deign to tell us."

Taking Klio's passive expression for approval, Stuart said, "And now it's your turn. Your face is veiled, but I would have you reveal yourself—figuratively speaking, of course. Who are you, Miss Vesper? What tales have you to tell? I imagine them to be extraordinary."

"I'm certain you have ways of finding out almost anything about me," Klio replied.

He shrugged. "Yes, but I'd prefer to hear what you have to say about yourself. For instance, the Coven believed your kind no longer existed. Too many generations of intermarriage with mortals. It's gone that way for most creatures outside the factions."

"The bloodline has been diluted," Klio said. "But on rare occasions the old traits manifest. Some choose to keep those qualities hidden, but my grandmother encouraged me to embrace my heritage. She knew that it would require a life of isolation, but

I agreed with her. I preferred to leave my home rather than suppress my powers."

"Your man—the djinn." Stuart rubbed at the stubble on his chin absentmindedly. "Is it the same for him?"

"Yes." Klio ground her teeth at Stuart's description of Whitby as "her man" for the second time despite having corrected him. She and Whitby had been drawn to each other because of their shared histories. Both of them were relics of days past, abandoned by family. Forsaken by the world.

"Was it difficult to find your way?" Stuart asked. Something flickered in his gaze. Klio wouldn't have named it sympathy. "Sixteen is young for someone to have already established the professional repute you possess."

"Every life faces its trials at some point," Klio said, keeping her expression passive. "Mine came earlier than most, but I have thrived nonetheless."

Klio's powers had manifested in the twelfth year of her life, the same night her belly cramped and she woke with blood on her underclothes. Coming of age hadn't been the beginning of a transformation from girl to woman. It had marked the moment at which she would no longer be part of the family she'd known but would walk in a different world. Apart. And, until she met Whitby, alone.

Stuart's gaze shifted to Klio's arms, sheathed from fingertip to elbow by silk gloves. "May I see them?"

"I'm a professional, Hamilton." Klio smoothed her skirt before folding her hands on her lap. "Not a performer."

"That's a shame." He sighed.

Klio smiled for the first time since she'd arrived in Stuart's cabin. "You're the only person I know who has longed to see what my gloves keep hidden."

"But those who've had the privilege to see—" Stuart's eyes were alight with eagerness. "Do they find your secret to be marvelous?"

"I don't know, Hamilton. They're all dead."

Whitby had gone by the time Klio returned to her cabin.

Klio stood in the middle of her sitting room, feeling a twinge of disappointment. Though he played the role of servant, Whitby was much more of a partner. He scouted and strategized with her before she entered the field of combat. While she fulfilled a contract, he acted as her eyes and ears around the perimeter of any kill site. Ever alert, Whitby secured the locations in which Klio did her work. Should she get into trouble, he would come to her aid. If Whitby had deemed it necessary to begin his surveillance of the steamboat immediately, Klio didn't doubt his judgment, but she would have taken comfort in conversation with her closest friend before the work of the night began. Selfishly, she'd also hoped to steal a few moments of laughter at the expense of the snobbish Mr. Stuart. Klio and Whitby had little regard for the archaic customs and exclusivity of the factions. Mr. Stuart was the embodiment of all those traits they found intolerable, but that shared dislike could have offered a much-needed reprieve ahead of what would be a span of tense hours as the night grew long.

Despite the taciturn nature Whitby presented to the outside world, to Klio he was confidant, adviser, and irreplaceable man-at-arms . . . so to speak. Although clients contracted for Klio's services, she split payment evenly with Whitby. Like his djinn ancestors, Whitby commanded magics that could mold the perceptions and actions of those around him. He could more than hold his own in a fight. But the *Fortuna* was a far different arena from those in which they usually battled. If Whitby came by information Klio needed, he would find her. She needn't waste her time worrying about anything else.

Klio changed her clothes and went back to Stuart's quarters. Talbot opened the door, and upon entering, Klio found her client freshly shaved and boasting a head of neatly combed hair. He shrugged on his jacket.

"I trust all is well, Miss Vesper?"

Klio nodded.

He smiled, casting an appreciative gaze upon her form. Like Stuart, Klio had taken the time to shed her traveling garb for clothes more suitable for the night's event. Her gown was emerald satin, but its shade bore a depth that gave the fabric a mottled effect whenever she moved—a quality emphasized by her skirts' fullness, which spread around her like the broad leaves of an exotic plant. The gown's low-cut bodice had a dusting of lace that shimmered the white and silver of moonstone, and while her neck and shoulders were bare, Klio's arms remained sheathed in black silk from elbows to fingertips. A veil of the same lace at her bodice kept her eyes from view.

"You make me regret that you accompany me for business tonight," Stuart said. "I'd much prefer an evening of pleasure with you at my side."

"Think on the pleasure of living rather than falling prey to your opponents," Klio replied.

With a snicker, Stuart offered Klio his arm. "I would be pained at your rebuff, Miss Vesper. But instead I'll take comfort in how difficult it is to lead you astray when your path is set."

"That would be wise of you, Mr. Stuart." Klio hooked her arm around his elbow. "Very wise."

The confines of the ship limited the number of spectators who could attend the Game. Even so, Klio marveled at the array of onlookers.

Tiered rows of seats ascended from the floor of the deck, allowing a clear view to those unfortunate enough to be seated farthest from the players. The rows had been divided into six sections. Entrance into each section was carefully monitored to ensure there would be no mingling between the factions. In other settings, interactions between the groups wasn't unheard of, but at this juncture, with so much on the line, such meetings could prove too volatile.

Klio walked at Stuart's side to the front of the Coven's section. The seats in each row were filled with richly dressed men and women, most bearing haughty expressions that vanished when they turned smiles of admiration or envy on their appointed champion. Those appreciative looks became curious, suspicious, or downright disdainful when they shifted from Stuart to Klio.

The opinions of these witches and warlocks troubled Klio not at all, but her skin crawled with the power that emanated from their ranks. The use of any kind of magic was strictly forbidden at the Game, both to prevent cheating and to protect the players from an arcane assault. That restriction, however, couldn't prohibit existing magic that seeped from the very pores of this faction. They reeked of it.

The Coven wasn't unique in its power, only in the form it took. To one side of the Coven were the sidhe. While the air around the Coven crackled with magic, the sidhe bathed in starlight. Fireflies and songbirds danced in the air around them as they indulged in food and drink. It was difficult to look upon the faeries without longing to join them; to gaze on their beautiful forms was to hear the song of a siren. A beautiful torment.

An altogether different lot sat on the other side of the Coven. While the sidhe suffused their surroundings with the tinkling chimes of their chatter and the silvery cascades of their laughter, the goblins offered a cacophony of screeches, roars, hisses, and snarls. Their ranks were made up of the small and gnarled and the tall and stick limbed, with skin in every hue of green, purple, brown, and gray.

Beside the goblins sat the wolves. Of all the factions, the wolves had the fewest spectators. Many of the rows in their section sat empty, and the handful of attendees was half human and half wolf, the latter roaming the aisles restlessly.

The next two factions, necromancers and vampires, were indistinguishable in their ghost-pale skin, but the necromancers favored hooded robes that shadowed their faces, while the vampires were attired in the finery of the moment, interested in attracting admiration rather than avoiding attention.

Klio's gaze moved from group to group. The wolves might present the most significant risk—the absence of spectators could be the result of others aboard the ship yet not at the tourney, giving them the chance to stir up trouble elsewhere. The vampires were difficult to assess. The atmosphere of their section emitted ease and celebration, but few creatures could rival vampires when it came to deception and misdirection.

"It's time." Stuart drew his arm away from Klio but surprised her when he caught her hand in his and lifted her silk-gloved fingers to his lips. "My life is in your hands."

Crackling anticipation exploded into shouts, roars, and applause as the six champions descended the steps from their sections to take their seats at the round table where the Game would be played: the hooded necromancer, whose robes obscured even his or her sex; the pale vampire woman with flaxen curls piled atop her head; a goblin with chartreuse skin and long bony fingers; a wolf in human guise, hulking and resentful as he glowered at his opponents; the faerie with skin like bark and hair of leaves; and finally Stuart, a warlock who approached the table with the swagger of someone who'd already won.

As the pastimes of each era changed, so changed the Game to mirror the world of the war whose fate was to be decided. Klio knew that the Game had taken many forms: the hunt, a footrace, a match of wits. In 1861 the Game would be poker.

The dealer was a woman called Naomi. Not precisely a woman — a shade, the spirit of a mortal summoned for the sole purpose of serving this role. Her neutrality was guaranteed by the summoning itself, a feat accomplished by the cooperation of a delegate from each faction.

While Naomi expounded upon the rules of the Game, Klio began to sweep the room with her eyes, alert to any sign of danger. The first hand was dealt. Play began.

No visual cue caused Klio alarm. Rather, a subtle prickling along her spine made her turn just in time to catch a figure darting out of her peripheral vision. The furtive quality of movement was enough to compel Klio to investigate. She felt a pang below her ribs as she wished Whitby were with her and could remain to watch the Game.

Keeping her stride casual and her expression diffident, Klio traced a path to the place she'd seen the figure vanish. She briefly considered the door that offered exit, but instead turned her attention to the space beneath the rows of spectators. This deck of the *Fortuna* had clearly been repurposed to host the tournament. Whether it served as a dining hall or ballroom under normal circumstances, the tiers of seating had been erected for temporary use. Below the rows of spectators was a skeleton of wooden beams that supported the weight of those above.

Klio glanced at the exit once more, then slipped into the darkness beneath. She couldn't see her prey, but a trail of magic lingered that she could follow. What she sensed at the moment was simply power, the potential for devastating acts but not the execution of such. Whoever she pursued commanded the arcane with prowess.

After loosening each of the fingers of her gloves, Klio slid them off and tucked them into the small silk purse that hung from her wrist. Her skin warmed, and she felt the shifting of her flesh in anticipation of a fight.

Tension hummed in the air as the crowd above vacillated from rapt silence to outbursts of delight and dismay. Klio moved with light steps, taking care to avoid catching her full skirts on the crisscross of wood beams. She ducked, twisted, and shimmied, letting her gaze float freely to spot any sign of her quarry. Parting her lips, she took a breath, hoping to pinpoint the elusive figure, but the mingled odor and taste of so many bodies packed into this enclosed space made it impossible for her to discern anything specific.

The quality of light began to shift as she neared the edge of the Coven's section. In another few moments she'd emerge from beneath the block of seats and into the walkway that separated the Coven and the sidhe.

Where had the stranger disappeared to?

Klio didn't know whether to wait for another sign of movement or continue on to the space below the sidhe. She slowed. When she drew her next breath, she tasted ash.

"Whitby?" Had she been tracking her own partner? She'd never made such a foolish mistake in the past.

The crowd erupted into a chaos of sound. Someone had

played an astonishing hand or pulled off an incredible bluff. The sound was so great, Klio almost missed the rustling above her.

The heavy weight of a hard masculine body dropped onto her shoulders, knocking her to the ground. Pain flashed through her right shoulder when she fell against a beam, its corner biting into her flesh. Her adversary had the advantage of surprise, but he'd given up control by choosing to fall onto her. Klio seized the opportunity to push off the beam and throw her weight against her attacker, taking them both to the ground.

She pinned her opponent, digging her knees into his chest and stretching her arms toward his throat. Heat radiated from his body, discomfort that promised to become pain. Despite the threat of imminent injury, Klio went still. Cold flooded her limbs even as she felt heat scorching through the satin of her skirt.

Only one creature had this defense.

Silver flashed at Klio in the dark. Silver eyes.

"Whitby." Klio choked out his name.

"I'm sorry, Klio." Whitby's voice, so seldom used, rasped like desert wind. "I can't fight it."

Klio rolled off her friend, ignoring the way her skirts smoked. "What are you talking about? Fight what?"

To Klio's alarm, Whitby jumped up, looming over her.

His voice was like a crack of thunder. "I didn't think it could be done. I thought the magics long lost."

"Tell me what you mean." Klio stood, though she felt tremulous and childlike in comparison to Whitby's menacing stance — something she'd never seen directed at her before.

"He found, he made." Silver tears gleamed on Whitby's cheeks. "I must obey."

He lifted his hands. Cracks ran over them, up and down his arms, gold and scarlet dancing beneath his flesh.

"Whitby, don't!" Klio took several steps back until she came up against a beam. "Stop this."

"I can't, Klio." He still wept, even as he advanced on her. "Forgive me and do me one last honor."

"Whitby . . ." Klio was shaking. She understood none of this, only her terror and the sorrow of betrayal.

"Honor me, dear friend." Whitby was terribly close. "Take my life, so that I cannot take yours."

"No."

"I beg you." Flames rippled along his fingertips. "Do not make me serve him. Save yourself."

Rage had overtaken Klio's fear. What monster had stolen her friend's will? Who dared make Whitby a slave?

Whitby stopped mere inches from Klio, and she could see it took immense effort for him to hold off his assault. "I will not harm you." Whitby's voice shook from the strain of battling whatever unseen force controlled him. "You are the only solace I've found in this world. You must know that."

Klio choked on her sob. "There has to be something, some other way—"

"You can only free me with death, Klio." Whitby's teeth gnashed as he struggled against his unseen master.

Klio knew she couldn't hesitate. Couldn't think. Whitby held on to the barest shred of control. Forcing herself into action and banishing all emotion, she dove to Whitby's right and rolled past him. She paused on the balls of her feet, then pivoted and rose. Standing directly behind him, Klio lashed her arms out, aiming for the back of his neck.

The twin serpents coiled around each of Klio's arms sprang to life. Four hissing heads lifted and struck, fangs burying themselves in the flesh of Whitby's neck. With a gasp, Whitby stiffened. The serpents released their prey and drew back. Only when Whitby collapsed, falling face-first to the ground, did the snakes return to their slumber—living, deadly creatures dormant as if they were ink needled into Klio's skin.

Klio dropped to her knees at Whitby's side. The searing heat had fled his body. His breath came in dry, shallow rattles. He turned his face toward Klio, offering her a weak smile.

"Thank you, my friend."

Whitby shuddered as his body began to crumble.

For a long time, Klio sat and wept silently, letting the pile of sand at her side pour through her hands.

Hamilton Stuart entered his cabin, bedecked in the glow of victory. Klio awaited him on the same sofa she'd occupied just hours before.

Stuart paused in the doorway when he saw her.

"Did you hear the good news?" he asked her. He went to the side table to decant himself a drink.

"You won," Klio replied. "Congratulations to Mr. Cromwell on another century of rule."

"I wouldn't congratulate Cromwell just yet." Stuart took his seat opposite her. "He didn't win the game. I did."

"From your tone I gather you expect more than praise for your victory?"

"Indeed." His gaze traveled over her singed dress, pausing on the brass oil lamp she held in her lap. "I'm sorry to have put you through such an ordeal, but I needed to know just how good you are. You see, I didn't bring you here to protect me during the gaming."

"I gathered as much," Klio said, watching him calmly. This exterior serenity was a boon of her kind. She could keep her most turbulent emotions in check until the appropriate moment to unleash them arrived.

"But I do want to engage your services," Stuart continued. "Permanently. You belong among those who are likewise the paramount of their kind. The Coven outmatch all the other factions, but many within our ranks believe it's time for Cromwell to step aside—"

"And you've just proven you're the one to take his place," Klio finished.

"I know you have long been isolated, but there is much, much more I can offer you. I will lead the Coven into a new era. After this ridiculous war ends, the West will be open and it will be the visionaries, the innovators, who shape the future. Surely you see that."

"And Whitby? Had he no future, in service to the Coven or otherwise?" Klio's fingers traced the shape of the brass lamp.

"A creature of his nature could only hold you back," Stuart said with a disapproving frown. "I've had you watched for months now, and while it was clear you needed no one other than yourself to thrive in your work, you chose attachment to one lesser than yourself. I pitted the djinn against you to show you that."

"I see."

"And to be perfectly frank"—Stuart smiled, pleased with himself—"it was to indulge my own curiosity. No one has attempted to entrap a djinn in centuries. The magic required to complete the task seemed simple enough, but I didn't know if it would be possible, particularly on one like your Whitby, who was only part djinn."

"But you succeeded." Klio set the lamp beside her on the sofa. "I must confess that your experiment puzzles me. Did you not imply that I would accept this contract because I abhor slavery?"

"I do remember raising that point," Stuart replied, with a faint crinkling of his brow.

"Yet you chained Whitby with your spell." Klio tamped down the welling grief that tried to climb from her belly into her throat. "You took his freedom and made his body and his magic subservient."

"Yes," Stuart said, still smiling. "You could interpret my actions in that way, but I'd advise you to think of the djinn's role in this little play of ours as the sacrificial hero. His death elevated you to the station you deserve. While you may grieve the loss of your companion, he was a djinn, and you must know that in the natural order, djinn were meant to serve."

"I understand." Klio stood. "You only meant to help me. To show me how I'd misjudged my place, and Whitby's place."

She began to pull off her gloves, and Stuart drew in a sharp breath.

"I can kill you before you blink again," he snapped.

Klio laughed. "I know that, Hamilton. But you wanted to see what I have hidden. That's all I'm doing. Showing you."

Stuart relaxed a bit, but his eyes were still sharp, his posture wary.

Klio let her gloves drop to the ground.

"Oh, my." Stuart forgot his reservation and leaned down, gazing at the twining serpents on Klio's arms. "Marvelous."

"Thank you," Klio said. "They are the primary manifestation of my ancestry, and my weapon of choice."

"A fine, fine weapon, Klio." Stuart dared to lift her hand to his lips. "They are almost as beautiful as you are. Almost."

"You flatter me, Hamilton," Klio demurred. "Do you know that my ancestors had more than the serpents in their arsenal?"

Stuart tilted his head, regarding her curiously. He still held her hand in his. "I know the history of the gorgons, my dear girl. But it's been well documented that the other traits of your kind were bred out generations ago. The only lingering evidence of your heritage being the serpentine shape and color of your eyes."

"Of course you must be right." Klio gripped his fingers tight and smiled. "Since you understand the true nature of all creatures so very well."

She lifted her veil.

❧ *Author's Note* ❧

History and fantasy have long been twin passions of mine. Having earned a PhD in early modern history, I've spent many hours poring over crackling papers and aged maps in search of hidden narratives within the historical record. Writing historical fantasy presents a particular treat of taking the known and infusing it with magic and mystery. "High Stakes" let me delve into the world of one of my favorite, and much-maligned, creatures of myth while also examining the volatile culture of America on the brink of civil war.

The Red Raven Ball

Caroline Tung Richmond

EVERY AUTUMN, AFTER THE LEAVES have faded from emerald to gold, my grandmother throws the most magnificent ball in Washington. No expense is spared—for Grandmama says that this is the Van Persies' way—and she opens our coffers to purchase crates of champagne, platters of baked oysters, and bouquets of hothouse flowers so delicate that they wither come morning.

It's quite the lavish spectacle.

And I'm afraid it's all a terrible waste.

For over a year, our nation has been torn asunder between North and South, but will a war stop Grandmama from hosting her favorite fete? Certainly not. Because this year she has made *very* special plans.

"Elizabeth, dear," she has been saying for weeks, "now that your schooling is finished, you must turn your thoughts to marriage.

No, no, don't shake your head at me. I've invited the city's most eligible bachelors to that ball, and I'll see to it that there'll be a wedding by Easter."

"But Grandmama—" I've said every time, hoping that she'd put such thoughts out of her mind and that she'd call me Lizzie for once.

"That's quite enough! Now then, come rub my shoulders."

I sighed and sighed again, but I did as she asked because Grandmama reigns over our family (and the entire capital for that matter) with a gloved fist. I swallowed my protests too because she'd box my ears if I shared my opinion about a springtime wedding—for I find the idea to be horrifying. I'm only seventeen just! My own mother, may she rest in peace, didn't wed my father until age twenty-two, which allowed her to finish her schooling, write columns for an abolitionist newspaper, and eventually find a love match. I dream of a similar path for myself.

That's why I've wrung my hands for weeks over Grandmama's matrimonial plans. A bride by spring? I'd rather parade through the halls of Congress wearing nothing but pantalets. I don't know how I'll change my grandmother's mind, but I do know this: I've no intention of catching a fiancé or even a beau at our ball.

Instead, I intend to catch a spy.

A Confederate spy, to be precise.

If Grandmama knew of my plans, she'd lock me in my room until I sprouted gray hair, but I've made a promise that I will keep. That I *must* keep.

Even if it means defying Grandmama.

On the evening of the ball, I act the part of the obedient heiress. I sit very still while my maid, Mary, pins my pale hair atop my head

THE RED RAVEN BALL -

and cinches my corset tight. Beyond my window, I see the well-groomed trees of Lafayette Square and the broad road that leads up to our handsome brownstone. Soon the road will be filled with horse-drawn carriages that will deliver our guests to our front steps, from senators and senators' wives to attorneys and ambassadors, and—if all goes according to plan—the very spy himself.

Fear tremors through me. A traitor in our home. What will he look like? Does he hold any remorse for his actions? Or perhaps—

"Here are your earbobs, miss," Mary says.

I smile at her in my mirror. "Won't you fetch the pearls from Sophie's room instead?" I nod across the hall toward my fifteen-year-old sister's bedroom. As much as I like Mary, I yearn for a moment alone to gather my thoughts for the mission ahead.

Mary pales. "But Mrs. Van Persie set these aside just for you. Her own rubies."

"I'd like to wear my mother's pearls tonight." Fear creeps into Mary's round eyes, so I pat her hand. "Don't you worry. I'll tell Grandmama that it was my idea."

"Yes, miss," she squeaks.

Once Mary departs I release a sigh, which is rather difficult considering how severely my corset suffocates me, and I unlock the desk drawer. Inside, I find my most precious possessions: my mother's gold ring, a lock of Sophie's hair, and a stack of letters from my mother's younger brother, my dearest uncle Ambrose. Or *Colonel* Ambrose Chamberlain, as he is better known, of the Pennsylvania Fourth Regiment. Most of his letters arrive via post, but his most recent was delivered by courier from his camp in Sharpsburg, Maryland. At first I thought something awful must have happened to my uncle, but once I read the letter I knew why he needed a more private correspondence. I open the envelope gently.

Dearest Lizzie,

I hope this finds you well, and that you're not cross with me for not writing sooner. I've received your letters and appreciate your desire to send a collection of books to my regiment to lift our spirits. It's very thoughtful of you, but I'm afraid my men are far more interested in dominoes and cards — and other pastimes I best not mention — and I'd hate for your novels to go to waste.

I'm in need of your help, however, for another endeavor. I've vacillated for days over whether to include you in these plans, and may your mother forgive me for my decision, but I'm left with no other option. I leave it to you to decide if you will participate, but I strongly believe your actions could save hundreds of Union lives, if not more.

It has come to General McClellan's attention that the Confederates have planted a spy within Washington. We know little about this traitor, only that the Confederates call him the "Red Raven." As luck would have it, we've intercepted a correspondence between the Raven and his Confederate compatriots — a message carried by a raven, in fact — in which the spy revealed that he will attend your grandmother's ball. Thus, I shall require your assistance. Here is what I propose . . .

There's a knock at the door, and I nearly leap to the ceiling when Sophie pokes her head inside my bedroom. I stow the letter in my dress pocket, but not before her eyes land upon it.

"I brought the earbobs you asked for." Her pink skirts swish as she enters, and her sweet-as-pie face tilts toward my pocket. "Hiding a love letter, I see?"

I quell the flutter in my voice. "Of course not, you silly thing."

"Do you have a secret admirer?" She makes a playful attempt to snatch the letter from me, but I swivel my hip away from her.

"It's from a schoolmate at Westacre," I lie, referring to the Quaker school in Pennsylvania where I lived these past three years. Our mother was educated at Westacre, and it was her last wish that Sophie and I would study there too. After she passed, Father sent us to the school to honor Mother's request, but Sophie grew homesick after a single term and returned to Washington. I, however, continued on at school and adored every minute . . . until Grandmama stepped in two months ago, deeming my education complete and ordering me home. I refused, but Grandmama stopped paying my tuition. It pains me that she thinks so little of a female's schooling, especially her own granddaughter's. I had hoped to teach at Westacre myself one day.

"A schoolmate?" There's a glint in Sophie's green eyes. "Or a beau?"

"You're nearly as bad as Grandmama." I roll my eyes, but I'm not bothered by her prying. Being near Sophie again has been the one bright spot in returning home.

Sophie insists on helping me into my dress, a russet-colored gown that sits low on my shoulders. It's the latest fashion in the city, but I feel entirely too exposed. I had no need for ball gowns or earbobs at Westacre, but now I have a wardrobe filled with velvet dresses and pretty jewels the size of my knuckles. All of this finery feels like the slippers that now adorn my feet: glittering and gleaming yet pinching my toes with every step.

I may be home, but I feel rather homesick.

Sophie hands me the pearls. "The suitors Grandmama invited aren't all terrible. Samuel O'Hara is rather handsome, and Elisha Noble is . . . Well, he owns many nice shoes. And you may take a liking to Abraham Radford."

"Radford? Do you mean William's cousin? *Your* William?"

She blushes as red as one of Grandmama's hothouse roses. "He isn't *my* William."

"Not yet, anyhow." I grin. My sister and William Radford have had eyes for each other since childhood, and their romance blossomed while I was at Westacre. Grandmama has given her blessing for the union, although she sniffs that the Radfords aren't as prominent as the Van Persies. "He'll attend the ball tonight, won't he?"

Sophie's gaze darts away from mine, and she chews upon her bottom lip. "Why, yes, of course."

"Did you two have a row?"

Before she can answer, Grandmama calls for us from downstairs and Sophie clasps my hands. "We best not keep her waiting." She tacks on a bright smile, but I can see the brittleness behind it.

"Did William say something to upset you?"

"Nothing! It's nothing at all." She drags me away before I can wheedle another word out of her — and before I can hide Uncle Ambrose's letter.

My stomach flutters. Not only have I lost my chance to stow away the envelope, I must soon undertake the mission he has entrusted to me. I agreed to help my uncle, of course. I'd do anything for him and the Union that my mother loved so much, but a dizzy spell hits me now that this moment has arrived. The Raven may be armed. He's likely dangerous too — for if he's willing to betray his country, then what else might he be willing to do? And here I am dressed in a pretty frock with nothing to defend myself with, unless you count my fists, and I wouldn't count them for very much. But I can't fail Uncle Ambrose and I won't fail the men who serve him. If capturing the Raven means saving just one Union life, then I mustn't falter.

We descend the staircase together and pass by the portrait

of our great-grandfather Joseph Van Persie. Dutch by birth, he journeyed to America at the age of seventeen and made his name first in the steamboat industry and later as a congressman from Maryland. In the painting he possesses a furrowed brow and a weak chin. Grandmama says that I must take after him.

When I near the bottom of the stairwell, I gasp at the transformation of our home. I've not attended our ball in three years, and I'd forgotten the grandeur of it all. Candles abound throughout the first floor, casting a flickering light over the foyer and the three adjoining parlors. My eyes collide with the colors of autumn, from the boughs of golden leaves coiling around the banister to Grandmama's deep-crimson dress. It looks as if the fall has blown in through the front door.

My grandmother, however, appears much more like winter with that icy glare upon her face. A shiver whispers down my back, and I feel like I'm a child again, cowering under Grandmama's scowl when she'd come for a visit. I straighten my shoulders, reminding myself that I'm no longer seven years old.

"Girls! Let me take a look at you," she says from the bottom step. She's dressed in a long-sleeved gown trimmed with ruches of black silk, and her gray hair is pulled neatly behind her ears. Unlike me, she shows no trace of nerves or unease. After all, Grandmama has hosted balls, dinners, and her famed afternoon teas for nearly four decades. Playing hostess comes as naturally to her as nibbling on her morning scone.

Grandmama studies Sophie, and her prune lips twitch in approval. "Quite sufficient, Sophia."

As she studies me, however, her mouth takes a noticeable downward curve. She scowls at my mother's pearls, and her scowl grows fiercer when she notes the—pardon my language—ample bosom that presses against my bodice.

"I suppose there's little we can do about *those* now," Grandmama mutters. "You clearly inherited them from your mother."

And what if I have? I think, but bridle my words.

Grandmama prods a bony finger into my side. "Back straight! Chin up! What sort of gentleman would want a wife who slouches?" Her sharp eyes land upon my pocket. "What's this I see? A letter?"

Heat inches up my spine. "It's from a schoolmate, that's all."

"A schoolmate, hmm? From that fanatical institution of yours?"

I bristle in silence. She's referring to the abolitionists at Westacre, teachers and students alike. It is a Quaker school, although I wouldn't call us fanatical. Grandmama, however, has deemed everything "radical" where my mother is concerned.

"I'll return the letter to my desk," I say, and pick up my skirts.

For some reason, Grandmama glances at Sophie before she takes me by the elbow. "You'll do no such thing. Our guests — and *your* suitors — will arrive at any moment."

Her words prove prophetic. Soon our home swells with the most prominent men and women in Washington, all dressed in their very best: tailcoats for the men and ball gowns for the women. Many of them fawn over Sophie and me, asking us who made our dresses and what sort of fabric was used. My sister answers each question with ease, and I can't help but gape at her. In my absence she has transformed into quite the accomplished hostess, and I'm left wishing that I could flit through the crowd as she does now. But I fumble to say the right thing and I keep tugging at my bodice because it's far lower than I'm used to. I long for the simple muslin dresses that I wore at school, but I tell myself that if I'm to catch the Red Raven, I must look the part.

My gaze rakes the parlor, and I wonder if the Raven has already arrived. Will he be young or old? Plump or thin? With each new face, I wonder. And I keep my ears tuned for three names in particular.

"Blackgrace, Crandall, and Duchamps," I murmur.

Sophie turns to me curiously. "Do you mean Senator Blackgrace? Or Congressman Crandall?"

My cheeks flame when I realize I've spoken aloud. Thankfully, Sophie soon forgets about me because the Radfords arrive next, with William looking very dashing in a black two-breasted tail-coat. With my sister occupied, I repeat the three names once more, this time in silence, and I recall my uncle's letter:

General McClellan suspects three men to be the Raven: Senator Benjamin Blackgrace, Congressman Joshua Crandall, and the French diplomat Laurent Duchamps. Each man possesses past ties to the Confederacy, and you'll need to ensure that they receive invitations to the ball. On the evening of the ball itself, I've concocted a means for you to uncover the Raven, based on intercepted Confederate intelligence. Read this carefully, Lizzie, for I don't wish you to come to harm . . .

Grandmama beckons me from the front parlor. "Elizabeth! Come say hello to Mr. Noble," she says, motioning toward a man whose height may rival that of President Lincoln himself.

I've no choice but to heed her, but I halt when I hear Sophie welcoming an older couple.

"Why, how do you do, Senator and Mrs. Blackgrace?" she says, her voice carrying into my ears like the school bell at Westacre.

Senator Blackgrace!

I spin around and let my eyes lay claim to the senator. Well over sixty, he possesses oil-black hair and shifty dark eyes, like the crows that loiter in the square outside. Or even a raven. My heartbeat gathers steam.

"Elizabeth!" Grandmama says.

I step toward her automatically—loath to face her wrath—but then I pivot in the other direction toward the senator. She calls for me again, but this time I pretend not to hear her. A strange thrill courses through me at my rebellion. I'm not in the habit of disobeying Mrs. Lydia Van Persie. No one is.

As I approach the senator, I nod politely to his prim wife, who hails from South Carolina and who may be her husband's connection to the Confederacy. I let Sophie converse with Mrs. Blackgrace, and I give the senator a smile, crooked as it might be.

"I don't believe we've met, Senator Blackgrace," I say. "I'm Lizzie Van Persie."

"I see," he says in a gloomy tone that matches the winters in his home state of Maine. "I'm acquainted with your father. Will he be in attendance tonight?"

"Unfortunately not. He's out west handling our family's affairs."

"The railroad business, if I remember correctly?"

"You have an excellent memory." My father travels often to oversee our family's business endeavors in the rail industry. At my mother's urging, he sold off the Van Persies' steamboat holdings because many of our ships were built with slave labor. Father's own feelings about abolition were more ambiguous than hers, but he would have done anything for her.

"Is your father well?" Senator Blackgrace continues.

"Quite well. The drier air in the West has done wonders for his lungs." My father's coughing fits have kept him out of uniform and away from home. He seems to avoid Washington—where he shared so many happy times with Mother—as much as he can. I've no doubt that he also wishes to avoid Grandmama's nagging tongue, which constantly tells him to buy back our steamships or to eat more of his dinner. He has never possessed the backbone to stand up to her, aside from his decision to marry an abolitionist spinster from a no-name family.

"Excellent, most excellent," Senator Blackgrace mutters. He appears ready to take his leave, but I can't let him until I ask the question that Uncle Ambrose readied for me. My fingers tremble, and I shove them behind me.

"I've heard your wife comes from the Carolinas," I start.

He arches a furry brow. "She does, though she prefers Maine."

"I hope to visit Charleston one day, perhaps after the war." I cringe inwardly at what I must say next. "I've always admired South Carolinians and their tenacity to fight for their convictions."

He sniffs. "If you'll pardon me—"

I step in front of him. It's rude of me, I know, but I let my uncle's question tumble free: "Forgive me, Senator, but have you met my dear friends Mr. Alexander and Mr. Stephens?"

My heart clashes against my chest. I search the senator's eyes. Will he understand the meaning behind my words?

But Senator Blackgrace only blinks at me. "I'm not acquainted with those gentlemen. Good evening, Miss Van Persie."

He stalks off, and my arms fall to my sides.

He must not be the Raven.

If he were, he would've recognized the code phrase "Mr. Alexander and Mr. Stephens" that would mark me as a Confederate ally—for Alexander Stephens is the Confederacy's vice president. And upon hearing that, the senator would have uttered a code phrase in return.

I wring my hands and wonder if I followed my uncle's

directions correctly. Could I have made a mistake? But the senator's eyes didn't even flicker when I mentioned the names.

Before I can take another breath, Grandmama thunders toward me with the force of a tempest. "Elizabeth! Mr. Noble has gone off to speak to Maud Ingersoll because you tarried here for so long. An Ingersoll! Her father, Robert, is an *atheist*, I'll have you know."

"I couldn't interrupt my conversation with the senator. Wouldn't that be impolite, Grandmama?"

"I'd define rudeness as disobeying your grandmother," she retorts, and pinches me. "Posture, Elizabeth."

I wish once more that she'd call me Lizzie, but I'm sure she'd simply pinch me again if I spoke up. I attempt to slip away, explaining that I haven't had a bite to eat all night, but Grandmama shushes me.

"You may eat *after* your engagement." She takes me by the wrist to haul me toward another suitor, but we're soon swarmed by a flock of her elderly friends, and I gladly make my escape.

Hurrying away from Grandmama's glare, I head into the library to gather my thoughts, but I find the room already occupied. In the far corner, Sophie stands beside Father's globe, on the verge of tears. William paces beside her, equally distraught.

"Won't you tell me what's wrong?" he asks her.

I shrink back into the shadows, forgetting about the Raven and thinking only of my sister. Something is bothering her: that much is obvious.

William catches sight of me and straightens. "Lizzie, how do you do?"

"I'm—I'm well, thank you," I say. "Forgive me, I didn't mean to intrude."

"Nonsense, not at all." He slides Sophie a look. "I'll take my leave."

He strides out of the room, leaving Sophie and me alone. I hurry to her. "What in the world has happened between the two of you?" I ask.

"It's nothing—"

I take her hands. "It's not nothing. Please, Sophie. Tell me what's wrong."

She smiles a bit too brightly. "There's no need to fret. William and I had a misunderstanding." She frees her hands from mine and asks breezily, "How were Grandmama's suitors? Or do you prefer your Westacre beau?"

I sigh. "What beau?"

"Your letter." She gestures at my pocket and makes another grab for it. "What's his name? Is he handsome?"

"Don't change the topic. Has William done something to upset you?"

Her eyes widen—in the dim candlelight I cannot tell if it's in anger or fear—and I expect her to storm off at my prying. Much to my surprise, she embraces me instead.

"Are you unwell?" I say with a startled laugh.

"Far from it. I'm simply happy to have you home, even if you won't tell me about your beau."

"I don't have a beau, for the last time."

"If you say so." She pulls back just as quickly as she wrapped her arms around my waist. "I best return to the party."

I look at her, puzzled. She seems as jittery as a caged cat. "Sophie?"

"William asked me for the next dance!" Then she skitters out of the room, leaving me to stare after her. She's acting very oddly, although I've no idea why. Shaking my head, I resolve to get to the heart of the matter—but after the ball is over.

I leave the library to seek out Crandall and Duchamps, but I find Grandmama and Sophie in the foyer instead, whispering furiously to each other. About what, I don't know. Most likely gossip. I attempt to skirt past them, but Grandmama possesses the eyes of a hungry hawk.

"There's no use avoiding me," she says. "We've much business to attend to, you and I."

Grandmama then snatches my hand and drags me through the house from bachelor to bachelor. There's Judge Jarrett's son, followed by Ambassador Eckhart's cousin, followed by a gentleman I don't even remember the name of. I feel like a Thoroughbred on the auction block, with Grandmama ready to sell me to the highest bidder. As if the Van Persies' coffers aren't piled high enough ...

After thirty minutes of these how-do-you-do's, Grandmama pulls me toward the third parlor, which has been cleared of furniture to serve as a ballroom for the evening. A string quartet tucked away in one corner plays a lively song for our guests.

Grandmama peers into the crowd. "Ah, there he is."

"May I ask who 'he' might be?"

She ignores me. "Do smile, or he'll think that you possess no teeth."

Grandmama tows me toward a portly man who's chewing a cheese tart and licking his fingers. I stare at him, aghast. He looks older than my father. She can't be serious.

The man turns around, and buttery crumbs fall from his lips. "Madame Van Persie!"

"How wonderful of you to come to our ball." Grandmama's own lips curl at the man's ill manners, but she masks her distaste.

"I don't believe you've met my elder granddaughter. Elizabeth, dear, this is Monsieur Duchamps."

Duchamps? I force a smile despite the disgust rolling through my stomach. "How do you do, monsieur?"

"*Enchanté,* mademoiselle." He takes my hand and kisses it, his mouth flopping against my skin like a freshly caught trout. "Your grandmother did not mention what a beauty you are."

I flush, not from the compliment but because Duchamps wiggles his brows at me in such a way that I'm tempted to slap him.

Grandmama nudges me forth an inch. "Why don't you and Monsieur Duchamps enjoy a dance?"

I'd rather flee to France, but I say, "I'd be delighted."

As the quartet begins a waltz, Monsieur Duchamps leads me to the floor and I rifle through my memory of what Uncle Ambrose told me about him, which wasn't much. Apparently he once invested in an Atlanta cotton mill, and rumor has it that he still carries sympathies for the South.

"I do love the waltz," I say, trying to ignore the crumb dangling from his bottom lip. "Are you enjoying the evening?"

"Very much, and even more so in your company." His left hand drifts toward my hip, and I squelch the impulse to bat it away. Grandmama instructed me to smile, but I wouldn't mind if Monsieur Duchamps believes that I'm toothless.

"I've never traveled to France. I'm curious what your countrymen must think about our current war?" I hope my talk of politics will distract him, but his gaze falls upon my bosom, and he makes no effort to hide it.

"I wouldn't know. I've not stepped foot in my home country for many years."

"Then what are your own opinions about the war?"

At last, his eyes flicker toward mine. "War is always unfortunate," he says, ever the diplomat. "Wouldn't you agree?"

"Yes, most unfortunate. Concerning your work—"

"How old are you, mademoiselle? Eighteen?"

"I'm seventeen just."

"Have you always been so"—his brows wriggle at me again—"*mature* for your age?"

I'm tempted to retch upon his shoes, but I ask him a question of my own, ready to be done with this dance and with him altogether. "Tell me, have you had the chance to meet my dear friends Mr. Alexander and Mr. Stephens?"

"I don't believe I have." He pulls me so close that I smell onions on his breath. "But you should forget about those gentlemen. Perhaps you and I could be friends instead?"

My cheeks flame. "I think not!" I should slap him—twice, even, and very hard—but I won't spare him another second.

"Mademoiselle—"

"*Au revoir,* Monsieur Duchamps."

Free from his filthy hands, I gulp down a glass of champagne, but it does little to wash away the memory of the Frenchman. I take comfort in knowing that I won't have to speak with him again, because he didn't utter the code phrase I needed to hear. That leaves me with Congressman Crandall. I need to find him. He has to be the Raven . . . unless Uncle Ambrose has made a mistake.

I frown at that thought. Could it be possible that the spy's true identity has slipped through my uncle's fingers? If so, the Raven could be anyone, a district judge or a foreign diplomat or someone else entirely. My eyes flicker over the parlor, and I wonder if he's here, sipping our champagne or smiling at our other guests. I dart quick glances over my shoulders.

Don't be premature, I tell myself. I must still speak with the congressman.

Smoothing my skirt, I search for our butler to tell me the whereabouts of the congressman, but when I pass by the servants' staircase another idea tickles at the back of my mind. I could run to my room and stow away my uncle's letter before Sophie or Grandmama inquires about it again. It wouldn't take long. I take the stairs two at a time and reach into my pocket ...

And find it empty.

My pulse halts. My gaze claws down the hallway, but I don't find the slip of paper. I hurl myself toward the staircase to retrace my steps, but when I walk past Grandmama's bedroom, my feet lurch to a stop. I blink hard. My grandmother is nowhere in sight, but her room is occupied. From her windowsill, two dark eyes fix on mine.

The eyes of a raven.

The creature hops onto my grandmother's desk and settles next to the bedroom key that she must have forgotten. At first, I wonder if the bird has lost its way, but when I try to shoo it through the window, I notice a piece of parchment tied around its leg. I go still. Uncle Ambrose mentioned that the Red Raven used a raven to correspond with the Confederates.

While the bird cleans its feathers, I tiptoe toward it and remove the parchment and read:

> *Have you gleaned more information concerning our enemy's troop movements? It may be time to arrange for another after-noon tea ...*

I stumble away from the desk.

Another afternoon tea?

"So here you are."

I jump and spin around. My grandmother stands in the door-way, her chin tipped high.

"I don't believe I granted you permission to enter my quarters, Elizabeth," she says.

My face drains of color. "Grandmama?" My instincts tell me to apologize quickly and exit even more so, but I can't ignore the letter in my hand. I thrust it behind my back, but Grandmama clucks her tongue at the sight of it.

"I see you've been trespassing where you're not welcome." She doesn't even address the parchment or the bird. "What do you have to say for yourself?"

"What . . . what do I have to say for myself?" There's a wobble in my voice. *Another afternoon tea.* Those words echo through me once again. "Why has this raven flown directly to your room?"

"How dare you question me," she snaps, and drags me toward the door. "We'll address your punishment later. For now, we're needed downstairs."

"That bird —"

"Is none of your concern."

"But —"

"Hush!" Grandmama halts in front of the window to give me a good shake, and the moonlight illuminates her from hairline to toe.

I try to speak but can't form any words.

"What are you gawking at?" she demands.

Goose bumps cover my skin, and I stare at my grandmother's dress. It's bloodred silk. *Red,* her favorite color.

"The letter was intended for you, wasn't it?" I whisper.

Grandmama snatches the parchment from me. "That's my private correspondence, and I've no need to explain myself."

"Then you don't even deny it?"

She merely picks at a loose thread at her wrist. "I'm well acquainted with Mr. Alexander and Mr. Stephens, if that's what you mean."

I brace a hand against the canopy bed. At last I've heard the words I've waited to hear all night, but they weren't whispered by Blackgrace or Crandall or Duchamps. Uncle Ambrose was wrong. We were both so very wrong.

Grandmama lets out a noisy sigh. "There's no use in lying to you. Your sister may have inherited my looks, but you were blessed with my mind."

"*Blessed?*"

"Do watch your tone. I've no patience for insolence."

Out of habit, I'm ready to utter an apology and slink away— but I clench my teeth and tell myself *No more.* I've allowed Grandmama to pull me out of Westacre and parade me through this ball like my marriage vows are for sale, but I cannot condone her treason.

"How could you?" I say. "How could you willingly work for the Confederates?"

She scowls. "I'm saving this family from ruin, I'll have you know."

"You call *this* 'ruin'?" I point at her jewelry box and the Chinese silk curtains cloaking her windows.

"Where did 'this' come from? I'll tell you where: from the fortune your great-grandfather made building steamships—in the *South.*"

"That was years ago! Father works in railroads now."

"And he's a fool for that. If your insipid mother hadn't persuaded him—"

"Insipid? How dare—"

"Her ridiculous convictions led us straight to the poorhouse! I possess the proof of it right in this very room." She nods at her jewelry box. "Open it."

"Why?"

"Open it."

I reach for the box, knowing that I'll find a trove of sapphire rings, ruby bracelets, and the largest pearls in all of Washington. But once I open it, I nearly gasp. It looks like Grandmama has been robbed. The rings, gone. The rubies, depleted. Only a strand of pearls remains, sitting lonely against the black velvet.

"I had no choice but to sell them," Grandmama says, pain lacing her words. "We're almost bankrupt due to this railroad venture. I'd no choice but to accept the Confederacy's offer. They pay me quite well in exchange for the secrets I glean at my afternoon teas. How else could I have bought the dress you're wearing?"

I sink onto the bed, dizzy from her revelations. I wish I could tear off this dress and burn it.

"So now you understand the importance of you marrying well," she continues. "The Confederates' money may keep us afloat, but we're standing upon a sinking ship. I *will* find you a husband — and a wealthy one at that — especially with your father off to who knows where."

My thoughts immediately shift to Father. "Does he know what you've done?"

"Of course not," she says. "Your sister, on the other hand. . . ."

My gaze bores into hers. "Whatever do you mean?"

With great flourish, she reaches into her dress pocket and pulls out my letter — the letter from Uncle Ambrose.

It grows difficult for me to breathe. "How did . . . ?"

"It appears I'm not the only spy in the family," she says, fanning herself with the letter before I yank it from her. "Sophia was kind enough to retrieve this for me."

My mind reels. No, I won't believe it. I can't. "She wouldn't do such a thing."

"She would and she did, while you two spoke in the library earlier."

My memory skips back an hour to Sophie's odd behavior in the library. Has my sister changed so much since I've been away at school?

"Why?" I whisper.

"Because I asked her to read all your correspondences," Grandmama replies. "It's my duty as your guardian to be privy to such matters, although little did I know that your uncle's letters would prove so interesting." She glances at me in her mirror. "Oh, don't be too cross with Sophia. She didn't want to read your letters — at first — but I told her that I'd never give her my blessing to marry that Radford boy if she didn't."

I don't think I can speak. This is all too much. My grandmother, a spy? My sister, an accomplice? I want to believe that Grandmama is lying — that Sophie would never betray me — but my heart severs in half just the same.

"Wash your face and gather your wits, Elizabeth," she orders me. "Now that you know the truth, we can return to the matter at hand: your nuptials."

My jaw slackens. "After what you've told me, you expect me to rejoin the ball as if nothing has happened?"

"You saw my jewel box. Our family's good name is in jeopardy — and *you* shall save it."

Despite my trembling legs, I stand. "If anyone has jeopardized the Van Persie name, it's you, Grandmama. You've committed treason."

She laughs. *Laughs!* "Call it what you want, but I've done this for our family. If I hadn't, we would have lost this house and the very clothes on your back." She tucks a strand of hair behind her ear. "You're a smart girl. Do you wish to spend the rest of your life in the poorhouse?" She looks me up and down. "Well, do you?"

I struggle for an answer. I struggle even to think. She expects me to wilt, like I've done so many times before.

Grandmama takes my silence for assent and marches for the door. "Come along."

I don't move.

"Stop dallying."

I refuse to budge. I don't wish to end up in the poorhouse. But how can we live a life funded by our grandmother's traitorous acts?

"Move your feet," Grandmama says.

Two choices fork in front of me. I can do as she says and preserve my family's name. Or I can take another path. My fists clench and unclench, and I think of my mother.

"No," I whisper.

Her eyes slash into me. "I beg your pardon?"

"I won't play a part in your deceit."

She hurtles toward me, her hand raised to slap me. "Listen to me, you —"

I block her blow. She grabs at my collar, and I realize she won't let me out of this room until I bow to her demands. I yank the bedroom key from the desk and wrench away from her, my heart beating so quickly that I fear it might burst.

"You wretched thing!" she cries.

I reach the door and catch a flash of Grandmama's murderous gaze before I shut the door behind me and lock it tight. She pounds her fists against the wood and spews terrible words at me, but I stuff the key into my pocket.

"Open this door at once, Elizabeth!"

I stare down the door. I quell the tremble in my voice and say, "My name is *Lizzie.*"

I force my legs down the hallway and stumble into my room. I'm unsure of what to do next, but I know I mustn't tarry in the house, not with Grandmama yelling and pounding at her door. I throw a cloak over my shoulders and gather my mother's ring and a small stack of spending money from my desk. There isn't time for anything else. As I descend the servants' staircase, my mind scrambles for where I should go—but I'm stopped midway by my sister.

"I heard shouting," she says, her bottom lip quivering. Her gaze falls upon my left hand with my uncle's letter still clutched inside it, and her face turns as white as her petticoats. "Where's Grandmama?"

"Upstairs," I mutter, her betrayal stabbing through me once again.

"Lizzie, please—"

"Grandmama told me everything. *Everything.*"

"Let me explain!" Her hands grab on to mine to anchor me next to her. "I never wanted to betray your confidence, but Grandmama said—"

"That she wouldn't give her blessing for you to marry William."

She nods with teary eyes. "What was I to do? I love him."

What of me? I'm tempted to ask her. *Do you possess no love for your own blood?*

Sophie dabs her eyes with her sleeve. "She forced me to do it. I've barely eaten or slept in weeks because of the guilt. You believe me, don't you?"

She cries harder, and I can't muster the strength to push her away. Despite the anger flaring inside my chest, I know that Sophie acted out of fear, not malice. And for that reason alone, I place my hand on her shoulder.

She laces her fingers against mine. "I'll write to Father. I'll tell him what has happened."

"There's no need." I pull away. Grandmama's shouting grows louder by the second, and I need to depart.

But how can I leave without Sophie?

I take her hand. "Come with me."

"Where are you going?" she says, baffled.

"Away from this place. Away from Grandmama. Do you wish to keep living under her thumb?"

Sophie steps back. "We . . . we mustn't be rash. This is our home."

It isn't mine anymore, I think. It hasn't been since Mother died.

"It's Grandmama's home," I say.

"Not only hers. It's ours too." She gives me her best hostess's smile. "Come, let me fetch you a glass of wine and a piece of cake. We'll all feel better in an hour." She tries to lead me down the stairs, but I shake my head sadly. It's clear that she has made her choice.

I kiss her cheek and whisper into her ear: "Marry William. Make a new life with him, away from the city."

That's all I can wish for her now: a new home. A new future without Grandmama.

I wrench myself free from her and race toward the carriage house, where I saddle a gray mare and guide her into the street. I should urge her into a gallop, but I glance back toward our brownstone — the homestead of my family for so many years. Only a minute ago I was one of the mistresses there and one of the most eligible young women in our fair capital. But now here I am, with a few bills in my pocket and a workhorse to my name.

Fear thrums through me. For a moment I wonder if I should run back into the house and beg Grandmama for forgiveness. She'd likely make me grovel, but she wouldn't turn me away. I'd have a bed to sleep on, fine food to fill my belly, new ball gowns . . . and it would all be a farce. A traitor's sham. I shake my head and tap my heels against my horse's sides. I can't turn back.

I *won't* turn back.

The mare trots forth, and I don't know where to lead her. I could return to Westacre, but I've no money for tuition and I'm too young to be taken on as a teacher. I suppose I could seek out Father, but he'd likely send me back to Washington. Besides, we've become strangers these past three years. A thought strikes me then. It's preposterous, not to mention dangerous, and I almost brush it away.

But it's the only place left for me.

I urge my mare down the street. I'll use what little money I have to spend the night at an inn, and come the morning I'll head toward Sharpsburg—and my uncle. I'll tell him about the Red Raven and the role my grandmother has played in this war. Whether he sends her to prison or not, that shall be his concern and not mine any longer.

I don't know what lies in front of me. I have little to offer Uncle Ambrose aside from a half-finished education and a soon-to-be sullied surname. Yet I know one thing: whatever path I choose, I shall make my mother proud. I hold tight to this thought.

I pin a brave smile to my lips and bring my mare to a canter. The pounding of her hooves matches the thud of my heart, and I breathe in the crisp air that carries the scent of a new day ahead. A new start.

"Head north, girl," I whisper into the wind. "We're going home."

🎔 *Author's Note* 🎔

I'm a native of the Washington, D.C., area, and as a kid I was fascinated by the rich history of my little corner of the world. I was especially intrigued by the Civil War and how D.C. played a big part in it, and how the city was mere miles from the South. It seemed as if the Confederates could've swum across the Potomac at any moment and claimed the city for themselves. So when Jessica Spotswood kindly invited me to contribute a short story to this anthology, I knew that I wanted to set my story during the Civil War and use Washington, D.C., as a backdrop. That's how the idea of "The Red Raven Ball" was born.

As I started my research, I became fascinated by the lives of Civil War spies, specifically the hundreds who were female. These women came from all variety of backgrounds, from freed slaves to poor actresses to Washington socialites. One of these socialites, a widowed secessionist named Rose O'Neal Greenhow, used her connections to gather information on the Union military for the Confederates. Mrs. Greenhow was the inspiration for the character of Grandmama.

Although most of the characters in this story are fictional, the atheist Robert Ingersoll was real (and an ancestor of my husband's). Ingersoll was a famed orator and politician—the *Washington Post* once dubbed him "the most famous American you never heard of"—but he was best known for his disdain of organized religion, which was a shocking proposition to nineteenth-century Americans and earned him the nickname "the Great Agnostic."

Pearls

Beth Revis

I HAD DONE EVERYTHING RIGHT. IT brought me no comfort to know that now, but I *had* done everything right. It helped, of course, that I'd been born into the right family. My papa had invested heavily in the rail system before the trains connected east and west, and before that, his papa had invested in the War, and before that, *his* papa had invested in ships crossing the Atlantic. But it was more than just being born into the right family. I had cultivated the right friends, gone to the right parties, flirted with the right men.

Well, I thought I'd flirted with the right men.

And when one of the so-called right men had proven to be anything *but* right, well. Everything changed.

At breakfast the morning after, my father had been waiting for me. All I had wanted to do was pretend that nothing had happened, nothing at all, but Papa had stood in front of the door, not even allowing me into the dining room and the comfort of a warm breakfast made by our cook, Maggie.

"You were *seen*," he had hissed at me.

I hadn't even had the courage to speak. Again.

"You were seen with that man. Everyone knows you let him have you."

Let.

"You could have done better, Helen. You could have married a Rockefeller, or a Vanderbilt at least. This one'll do. But you could have done better."

And then he had left, yelling for Maggie to bring coffee to his office. That had been my one chance to talk to my father about that night, but it wouldn't have mattered even if I *had* found the courage to speak. He'd already decided what he would believe, and nothing anyone could say or do would have changed his mind.

Just like nothing I could ever say or do would change that night.

Richard said I hadn't been pure to start with. He said I had led him on.

He said I had wanted it.

That morning, Maggie had made soft-boiled eggs and toast with fresh cream butter. She had presented the eggs to me in the little porcelain cups Mama had had imported from Japan when she married Papa, the ones with wispy blue lines along the rims. I'd cracked the top of the egg with that ridiculously tiny silver spoon in that ridiculously pretty little cup, peeling off the top of the shell and exposing the gooey insides. And there was something about it all—the broken egg exposed and the bleeding yolk inside its shell in the perfect little cup—it was in that moment that I realized just how much of my life I'd lost.

I haven't had eggs since that day.

After . . . after what he did to me—Richard had said I'd be forced to be his, or be every man's.

And maybe if I didn't have all my fancy education, that'd be true.

Instead, I'm going to run.

So while Papa and that man negotiate a dowry that suits both of them, I make my own plans.

I turn to the newspaper first and find a handful of personal advertisements seeking a bride. Each advertisement requests females to write letters so that the man can select a suitable companion for life. She would have paid passage out west, a guaranteed husband, and a promised life of security.

But I am done with men owning me.

Near those advertisements, I spot a small clip sponsored by the National Board of Education for the Populace. I memorize the address of the office and go there on my own under the pretext of hat shopping the next day.

The man in charge of the office is dour and is unhappy that I have no proof of the kind of education I'd need to be a teacher— no certification or proper training. I'm able to give enough evidence that I'm adequately intelligent for the job, though.

"I *did* get a request," he says finally, after quizzing me skeptically. "It's a rough school, just starting, and I doubt they'd be picky about certification. They had one teacher for a few months, but the area gets cold, and he left at the first hint of winter. It's in the territory of Wyoming. A subscription school. We don't usually deal with those, but they sent a request."

I have no idea what a subscription school is, but I nod my head eagerly.

"Look, you look like a nice girl," the stodgy old man says,

peering down his glasses. "If you got yourself in a bit of trouble ..."
His gaze moves down my body.

"Please tell me more about this Wyoming school," I say coldly.

"They'll pay for your passage on the Union Pacific, and you'll
have a room and board, taken directly out of your fees by the families setting up the school," the man tells me. "But it's dangerous
out there for a woman of genteel nature."

"That will be fine." I stand, holding my hand out for the card
with information on it. "I'll go there."

The program arranges the details. I am to take a train from
Chicago to Cheyenne, and then a coach. My students will be aged
seven to sixteen, as the new law stipulates their education. I am
only nineteen myself; the idea of teaching people just three years
my junior is rather intimidating.

The idea of leaving home with nothing but some books and
clothes is rather intimidating too.

But then at supper the night after I receive my Union Pacific
ticket, Richard touches my knee under the table. I startle and
move away, but when I look across the table, I see my father
frown, just a bit, and shake his head subtly.

I can't leave soon enough.

I try, one last time.

Papa sits in his office, the rich smell of cigar smoke wrapping
around the books lined up neatly on the shelves.

"Don't make me do this," I say from the doorway.

"What? Helen, don't mumble, come in." Papa leans back in his
chair, puffing.

"Don't make me marry him," I say, louder. "It's not right."

Papa lowers the cigar slowly, letting it drop ash over the side
of the desk. "You didn't give yourself many choices."

"This is a choice," I say. "Not marrying him is a choice. I don't care about scandal; with my dowry, I doubt any man will care in a year or so. Don't make me do this."

Papa starts to speak, but I cut him off.

"You raised me for better. You know I deserve better."

"Richard's a decent enough man."

"He's rich," I say, "but he's not decent."

Papa shrugs and picks his cigar back up.

"Mama wouldn't make me marry him," I say.

The end of the cigar glows red, the smoke obscuring Papa's face.

"Dead women have no voice," he growls.

I gasp, shocked that he would dismiss Mama so easily.

Papa leans over his desk. "Listen, Helen, you're old enough and God knows you're experienced enough to know the truth, and the truth is, it doesn't matter who you marry, as long as your position is secure. People go. Money stays. It's the only thing that does."

Without another word, I let the door close softly behind me. There is no going back now, that much I know for sure.

I never knew how easy it is to escape if you don't mind leaving nearly everything behind.

The only thing of value I take with me out west is in my head. I pack a trunk with clothes and books and a bit of money, and I pay Maggie with love and some of the cash I've hidden to ship the trunk out to Cheyenne, and then to the general store of the little town where I've procured a position. Maggie is reluctant to help me. She calls Richard my "dashing gentleman" in her soft Irish accent, and she feels our quick engagement is romantic, and I cannot find the words to tell her it was anything but. Her nose has always been in the gothics, ever since I taught her to read, and she hasn't plucked the stars from her eyes ever since Richard smiled at her when she served him at dinner.

Regardless, she sneaks the trunk out for me the day before I leave, so as I adjust my hat and take a deep breath, the only thing I walk out the door with is my reticule, filled with innocuous things, and my brain, with the education I hope will save me clattering around.

Knowledge is my only real value. My papa ensured that I was taught well. Education was what helped his great-great-grandfather rise to the top of society so many years ago; education meant that the family hasn't failed in the harsh years since. The things that separate us from the grime-covered workers in the factories are education and knowing that education makes us better. My papa never intended me to take over the family accounts after his death, but he also hadn't intended me to be a simpering wife with no thoughts of my own, despite his attitude about Richard. And while my papa is wrong about many things, he was right about the fact that when I have nothing else, I have my education.

But I also have my memories.

And my regrets.

I clutch the ticket in my hand at the station. The thin paper seems flimsy and weak, nothing at all what freedom should feel like. *This ticket*, it says underneath the emblazoned UNION PACIFIC logo, *entitles the holder to one second-class passage from CHICAGO to station canceled*. A little mark by *CHEYENNE* is the only assurance I have that I'm actually going somewhere . . . away.

The train pulls into the station, all billowing steam, and activity swirls around me.

And that is it. Just a piece of paper and a train and a promise of a job in the West, and a new life is within my grasp.

I step into the train with trepidation, my hand clutching the porter's as he helps me up. Wooden benches line the train car, but it's thankfully not as crowded as it might have been. A family of eight takes up two benches in the front; a group of men sits in the middle. An old man in a worn but neatly pressed suit sits primly near the back, and there are several empty benches before him.

"May I?" I ask, indicating the seat by the old man. He nods genially. Best to sit with someone who looks safe than to sit by myself and run the risk of someone less safe down the line.

"By yourself?" the old man asks.

He's just making conversation, I think. I smile despite the lump rising in my throat and say, "Meeting someone soon."

My eyes go to the window, half-expecting someone—my father, Richard, Maggie—to be raising a fuss, trying to stop me.

But I'm alone.

I don't breathe again until the train chugs to life, pulling me farther and farther away from this life I no longer want.

The rhythm of the train lulls me to sleep, and in my dreams, I'm wearing the glittering gown I wore that night to the opera, almost as sparkling as the bubbles of the champagne I drank with abandon. The world was my oyster.

And in my dream, Richard is like he was before. Dashingly handsome, with a smile that could melt the knees right out from under you. The perfect gentleman. When I leaned in to whisper conspiratorially about the opera to him, I felt . . . exhilarated. He had an edge to his shine, but he felt safe too. Someone I could confide in, someone who would smile when I touched his elbow or tapped him with my fan.

And then I woke up.

The train is hot and stuffy and unbearable. It's already well into autumn, but despite the cooler temperatures outside, my dress sticks to my skin, and my hair clings to the back of my neck.

The coach that picks me up in Cheyenne is miserably cold but equally stuffy. The man sharing the coach with me makes a point of telling me that Cheyenne just got its first public schoolhouse last year. We don't pass the building, but I suspect it is far nicer than anything I'm heading to.

But this life will be better than what I'm leaving behind. The farther we go, the farther I am from Richard. I promise myself that the school will be a haven, an ivory tower I can live in with books and students and no Richard.

It's a hovel.

Well, more accurately, it's a small house attached by one wall to the local Episcopalian church. Mr. William M. Jeffers greets me at the coach stop, and we walk together the half mile to the church at the end of the main street. The church is long and narrow, made of logs; the shack attached to it is made of planks, with cracks big enough to show daylight through.

I step inside the "schoolhouse" tentatively. There are a few split-pole benches, a rough table that's clearly meant to be my desk, and a writing board hung on pegs on a wall. The only heat comes from the stove at the back of the room — or it would, if it were lit.

"You're awful young to be out here alone," Mr. Jeffers says as I stand in the center of the one-room schoolhouse, turning slowly to inspect everything.

"I thank you for the compliment," I say coolly. "I'm quite the spinster, though." I've pulled my hair back into a severe bun, so tight it hurts my head, and I'm wearing my most dour dress.

"See that you stay that way," Mr. Jeffers says in a fatherly tone.

I nod. Only single women are allowed to be schoolmarms. But I have no intention of marrying.

"The Cookes gave a steer to pay for this," Mr. Jeffers tells me proudly, sweeping his arm to indicate the building. "We've got a collection going for improvements, to make this a real school-house. The Cookes got ten young'uns for your class; they're the ones what pushed for a school here, that and the new law. You'll probably get about ten more. Some'll pay in goods. Mr. McHenry will give you a fair price for things at the store if you don't have no need for them."

My classroom was paid for by a cow.

And it looks like it.

Greased paper covers the only window, letting mottled light inside. "We got glass comin' in. Mr. McHenry ordered it himself," Mr. Jeffers says quickly when he sees where I'm looking. "You're from Chicago, ain't ya?" he adds. "I mean, I know the train came from there, but you're from the city proper. You talk like it."

I nod.

"Wyoming's a bit different from Chicago."

I don't bother responding; that much is obvious.

"It's a good school, Miss Davies." Mr. Jeffers, for the first time, sounds defensive, almost angry. I try to see myself through his eyes. My dress may be plain, but it's still fine. And while I've tried not to show it, there must be something in my face that betrays my emotion.

"It is indeed a good school, Mr. Jeffers," I say. "And I am right grateful to be here."

"If it gets too cold, you can use the church," Mr. Jeffers allows. "And there's a good stack of wood for the stove."

"Thank you." The words are almost a whisper.

"We've arranged for you to room and board with Mrs. Franklin, down the street. She runs a ladies' home. Got three seamstresses there already," Mr. Jeffers says. "After this month, though, you're to pay her direct with the fees you collect from the children."

"Thank you," I say again. "I had a trunk that was sent ahead. Will it be there?"

Mr. Jeffers laughs. "That'll be at the general store," he says. "One of the boys there'll help you cart it back to the house."

The general store isn't hard to find—there aren't that many buildings on Main Street, and the painted sign above the large windows reads MCHENRY'S STORE in large blue-and-gold letters. The paint is peeling a bit, but the windows sparkle and the floor is immaculately swept.

The shopkeep, McHenry, has my trunk waiting for me. I breathe a silent prayer of thanks to both God and Maggie.

I might just survive this after all.

The room Mrs. Franklin has for me is small and plain but serviceable. The same can be said of the food she serves for supper.

I don't allow myself to open my trunk until that night. At the top of the trunk is my mother's wedding dress, made of pale-blue silk covered with ivory lace and seed pearls. It was a last-minute addition to the trunk. I do not expect to ever wear it. But the idea of leaving behind this last piece of my mother . . . I couldn't do it.

I imagine the way my mother felt when she wore this dress. I used to have a portrait of my parents after the wedding, their faces still and stoic. But when she wore the dress, she must have been filled with hope and joy. She truly loved my father, and I think he truly loved her. Before she died, I think my papa cared about things like love and happiness.

The dress crumples in my hands, and I hold it against my face, breathing in the scent of cedar from the chest where it was stored. The tiny seed pearls at the neckline dig into my skin.

As a little girl, I dreamed of picking apart the seams of this dress and refashioning it into my own.

I take a deep breath and fold the gown carefully. Best to avoid wrinkles.

At the bottom of my trunk are the eight books I felt most important to bring with me. *King Lear* is the most worn, my favorite play, but I've read my translation of *Les Misérables* almost as often. The McGuffey's Reader I used when I was learning my letters. My father's favorite book, *A Pictorial History of the United States*, is something I took just because it is something he loves.

The other books—philosophies—used to bring me comfort. My fingers linger over Socrates, but the book I select is my old favorite, Thomas More's *Utopia*.

The words inside, however, do not calm my fears. They speak of a land I'll never know, of happiness and peace I only thought I knew.

The book drops from my fingers. I have been so, *so* stupid. What makes me think I can teach children? They don't need philosophy in a schoolhouse made of planks. They don't need pretty ideals for a life they will never have. They don't need *me*.

As Mr. Jeffers informed me, I have ten students from the various branches of the Cooke family. They are easily identifiable: they are the ones with clean faces and slates. The head of the family— Old Man Cooke, who owns the largest ranch in the area—sends them all to the school on a wagon.

I have seven other students. Four are from the McHenry family, who own the general store in town; two are twin daughters of the preacher of the Episcopalian church with which we share a wall; and one is a little slip of a girl named Phoebe Ann. She's the only one without her own slate, the only one without a lunch pail and no intention of returning home for a midday meal, and she squints so badly I'm not sure she can see the front of the room.

"She won't last," one of the Cooke children informs me in a loud whisper.

But Phoebe Ann—Annie, as she quickly tells me she likes to be called—pays me for a month of schooling with a small jar of berry preserves. She warns me she can only come now that there is no harvest and her momma hasn't just had another baby for her to take care of and the next youngest has died of a fever, and if things change, she'll have to go. She asks if she can pay with rabbit skins next month, since that's the last jar of berries they have. I say she can.

That's how the subscription school works, I learn. The Cooke family bought the schoolhouse, and the McHenrys donated some money to get it all started, but that was only for the beginning. Now that the school is established, everything comes from the subscription fees the students give me. They all pay by the month. And I'm to use these fees to pay the church rent, to pay for the supplies I need to run the school, and to pay for my own needs with whatever's left. Which won't be much, as the teacher they hired originally scampered at the first sign of winter and took some of the supplies for the school with him.

Despite living the farthest away, the Cooke children are the first to arrive. The boys load the stove with wood, and the girls help with the washbasin. They each have their own seat, arranged from youngest to oldest on the benches, two children to a little table. They have to shuffle around to accommodate Annie, who hadn't bothered to come to school while the previous teacher was here, as she'd been helping her family on the farm—but none of the children really seem to mind. They make a point to remind me that all the Cooke boys will miss months at a time in the spring when new calves are born.

We recite the Lord's Prayer.

Then the children look at me.

Waiting.

My stomach twists. I had planned what to do in this moment, but now that it's here, now that all their eyes are on me ...

"Mr. Brooks started with numbers," the oldest Cooke girl informs me.

I cannot let them think of me as just a replacement, a poor imitation of their former teacher. I snatch up my McGuffey's Reader from the table I use as a desk. There are no books, not aside from the ones I brought with me and a spare Bible.

"We shall start with reading. Bridget McHenry," I say, pointing to the eldest girl in the class, "you shall go first."

She swings her legs into the aisle, stands, and strides to the center of the room. She is only five years my junior, and she carries herself with more confidence than I have ever had.

No ... that's not quite true. I used to have more confidence. I used to think the world would bend to my will too.

Bridget takes the book from my hand.

"Page one hundred and seventeen," I say in a loud, carrying voice that betrays none of my nerves. "Read the story of the gouty merchant, please."

Bridget clears her throat and reads the tale, her voice loud and clear. It's a very short piece, about a rich man doing his accounting when a stranger enters his building. The stranger at first acts kind, telling the man that he found the door ajar and that there seemed to be no one home, so he wanted to inform the rich man of the danger of leaving his door open. The rich man thanks him, telling him he'll have his footman thrown in jail, that he is home alone and quite vulnerable.

At which point the stranger smiles, thanks him for confirming he's alone, blows out the candles, and robs the rich man blind.

Bridget hands the book back to me and returns to her seat when she's done reading. Before she can sit down, the eldest Cooke boy stands.

"Yes, Joseph?" I ask him, hesitating only a moment for his name.

"I read after Bridget. That's how Mr. Brooks had us do it."

"We are going to discuss the story of the merchant and the stranger before we move on," I say coolly.

"Mr. Brooks didn't have us discuss."

"I believe I have already confirmed that I am not Mr. Brooks," I say, leveling him with a stern eye. Inside my head, I think that should this boy go home and complain to his father, who bought my classroom with a cow, I may be fired. Or worse—he could lead a revolt against me himself, getting the other children to turn on me. There are far more of them than me.

But he just sits.

"Let us, ah, discuss the tale, then," I say awkwardly, leaning against my desk.

Little Annie's hand shoots up. I nod at her, and she stands and faces me as she answers. "That rich man was right stupid," she says, then sits down.

I motion for her to stand again. "Elaborate."

Her eyes are fierce. "It's like the story of the possum and the snake my momma tells."

One of the Cooke boys snickers at her but is silenced the second my gaze swivels to him. "I don't know this story," I say.

"Snake asks the possum to tote him across the river in his pouch. Possum says no, can't trust no snake. Snake begs and begs, and finally the possum totes him 'cross the river. Get to the other side, snake sneaks out and bites the possum. Possum cries out, but the snake says, 'You knowed I was a snake 'fore you put me in your pouch.'"

The snickering Cooke boy—Jebediah—stands up. "That's not what it means *at all*," he says. "The story means that people are generally good, unless you give 'em a chance to be bad. Can't blame a man for stealing something you leave unguarded."

Before I can do anything, Annie spins around to face him. "So it's all right to hurt someone, long as they can't fight back?"

"That's not the same at all!" Jebediah says.

"Why ain't it?" Annie snarls. "Just cause something's easy to steal don't mean God ain't watching you steal it."

"You got something worth stealing, it's your job to protect it. But," Jebediah adds, his voice lowering, "not like you got anything worth stealing, no need to worry 'bout that."

"Enough!" I roar. I can feel heat rising in my face. I had picked the story with the intention of talking about theft, perhaps seeing if the students would be interested in reading a translation of *Les Misérables*, but this conversation has hit far too close to home for me.

"Annie is right; if you know someone's a snake, you can't trust him. The only problem is, you can't always tell who the snakes are." My gaze settles on Jebediah. "And I confess to being deeply concerned with the way you think theft is to be so easily forgiven. Taking something from someone just because you can is still a sin, Mr. Cooke. Go outside and chop more firewood for the class until you understand that lesson more thoroughly."

Jebediah starts to protest, but whatever fears I had of the students have been burned away by my rage, and they can all see it. He snaps his mouth shut and stomps outside.

"Annie, would you like to read the next story?" I say.

"Can't," Annie says, sitting down.

It takes me a moment to realize she means she can't read at all.

A week later, Annie brings a gun to school.

Well, that's not fair. Annie—as well as several of the Cooke boys—always brings a gun to school, but they've been revolvers, carried in case they run across snakes or something else dangerous on the way to school or back home. It shocked me the first time I saw the glint of metal at one of the boys' waists, but I'm becoming accustomed to not showing my shock anymore.

But it seems like everyone is shocked by the rifle Annie brings to school on Monday and sets in the corner near her seat.

"This is way too nice," Jebediah says, hoisting the gun to his shoulder.

"It's not; the sight's broke off," his brother Joseph says. "And look at the stock."

"Give it back," Annie protests.

Jebediah is right—the gun *is* nice. Even I, who know very little about guns beyond a passing ability to shoot them, can see this, despite the damage to it. The sight's been replaced with a silver dime sawed in half, and a crack in the stock's been reinforced with wire, but beyond these flaws, the gun looks nearly brand-new. The octagonal barrel gleams and, aside from one deep scratch, looks perfect.

"Give it back!" Annie demands again.

"How'd your daddy get this?" Jebediah taunts, not bothering to return the rifle. "Steal it? Win it in a poker game?"

"Maybe he killed an Indian for it," Joseph says.

"Not very likely an Indian would have a gun like this," Jebediah shoots back.

"Give it here!" Annie shouts.

"Sight's broke off, like the Indians do," Joseph points out.

"My daddy was *given* this gun, and you give it back to me now!" Annie stomps her foot.

"Who'd give your daddy anything?" Jebediah says.

Annie snarls and delivers a sharp kick to Jebediah's knee, snatching the gun the second he lowers it. She races out of the room, but I see a sparkle of tears in her eyes.

"Poorly done," I tell the boys in a low voice. They're decent enough to look ashamed.

"More chopping?" Jebediah asks.

"We're running out of wood that needs chopping," I tell him, cocking an eyebrow. "At lunch, you're cleaning every single slate."

I find Annie sitting on the steps outside. Her tears were of anger, not sadness, and have already burned from her eyes.

"He's so mean," Annie mumbles. She glances up at me. "Just like a snake."

I smile, remembering her story on the first day of class. "Maybe not quite a snake," I say. "I've known snakes; they're worse. Jebediah's just a . . . just a lizard."

This earns me a smile, but it disappears quickly.

"My daddy *was* given this," Annie tells the gun, not me.

"I believe you," I say.

"Some rich man came from Chicago. Hired my daddy to help him hunt, guide him around the land. They were gone for weeks." She glances up at me. "You're from Chicago, ain't ya, Miss Davies?"

"Yes."

"Did you know the man? He was named Franklin Smithfield."

"Chicago is a big place, bigger than this little town. I didn't know him."

"Wish I lived somewhere people didn't know me," Annie mutters.

I start to rub her back but hesitate. Annie can be prickly. I don't want to scare her off.

"My daddy saved that man's life, though. His horse threw him when a grizzly attacked. That's how he broke the Ballard." She strokes the wire holding the stock on the gun. "He gave it to my daddy after my daddy killed the bear for him."

"Your daddy sounds like an honorable man," I say.

"He is," Annie mumbles. She stares at the gun. "Maybe I should go."

"Go?" I ask. "Where?"

"Home."

"Why?"

"Momma's pregnant again. Half a year, I won't be here anyway. Probably sooner."

I swallow, surprised. I shouldn't be. But I am.

I want to tell Annie that a lot can happen in half a year. That she is worth more than a caretaker for her siblings. That her own mind has value, and her own will, and that what she wants matters.

But all I say is "Stay at least for today."

One of the McHenry girls tells me that the package I ordered from their daddy at the general store arrived, so the next morning before school, I walk down the street.

Annie's mule is hitched in front of McHenry's store, and when I enter, I'm surprised to see Mr. McHenry sliding some

coins across the counter to her. Her fingers are covered in dirt—
no, dried blood. Mr. McHenry stacks up a pile of fresh rabbit furs
she just sold him.

"What'd you do with the meat?" Mr. McHenry asks.

"Sold to Mrs. Hutchinson," Annie says.

"Bring me some next time; I'll give you a fair price."

Annie nods, pocketing one of the coins and handing the other
back to Mr. McHenry. "My daddy needs some more primers."

Mr. McHenry gets a small box for her. As he hands it to
her, he says, "Is it your daddy reloading the shells or are you
doing it?"

Annie doesn't answer.

"You giving him that other coin?" The shopkeeper's voice is
lower now.

Annie nods.

"Don't you let him buy more drink, you hear? Hide it if that's
what he's going to do."

Annie pockets the box of primers and turns to go.

"Miss Davies!" Mr. McHenry says when he notices me. Annie
starts in surprise, and red creeps up her cheeks.

Before any of us can say anything else, Mr. McHenry's children burst in through the back door, along with the twins. They
crowd around the front counter.

"See! I told you Daddy got more candy!" Bridget cries,
pointing.

The twins pull pennies out of their pockets, eyeing the glass
jars eagerly.

Mr. McHenry starts to serve me first, but I nod to the children. "Go ahead," I say, smiling as Mr. McHenry starts doling
out sweets.

"Why don't you get something, Annie?" I ask her gently.

"She doesn't eat candy," Bridget says around a lemon drop. "She only eats rabbits and rats."

"Bridget!" Mr. McHenry glares at his daughter. She looks immediately ashamed, even more so as Mr. McHenry threatens her with a switch for her rude words. But as Annie slinks from the store, I can't help but notice that Bridget still has the sweet in her mouth, and Annie has nothing.

"Get on to the school," I tell the children as they rush out. "I'll be there in a minute."

"Now, Miss Davies," Mr. McHenry says, leaning down the counter. "I just got the package you ordered. And I sold that pretty dress of yours for more than I thought, so I owe you an extra quarter." He gives me the coin and the slender box together. The words HOPKINS & ALLEN are written on the side of the box, and it weighs heavily in my hand, but not so heavy that it pulls down my skirt when I slip it in my pocket.

"Where'd you get such a nice dress out here?" Mr. McHenry asks. "Them little seed pearls were mighty fine."

"It was my mother's," I say, trying not to remember the way I once dreamed of wearing it.

"I could have gotten you a cheaper model," Mr. McHenry says, indicating my pocket where the box lies hidden.

I know he could have. "This is just right," I say. "Thank you."

Annie's attendance becomes increasingly sporadic in the next few weeks, and she shows up later and later in the day. Snow starts sprinkling down, dusting everything in white, and the promised glass for the grease-paper window still hasn't arrived, but the stove keeps us warm enough.

We're in the middle of saying the Lord's Prayer when Annie rushes in, snow already melting on her coat from the steamy heat of the stove. She carefully leans her rifle against the back wall and then whirls around to me.

"Miss Davies!" she gasps.

"Don't interrupt," I say, but it's too late—the rest of the children are thoroughly distracted by Annie's sudden appearance.

"A stranger's here!" Annie says, still catching her breath. "He was at McHenry's, looking for *you!*"

The children are abuzz, quizzing Annie about the stranger. For one brief moment, I think maybe it's my papa, that Maggie told him where I went and he realized he loved me more than my reputation. But Maggie never really did like Papa.

Not the way she liked Richard.

And there he is, standing in the doorway.

"This is him!" Annie says excitedly. "The stranger!"

Richard strides into the room as if he owns the schoolhouse.

"That's no stranger, Annie," I say, backing up. "That's a snake."

The entire class's attitude shifts immediately, although Richard doesn't notice it. Jebediah's and Joseph's hands go to the revolvers they carry. Annie slinks to the back and picks up the Ballard rifle.

But Richard just slithers forward.

"I knew I'd find you eventually, Helen," he says, his voice low and horrible. "You can't run forever."

"I'm not running, Richard," I say. My hand goes to my pocket.

Jebediah moves, and Richard must notice him from the corner of his eye. He turns, surprised, and sees Jebediah's hand on the grip of his pistol, not yet drawn. "Uh-uh, little boy," he tells Jebediah. Richard moves like lightning, knocking the boy to the ground, and pulls out his own pistol quicker than thought. Joseph tries to draw his weapon, but Richard already has the barrel of his pistol pointed at him.

"Richard!" I scream. "Leave the children alone!"

Richard kicks Joseph in the chest, sending him to the ground too. "You're coming with me, Helen. You're coming home. What's mine is mine, and you're mine."

"Miss Davies?" Annie's voice is quiet, quivering in fear. Richard doesn't turn around as he draws closer and closer to me. "Miss Davies, my daddy said I wasn't allowed to shoot nobody in the back, not ever, but I'm wondering if it's okay to shoot snakes in the back."

Richard turns around slowly. Annie's Ballard No. 4 Perfection Model is aimed right at his heart. And although she's white as a ghost, her aim doesn't quiver.

Richard snorts in contempt. "You're going to let a little girl like that play with a big gun just so you feel safe?"

"No," I say. "I'm not."

I pull my own pistol out of my pocket. A small gun, bought with my mother's wedding dress. I traded her seed pearls for the pearl grips of the .32.

"You'd never shoot me, Helen," Richard says, smiling, his fangs showing. "No woman of mine would shoot me."

So I shoot him.

"Get the law," I order Bridget as the twins scream. Jebediah and Joseph pin Richard down as he writhes in pain on the floor. I peer down at him dispassionately.

I only shot him in the shoulder; you'd think a man would have more respect for himself than to scream like that.

🎭 *Author's Note* 🎭

Sharp-eyed readers may note that the sharpshooting little girl in this story is based on real-life crack shot Annie Oakley, who said, "I ain't afraid to love a man. I ain't afraid to shoot him either." While Annie was famous for being able to shoot a cigarette from a person's lips or a playing card edge on, she learned to be a crack shot at a very young age in order to provide her family with meat. They couldn't afford to waste bullets, so if she missed, she went hungry. With such motivation, it's little wonder she learned to shoot well.

After the Civil War, many teachers were female. They typically had a cursory education from a "normal school," a school or college that trained teachers, and they could be as young as fifteen years old. Rules for female teachers were strict, commonly including a mandate that the woman not marry while teaching, and teachers had to uphold a very strict moral code. For all that, an average teacher's salary for a woman was around fifty dollars a year. A male teacher received around seventy dollars per year. Subscription schools were not rare in the mid- to late 1800s and were in fact the model used to develop the first school in Wyoming.

The author would like to gratefully thank Louis L'Amour's books and her father for inspiration and information.

Gold in the Roots of the Grass

Marissa Meyer

T HE PROSPECTOR ACROSS THE TABLE smelled of horse manure and two long months of summer sweat. I wished to tell him that his dead business partner wanted him to go back to camp with a bar of lye soap and soak in a hot bath, but I suspected any business partner of his wouldn't have been much for hygiene either, and the prospector's glare told me he was already skeptical enough.

"The spirits not always come," I explained as I lit the incense sticks. "But ask your question and we will hope." I spoke slowly, using the broken cadence I mimicked from my uncle and neighbors, even though I'd been born in San Francisco and was one of the few Chinese in the Badlands fluent in both languages. The miners valued the heavy accent. They seemed to think it made me a more authentic descendent of the Celestial Kingdom — their exotic word for *China*—and more connected with the spirits that spoke through me.

At least, on a good day they spoke through me.

"When you say *spirits*," the man said, watching my hands with suspicion, as if lighting incense were a dangerous pastime, "you mean just the one, right? I just need to talk to my partner. None of your pagan gods or nothing like that."

I pressed my lips, barricading my pride against the affront. "I invite your partner but cannot choose who answers." I lit the candle on the table and shook out the match. "You have gift for spirits?"

He snarled, showing yellowed teeth surrounded by grizzly whiskers. "Like a *sacrifice*?"

I stared at him over the flame, long enough that I hoped he understood he'd asked a remarkably stupid question. Finally, I responded, "Or perhaps a cup of rice."

He slowly sat back, but his glower didn't lessen. "What's a cup of rice gonna do?"

"Is customary to give gifts to the dead, as a sign of respect, and so they might have sustenance in the next life. If you do not have gift, we have spirit money for purchase." I gestured to the front room, where my uncle ran his laundry service.

The prospector spent a moment rocking on the wooden stool, then reached into his breast pocket and retrieved a pre-rolled cigarette. He tossed it into the brass bowl on the table. "He can have that. But just one. I ain't got more to spare."

Jaw tightening, I scooted the bowl to the side of the table. "His name?"

"Thomas Manning."

"Think on the question you would ask Thomas Manning."

He drummed his fingers on the table while I did my best to

concentrate. Sitting back, I shut my eyes and let my breathing calm. I imagined the drumbeats I had heard a hundred times during my mother's rituals, back when she was a respected *wu*-shaman in San Francisco's Chinatown.

I did not have high hopes that Thomas Manning would make his presence known today. If I'd been partnered with this man in life, I wouldn't come back to visit him either.

Which meant it was time for a performance.

Sometimes my patrons had simple requests—a fortune told by the wrinkles of their palm or a question answered by the *kau cim* sticks.

But usually they came to me because they wished to speak with the dead.

When my uncle first brought me to Dakota Territory, I refused to take for granted the traditions my mother had begun to teach me before she too became an honored spirit. I would light the incense. I would burn spirit money and paper effigies. I would sink into my trance so the spirits might use my voice to speak.

But I had never finished my training to become a true shaman, and too often my patrons left disappointed and angry. The rough-edged men of Deadwood had little patience for our traditions, and they didn't like being told that the spirits did not wish to speak with *them.*

After a week with sparse patronage and a threat from my uncle that he would soon have me scrubbing linens in the laundry, I dared to fake my first trance.

It had gotten easier since then.

I did not tell lies, after all. I told likelihoods.

Your departed lover is here, I'd whisper, *and she wants only your happiness, even if you need to take comfort in the arms of a soft-bosomed dove.* The lonely man would no doubt visit a pleasure house soon enough, even without my encouragement. Or I might say, *The spirits urge you to welcome the one-eyed man, for he will bring you prosperity.* Then I'd imagine the prospector chuckling to himself when the one-eyed knave of hearts came into his poker hand that night.

I was right often enough that they kept coming back, eagerly listening to my whispered fortunes, and always hoping to hear a single word.

Gold.

Satisfied or not, they all dropped a few coins into my tin cup as they left. It would not make me wealthy, but at least I didn't have to spread my legs for coin like the girls I saw hanging out the windows of the Gem or Bella Union.

"Well?" said the prospector. "Has old Manning got something to tell me or not?"

I caught a whiff of his rancid breath mixed with my incense and tried to disguise my grimace. Through my puckered lips, I whispered, "Yes. He is here."

The prospector's voice was lower now, following my example. "Tom?"

I swayed on my seat. "Thomas Manning. We invite you to speak. Please, answer our questions."

"Tom, are you there?"

It was amazing to me how easily their suspicions came and went. How strongly they wished to believe, despite how they scoffed at our ways and traditions.

The prospector began to speak in earnest. "You picked a right awful time to get yourself killed, Tom. We've got an offer to buy the claim, and it could be a good deal for me, but I need to know—"

I held up my hands. "Wait. Thomas speaks."

A silence. I shifted my eyes beneath my eyelids. "He is telling you to seek out your bright future."

"Bright? You mean like gold?"

I cocked my head to the side, pretending to listen. "He is unclear. But I see much joy. There is piano music in a dimly lit hall. A pretty girl is trying to catch —"

A crushing grip wrapped around my wrist, yanking me forward. I cried out, my eyes snapping open. The incense clattered to the floor.

The man sneered. "Do I look like a fool, you slant-eyed witch? You think I care about an overpriced whore? You think *Tom* did?"

I winced, as much from his rotted breath as the insult, which, truth be told, was one of the less creative my patrons had called me.

"Tom and me been working the same goddamn gold claim for nine months, with nothing but goddamn rocks to show for it. So you tell me if you can talk to his ghost or not, 'cause I need to know if he found gold, or if I should sell my claim and get the hell out of here."

"S-sorry," I stammered.

"You'd better be, 'cause if I think you're tryin' to make an idiot of me, I will gut you like a pig."

My gaze darted to the tattered sheet that divided my room from the front of the shop, but I knew my uncle wasn't back from visiting with the neighbors.

I tried to pull away, but his fingers only tightened. "We try again," I assured him, wrapping my free hand around the brass bowl that held the lone cigarette. "Thomas Manning come for sure this time."

His grip began to loosen.

I smiled submissively and, hard as I could, smashed the bowl against his temple.

The man reeled back, startled. I flipped the table, catching him in the jaw and sending him and his stool toppling backward. The candle on the table extinguished. The man released a stream of curses and slurs, but I was already at the desk on which we'd built our spirit altar, yanking open the top drawer.

I grabbed the pistol my uncle had given me when he said we were leaving San Francisco. Leaving behind the only life I'd ever known. Leaving behind my mother's still-wandering ghost.

I raised the gun and locked my elbow. I'd never fired the gun before, and I hoped the sight of it alone would persuade the prospector to leave.

Except, when the prospector spotted my tiny pistol, an amused grin showed his cracked teeth. In a blink, he unholstered his own gun, much larger than mine, and trained it on me. I guessed it would not be *his* first time pulling a trigger.

Panic scratched at my throat.

Then, all in unison, the candle flames on the altar flickered. The world hesitated. A familiar hum vibrated through my chest.

The prospector frowned and glanced at a shelf on the wall, where three candles dripped with old wax.

A chill of air brushed against my neck. Gooseflesh tickled down my arms. Not in fear, but not in relief either. I was used to ghosts on the streets and in the hills and drifting aimlessly through town, but I didn't care for those who came into my home, uninvited and rarely welcome.

"Tell him that gold has been found."

The deep voice tumbled and rolled with the measured cadence of the dead. Though I strained my eyes to the edge of their sockets, I could not see him behind me and I dared not turn my back on the prospector.

"What was that?" The man twisted his head. I couldn't tell if he meant the whisper or the flicker of candlelight.

I wet the roof of my mouth. "He says that gold has been found," I said, dropping the fragmented English to better echo the ghost. With so few chances to communicate with the living, spirits could be sensitive about being misunderstood, and translating them falsely could lead to more upsets than a few coins in a tin cup were worth.

The prospector turned wary. "What're you on about?"

The ghost appeared at the edge of my vision, gripping the straps of his suspenders as tight as one would grip a butcher knife. His messy yellow hair was full of dust, and a feather-tipped arrow jutted from between his shoulder blades, like a flag marking its territory. The shaft was striped in the traditional red and blue paint of the Sioux. Blood had crisped to dark brown on his shirt.

There was something unnervingly familiar about him, but I couldn't see his face, and anyhow, all the white men with their bushy mustaches and dirty linen shirts looked the same.

He was much too calm to be *è guǐ*, and I could be glad of that, at least. Even after all these years, the hungry ghosts terrified me. Perhaps he was *yuān guǐ*, a wandering spirit seeking justice for a wrongful death. The arrow would suggest as much.

"*Tell him,*" the ghost said, moving past me, "there is still gold to be found in these hills."

"A male spirit has arrived," I said, before repeating his words.

The prospector's eyes widened. He followed my look, but to him there was only empty air. Maybe a shadow. Maybe a spot of cold. Maybe his own superstitions creeping through the candle smoke. "Tom? Tom, that you?"

The ghost shook his head. "Thomas Manning is gone."

I wasn't surprised. "No, he says Thomas Manning has gone on to—"

The prospector spat onto the wood floor. The glob passed through the ghost's shoe. "You *are* a witch."

The ghost inhaled—a sharp hiss. "She told you what you wanted to hear, you ignorant ass." Though he was so close, I knew the prospector couldn't hear him, and I wasn't about to repeat *those* words. I thought again that maybe I should shoot the prospector before he shot me—the pistol was still warm in my palm—but then the walls and floorboards began to tremble, the candlesticks rattling, the brass bowl vibrating across the floor.

The prospector turned ashen.

"Tell him," said the ghost, "that while there is gold to be found, he'll see not one nugget nor a pinch of dust. Death is painted in ashes upon his forehead. He'll die if he stays in Deadwood."

I gaped at his back. Though I was willing to make up fortunes to satisfy my patrons, it was rare to hear one from the lips of a true ghost. They were secretive beings, and even now it was unclear to me how much of the future they could see, and how much of it could be changed.

"Is that true?" I whispered.

The ghost cut a glare at me, his pupils dilated with anger, and I gasped at seeing his face.

I'd been right before. He *was* familiar, and a sorry sight to my eyes.

"Just tell him," said the ghost, at the same time the prospector stammered, "Is what true?"

Again, I repeated the ghost's words. Perhaps the prospector could see the truth in my face, for he did not gut me like a pig after all, just lowered his gun and cursed, a lot. "You goddamn

Celestials and your goddamn superstitions," he railed, but there was more fear in his voice than gall. "You should all be hanged for bringing your curses down on us!"

Despite his hubris, he snatched up his filth-covered hat and fled, shoving his way through the curtain. I wondered if by morning light he'd be hitching a ride on the first stagecoach, or discovered whiskey-drunk in a saloon.

Summer heat seeped back through the walls as the ghost's fury began to ebb. My pulse stayed erratic. My palm would be ridged with lines where the gun's handle pressed into it.

I stared at the arrow in the ghost's back and waited for him to speak, willing away my distress at recognizing him.

He was a ghost now, and I would treat him no different than all the others. He'd helped me, and I knew he would want something in return. That was the way of the wandering spirits.

Perhaps if I didn't show gratitude, he might not realize how much I was in his debt.

He turned and watched me through reddish-gold eyelashes.

My traitorous chest tightened.

I didn't know his name, but all last fall I had seen the boy coming and going from the pest tents erected on the edge of the Badlands during the smallpox outbreak. Most men hid in their camps, but he'd helped the doctor tend to those poor quarantined souls and not once turned poorly himself. Then, he had been very much alive.

Once, I'd passed him on my way to the mercantile, and though he'd looked halfway to dead with exhaustion, he'd paused and smiled at me.

Then he'd tipped his hat, like a gentleman to a lady.

I'd turned away, fast, but that smile had clung to me for days. It had led to a great many fancies, most of which involved him coming to ask for his fortune to be told. I'd imagined tracing the lines on his palm and telling him of the many children in his future, and blushing like a witless little girl.

"Sorry for intruding upon you," he said, breaking our silence. Though he wasn't wearing a hat, he tipped an imaginary one at me anyhow, and it was by a force of will that I smothered a sad, pitiful sigh at the gesture. "My name is James Hill, ma'am."

I stared.

A hesitation. "I mean miss."

I swallowed, hard. "My name is Fei-Yen. Sun Fei-Yen."

I was prepared for scorn, but James Hill apologetically asked if I could repeat that before he attempted it himself.

"Soon Fay Yen." His atrocious accent prompted a weak smile from me, which I didn't like. I did not smile at ghosts. Not even *this* ghost.

After a long, long pause, James held out a hand. "It's a pleasure to make your acquaintance."

His sleeves were rolled up, and I could tell he had a miner's arms, strong and dark from the sun. Callused palms and dirt-stained fingernails. There was a presence about him that drew me in, a stickiness that was hard to resist. Few could understand the magnetism of spirits. How they could be simultaneously appalling and alluring, like the opium pipe to an addict.

James slowly pulled his hand back, embarrassed that I hadn't taken it. "Please don't be frightened," he said, not understanding. He gripped his suspenders again. "I intend you no harm, but Millie Ann said you might help me."

Finally my tongue loosened. "I cannot help you."

His eyes bored into mine. "I think you can."

I tempered my sympathy. I had gotten better at this over the years. After all the ghosts and all their demands. The angry ones, the sad ones, the wronged ones—they all wanted just one thing. "No, I can't. I'm sorry, James Hill, but you'll have no vengeance from me. Not against the Sioux."

His brow creased. "Pardon?"

"That's a Sioux arrow in your back. This land belongs to them. It is a sacred place upon which we are all trespassers. Maybe you deserved to be shot. Maybe we all do." I inhaled, bracing. "Besides. I'm one girl, and they are warriors. I cannot avenge you."

Then, unexpectedly, he smiled, and my heart thundered like a gong, remembering that smile.

"Did Millie Ann want vengeance after *she* died?"

I turned away and busied myself with returning the gun to the drawer beneath the altar and relighting the candles.

Millie Ann was *gū hún yě guǐ*—a sad, restless ghost who died too far from home. She had come to Deadwood after being promised work as a waitress. Spent all her money on a train ticket only to find a different occupation waiting for her, and it was too late to go back. Four months later she'd lain dying in a pest tent, covered in those awful sores and crying for her mother.

I often visited Millie Ann's ghost when she became agitated, listening to her sad tale over and over again.

"No," I said, setting aside the matches. "She asked to go home." A request I was powerless to help with. "Though some days she's just hungry, so I bring her sliced apples. But Millie Ann wasn't murdered."

"There's already a group of men plotting retaliation against the savages for the murders, whether we all deserve to be shot or not. I need your help with something else." He paused, his body flickering in the candlelight. A faint smile still lingered along the bow of his upper lip. "Though I wouldn't mind some sliced apples too, miss, if it isn't too much of a bother."

I'd seen hundreds of ghosts in my sixteen years, and Deadwood, barely a year settled, already felt like standing on the bridge to *Diyu* itself.

On every hillside I could see the ghosts of the Sioux, donning their animal skins and bear-claw necklaces and glowering at the trespassers who trampled their ground. A treaty had once promised that the Black Hills would be theirs for the keeping, but those signatures meant nothing once gold was found — so much gold it grew up from the roots of the grass, the newspapers reported.

Gold attracted its own ghosts. Diseases swept through the mining camps. Outlaws and horse thieves roamed the trails in search of easy targets. Whiskey led to brawls and gunfights, and the few who didn't take to drink found comfort in the opium dens.

Then there were the soiled doves, many of whom, like Millie Ann, had been promised good paying jobs only to find themselves trapped in a pleasure house with no money and no way out. The ghosts of women who had committed suicide, *nǚ guǐ*, frightened me almost as much as the hungry ghosts — those whose families forgot to honor them after their death. Hungry ghosts emerged from the gates of hell during the seventh month, seeking food to fill their bulging stomachs and dragging mischief and misfortune in their wake. They were hideous things to behold, some with long needle-thin necks, others with rotting mouths and flaming tongues.

But at least they came only once a year, whereas suicide ghosts never went away. They wore their desperation soul deep, realizing again and again, day after day, that they were still trapped here. That there was still no way out.

Ghosts are drawn to *wu*-shamans like mosquitoes to an oil

lamp. Here in Deadwood, I couldn't leave the laundry without seeing their shadows from the corners of my eyes or feeling them tug at the hem of my jacket. I often took circuitous routes to try and lose them, as it was bad luck for a ghost to follow you home.

Even now I could feel the ghosts of Deadwood drifting toward me as I followed half a step behind James, my eyes downcast to keep from drawing attention, both from the multitudes of men who filled the streets and the spirits that gathered in my footsteps. When I was little, my mother always sent them away—sometimes with bribes of food, sometimes by chasing them off with a straw-bristled broom. I hadn't realized what a nuisance they were until she was gone.

There was something unusual about the ghost of James Hill, though. Despite the arrow in his back, he maintained a light step as he walked down Main Street crisping on the apples I'd smuggled from my uncle's stores. (After gifting them to his spirit, I'd stashed the physical apples under the walkway behind the laundry, hoping they would rot away before they were missed.)

We were two blocks from Star & Bullock's hardware store when I noticed the commotion. A crowd of men was gathered in the street, screaming obscenities. The newspaperman was there too, trying to gather information from the shouting. Not far off, I spotted a finely dressed woman sobbing hysterically and clutching a boy—maybe seven years of age—against her hip.

Easing through the crowd, I spotted the source of the outrage. A wagon was being pulled by a couple of mules. It was loaded with two bodies and a swarm of flies.

My heart shuddered, but I didn't look away.

James Hill's eyes were faded in death, his corpse drained of color. Someone had snapped the arrow off at his back, but the broken shaft could still be seen protruding from between his shoulder blades.

The second body on the cart was one I didn't recognize. A full-whiskered man with one boot missing off his stockinged feet. Two arrows were stuck in his torso, a third in his thigh.

I scanned the dozens of ghosts gathered in my periphery, but I didn't see his spirit among them.

"Jeremiah was a good, God-fearing man!" one of the louder mouths was saying. "And his son, there, as selfless as they come! Now the Sioux come onto *their* land and murder them when they ain't done nothing but work hard to provide for their family. I've had enough lookin' over my shoulder for these savages. These murders must be answered!"

His words were met with a cheer and a gunshot that made me jump.

"I'll offer a hundred dollars from my own pocket for every dirt-worshipper scalp brought back!" the loudmouth continued, to more cheering. The stench of alcohol was already heavy on more than one of them, and the sight of the bodies was spurring their bloodlust.

I turned to James, but he wasn't watching the crowd. He was staring at the crying woman and the child. Her face was half covered by a handkerchief.

"Your mother?"

James gave a sad nod. "And my brother. Jules."

They made a pretty family, all yellow hair and faces like you'd see in a painting.

With a start, I realized I'd seen the woman before. "She came to me once."

James didn't take his attention from them. "I know. About five months ago, when Jules was sick." Some tension slipped off his shoulders. "None of the doctor's treatments were working, and we were desperate. Some of the men in the camp told us you might be able to help." His gaze slid toward me. "Ma said you called on the spirit of my grandmother, and she told her to make a special tea for Jules, out of plants she could only get from some of your neighbors. She followed my grandmother's directions to the word. The very next day, Jules's fever broke, and . . . there he is. Alive."

I stared at the young boy, remembering how desperate his mother had been when I suggested the tea, a combination of ginger, cinnamon, peony, and licorice. It was a common treatment, used to improve the healing energy of the body.

"I'm glad," I said.

"Me too." James rocked back on his heels. "Though I wondered how my Irish grandmother could possibly have known to give him Chinese tea, of all things."

James shifted closer to me. I looked away.

"Fei-Yen, I've spent five months making excuses to walk by your family's laundry, trying to come up with a reason to go inside. I never imagined I would be dead before I finally had the courage to thank you."

I dared to look up and hold his gaze again, even though my heart was thrumming as I thought of him walking by our laundry all those times. It was a strange thing to think—that *he* had wished to speak to *me*.

Our conversation had tugged us closer. We were standing nearly toe-to-toe.

I inhaled sharply and pulled back.

My heel crashed into a feed bucket and I gasped, arms flailing. James caught my elbow and pulled me upward, locking me firm against his chest for merely a heartbeat before he flickered and vanished.

I stood on the street, alone, my pulse in my ears. It was difficult for ghosts to affect the physical spaces of our world. Between
frightening the prospector earlier and now bracing my fall, he
must have used up too much energy. It would take some time
before he returned.

I was almost grateful—*almost*. At least it gave me time to
think, to let my mind clear without being pulled off course by his
friendly smile and too-easy gait.

Five minutes passed before he began to appear again, more
faded than before.

I greeted him with a nod, but I didn't smile or thank him for
catching him.

"You want me to be your voice," I said, as James gathered his
spirit back together. "So you can tell your family good-bye."

To my surprise, he shook his head. "No, Fei-Yen. I want you to
help me give them a future."

"A future?"

His voice crackled at first but became stronger as he watched
his family. "There's a businessman in town named George
Rinehart. He arrived a few months back and has been buying
up claims ever since, mostly placer mines that already ran dry.
Turning unlucky prospectors into paid miners. He's offered to
buy our claim. Not for much—says the land is barely fit for goat
grazing—but enough that Ma and Jules could pack up, go back
to New York. She signed the deed this morning, within hours of
hearing about the attack. Heartbreak, I suppose." A line formed
between his eyebrows. "I need you to get that deed back and
destroy it. She can't sell the claim."

"Why?"

"Because we found it, two days ago. There *is* gold. I've seen it
with my own eyes." He hooked his thumbs behind the suspenders.

"Enough to live comfortably—here or New York or wherever she wants to go. Jules could go to school. If you got that deed . . ."

A needle inside me said that Mrs. Hill had willingly sold the claim, so why should this businessman lose just because her son was stubborn enough to wander around after being shot rightfully dead?

"I don't owe you any favors, James Hill." I recited the words I'd silently rehearsed after he'd vanished. "You may have saved me this morning, but I already saved your brother. Five months ago."

His face showed no surprise. "I know. I needed to repay my debt to you."

"And I owe you *nothing*." I wanted to hear him say it. Freedom from a spirit's control was a valuable thing to someone like me.

"You owe me nothing," he admitted, his body no longer vague and wispy. "But I will beg you on my knees to do this, Fei-Yen. Please. Help me."

Sympathy seeped through me, and my hand twitched toward him, but I locked it firm against my side. Across the street, his mother was kissing Jules's head. The driver of the wagon was getting ready to haul the bodies of James and his father away to be prepared for burial.

Maybe, if she did end up the owner of a working gold claim, Mrs. Hill might be willing to pay a commission off it. In gratitude. Not just for saving the claim but for saving her son's life when he was sick.

Maybe it would be enough to take me back to California. I hadn't wanted to leave in the first place. I tried to persuade my uncle to leave me behind—my skills were more suited to the city—but he insisted we stay together. He believed he could provide for us both, and his laundry was doing well enough, but we both knew I didn't belong here. Whether or not he regretted bringing me, it no longer mattered. There wasn't enough money to send me back.

All I needed was a ride on the stagecoach and a train ticket out of Cheyenne. Enough to let a room where I could conduct the *wu*-shaman rituals.

Maybe, when I got there, I could find another shaman to complete my training. Maybe I could even find my mother's spirit, if she hadn't yet departed. Oh, how I yearned to see her again. To be home.

"All right, James Hill," I said. "I'll try."

I made myself small as James and I darted through the alley between a saloon and the newly constructed hotel. The sounds of clinking glasses, the hollow clatter of dice, and an upbeat piano melody spilled from open windows.

I was clutching a stack of rough-spun linens in both arms. It had been easy enough for me to persuade the man at the hotel's desk to give me a key, explaining in poor English that I had to deliver laundry to a guest. All he'd cared about was that I go in through the back door and stop taking up space in his lobby.

I rounded the corner and spotted a figure outside the hotel's door, her dress gauzy and her bone-thin arms wrapped around her hips. She was staring up at the second-story windows.

We both stopped, but it was James who spoke. "Millie Ann?"

Her head turned, although it took her haunted gaze a moment to follow. "James Hill," she said in her usual meek voice. "You found her."

"I did." James tipped his nonexistent hat. "She's been as kind as you told me she would be."

A frown carved its way across my brow. I didn't like to think of the spirits talking about me around town, appointing me their personal telegraph into the realm of the living.

"What are you doing here, Millie Ann?" I asked, never having seen her so far from where she died.

"I was looking for the post office . . ." Millie Ann scanned the walls of the alley. "I wanted to post a letter to my mother. But I seem to have taken a wrong turn."

I sighed. She'd most likely been pulled off course because of me. Even as I thought it, the faint ghost of a dark-skinned man in a derby hat drifted into the far end of the alley.

More would follow.

It was time to finish this task for James Hill and return to the sanctuary of my incense and altar, where only the strongest spirits could follow me.

I curled my shoulders over the linens and shoved through the hotel door, certain that Millie Ann would either find her way back on her own or still be waiting there when we returned. She could have followed me into the building, but passing through walls cost so much energy that most spirits never bothered.

The hotel was eerily quiet. James and I climbed to the second floor, where the walls smelled of fresh timber. I knocked when we reached Rinehart's room, but there was no response. Balancing the linens again, I slipped the key into the lock, heart pounding.

The room was furnished with a four-poster bed, a pedestal sink and mirror for shaving, a writing desk, and a reading chair with an ironed newspaper draped over one arm. A round-topped trunk sat at the foot of the bed, fastened with brass buckles and stuck with a dozen labels of different cities — San Francisco among them. My heart squeezed with homesickness.

"Try here first," said James, standing at the desk.

I set the linens down on the bed and joined him, opening the top drawer. Inkwells and envelopes. In the next, blank stationery. The bottom drawer held a newspaper clipping with a photograph of a well-dressed man who James told me was George Rinehart himself. Beneath the paper was a stack of document files. I pulled them out so James could puzzle out the labels printed in a neat hand.

One window was cracked open, and I could hear men down below, discussing weapons and horses and raving about the godless savages they'd soon be hunting.

We reached the last file, and James shook his head. "Accounting and travel papers. It's not here."

Leaving the papers, I crossed the room and dropped to my knees beside the trunk, pressing up the latches, grateful to find it unlocked. Inside, a bundle of heavy cloth was rolled up and tied with twine, and tucked beneath it—more papers.

James hunkered over them, attempting to decipher the tiny print on the top pages. His eyes brightened.

"This is the deed to the Johnson claim, just upstream from ours." He looked at me. "Albert Johnson was killed a little over a month ago, also by the Sioux. There've been lots of attacks lately, but things had gone quiet long enough that Pa and I thought . . ." His jaw tightened, but he shook the regret away. "I hadn't realized Johnson was looking to sell his claim too. Rinehart must be buying up the whole valley."

"Does he know gold's been found?"

"Could be. If we found it on our land, it's likely there'll be more deposits all along the creek."

"He can't be pleased that the Sioux have suddenly become so territorial over it too." I frowned. "Have all the killings been done by arrow?"

James shrugged. "Far as I know."

"Strange, isn't it? They have guns. But it's as though they want it to be known—*we're* killing you. This is our land."

"You said yourself, it is sacred to them." James dragged a finger along the lettering on the first page. "Can you pull out these papers? Maybe our deed is here too."

Nudging the bundle of fabric aside, I lifted the first stack and deposited it on the rug. The English alphabet swam across the page.

When I looked up, I saw that James wasn't studying the papers, though. He was still staring into the trunk. The bundle of fabric had fallen at an angle, revealing the feather-tipped shaft of an arrow.

Painted red and blue.

Reaching in, I untangled the twine and peeled back the fabric, revealing dozens of arrows painted in the Sioux's warrior colors. I picked one up, holding it in the loop of my fingers. It appeared unused.

I frowned at James, who seemed equally stunned.

James, who still had a Sioux arrow lodged in his back.

How many attacks had there been? How many had died? How many on the land George Rinehart wanted to purchase?

The land that until recently had given up no gold at all.

An enraged shout echoed from the street below—a battle cry from the gathered townsmen.

"The Sioux aren't doing this," I said. "Are they?"

Footsteps thundered in the hall.

I dropped the arrow and scrambled to my feet just as the door opened. An unfamiliar man stood with a key in hand, confused that the door wasn't locked. He was big in every way—big head, big shoulders, big hands. His gaze fell on me.

I grabbed the stack of linens from the bed, holding them like a shield.

"Laundry service," I said. "Ri-nu-hart?"

"That's Charlie Smith," said James. "Rinehart's right-hand man."

I looked again at those big callused hands.

"Who let you in here?" Charlie barked, taking in the open trunk, the scattered papers, the arrow.

"Laundry?" I repeated, trying at innocence.

With a snarl, Charlie lunged at me, and I ducked, tossing the linens into his face. He stopped just long enough to swat them away, giving me time to snatch the bundle of arrows from the trunk. I rushed forward, but the burly man sidestepped with me, reaching for my arms.

I spun away and ran to the window instead, shoving the pane upward and launching myself toward the balcony. A hand seized my ankle. I kicked my heel into Charlie's nose, and he reared back, taking one of my shoes with him. I pulled myself one-handed through the window and collapsed in a heap on the balcony.

The sun had dropped behind the hills, and Main Street was lit by gas lamps and saloon windows. But the men were still there, separating into groups, deciding which direction each would go on their avenging party.

Gripping the rail, I pulled myself up. *"Help!"* I screamed, glad when a dozen faces turned upward.

A hand landed on my arm. I tried to shake it away, but another was on me just as fast, dragging me back toward the window. I screamed again and, with a grunt, tossed the arrows over the railing. Someone yelped, followed by the crash of wood and arrowheads.

"Murderer!" I screamed. My head collided with the window frame. I flinched but kept yelling. "George Rinehart ordered those

men to be killed"—I yanked my hand away from Charlie's grip, leaving scratches where his nails had dug in—"and he's blaming the Sioux for it! He murdered them! He—" A hand clamped over my mouth, and I was pulled back through the window and tossed to the carpet. Air fled from my lungs.

Charlie slammed my head against the floor, straddling my stomach. A string of vile insults dripped from his mouth, but stars were creeping into my vision and I barely heard him. My hands scrambled across the floor, searching for a weapon, anything—

I heard a strained noise from James, then something was shoved into my hand. My fingers clamped around the shaft of the last arrow, the one I'd dropped before.

As my vision gave way to darkness, I swung my arm up, jamming the arrowhead into Charlie's throat. Something hot splattered across my forearm.

Release.

Air.

Charlie collapsed onto his side, blood already seeping into his shirt. He gripped the arrow but gave up easily. I think he saw his death coming.

I hoped his spirit would not come back to haunt me.

"Fei-Yen!" James dropped beside me, eyes wide. The edges of his body were blurred and flickering from moving the arrow, but I still felt the tender brush of fingers on my face. "Are you all right?"

I sat up slowly, groaning. I could tell James wanted to help, but he was too weak. "Thank you, James," I gasped, my voice roughened from the fight.

Was I back in his debt now? I'd lost track.

A click echoed through the room, and my attention snapped upward.

I recognized George Rinehart from the newspaper clipping. He was framed in the doorway, a pistol in his hand and fury playing across his brow.

"Who," he drawled, "is *James?*"

My lungs tightened. I searched for an answer. Something truthful and threatening. *James is the boy you killed, the ghost who is haunting you even now—*

But it seemed Rinehart didn't care who James was after all. Before I found my voice, he pulled the trigger.

It was the noise that startled me the most, throwing me back onto the floor. The shot was so loud it could have come from inside my head.

At first I felt nothing, and I thought, *He missed. He missed.*

But then my tunic grew wet and I felt for the wound and the blood soaking into the fabric.

The pain came last, but it was searing.

James screamed, trying to press his faint, flickering hands against my wound.

I stared at the ceiling and watched my death approach. I had seen death often enough that I wasn't frightened. I would be glad to leave these hills with their fallen timber and their gold and their ghosts, the manure stink and the slopping mud, the gambling and the piano music and the broken women who watched from upstairs windows.

A howl drew my attention.

James was shaking, violently. His fury had turned him into a storm, thrashing at the papers and files on the floor, twisting them like a tornado. He somehow managed to throw an inkwell across the room. It shattered—black ink dripping like blood down the wallpaper.

Rinehart, wide-eyed, was backed into the corner and waving

the gun at nothing. James went for him but was only strong enough to pull at the watch chain that dangled from a pocket. At James's touch, Rinehart squealed like a child and stumbled toward the door.

An icy wind burst in from the corridor, pushing him back. Rinehart crossed his arms over his face.

Blackness crowded my vision.

But I still saw them, the ghosts.

Some who had told me their sad stories in the months since I'd come to Deadwood. A few I had sneaked apples to when I could. Others I'd only seen drifting aimlessly through the streets.

There were mustached men with arrows like sewing pins in their bodies. Men who had died from bullet wounds and hangings. Women who had succumbed to laudanum or fever. Millie Ann was there too. She was vicious and beautiful, her hair streaming behind her as the battered spirits pushed Rinehart back. Back. His eyes spun around the room, not seeing, not understanding. Unable to get away from the vengeful spirits.

They threw him from the window.

I would remember only his scream, and then the cool, ghostly palm of James Hill settling against my cheek.

I had no use for wandering, no interest in vengeance or haunting. And still I came back.

James Hill sat cross-legged beside me when I opened my eyes. His smile was a rush of relief, his hands cupping both of mine as he bent over and pressed his lips against my thumb.

"I wasn't sure if you would stay," he said, lifting me from my body. "But I'm glad you did."

My body was taken to Ingleside Cemetery, just above Whitewood Creek, a mere stone's throw from the freshly dug graves where James and his father rested. My burial passed in silence. I had no children to say prayers for me or leave me gifts of rice and peaches, and yet I watched my burial with the calm certainty that my fate was not to become a hungry ghost. In spite of the violence of my death, I felt content. Having known the spirit world all my life, being a part of it now was almost like a homecoming. I imagined my body turning to dirt. I pictured the grass and wildflowers that would someday grow here, and how there would be gold at their roots.

A shovel crunched into the loose soil. Rocks and dirt scuttled across my coffin. My uncle, who had wept only in private, turned away.

I was surprised to see non-Chinese among those gathered. The scandal associated with my murder, followed by what was believed to be Rinehart's guilt-induced suicide, was all anyone was talking about. With the impostor arrows as evidence, Rinehart's actions had fast become suspect, and a hastily constructed jury had soon nullified all of his recently purchased deeds. James was confident his father's secret would be revealed soon enough.

"What shall we do now?" said James.

"I don't know." I traced the open wound on my stomach where the bullet had entered. There was no pain now, only a reminder. "I never expected to die in these hills."

James ran his thumbs along the inside of his suspenders, surprisingly jovial for one so recently dead. "And ghosts must haunt the place where they died?"

I hesitated. A part of my spirit would watch over my body for a while, then depart for the underworld. It already knew the way. But the rest of me, the *restless* me . . .

"I need to find my mother," I whispered, meeting his gaze and suddenly sure, so sure, that this was why I had stayed. To find her. To honor her. To say good-bye—or not.

"And where is she?"

"California."

"Ah. I see." His gold-red lashes dipped in thought. "If I'm not mistaken, there'll be a stagecoach heading west in the morning."

I tried to picture the calendar in my thoughts, though days and nights had begun to blur. "You're right." Finding it painful to look at him, I began picking my way through the cemetery. "I suppose this will be good-bye, then."

"*Good-bye?*" He stayed at my side, so close I could feel the tickle of his arm hairs on mine. "Miss Fei-Yen, you did me and my family a great service, and got yourself killed for it. By my estimation, I'll be in your debt for some time. *Ages,* even. It'd be difficult to pay off my dues if I'm half a continent away."

My feet stalled. I looked up.

James was right. He *was* in my debt. And yet he didn't seem at all upset to find himself beholden to the will of a wandering ghost.

He smiled the same smile that I remembered from last fall and tipped his invisible hat. I felt the pull of him, drawing me closer.

This time, when he held out his hand, I took it.

❧ *Author's Note* ❧

My husband and I go on a lot of road trips together, but one of our most memorable was the drive from Minnesota to our home in the Pacific Northwest that took us through Deadwood, South Dakota, for the first time. After all the prairies and cornfields, entering the ominous Black Hills and driving into Deadwood Gulch felt like going back in time—at that moment, riding in a horse-drawn carriage would have felt more appropriate than my VW Bug. I became fascinated with the city that prides itself on its reputation as the last great Wild West town. Sure, the slot machines are now electronic and prostitution has been outlawed for over half a century (though the last brothel didn't officially close until 1980), but you can still sense the area's rich, often-savage history around every corner. It's in the imposing hills that creep right up to the edges of town. It's in the Victorian architecture rebuilt in brick and stone after a fire claimed the original timber structures. It's in the shady graveyard that marks the final resting places of gunslingers like Wild Bill Hickok and Calamity Jane.

Conducting research for this story was a joy—one of those times when it was difficult to stop researching and start writing. The characters and the story are entirely fictional, and some liberties have been taken, but I've done my best to write a story that would fit in with the history texts (supernatural elements notwithstanding). Though the Black Hills gold rush lasted only a few years, it left Deadwood with an abundance of tales full of real-life bandits, brawls, and all those assorted vices that usually follow in the wake of man's greatest weakness: *gold*.

The Legendary Garrett Girls

Y. S. Lee

They now say there are more liars to the square
inch in Alaska than any place in the world.
— *Seattle Daily Times*, August 17, 1897

W HEN THE STRANGER WHIPS OUT A
pistol, everyone hits the floor.

Everyone except John and me, that is. He goes perfectly
still, one thin brown hand flat on the table. The gun is pointing
straight at him, yet his dark eyes are calm. Me, I just feel exasperated. It's been such a long day, and it's only midnight. "Put that
down," I say in my sharpest tone. I touch my hip and feel the
reassuring handle of my bullwhip, looped to my belt.

The newcomer's gaze bobs around the dimly lit tavern
and finally locates me beside the bar. "You trying to tell me
what to do, little girl?" He gives me a once-over that might be

insulting, except he can't focus properly. Still, the gun droops in his hand.

"I'm not trying; I'm giving you an order." I point to the hand-written sign tacked above the bar:

GARRETT'S RULES FOR BAR-ROOM BRAWLS
1. Don't do it.
2. Really. Don't do it.
3. You will regret having done it.

His gaze slides over the sign, and a faint frown appears between his eyebrows. Good grief. Too pie-eyed to read.

"I'll save you the time," I snap. "Put the gun away."

He glares at John. "I can't drink with that dirty Indian in the room."

My pulse rockets. "Then get the hell out of my saloon!"

"This here is *your* saloon? Thought it was called . . ." He scratches his head with his free hand.

Leave it to a drunk to focus on petty details. "Garrett's Saloon. And I am Miss Lily Garrett. Proprietress." As I speak, I uncoil my bullwhip. It'll be downright satisfying to use it on this pustule of a human being.

"Co-proprietress," corrects a sweet, husky voice. My sister swishes into the building on a gust of frozen air and takes the stranger's arm as though they're off for a stroll through Central Park. "Allow me to introduce myself: Miss Clara Garrett, co-proprietress. You must be new to Alaska, Mr. . . . ?"

He gapes for a full minute at her glorious red-gold hair, her startling violet eyes. He wobbles visibly—a common response to Clara—and actually attempts a bow. "F-Fenton, miss. Stanmore Fenton. It's a real honor to meet you, miss."

Clara smiles, reaches over, and plucks the pistol from his limp fingers. "It's a pleasure to welcome you to our humble town, Mr. Fenton. I know our ways are different from those Outside, but let's start with this: the Indian gentleman in the corner is a member of the Tlingit tribe and a respected trader in town. He's also a friend of ours. Why don't you sit down and refresh yourself? I suggest you stand John a drink, to show there are no hard feelings. We have scotch, bourbon, gin, brandy, and beer. And champagne, of course."

Her smile stays frozen in place until she gets to the bar, where only I can see her expression. "Come on, Lil," she says in a fierce whisper. "You catch—"

"I know, I know. You catch more flies with honey than with vinegar."

She whips off fur-lined mittens and sheds her Indian-style parka. "If you know it so well, why can't you act on it?"

"I stopped him from pointing the pistol at John," I mutter. It's pathetic, a classic kid-sister kind of protest, but she isn't giving me any credit at all.

"Yes, but it took me to confiscate the gun and sell him another round of drinks."

"Well. Want me to mix him a vinegar cocktail?"

Clara snorts, a sound of amusement. Her ire never lasts. Unlike mine. She checks the gun—unloaded, which only confirms Fenton's stupidity, to my mind—and drops it into a box under the bar, where it clanks against a motley array of other weapons. That's another of Garrett's rules: all firearms must be unloaded. Even our hunting rifle, which hangs discreetly along the side of the bar.

Our mother, Lucinda Garrett, made the rules. She raised Clara and me single-handed while running taverns from San Diego to Seattle. She taught us everything we know. When Lu died last year of influenza, we couldn't bear to stand in her place behind the bar. Still, we wanted to keep up the Garrett tradition. We sold everything, took a steamer north, and were among the first to wade ashore along the mudflats of Skaguay.

Clara pours a tray of double scotches—that's one shot of cheap whiskey, the same again of melted snow—and delivers it to Fenton's table. John's expression is serious, but he accepts his drink and takes a sip before slipping out the door with a brief nod of farewell. Fenton orders another round for his table. I slide a pair of logs into our wood-burning stove. Life in a gold rush town roars on.

"We need to be on the lookout," murmurs Clara, setting the empty tray on the bar.

"What for?" I fiddle with the weigh-scale, and my fingertips come away glistening with gold dust, the second currency of Alaska. Sure, we prefer old-fashioned paper dollars, but with so many big spenders wandering around with pokes of gold dust looped through their belts, half our profits are weighed out in ounces.

"There's a new con man in town. Name's Soapy Smith."

"'Soapy'? That doesn't sound so dangerous to me."

"He was here for a spell last fall, running shell games and card scams out on the trails. Left at the start of winter. But now he's back," says Clara. "Apparently he's greedy, ruthless, violent, and completely amoral."

"I sure hope," interrupts a silky male voice, "your sources also mentioned my considerable charm."

Clara spins around. The speaker stands just behind her, a man with a thick black beard that hides his mouth and threatens his cheekbones. He has two friends with him, one at each elbow.

Fear twists my gut. The trio has been sitting near the bar this whole time, quietly drinking spruce beer. I'd written them off as *cheechakos* in their stiff boots, new coats, and inadequate gloves. We see hundreds like them stumble into town each week, fresh from the Outside, their pockets stuffed with cash and their heads with cotton wool. They roll into our saloon, certain that they're just a couple weeks away from striking it rich, and celebrate in advance.

But if what Clara said was true, these three are entirely different.

"Evening, ladies," says Soapy, tilting his hat to each of us. "Jefferson Randolph Smith the Second, at your service, although I hope you'll call me Jeff." He speaks with a soft southern lilt. "I believe I heard you introduce yourselves as Miss Clara Garrett and Miss Lily Garrett?"

We nod.

"Well, on my way up to Skaguay, I heard the rumors about a pair of heartbreakingly beautiful sisters running the most elegant drinking establishment in Alaska. But I confess, the story sounded too good to be true." The beard stretches sideways, and I realize that he is smiling. "And yet here I am, pinching myself repeatedly to wake from this dazzling dream, and it all seems just as true as true. I'll bet you can pick up gold nuggets the size of walnuts along the side of the road, too."

He's laying it on way too thick. For one thing, Garrett's Saloon is far from "elegant." It's nice for Skaguay, but that's only because it's built of wood, while most of the town is still a row of canvas tents. Furthermore, while Clara is indeed "heartbreakingly beautiful," I am not. Honey and vinegar, etc.

Soapy must see the glint in my eye, because he hurries on. "It's a real pleasure to meet young ladies with so much courage and business sense. Why, neither of you can be a day over eighteen, and here you are, running a thriving saloon, in the wildest frontier on earth."

"What brings you to Skaguay, Mr. Smith?" Clara's arm vibrates against mine and I can feel her thinking at me: *Honey, not vinegar.*

The beard ripples again. "Why, business, of course. Just like you two little ladies."

I despise coyness in both women and men. "And what kind of business is that?"

"Well, I have very diverse interests, but certainly one of them is drinking saloons, dance halls, and such."

Clara's lips curve, but her smile stops short of her eyes. "There's plenty of room in town for another bar or three. And we won't be competing with any dance halls. My sister and I sell beer and spirits, and nothing else."

Soapy smirks at that. "And you're doing a roaring trade. I believe that's all down to you as the main attraction, Miss Clara." His gaze flickers to me. "Not forgetting you, of course, Miss Lily."

I forget all about honey. "I'd rather you were honest than polite, Mr. Smith."

He grins even wider. "A girl after my own heart."

"No, thanks. I'd rather have your wallet."

Clara elbows me, hard, but Soapy only chuckles. "In that case, Miss Lily, I'll put my proposition to you. You and your lovely sister already know it's a dog's life, running a saloon in a lawless town like Skaguay. Uncle Sam's two hundred miles away in Sitka; might as well be two thousand miles, for all practical purposes. Sometime soon, you and Miss Clara'll need a business partner who can really crack the whip." His gaze falls to the bullwhip coiled at my waist. "You can keep order among a handful of harmless drunks, I'm sure, but what about the nasty ones? The ones whose pistols are loaded and who aren't scared to use them?

"No," he continues, "you need me. I've owned a string of successful saloons and dance halls all through Colorado, and I'm real good friends with the marshal. With me as your business partner, there'll be no delays in shipments of liquor, no fuss over paperwork, no hassle with the law. I'll take care of it all."

I start to object, but he barrels on. "You're also not making as much money as you should, with this sturdy wood building. Bet it cost thousands to build, what with the price of lumber and labor up here. And how much are you taking in every night?"

We stay silent.

After a moment, he shrugs. "Doesn't matter. I'll double your bar takings and triple your overall profits. I'll knock out this back wall and build a stage for dancers and musicians, and add a cook shack outside. No customer will ever need to leave . . . till he runs out of money, anyway. Garrett's Saloon'll be the finest entertainment emporium in . . ." He gestures widely, made breathless by his own vision.

"Skaguay?" suggests Clara. "It already is, Mr. Smith. Now, my sister and I appreciate your creativity and willingness to lend a hand, but we like *our* business the way it is. I'm sure your saloon will be a booming success too. Once you've built it." There's a faint hardness to her tone that tells me how riled she is, but her expression is as smooth as ever. "Now, would you like another round of drinks, or will you be on your way?"

I scan the room. It is silent, with all attention on us. When I glance back at Soapy, I almost choke on my own breath.

His eyes are hard and beady, his neck flushed red. The charming facade is gone, like someone smashed out a window. "Miss Clara, I don't believe you girls understand me properly. I meant what I said."

I curl my fingers around the handle of my bullwhip, although he's too close for me to use it on him. "So do we, Mr. Smith."

He bares his teeth in a grimace that is technically a smile and puts his hand to his hip. There, half visible inside his coat, I see the curve of a handle, the gleam of a polished steel barrel. My stomach rolls and I glance toward Soapy's friends. They face us, arms akimbo, the better to give us a glimpse of their own pistols. I swallow hard and think of the threats embedded in Soapy's previous speech: the marshal snug in his pocket, the government hundreds of miles away, nasty drunks with loaded guns.

Clara glances toward the end of the bar, where our rifle hangs concealed. I take her arm firmly. She'll never reach and load a firearm before these three can draw theirs.

Soapy looks at me with a flicker of approval. "Good girl," he says, a portion of his southern polish restored. "No beauty, but at least you've got a brain. Now, I've given you my pitch. You'll both stay and work the bar." He eyes Clara. "Unless you want to try dancing." Her expression should disembowel him, but he only shrugs. "Suit yourself. You work the bar, Miss Lily will manage dancers and musicians, and I'll organize everything else. Deal?"

I shake my head, trying to clear it. "Not yet. What's the split?"

He actually winks at me. "I do believe I like you, Miss Lily. Eighty-twenty is what I'll do for you, if you'll shake my hand here and now."

That doesn't sound so terrible, if we can just set aside the threats, the guns, and the sick fear I feel in his presence. "Eighty percent . . . for us?"

His mirth is sudden, immense, and genuine. When he can stand straight again, he mops the tears from his cheeks and beard, and even his henchmen are snickering. "Did I say you had brains?

It's eighty for me, you numskull. And that's only tonight. You can sleep on the decision, but it'll cost you. Tomorrow's split is ninety-ten. And the day after that, this here saloon is mine." He looks around, taking in the polished oak bar, the bright oil lanterns. "I think I'll call it Jeff Smith's Parlor."

I hate his greasy condescension, but that's not why my skin feels aflame, my throat strangled. I stare at him for a long minute. At last, I manage to croak, "This is flat-out extortion."

Smith beams at me. "Welcome to Skaguay, m'dear."

"I'd rather burn it to the ground than hand it over to that bastard," Clara snarls, slamming down the last tray of whiskey glasses.

It's four o'clock in the morning and we are finishing the dishes. The ones Clara hasn't broken, anyway. "I know," I say. "But we can't burn down just one building; the whole town would go up in flames in about ten minutes. We'd destroy everyone's future."

"So what? They're all hiding under their beds while that festering scab of a *cheechako* destroys our lives."

It's true. Smith and his henchmen left soon after his ultimatum. While I took care of the bar, Clara slipped out to talk with other Skaguay business owners. It seems there's a lot to know about our would-be associate, none of it good. He was a street-corner flimflam man turned card shark. He earned the nickname "Soapy" for his most famous racket, in which he auctioned off bars of soap. His many saloons and gambling dens in Colorado were the perfect fronts for his cons, all of which involved stealing from unsuspecting marks.

With so much gold dust flying around the Klondike, and thousands of feverish tenderfeet stampeding their way up here, it's no wonder Soapy reckons he can strike it rich too. He doesn't need to pan for gold; he can steal it right out of everyone else's pockets. And it's no mystery why he's chosen Garrett's Saloon as his first target either. We are young. We are women. If I were Soapy, I'd have picked on us too.

Clara twirls the front-door key around her finger. "What do you say, Lil? I'm all for dousing the place in kerosene and lighting a bonfire so big they'll see it in Canada. Then I'll bury this key in a dog turd and leave it at Soapy's door."

I've never seen my sister like this. Then again, we've never faced this kind of threat. Lu Garrett didn't have a rule for dealing with brazen extortion. "Where would that leave us, Clary? Homeless and destitute."

"Not destitute: we have our savings. We'll get the first boat to Seattle tomorrow morning."

"D'you really think Soapy would wave us off from the dock after we destroyed the saloon? From his perspective, we'd have burned down his property. How many hoodlums does he have? Do you think we'd even make it on board?" I shiver. "I don't think he'd be merciful just because we're young women."

She goes very still. "The opposite, I think."

"Yes. He'd make an example of us, to whip everyone else into line."

"We could give him the slip, head north over the White Pass."

I raise one eyebrow. Locals know that the nearest trail to the Yukon is, well, impassable. Even now in midwinter, when the ground is solid ice instead of boggy mud, the route is narrow, treacherous, and putrid with the half-rotted corpses of hundreds of starved and overworked horses abandoned by their owners. Only the greedy and stupid attempt the White Pass. They try by the hundreds each week.

Clara's eyes are wide, her face milky pale. After a long pause, she whispers, "Then we're trapped. We have to agree to his terms."

"The others won't stand with us against Soapy? If we all worked together, we could run him out of town."

"I went everywhere. 'Every man for himself,' they said. Others told me to take Soapy's offer and be grateful." Her lip curls. "Most of them couldn't even look me in the eye."

"You think he bribed them to say that?"

"He doesn't need to; they're terrified of him. Madame Robillard says he's got spies all over town, fingers in every pie. The neighbors are just grateful he's after us, not them."

"What did they say at Clancy's?" The Clancy brothers own the second-most-popular saloon in Skaguay. They have always resented our success.

"Pat Clancy laughed and said girls had no business running a saloon anyway."

I hesitate. "Soapy's offering us ten percent of the profits. That's only twenty dollars a night. Maybe forty if he doubles our takings, like he said." That's a lot more than pocket change anywhere else in America, but Alaska is different. Sometimes an egg costs a dollar.

Clara nods. "And what happens when Soapy reneges on his offer and kicks us out? That's just a matter of time." Her eyes are dazzling with unshed tears. "We've already lost, Lil. The saloon is gone."

When confronted with an abstract threat, it's easy to roar, *Over my dead body*. But this threat is real. It's the realest thing I've ever faced—more real than frostbite in January, more real than the stink of hops and tree sap as I brew beer, more real than the transcendent glory of the northern lights. And I can't think of a single argument in our favor.

I fill a pot with water and set it on the woodstove. I carefully grind the last of our coffee beans. Normally, I'm stingy with the coffee, trying to eke it out until the next boatload of supplies comes to town. But tonight we'll enjoy it while we can. We sit at a small table, side by side, steaming mugs in our hands.

"What are you thinking?" asks Clara quietly.

"All kinds of things." My heart is pounding so hard I can barely hear her. My brain is equally frantic.

"I love you, Lily Garrett," she says, her voice tight. "And I love being alive. I want us to stay this way."

I grip her in a fierce hug. "I love you too. And we will live. If Lu were here, she'd make a new rule: we don't buckle under to *cheechakos* named Soapy."

Clara makes a sound that is half laugh, half sob. "Promise?"

"I promise." We hug for a long time, and then we straighten up. We sip our coffee. "I think you're right: we're going to lose the saloon. But we're going to leave it on our terms."

Finding Soapy is easy. Next day—or rather, later the same day—I walk down Broadway to Skaguay's least-squalid hotel and ask for Mr. Smith. The hotel's owner, Mrs. Braun, doesn't blink, but I know the gossip will be halfway around town almost before I finish my sentence. "Mr. Smith, yes," she clucks. "You sit in the breakfast room, dear. I'll fetch him for you."

The "breakfast room" is a medium-sized tent pegged to the main building, furnished with a few rickety tables and stools. Its kerosene stove is no match for the piercing breeze that leaks in under its canvas hem, and hungry guests shiver in their overcoats as they gobble congealing bacon and stiff toast. Not me: I have my nerves to keep me warm.

In a few minutes, Soapy materializes. "A good morning to you, Miss Lily. I hope you slept well; I know I certainly did."

I don't bother with a greeting. "I have a counterproposal for you, Mr. Smith."

He glances around before sitting down. I notice two hoods place themselves at the next table, their attention clearly fixed on us. "May I offer you some refreshment?" Soapy asks. "The coffee's never hot, but it's better than the tea."

"No, thanks. This is purely a business call." I'm pleased to find that my voice barely shakes.

"I'm keen to hear it."

"I'd like to propose a short-term partnership. My sister and I will offer you a fifty-fifty share of the saloon's nightly profits for the next month." I take a deep breath. This next sentence will hurt. "After that, we will turn over the business to you — and leave town."

Soapy smiles flirtatiously. "Just like that? Why a month?"

If I try to smile back, I'll cry. "We don't have any savings. A month will allow us to build up a cash reserve. It'll pay for our tickets out of town and help us set up a new business in our next home."

"Where do you plan to go?"

"That's not your concern, Mr. Smith. I promise we'll leave Skaguay."

He thinks about that. "How much does the saloon take each night?"

"About two hundred dollars, on average."

He whistles low. "And you want an extra month? At fifty-fifty, that's three thousand dollars in your greedy little purses."

I don't point out the utter hypocrisy of his lecturing me about greed. "Like I said, that's our journey out and capital for the future."

He glances toward his men at the next table. "I should say no. Why would I settle for a measly half when I'll be getting ninety percent from you tonight anyway?"

"You might not," I reply, and the anger in my voice surprises even me. I hold his startled gaze and do not blink. "You have no idea what we are capable of, Mr. Smith, if pushed too far."

There is a long silence. I sit completely still and continue to stare at him, and he at me. It's fifteen degrees outside, and I am sweating from neck to knee. Eventually, he forces a chuckle and says, "Well, then. Fifty-fifty, and you'll hand over the deed?"

"Deed, keys, and contents. There's even a barrel of genuine French brandy in the storeroom."

He shrugs. "I always was a tenderhearted fool. One week of fifty-fifty, Miss Lily."

"Two weeks. That's my final offer."

A conniving smirk slides across his face. It's gone a moment later, but I know what I've seen. "You're a hard bargainer for a little girl. After the two weeks is up, maybe you'll consent to join my business."

"Do we have a deal, Mr. Smith?"

"Two weeks, you said?" he asks, dodging the question.

We shake on it. His hand is corpse cold. As I leave the hotel, I scrub my right palm against the rough wool of my overskirt until it's raw.

I walk all the way down Broadway, checking frequently over my shoulder. I can't see any of Soapy's sidekicks behind me, but that doesn't mean I'm not being followed. At Sikorsky's Outfitters, I purchase a few supplies, paying for them in gold dust: a pick, a short-handled shovel, a bucket, several oilcloth bags, a couple of canteens, and some cartridges for our hunting rifle. The oilcloth, canteens, and ammunition fit into a satchel slung beneath my parka. There's no subtle way to carry a shovel or a pick, but that suits my purpose. I walk tall as I stride homeward along the busy streets.

I pin a notice on the saloon door saying CLOSED UNTIL 8. Now that I'm alone, I have a sudden attack of nausea. It's one thing to cut a deal with Soapy, another thing entirely to go through with our plan. Still, what choice do we have? If we're going to lose the saloon and leave Skaguay, at least we'll do it our way.

I walk behind the bar. There, carefully hidden by casks of booze and crates of empty bottles, is a trapdoor wide enough to admit a man. I raise the lid and haul out the shoe box that holds our life savings. I know precisely how much cash is in that box. But for now, I'm interested in the empty hole.

Digging frozen soil is almost impossible. But here in town, stoves and fireplaces burn constantly. The buildings are all huddled together, and they keep one another—and the ground—warm, like a pack of sled dogs bedding down for the night. Having said that, it is still 100 percent thankless and exhausting work. I'm about three feet down and coated in muck when Clara finally comes home.

"Sorry I took so long," she says, stamping ice from her boots. She must have done a good clip: she's sweating despite the knife-like winds outside. "John's on the trail, so I hiked up to his clan house to leave a message."

"Any idea where he's heading?" As a trader, John is often away for weeks at a time.

"They're not sure. Probably not Dawson."

Dawson City is more than four hundred miles from here. If John is traveling to Dawson, we really are doomed. "You think he'll help us?"

"Of course he will. We've been friends forever."

My mouth twists. "About six months, actually."

"That's a lifetime in frontier land," she argues. "It's as long as the town of Skaguay's existed. We three have a history."

It's true. When John first trekked into town with a heavy pack on his back, everybody wanted his goods but nobody wanted to deal with an Indian. That changed when Clara and I bought his best furs to make winter parkas. Our friendship grew from there: he taught us how to paddle a canoe and showed us the best places to gather salmonberries. We told him stories from the Outside—wild tales of growing up in saloons all along the Pacific Coast—and helped him learn to read English. We even know his Tlingit name. We're the only white people who do. Still, I'm worried. "He'd better come back to town in time to help us."

Clara comes around to inspect my work. "What did Soapy say?"

"Two weeks. I had to shake his hand."

"Ugh. Poor you." She reaches out to haul me up. "Here, let me have a turn."

The next five days, we only stop digging to open for business between eight p.m. and two a.m. At all other times, one of us is deep in that blasted hole, which is slowly becoming a tunnel. The other person cooks meals, keeps the saloon looking decent, and dumps hundreds of bucketfuls of soil out back, beside the privy. The sun sets around three in the afternoon, but, as we hope, plenty of folks have a chance to notice Alaska's newest mountain. A lot of regulars tease us about it and we smile mysteriously. They complain about our shorter hours and we smile mysteriously. They ask if we're going to work for Soapy and we smile mysteriously.

All of Skaguay gossips about Soapy's latest grab game. Rumors multiply like wild hare on the tundra. Still, we can't sleep at night. Clara looks more ethereal than ever. I am plain haggard.

John finally stops by the saloon almost a week after Soapy's first visit. He is travel weary and unshaven, and I have never been happier to see anybody in my whole life. He pulls up a stool at the bar and says, "I got Clara's message."

I pour him a double brandy—no melted snow—and wave away his money. "Are you able to help us?"

He turns and looks slowly, deliberately, around the room. "I've never seen it this busy." He's right. Despite the shorter hours, our takings are better than ever. The rumor mill helps with that: the men worry that Clara might leave soon.

"Only for a day or two longer," I say. "A week at the outside."

"And then?"

"We need your help skipping town. We have to use a route known only to your people."

He pauses midsip. "You're leaving? Just like that?"

"Would you stay, if you were us?"

His mouth twists. "Of course not. But I will miss you."

"Everyone says that," I snarl, "but they're still just twiddling their thumbs while Soapy runs us out of town."

He holds my gaze. "I won't. How can I help?"

"We need to paddle down the coast, maybe as far as Juneau. We'll have very little with us."

He nods. "I'll wait for you at the clan house."

"Thank you." I glance around the bar. All eyes are on Clara, holding court in the middle of the room, so I press a small, heavy bag into John's palm. "A deposit," I say. "For supplies."

He frowns. "That is unnecessary. We are friends."

"Desperate, high-risk friends."

His lips curve very slightly, not quite enough to call it a smile. "And what will I do with your gold dust? We Tlingit don't value it."

"A trader like you?" It feels good to joke, however badly. "I can't imagine."

Exactly one week after we shook hands, Soapy Smith storms Garrett's Saloon. He doesn't kick the door in; his henchman does that for him. Both their guns are drawn. And while Clara and I are braced for something just like this, we still scream in genuine terror. After all, if he knew what we were planning, he'd shoot us on the spot.

"Miss Lily and Miss Clara," he says in that smoky-soft drawl. "How delightful to see you again. I've been meaning to drop in for a drink, all this past week, but you've been keeping different hours." He pauses and looks around the saloon. "I can't help but wonder why."

Clara, who's been on digging duty, drops her tools into the hole. We stand together, shoulder to shoulder, in a pathetic attempt to hide the mouth of the tunnel. "We have your sh-share of the money," I say, stuttering in earnest. "Our nightly p-profits have actually gone up. I think it's because of the new hours."

Soapy isn't listening. "What are you doing hiding behind the bar? Walk out slowly, both of you."

I obey, keeping my hands in plain sight. Clara follows, but not until she's kicked the trapdoor cover into place.

"What was that sound?" yells the hoodlum. I recognize him from the hotel: short, squint-eyed, none too bright. Maybe it's borderline hysteria, but despite the pistols aimed our way, I begin to feel mildly optimistic. If Soapy has brought only one thug, one from the farm team at that, he doesn't consider us much of a threat.

Soapy strolls behind the bar and looks down. "I suspected as much," he says. "Miss Clara, didn't you know that all the gold is buried in the creek beds, not the town?"

He's still chuckling at his own joke when Clara sticks out her chin and says, "Shows what you know."

"Shut up!" I hiss, elbowing her.

Soapy's gaze sharpens. "Cover them, Red." He kneels, and the trapdoor creaks open. He whistles long and low. "My, you girls have been busy. This is practically a mine shaft. Red, you got a candle on you?"

"No, boss."

Soapy sighs. "Fine. Get over here." He keeps his gun loosely trained on us, but his attention is on Red.

"Can't see nothing, boss."

"Then climb in, you idiot."

"'S awful dark in there, boss."

"Guess you should've brought a candle." Soapy turns to us and says with a simper, "Good help is so hard to find."

Red gives a muffled grunt. "It's real deep, boss. Height of a man, at least. And that's not the end of it."

Soapy strides behind the bar to look for himself. Then he turns to us, hands on hips. "Seeing as this is now my bar, why don't you girls tell me what's going on? Why the hell would you spend your last week in Skaguay digging a tunnel to China?"

"Our deal was for two weeks!" I object. "We shook on it!"

"New day, new deal: tell me where this tunnel goes and what you were planning to do with it, and you get a pair of one-way tickets on the next steamer out of town." He pauses. When he next speaks, his voice is viper-like. "Refuse, or lie, or try to double-cross me, and you dear, sweet girls will wish you were never born."

Clara blanches to the lips. "We understand," she whispers.

"You changed your mind once," I say, not even trying to control the shaking of my voice. "How can we be sure that you won't change it again after we've told you?"

His smile is even more frightening than his voice. "You can't."

There is a long silence. Then, as though against our wills, Clara and I step toward the bar. From my position at the side, I can see both the hole and Red's head just inside it.

I take several deep breaths. "It's simple, really. Our neighbor Madame Robillard runs a boardinghouse. She has a safe where she keeps valuables for her lodgers: jewelry, gold nuggets, cash. And, well, we happen to know the combination." Most of this is true.

Soapy's eyes gleam. "How did you learn the combination?"

I fidget. "Her maid told me."

"So you girls *were* digging for gold after all." Soapy sounds impressed.

"If you had a light, you could see the direction of the tunnel," Clara says helpfully. "Maybe if Red goes in deeper and sort of waves to you?"

Soapy motions Red to obey. The henchman slides farther into the tunnel and lets out a howl of pain.

"Oops," says Clara. "Sounds like he spiked himself on the pick. I threw it down there when you first burst in. Sorry, Red!"

As Red inches through the tunnel—it's a tight squeeze for a man, especially a broad-shouldered one—Soapy dips his head and watches. His grip on the pistol slackens.

"We're making a beeline for Madame Robillard's private parlor," I explain. "See how the tunnel curves?"

"It's at the very back of her house," adds Clara. "About twenty paces from this wall, we reckon."

Soapy kneels, pushing his face into the tunnel's mouth. His gun lies just beside his right hand. "How far along did you get with the tunnel?"

In one practiced motion, I slip our loaded rifle from its hook on the side of the bar and press the muzzle to the back of his head. Hard. "About this far."

Soapy freezes.

My whole body is trembling, but that probably makes things

scarier for him. "Now," I say, "very slowly, slide your right hand away from your gun."

"What's up, boss?" comes Red's muffled voice.

"Tell him nothing, it's all right, keep going."

Soapy obeys, his voice stiff with outrage.

"Now stand up very slowly. That's right. Hands in the air."

Despite the chill of the room, streams of sweat trickle down Soapy's face. Still, I admire his nerve. Two feet from the end of a loaded rifle, and he's swearing at us using curses so inventive that even I, who grew up in a saloon, find them educational.

"Hey, Red," sings out Clara, "can you catch?" She clocks Soapy over the head with our cast-iron frying pan. His eyes cross, his knees buckle, and with a little shove from Clara he drops, like a sandbag, down into the tunnel.

To the sound of Red's much less creative swearing, Clara thumps the trapdoor into place and slaps a sheet of iron, salvaged from our woodstove, on top of it. Together, we roll a keg of beer on top of that, to weigh it down. We pause, panting and shaking from our exertions, and listen with satisfaction to Red's muffled curses.

"Hey, Red," calls Clara. Her curls are damp with sweat, and she's grinning like a fool. "Did you find the shovel I left you?"

More swearing.

"You'll never get out this side," she says. "Trapdoor's lined with iron and weighted. I suggest you make your way to the other end of the tunnel and dig straight up."

We don't linger to hear Red's answer. Our supplies are already packed in satchels, our cash folded into oilcloth bags we've worn strapped under our skirts all week. We step out onto Broadway, and Clara catches the arm of Old Tom Hines, one of our faithfuls.

"Tom," she says in her perfect hostess's voice, "the liquor cabinet's wide open. Why don't you go treat yourself and a hundred of your closest friends?"

We make our way up the street, spreading the word: drink Garrett's dry, keep the glasses, take the furniture. By the time we stop at Shaw's lumber merchants, telling him to help himself to the wood planks the saloon is built of, we have to shout to be understood. We link arms and fight the human tide to the very top of the street, to survey the full extent of the chaos we've inspired.

After a few minutes, Clara squeezes my arm. "Hey, why are you crying?"

I touch my face, and she's right: I am. "It's all over. All that hard work ... gone." I gesture to the saloon. It was more than just our business. It was our life. Our inheritance from Lu.

"It is," she concedes. "But I think we've gained more than we've lost."

I shake my head. "I don't follow."

"Look at all those happy people: talking about us, drinking to our future, finishing our revenge for us. We're forever part of Skaguay's history now. You and me, Lil. We're going down in legend. The infamous Garrett sisters."

I suppose it's something. Eventually, I draw a shaky breath. "You were very specific about where they should start digging. Where do you have them coming up?"

Her eyes sparkle. "Well, it's hard to be precise when you're that far underground."

"But?"

"If they dig straight up?" Her lips twitch. "They should surface pretty much in our outhouse."

❦ *Author's Note* ❦

"The Legendary Garrett Girls" was first inspired (though I didn't know it at the time) by a family vacation to Alaska, where I rode the White Pass railway and saw the grave of Soapy Smith. I even started my research, accidentally, when I bought William B. Haskell's memoir, *Two Years in the Klondike and Alaskan Gold Fields, 1896–1898,* as a souvenir of the holiday. Many details of daily life in this story come straight from Haskell, including the use of gold dust as currency.

One of the tricky things about researching Soapy Smith is the proliferation of legend and rumor around his rather murky life. It's safe to discount the wildest legends ("He was the new Napoleon of crime!" "Moriarty had nothing on Jeff Smith!"), but there are clear factions in the interpretation of Smith's life and times. For a writer of fiction, this is ridiculously liberating: I was free to cherry-pick the details that best suited my dramatic impulses.

My research into Tlingit culture suggests that formal names are private and not to be used lightly. In homage to Kate Carmack, Jim Mason, and Dawson Charlie, members of the Tagish and Tlingit First Nations who discovered gold and triggered the Klondike gold rush, I've given my Tlingit trader, John, an English name of convenience.

If you're curious about Soapy and the Klondike gold rush, please visit my website, where I've posted a short bibliography. For readers and writers of historical fiction, it's never too late to stake a claim!

The Color of the Sky

Elizabeth Wein

ANTONIA'S TIMING WAS PERFECT. The sun was just flaming over the horizon, making insects shimmer and lighting the green glass insulators in the new electric poles that marched up and down the empty streets. This far north on the Kings Road, buildings stood at a distance from one another and looked like they'd been thrown together in a day. Everything felt unfinished and exciting, changing minute by minute—blink and you saw something new. Five years ago Tony's father had brought her here to see horse races at the track—now the same racetrack served as an airfield and hosted flying shows.

Today, Tony was here to see the flying.

There were a few other people waiting across the street from Paxon Field, early risers like herself who'd been lucky enough to get a tip-off about the informal flying show that was going to happen this morning. Bessie Coleman, Queen Bess, Brave

Bess—the only black woman in the world with a pilot's license—was coming out here to do a test flight before tomorrow's air display.

Tony hesitated for a moment at the closed door of the airfield office. Traffic amounted to a milkman's horse and one rattling old Tin Lizzie Ford, which didn't even slow down as it passed, but someone had decided the test flight was important enough to warrant a young white uniformed policeman patrolling the front of the wooden office building. The policeman came out to stand in the middle of the street and waved the car on importantly. As Tony stood wondering whether she should go into the office and explain that she'd been invited, or if it would be better just to wait until Miss Coleman and her escort got here themselves, the policeman turned and saw her.

He tried to shoo her away like a stray dog.

"This show ain't open to the public," he told her. "The parachute jump is tomorrow, over at the racetrack. If you want to watch just now, you can stand on the other side of the road."

"Miss Coleman's publicity manager invited me," Tony explained. "He's Mr. Betsch, from the Negro Welfare League. Yesterday she came and lectured at my school—I go to Edwin Stanton—"

The policeman's lips parted as though he were about to interrupt. Tony plunged on, speaking fast: "She's got a moving picture of her aviation stunts in Europe, and yesterday while she was rewinding her film reels, Mr. Betsch told me I could come along today so I can interview her for my Physics Club—" She realized she was talking *too* quickly, sounding a little desperate.

"Other side of the street," the policeman said, pointing.

Darn it. I knew it, Tony thought. *I should have planned a good argument—*

THE COLOR OF THE SKY

"You can stand over there with all the other niggers and get a view of the whole sky," the man said blandly. "Nobody's charging admission. It's a free country."

Tony's face grew hot at the hated word. What infuriated her most of all was the casual way people used it: *Outta the way, nigger; I'm in a hurry. Hey, nigger, which way to the train station?* Tony caught her breath, clenched her toes in her worn oxford school shoes, and thought hard. No point in bringing up the questions her senior high Physics Club had put together about the flight characteristics of Bessie Coleman's new aircraft—or Bessie Coleman's commitment to opening an aviation school for young Negroes of both sexes. And absolutely no point in mentioning Tony's own interest in the Dutch aircraft designer she knew Bessie had met in Europe.

Tony swallowed frustration and ambition and tried to play the part of a winning and innocent schoolgirl. Her cheeks were still aflame. She felt like she was being dishonest: hiding her interest in science, which always made men suspicious no matter what color they were, and trying to be pleasant to someone who'd insulted her without even realizing it. She tried a simpler tactic.

"I was just hoping to get Bessie Coleman's autograph when she gets here." It was true enough she'd like to have that autograph, and maybe if she could speak to Miss Coleman herself, things would turn around.

"You can do that tomorrow." The policeman was growing impatient. "The air display tomorrow's gonna be for a mixed audience—pay to get in like everyone else. I'll be there myself."

"I'm looking forward to that!" Tony knew the flying show would be for a mixed audience—Bessie Coleman had fought for that privilege and won it. The whole Physics Club, and probably the rest of the school, were coming to watch. Thinking of

Bessie's persistence, Tony made one last attempt to win over the policeman.

"Look!" Tony had two schoolbooks, a couple of ham-filled biscuits wrapped in paper for her dinner break, and her cardboard notebook with her newspaper clippings about Bessie Coleman and the questions for the Physics Club tied together with a piece of twine. Tony slid the notebook free; as luck would have it, it fell open to a photograph of Bessie posing beneath the wings of an aircraft with a white cameraman holding a huge Pathé moving-picture camera. The aviatrix and the filmmaker were both grinning conspiratorially, and the caption read, "Snapped in Berlin, Germany."

"Look," Tony repeated. "She did a tour through Europe doing test flights for aircraft designers. She flew over the kaiser's palace! She's not just a circus performer—"

The policeman bent over the page. The picture held him for a moment. Then he let out a grudging sigh.

"Okay, you go wait across the road with the other niggers and when she gets here you can come and ask for her autograph. But if any of those little kids follow you over here, I'm gonna chase you *all* away. You got that?"

It was a small victory made sour by the relentless casual insult. Stung and triumphant, Tony closed the notebook carefully. "Yes, sir," she mumbled, lowering her eyes.

"Get going, girl," the policeman said, jerking his head in the direction of the fence on the other side of the road.

Tony went, clutching the notebook under one arm and her schoolbooks under the other. It was unbelievable how polite you had to be when somebody cut you so low, so carelessly, that you wanted to spit at him. Would he call Bessie Coleman a nigger? He probably would. Some things never change.

Knowing Bessie Coleman was a southern girl herself gave Tony a little comfort. She knew Miss Coleman's story, and getting people to take her seriously must have been even harder than it was for Tony. Half a generation older than Tony, Bessie Coleman had been born and raised in Texan cotton fields. Already Tony had more schooling than Miss Coleman, who'd completed eighth grade and one term of college. But even as a schoolgirl, Brave Bess had been interested in flight—she'd written an essay about the Wright brothers and their history-making flying machine.

She didn't complete college because she ran out of money. She went home and earned her living doing people's laundry, until the dead-end pointlessness of the work drove her north to Chicago. There she pestered and pestered people to teach her to fly. When no one would—because she was a woman or because she was black or both—she managed to get herself sponsored by a local newspaper, went to France, and learned to fly there.

And now she was trying to raise money to establish a flying school for Negro boys and girls.

Maybe some things do *change,* Tony told herself. She stayed on the edge of the small crowd, watching the road and considering how she was going to get Miss Coleman's attention without a crowd of truant schoolboys following her like gnats.

"Hey, here they come!" yelled one of the boys, pointing at a dust cloud rising in the near distance.

The car pulled up in front of the new frame building, and the driver got out. Tony recognized the handsome young man in the dark business suit as Bessie's chaperone, John Betsch, who'd invited Tony to come along today. A white man emerged from the backseat, wearing a leather flying jacket and carrying a satchel made out of a flour sack. He got to the front passenger door before Betsch and opened it, and out stepped the woman flyer herself—Brave Bess, Queen Bess, queen of the air, queen of the sky. Bessie Coleman was little and pretty and official-looking in her jodhpurs, every inch a modern woman.

John Betsch took a moment to survey the crowd. Then he shouted, "Hey there, Tony!"

He'd recognized her. Thank goodness Tony had been bold enough to go up to him and shake his hand after the school lecture! She'd told him about the Physics Club. She and Betsch had talked about Miss Coleman's moving-picture projector, making guesses about how it worked while Miss Coleman rewound the reels.

Tony's mother always did say *You make your own luck.*

"It is Tony, right?" Betsch called. "Short for Antonia?"

"Yes. Hello!" Tony waved the cardboard notebook as a greeting, feeling her cheeks flushing again. Now the kids were gaping at her; she knew that if she crossed the street uninvited they'd be sure to follow, and then the cop would shoo her away with the rest of them. She held her breath. At least she'd gotten Betsch's attention.

"Come say hi," Betsch invited. "Miss Coleman was sorry she didn't get to meet you yesterday." He turned to the white policeman, who stood barricading the famous woman from the other spectators. "Okay if Tony joins us, Officer?" he asked politely, tipping his hat.

Antonia, miraculously, was allowed across the street.

"Hi, Tony," Bessie said to her warmly. "Great timing! Can you stick around after the test flight? Mr. Betsch said you have questions for me." Bessie glanced at the notebook in Tony's hand. "How about I give you an autograph now, in case you have to leave for school before I'm back on the ground?"

"I—sure!" Tony flipped the notebook open against the warm hood of the car. Miss Coleman laughed when she saw the clippings.

"It's all about me!" she said with pleasure. With her round face and petite features radiating delight, she seemed almost younger than Tony.

Tony laughed. "The questions I've got for you are about your plane's flight characteristics," she said. "Not about you."

"Well, I'll know more about that after the flight! Stick around. This plane's just come from Texas, and I've only flown it once before. It's not new, but it is going to be the first of my fleet," Bessie Coleman boasted. "I already put in an order for three more. Maybe you'll come learn to fly with me when I get that flight school open!"

She paused a moment, scanning the Physics Club list of questions about aerodynamics. Her youthful expression grew suddenly shrewder. "You and your friends have pretty good heads on your shoulders!" she said. Then she took Tony's pen and wrote in a firm, clear, confident script on the blank page right opposite the list. After a moment she lifted the pen and read aloud, as though she was pleased with what she'd written: "'To My Dear Admirer Antonia. Only you can make your dreams come true. Always reach for the sky and soon it'll be time for you to take flight. Your friend, Bessie Coleman.'"

She handed the pen back and patted the notebook. "Hey, Bill, come take a look. These kids aren't just autograph hunters — they're serious about aerodynamics! Tony, meet my mechanic, William Wills."

The white man in the leather flying jacket put down his satchel and offered Tony his hand. She took it, surprised, and he shook hands with her very briefly. He didn't smile, but he bent over the page of questions and scanned them briefly.

"Bill Wills brought my new plane here from Love Field in Dallas a couple of days ago," Bessie said.

"And it wasn't easy," Wills said. "Wait till I give them a piece of my mind back at Love Field—they're going to get a reputation for just being a junkyard for old army flying machines! I had so many mechanical problems on the way, I had to make two unscheduled landings. Took me a whole day to fly here." He glanced up at Miss Coleman. "You want to treat this baby gently when you fly her. I feel like I'm just getting to know her tricks!"

"Now, Bill, that's why I'm letting you do the flying this weekend," Miss Coleman answered cheerfully. "This morning we're just going to take a look over the racetrack to make sure it's safe for my parachute display tomorrow. And I expect you to treat my new baby gently, 'cause I'm going to leave my safety straps off so I can see over the side of the cockpit. I want to get the big picture."

"Well, the Jenny's got dual controls," Wills said. "We can take turns. You can give her a test run."

Bessie Coleman turned back to Tony. "If you're staying to watch, you can come out on the field with Mr. Betsch while we take off. Maybe I can take you for a flight myself later this weekend!"

"I'll go check out the Jenny," Wills said, and headed around the office building out to the landing field. Miss Coleman turned to the eager little crowd on the other side of the road and gave them a beaming smile and a sweeping wave, then followed Wills.

A couple of boys tried to edge closer to Betsch's car. The unpleasant policeman herded them back, truncheon in his hand, eyeing everyone menacingly.

"Come on, Tony," Betsch said.

Tony realized that the distracted William Wills had left his flour-sack satchel sitting on the ground by the car. She had an excuse as well as an invitation now. She picked up the sack, slung it over her shoulder, and headed after Betsch to the airfield. Once again she felt triumphant, but she didn't dare look back to see if the policeman noticed.

Tony couldn't make out the pilots' faces as the little Jenny aircraft began to rattle across the grass field—their heads were covered by helmets and goggles, and the taxiing plane kicked up a cloud of dust. The morning haze hung still in the sky, and the sun was higher now. Suddenly the flying machine soared, lifting over the roof of the office and creating a wind that rattled the airfield fence.

Tony's heart soared too. Understanding the principles of flight didn't make it any less amazing to watch. It seemed a perfect miracle that the flimsy machine could be lifting two human beings into the air—people Tony had spoken to, even *touched*, half an hour ago, and now they were *flying*. Tony watched the little Jenny turn, heading out over the racetrack in a steady, noisy ascent. It circled the track and Tony imagined the aviatrix giving directions to the pilot seated ahead of her: *Go higher. I want to get the big picture.*

The flying machine climbed.

Now it was nothing but a speck in the sky, three-quarters of a mile up, and Tony couldn't make out any details. She strained to see, worried that if she took her eyes from the aircraft she'd lose sight of it and not be able to find it again.

Then the aerobatics started.

The machine plunged so fast that Tony imagined she could faintly hear the wires between the wings screaming with the speed of the descent.

You can give her a test run, the mechanic William Wills had said. Tony wondered which of them was flying right now. Bessie must feel it was safe, since she'd said she wasn't going to wear her straps.

Tony had seen this trick before—over this very track she'd seen other pilots throw a machine into a dive, spin, then pull out and up at the last second and soar back into the sky. A dive like that was exactly what the little Jenny biplane did now, tearing a thousand feet down the sky and then suddenly dropping into a spin, corkscrewing around and around its own tail as it descended, like a winged sycamore seed. As it spiraled downward, lower and lower, Tony wondered with excitement if Miss Coleman had seen the question about the Jenny's spin characteristics—if maybe she'd mentioned it to the pilot and now they were trying out the daring display.

Tony held her breath, waiting with her heart in her mouth for the moment when the Jenny would stop spiraling and the wings would swoop steadily skyward.

It never came.

Five hundred feet above the ground, the spinning plane flipped over backward. A small, dark silhouette suddenly detached from the rest of the machine. The figure dropped like a tumbling stone through the sky. One moment it was part of the plummeting plane, and the next it was the living body of a brave and desperate pilot, and then it was gone.

In the first seconds after a catastrophe, you can't believe it really happened.

Part of Tony's brain insisted that both pilots were still in the aircraft she was watching, both still alive and fighting to stay in the sky. She stood rooted to the spot, straining to see the plane as it screamed back toward the airfield. She found her lips moving in a silent plea to the pilot: *Straighten up, please straighten up*—and then it became a prayer. *Please, God, let them straighten up.*

And she didn't even know who she was praying for.

The pilot straightened up, but not in time. The Jenny was too low now—trees loomed ahead of it at the edge of the farm field across from the racetrack. For one more vain second, Tony hoped the plane would miss the treetops. But the landing gear hanging down from its belly got caught in the top of one of the tall slash pines, and the aircraft took the tree's highest branches with it as the plane flailed and flipped itself over and hit the ground.

Then everything was quiet.

Tony had forgotten John Betsch, who'd been standing right beside her watching the whole thing too, until the moment when he tore across the airfield, running as fast as he could go. The policeman pelted after him. So did the boys who'd been watching from the road.

Dazed, Tony ran a couple of steps after them, when suddenly she remembered the figure who had fallen out of the tumbling aircraft. It hadn't happened directly above the airfield, but over a neighboring cross street. Tony ran away from the fallen plane, along Edgewood.

There was a little crowd gathered ahead of her. Something about their sober silence made Tony stop in her tracks before she got close enough to see what they were gathered around. A knot of men knelt over the inert form in the middle of the crowd, talking to one another in hushed tones. Around the edges of the crowd, sobbing women stole agonized glances at the scene and quickly looked away again, holding one another by the hand and around the waist.

There was something in their quiet reverence—the way the women were wiping one another's tears, as though the broken body in the center of the crowd was family—that made Tony sure the body was that of the famed Bessie Coleman.

After a moment a couple of people stepped back, but no

one moved fast—no one went running for an ambulance or a doctor.

Then suddenly the young policeman who'd tried to turn Tony away from the airfield was back on the scene.

"Hey!" called the policeman. "Hey, you, nigger girl with the questions! Get over here!"

Tony closed her eyes for a moment, reeling with the shock of what she'd just seen and the sheer horror of the law singling her out in a crowd of onlookers.

"You!" He was advancing on her now. She thought about running and suddenly became aware that she was carrying her books on their string over one shoulder and William Wills's satchel over the other. If she ran, it would look like she was trying to steal the satchel.

Oh, Lord have mercy, maybe it already *did* look like she was trying to steal it?

A sudden wave of anger drowned Tony's unhappiness for a moment. She'd run to the fallen pilot because she'd been trying to *help*. One of America's great heroes was tragically dead, and wasn't that more important than tracking down an anonymous school-girl? Tony stood her ground as the policeman stomped toward her, his eyes narrowed in a suspicious frown.

That was when they heard the rush of thunder as what was left of Bessie Coleman's Curtiss Jenny flying machine, a quarter of a mile away, exploded into a tower of flame.

The policeman escorted Tony back to the airfield office. He told her she was a witness; that's all he'd tell her. For half an hour he drank coffee with the man who was handling the telephone, but they didn't offer any to Tony. They didn't offer her a seat, either, so she stood warily in a corner of the office, trying to be invisible.

She didn't dare set down the bag or her books. Her arms began to ache.

But she couldn't help overhearing what was going on, as the man on the telephone relayed information. The police and three technicians were already attempting to pick over the wreckage to find out what had gone wrong with the plane, newspapermen were out there ghoulishly taking pictures, and a pair of undertakers were on their way.

"Can you beat that—having to call two different undertakers?" the telephone man exclaimed to the policeman. "One for the pilot, one for the nigger girl! Nobody having a good day except the undertakers."

At that moment, a man in overalls came slamming into the airfield office. He was so soot covered from head to toe that he looked like he was performing in a minstrel act. *"God-damned loose wrench!"* he swore, his mouth and lips garishly wet and red in his filthy, blackened face. He announced to no one in particular, "There was a God-damned wrench jammed in the works of that plane. That poor bastard Wills didn't stand a *chance*. No pilot in the world could have straightened a machine in that kind of trouble. A *God-damned loose wrench!* I don't blame the pilot. I blame the mechanics who left it there!"

The furious mechanic suddenly noticed Tony. "Pardon my French! But I guess you hear a lot of cussing where you live. Well, it's *bad*, girl, bad." He turned to the policeman and the receptionist, dismissing Tony as someone who got cussed at a lot. "The explosion was caused by that Negro Welfare League boy lighting a cigarette to calm his nerves. Tossed his match on the ground and whoosh! There was fuel spilled everywhere, and the plane and a couple of trees just went up in flames. One cop's pants caught fire. They hauled the colored boy off to jail."

Tony tried to hold back her own strangling anger, but words burst out of her. "You mean John Betsch? They took him to jail? What for?"

"For being a fool." The soot-covered man eyed Tony slantwise. "Maybe for getting too many colored folk excited about aviation."

The white policeman looked over at her in surprise, as though he couldn't remember why he'd thought she was so important half an hour ago. It was obvious she couldn't add any useful information to what the mechanic knew.

"Go on, scoot on home, girl," he snapped. "Nothing you can do here."

Seething at the pointless panic they'd made her endure, raging over their easy dismissal of Bessie's pioneering ambition, Tony didn't need to be told a second time to leave their mean-spirited company. She nodded once to the mechanic who had given her the awkward apology for his bad language. Then she walked with dignity out of the building. At the end of the block she ran for the Kings Road streetcar that would take her back to the center of Jacksonville. She was breathless with sobs by the time it came.

She'd already climbed on and was making her way to an empty bench before she realized that she was *still* carrying William Wills's flour-sack satchel over her shoulder.

She couldn't carry it around with her at school all day. But her heart galloped with fear and fury at the thought of taking it back to the airfield. Better just to drop it on someone's trash heap . . . But then, what if someone *else* found it and brought it back to Paxon Field? They might ask John Betsch about that "nigger girl" who'd been following Bessie around, and he knew Tony's name. She couldn't just abandon the bag. Why in the world hadn't she put it down in the airfield office? Getting noticed while she was already there, waiting for them to accuse her of stealing, couldn't possibly have been worse than going *back* and *volunteering* for it.

The streetcar rattled slowly on its way into the city. Now the bag sat on her lap like some mischievous magic object out of a folktale, waiting to get her into trouble. The shoulder strap made it easy to carry, and it wasn't even as heavy as Tony's bundle of schoolbooks. She hesitated. Then she opened the canvas sack and reached inside, trying to look like she knew what she would find.

The cardboard notebook that she pulled out was very like her own but more heavily battered. Too deep in now to let herself consider the moral implications of invading a dead man's privacy, she opened the book.

It was a maintenance record for the crashed Curtiss Jenny. Inside the front cover, Bessie Coleman had written her name, proudly declaring ownership of the aircraft. The confident sweep of her signature with its rounded *O* and *A* exactly matched the autograph in Tony's own notebook. Tony's breath caught in her throat.

She turned the pages.

The entries went back only a couple of years, though the notes in the beginning suggested the plane was older than that. The last few pages were dated like diary entries, describing work that had been done in the past couple of days. Tony guessed that Wills had made these notes during his unexpected landings in Mississippi on his way from Love Field in Dallas to Paxon Field in Jacksonville—a careful record for the aircraft's new owner. It felt almost private to read it, intimate secrets intended for the woman who would have someday known that plane from the inside out.

Tony slid the notebook back into the bag. There was a soft

cloth in there as well—a clean, folded shirt. And a rolled felt bag that Tony thought contained shaving equipment.

Tony folded the flour sack shut and closed her eyes, feeling the rhythm of the streetcar clattering over the rails. The only thing to do was to take the bag home and shove it under her bed and hope no one ever found it. Bury it in the backyard. Burn it. Try to forget the way those white men had talked to her. Try to forget the way they'd talked about *Bessie*. Try to forget the sight of Bessie Coleman's falling body and the roar of the explosion that had incinerated William Wills.

Tony went to three church services that Sunday—her family's usual one in the morning, then a funeral for Bessie Coleman in the afternoon at the Negro Baptist church, and then another funeral service for Miss Coleman that evening at the Negro Episcopal church. Tony got her whole family to come along to the afternoon funeral, even though they had to stand outside—only about a third of the mourners fit in the church. You couldn't hear the eulogies, but everybody outside joined in singing the hymns. Maybe Bessie Coleman would have been cheered by a mixed crowd at the flying show that weekend, but Tony didn't notice any white people at her funeral—it looked more like the entire Negro population of Jacksonville had turned out to say good-bye. Tony caught her mother wiping her eyes.

Her own eyes stayed dry. She couldn't cry. How did you mourn a dead dream?

Nobody in her house wanted to go to the evening service, so Tony asked if she could go by herself. Her parents weren't happy about it. "Too much, Tony," her mother said. "It's too much. You are spending a whole day mourning a stranger!"

"Bessie Coleman is not a stranger to me. I've been following her career since 1921. Watching how people came to respect her is why I wanted to go to high school—you and Daddy both know that! That's why you agreed to let me go to Edwin Stanton! Why do you think five thousand people turned up at her funeral?"

"So long as your schoolwork's done," her father said, which was his way of giving permission.

So she went to the evening funeral too. When the service ended, Tony found herself swept up in the crowd that escorted Miss Coleman's casket to the Jacksonville railway station. Five hundred people stood on the platform watching the porters lift the coffin into the baggage car. Someone behind Tony began to hum softly in the warm spring evening gloom. After a bar or so, another few voices joined in. Tony did too, buoyed by being part of such a unified crowd. Words in her head accompanied the tune:

> *My country, 'tis of thee,*
> *Sweet land of liberty,*
> *Of thee I sing. . . .*

Later that night, after she got home, Tony sat on the creaky porch of the shotgun house that still belonged to her grandmother. The magnolia her grandfather had planted when her mother was born was now in glorious full bloom, scenting the whole street, and stars glimmered through its leaves. Their rustling mingled with the sound of Tony turning pages as she leafed through the pile of newspapers, both white and black, that she'd collected in the past three days. They'd cost her a week's wages from the milliner's where she worked after school.

Her mother came out to coax her gently to bed. "Child, you're going to go blind there, reading by one candle like that."

"Daddy said I had to put out the lamp. Tomorrow there's

going to be another funeral in Orlando, where Bessie lived, and then one up in Chicago, where her family lives."

"Your daddy is worried about you. You are acting a little crazy, Tony."

Tony was sick of the papers anyway. The way they reported the crash fueled the rage seething in her chest. Worrying about the aircraft's maintenance log in the flour-sack bag under her the mattress wasn't helping.

"See here, Momma, this article says her mechanic was *teaching her to fly!*" Tony flourished the paper. "And this one has got the story all the way at the back, and it just has a picture of the dead white pilot and it doesn't even mention Bessie's name, just calls her 'the woman'! She is a 'daring aviatrix' in the *Chicago Defender.* But these white papers just don't care about a colored woman— no matter *what* she does."

"Well, that's the truth." Her mother sighed. "They *don't* care. Come on to bed, Tony honey." She hugged a thin arm around Tony's shoulder and kissed her cheek with dry lips. Tony couldn't see her face, but she could smell the Madam C. J. Walker oil in her hair.

"Momma!" Tony gasped in frustration. "Doesn't it make you *mad*?"

"Would I be sending my daughter to the only colored high school in the city and letting her study physics if it didn't make me mad?" her mother answered quietly. She began to gather the strewn newspapers.

Tony blew out the candle and stomped into the house. The porch shook.

She lay awake. Her mind was too full of the day's images and the words on paper and the crowds of mourning people and the fact that *none* of it actually felt like it had anything to do with the warm, excitable person who'd shaken Tony's hand and made promises to her three days ago. That dream of a flight school, the newsreels and the lectures and the encouragement—who was going to keep that going? All those thousands of people at the churches today—maybe one of them would step up and keep that dream alive, but right now, for Tony, her only connection to the sky was the guilty bag under the mattress, with the aircraft log book hidden inside. And Tony couldn't show that to anyone, ever.

Tony listened to her sisters' breathing. She tried to calm herself, running the wonderful scene of the humming crowd at the train station through her head like one of Miss Coleman's film reels. The quiet music swelling in the dark had been one of the most magical things she'd ever witnessed: a crowd of strangers united in one moving voice.

From every mountainside,
Let freedom ring.

But other voices crowded in her head, jammed in the works of her mind.

A God-damned wrench.
Guess you hear a lot of cussing where you live.
One for the nigger girl!
For being a fool.

And then she remembered a woman's voice.

You make your own luck.

And another woman, friendly, warm, and encouraging:

Soon it'll be time for you to take flight.

Brave Bess, people had called Miss Coleman. How had she managed to fly free in a land so tangled in unfair rules? She wasn't a lawbreaker.

She did things herself, Tony thought. *She went places. She went to Chicago and found people who gave her work; she went to France and found people who taught her to fly. She came back here and found people who respected her enough to sponsor her, to manage her shows. And she went to Texas and found people who would sell her a plane. She took control. She made her own luck. Those places she went and those people who helped her are real. The editor at the* Chicago Defender. *John Betsch. William Wills. The people who sold her the plane. I can find people like that too.*

I wish I could give that Curtiss Jenny's maintenance book to some-one who would care about it, Tony thought. *Someone who knows what it means. Not just someone who believed in Bessie's dream, but also someone who understands the mechanics of flight. Someone who knew her, or who knew the man who wrote it out . . .*

Then she realized there *was* something she could do with William Wills's satchel. There was a place she could take it and people who would care about it.

She was going to take that book and that satchel back to Love Field in Dallas, Texas, where it had come from.

Tony got dressed in the dark. Her sisters were awake the second she got out of bed.

"Where are you off to?" baby Alma Mae asked.

"I am going to Chicago," Tony said. This outrageous lie was less outrageous than her real plan. "I am going to Bessie Coleman's Chicago funeral, to her family funeral in her hometown."

"Are you crazy?" hissed Sarah, who was jealous that she wasn't in high school yet and had missed the lecture on Thursday.

"I gotta leave before Momma gets up. 'Cause I have to catch the six fifteen a.m. train."

"I bet you gotta leave before Momma gets up 'cause you ain't asked her if you can take the train to Chicago all by yourself," said Alma Mae.

"How much school are you going to miss?" Sarah gasped, and repeated for effect: "Are you *crazy*? Are you really gonna spend all your saved-up money on a train ticket to Chicago so you can go to a funeral for someone you don't even know, when you already *went* to two funerals for her?"

"Just don't tell Momma till after the train has left, okay?"

Sarah didn't answer. Tony wasn't sure if that meant she would or she wouldn't tell, but Tony guessed that if her sisters didn't kick up a fuss now, they wouldn't tell on her till later.

"You wearing your Sunday clothes? You'll look good on the train," Alma Mae said approvingly.

"Yeah, all dressed up so I can be squashed on a wooden bench for twenty hours in the colored car."

"Least you got a good job to pay for your ticket," Sarah reminded her sharply. "Least they let you ride. Least it's 1926 and not 1826."

"Yeah, least there is a train!" said Alma Mae.

"You two sound like Grandma. Times have changed since she was your age."

Grandma had been a plantation slave when she was Sarah's age.

Tony pinned on her hat. She felt under the mattress for the flour-sack bag and tucked her schoolwork, her notebook, and her coin purse inside it. Alma Mae and Sarah listened to her blind last-minute packing without saying anything else for a short while.

Then Alma Mae told Tony reassuringly, "Daddy is gonna tan your hide when you get back."

"You hush," Sarah told Alma Mae, and Tony knew she could trust them.

"Thank you," Tony said, and kissed each of them good-bye in the dark.

$$\times \quad \times \quad \times$$

It took Tony nearly two days to get to Dallas. The colored car was crowded and stifling and stank of sweat and the one toilet—Tony had no choice but to contribute to both. The last three hours of the journey through the fields and banks of tossing bluebonnets made her so crazy for fresh air that she began to contemplate leaping from the train to join the workers hoeing the cotton fields just so she could be outside. She ate the last of Momma's biscuits, the ones that were supposed to be her school dinner. She had Booker T. Washington's *Up from Slavery* open on her lap, because she was supposed to be reading it for school, but she kept putting it down because *yes, she knew* that education was going to lift her above her grandma's past. But she couldn't write out any of her missed work on the swaying, crowded train.

The flour sack and its contents didn't weigh heavy on her cramped knees, but they did on her heart.

When Bessie Coleman rode this train, which maybe she did just last month, she'd have had to sit in this car just like me, Tony thought. *Queen Bess, the queen of the sky, jammed on a wooden bench in the stinking colored car.*

Tony looked out at the bluebonnets and thought, *Blue, blue, the color of the sky.* Not white. Not black.

Blue.

There was a jitney bus that ran from the middle of Dallas out to Love Field, but Tony didn't realize that until three of them had passed her on the five-mile walk. When she set out from the train station, she was so rumpled and frazzled and exhausted she didn't actually know what time it was. She didn't notice the city around her until it was almost gone, and the last quarter of a mile was so rural that she started passing cotton fields again. Gray people bent over their monotonous hoes, and no one looked up at Tony as she passed, bedraggled and gray with travel dust herself. No one waved. A strange dreamlike daze began to creep over her, and she began to feel she no longer even knew what *year* it was. Surely this was what these fields looked like when her grandma had worked them under the overseer's lash. There was no overseer in sight. That was the only difference.

Then an engine began to clamor and rattle not too far away.

The spell was broken. It was like a kiss in a fairy tale. Suddenly Tony was wide awake.

People looked up for a moment, stretched, and grinned. Someone waved at Tony at last. An aircraft appeared, flying low over a stubborn row of scrawny young live oaks along the edge of the field, and climbed steadily overhead.

"Looks like they got another of those old Jennies back in the sky," someone said knowledgeably.

"Go along with me to Love Field and take a look before dark?" said his friend in the next row.

Tony adjusted her hat against the sun that dazzled her stinging, tired eyes. Now she noticed how far down the sky the sun was, and she realized she was going to arrive at her destination just before sunset. And there she'd be, in the dark, five miles out of town, with no place to stay and nothing to eat.

Least she wasn't dead. Least it was 1926 and not 1826.

She was nearly there. There wasn't any point in turning back.

Love Field was so big, and there were so many aircraft sheds and so many actual aircraft standing in front of them and on the field, that for a moment Tony was overcome with a feeling of unreality.

This wasn't 1826. But it couldn't be 1926, could it? This must be what 2026 was going to be like.

She had a moment of terrible panic when she saw the two white men in greasy caps and overalls standing on the porch of the office with a newspaper spread over the rails, shaking their heads. This was going to be the Paxon Field office disaster all over again. Texas had the worst Jim Crow segregation laws in the country—what in the world had made Tony think she'd be better off revealing her accidental theft here than at home, even if these people had tolerated Bessie enough to sell her a plane?

Both men watched Tony as she straggled to the foot of the porch steps, and she wished desperately she could spruce herself up a little before she had to face them. What could she possibly say? Calling her names was the least they might do to her. Putting her in jail wasn't even close to the *worst*. She'd been crazy to come. Sarah was right.

Tony stood at the bottom of the porch steps, feeling fully ready, for the first time since watching that terrible plunge from the sky five days ago, to burst into baby tears.

One of the men had a pipe clenched in the corner of his mouth. He took it out and gave her a pleasant smile. "Any chance you're the next Bessie Coleman?" he said.

Tony's mouth dropped open.

"Aw, look at her. Don't tease her," said the second man. He touched his cap with two fingers, a sketch of a salute. "You need help, kid? There's a telephone in the office." He called over his shoulder. "Hey, Louis! Got a sec?"

A young, slow-moving, mild-mannered black man stepped out of the office and onto the porch. "What's going on?"

The man who'd greeted her waved his pipe at Tony. "Don't

think she wants to buy a plane like the last gal," he said. "But it looks like she's come a long ways to get here."

"Welcome to Love Field," the black man said to her. "I'm Louis Manning. Mechanic, parking-lot attendant, receptionist, publicity specialist, parachutist, pilot!"

"He's kind of a jack-of-all-trades," said the man who'd saluted.

"You can call me Louis," said the jack-of-all-trades.

Still astonished by their friendliness, Tony was able to pull herself together a little. "I came by train from Jacksonville." She saw the sober shift in their expressions—all three of them stood listening and alert, side by side on the porch with their attention fixed. They knew exactly what "Jacksonville" meant this week.

"I saw it happen," she said huskily.

Now it was their turn to look astonished.

"Come on inside, honey, and sit down," said Louis. "You got a place to stay here in Dallas?"

Tony shook her head.

"We'll see what Pa and Ma Vencill can do for you tonight. They live over in the old officers' mess. Let's get you a cold drink. We are all mighty shook up over that crash—feeling kind of responsible, you know? Lost a good plane, a good mechanic, and the most forward-thinking woman flyer in the world. Come in and tell us what happened."

The man with the pipe offered her his hand to help her up the porch steps. Tony stared at him, astounded. She'd never seen any white man do such a thing for a black woman.

Louis laughed. "Go on, let him be a gentleman. Doesn't happen often!"

"But—!"

"But you're a colored girl? We're all colored here. Blue as the sky."

"Bessie Coleman was a caution! Terrible loss. Did you see the last newspaper interview that young woman gave?" rumbled Wade Vencill, presiding over a very full dining-room table. He and his wife, Myrtle, cooked for the handymen of the airfield. Tonight's guests were mainly young men and women, half of them the Vencills' grown children and the other half mechanics or pilots—Tony couldn't entirely figure out which was which, and some were both or all three. The crowd included Louis Manning and another black man, not to mention Tony herself. "Queen Bess said she'd just ordered four new planes! *Four!*" Wade Vencill gave a single, brief guffaw that managed to sound both fond and bitter at the same time. "That's Bessie all over. The good Lord knows she didn't have that kind of money. Four new planes! If I'd have known that antique flivver of a kite was going to be the death of her, I'd have loaned her another fifty dollars myself!"

"She talked as big as she dreamed," Ma Vencill said. "She wanted things so fierce it must have seemed to her like saying them out loud would make them come true. That flight school she's been raising money for! Teaching colored boys and girls to fly!" She wiped her eyes quickly with her napkin. "All right, Antonia, you have to tell these folks what really happened at Paxon Field. The only man we've heard from in Jacksonville is the undertaker, and all he wanted to talk about was how to get in touch with poor Bill's family. It breaks my heart to think of that young man going up in flames!"

The pilots and mechanics leaned forward around the table, quiet and expectant.

"It was a loose wrench," Tony said. "It got stuck in the machine's mechanism — I don't know how."

"A wrench! A loose wrench!" everybody echoed. "How in the world —"

"Mr. Wills was working on that plane the whole way to Florida," Tony said. "He had to make two unexpected landings because of mechanical problems." With a quiet settling of her heart, she said evenly, "I brought you his maintenance log."

It was the easiest thing in the world to say. *I brought you his maintenance log.* No one had any doubt about her honesty, or why she'd brought it *here.*

"We are mighty grateful for that," said Louis Manning. "But what made the wrench get jammed? Were they stunt flying?"

They all looked at Tony.

She nodded. "The plane dived. I don't know which one of them was flying. I thought Bessie might be doing it on purpose, testing the plane. Maybe she was."

"Why did she fall out? Wasn't she strapped in?"

"She wanted to lean up over the edge to look at the racetrack where she was going to do a parachute jump the next day. She couldn't get up high enough to see out of the seat with the harness on."

Pa Vencill said soberly, "There was that young fella killed himself falling out of a plane right here not ten months ago. I keep telling folk to strap themselves in, every time. Wish I knew why people still think they can fly without harnesses."

You make your own luck, her momma's voice reminded her drily.

Ma Vencill exclaimed, "What I want to know is why don't the dad-blamed white newspapers print Bessie Coleman's name?"

"So what happens now?" Tony found that the warmth and freedom of the company made her as bold as if she were talking to her sisters. "Miss Coleman's never going to buy a fleet of planes. She'll never start a school for colored pilots." Tony blinked back tears. "She'll never show that newsreel to another school or answer another Physics Club's questions about aerobatics."

"Well, shoot, girl," said Wade Vencill. "You can find out about aerobatics yourself, for a start. Just ask these fellas what you want to know."

"You got the jump on Miss Coleman," Myrtle Vencill said gently. "Don't you know you make your own luck?"

Tony was trying too hard not to cry to force a smile. "My momma says that too. But I don't get what you mean."

"You won't have to go to France to get someone to teach you to fly, like Bessie Coleman did. She sowed the seeds of change herself. Her dream is not going to die with her. We are *all* going to keep Bessie Coleman's dream alive."

"We're so glad you came, Antonia," Louis Manning said quietly. "But it's a long way to come and a hard journey for a schoolgirl. You could have mailed that notebook here and saved your train fare. Why'd you do it?"

Tony looked around. She'd come because she wanted to find people who cared about Bessie Coleman *and* who understood the science and miracle of flight. And she'd found them. She'd come for this.

For this. For this one evening under the electric light where her skin and being a girl didn't matter one bean. For these people whose heads were full of airspeed and wind speed and engine power and Bernoulli's principle. For the woman with a heart big enough to mourn two different people because they were both flying high and came to earth hard. To know that in some people's eyes, the only color was the sky behind you.

She looked around at the friendly faces waiting for her response.

"I wanted to meet the people who'd sell an airplane to a Negro woman," she told them honestly.

The Vencills laughed. The black and white pilots around the table answered nearly in one voice. "Here we are!"

Tony didn't literally leave the ground. But something inside her began to take flight.

🕸 Author's Note 🕸

This story is based on the true events surrounding the death of the pilot Bessie Coleman, the first black woman to gain a pilot's license and the first American, black or white, male or female, to earn an international pilot's license. Four enormous funerals were held for her in three different cities after her tragic death in 1926, a testimony to how deeply she'd won people's hearts.

Except for Tony and her family, most of the named characters in this work of fiction are drawn from real people: Myrtle and Henry Wade Vencill, Louis Manning, William Wills, John Thomas Betsch, and of course Bessie Coleman. I have put words into their mouths based on what little I know about them. I hope I have respected my characters' historical counterparts.

For the full story of Bessie Coleman's life, try *Queen Bess: Daredevil Aviator* by Doris L. Rich.

Bonnie and *Clyde*

Saundra Mitchell

C ALEB NEWCASTLE HAS WANTED ME since I turned thirteen. That's when I robbed my first bank.

He was only fifteen then, not even a real lawman. His daddy deputized him, and he was the cock of the walk after that.

Sitting up in a pecan tree, I watched him strut back and forth in the woods. His gun drawn, his hat tipped back, he stalked me. Eighteen now, he was cut out of all-American cloth, his blue eyes sharp and his long legs swift.

Too bad for him, and lucky for me, he didn't have the sense God gave a goose. If he'd looked up, even once, he'd have seen me. I'd picked a bad tree to climb. It wasn't real tall, and it didn't have a lot of leaves. Usually, my escapes were cleaner than this. I'd been caught off guard—Caleb had showed up while I was still in the bank this time. He got the jump on me, and I *still* got away. Which made it especially sad, the way he was carrying on.

Back and forth he went beneath me, until he lost his temper. Throwing his hat, he kicked a cottonwood tree. All he got for that was a stubbed toe and a shower of dead leaves.

I pressed myself flat against the trunk of my pecan and tried real hard to hold still. To keep from laughing, I bit down on the heel of my hand.

It was hard, though. He was cussing up a storm on account of nobody could hear him do it. In town, he was always saying "gol'dangit" and "dadblame"—he wanted people to think he was a moral authority. Butter wouldn't melt in that mouth, he'd have liked you to think.

Well, I had news for him. God could hear him cussing when he thought he was alone. And when he was alone, Caleb Newcastle's mouth was *filthy*.

Sometimes, though, his mouth was sweet as lemonade. Just right for a stolen kiss behind the church, or down the lane where nobody could see. Probably, he wouldn't want to kiss me if he knew I was number-one Most Wanted in Posey County. That would be his loss, though. Mine too, I guess. When he wasn't being awful, he was downright delicious.

Caleb stuffed his gun in the holster. Then he retrieved his hat. Didn't look a bit ashamed about his tantrum, but that's because he didn't know I was watching.

Shifting, I tried to get comfortable on my branch. It seemed like I'd need to settle in for a while. Then, the second of two things happened that just about ruined my day.

The branch I was on cracked.

It rained pecans down on Caleb's head. Hilarious. At least until he looked up. I wasn't caught quite yet, but I sure was spotted.

(The first thing came this morning—I read about Bonnie Parker and Clyde Barrow getting ventilated on a back road in

Bienville Parish, Louisiana. It's not that I approved of their shooting and killing people, I just did not. But I felt a certain kinship to Bonnie, being that we were sisters in crime.)

At the moment, that was their problem and I had plenty of my own.

Caleb knew I was there. There weren't no point in pretending I was a bird. From the bandanna around my face to the laces on my shoes, it was evident that I wasn't nesting. Gruffing up my voice, I raised my hat in a friendly hello.

"You kiss your mama with that mouth?" I asked.

Caleb cussed again and started up the tree. Now, the fact was, it wasn't much of a tree to begin with. From the cracking, he should have been able to tell that it was barely holding my weight, let alone his. But lack of sense and righteous indignation sent him shinnying up after me. That fool tried to pull out his gun as he climbed.

"You're under arrest," he informed me.

With a grin he couldn't see, I said, "No, I ain't."

The tree groaned once, then snapped. I crashed to the ground. A hail of pecans pelted me, leaves and bark and God knows what else raining down at the same time. I gaped like a goldfish out of a bowl, trying to catch my wind. But since I was down, and Caleb was tangled in the branches, this was my chance.

Scrambling to my feet, I stopped long enough to laugh at him. Then I hitched up the hem of my pants and bolted. Everybody always said I had long legs like a colt. Most of the time, they said it when they could admire them under my skirt. It was a shame none of 'em saw me run. I was just exactly like a foal, wild and free. Jumping everything. Barely looking back.

A shot echoed through the woods.

That cake-eating dog was shooting at me!

This posed a problem, what with him having a real gun and me without. Out of principle, I didn't carry one. If I ever got caught, I figured the judge would go easier on me if he realized I was never armed. If I wanted to hurt a bank teller, I guess I woulda had to take off a shoe and hit him with it.

Caleb fired again. I skidded down a hill. Brambles bit my hands. Thorns caught my clothes, and I was gonna have a hell of a time explaining this to my mama when I got home. Another shot hit the tree right next to me. Splinters flew, and my heart stopped. I didn't like to be pessimistic, but I was afraid I wasn't gonna make it home alive for Mama to take a strip off of me.

Nope, not acceptable. I knew the Wabash River wasn't too far. If I made it there, I could lose Caleb. Ducking another shot, I tried to count real quick. Was that three bullets or four? Did he have three left or two?

I decided it was two, because that was better odds for me. Grabbing a rock off the ground, I heaved it into the distance. As soon as Caleb shot in that direction, I took off running. I know I'm supposed to be a good girl. I know I'm supposed to be happy doing needlework samplers and baking potatoes in coals and whatnot.

But Lord, I love running from the law.

Now, I reckon some would say it ain't moral to rob a bank. I'd say I didn't have a choice.

Things had been going pretty good for my little family. Daddy was a supervisor over at the mill, and Mama made pin money selling eggs out our back door. Our pantry was full enough, our bellies round enough, our sleep sweet enough.

We were a lucky-sad family on account of my being an only child. Mama and Daddy always meant to have a houseful. It just never came to be.

I suppose, come fall of 1929, that was a good thing. One October Wednesday, Daddy come home from the mill with a gray face and lines on his brow. A bunch of fellas up in New York City lost *fourteen billion* dollars. I didn't see how you could misplace a number with that many zeroes, but Daddy said it blew no good wind.

Dinner was fried chicken, collard greens, and silence. Once that news was lying on the table, it took up all the air in our little house.

I was only ten then, so I didn't understand. By 1931, I understood.

Nobody but banks had any money left. People had to scrabble. They couldn't buy lumber for houses or fences or chicken coops, and the mill closed down. Mama still had her pin money, because chickens eat what they find. But it wasn't nothing close to Daddy's salary.

Swan's Holler wasn't a big town, so Daddy started hitching rides to the next town over, and then the next. He looked and looked for a job that nobody could offer him.

Mama let out my Sunday dress. Then she sewed a stripe out of the rag bag along the hem to get it back to my knees. I wasn't the only patchwork girl in town, neither. Things were rough all over, and only got worse when the new banker came.

The old one, Mr. Pickery, was big on grace. He understood didn't nobody have any money. Everybody wanted to pay their loan receipts, but they couldn't. He said, all right, maybe next month. And Mama would say, I just fried a chicken: you take some home to Eugenie. It went on that way for months, Mama sending Mr. Pickery away with eggs or chicken or soda bread instead of money.

By the end of the year, Mr. Pickery moved on to his final reward. The way my parents said that, I got the impression it was a trip he neither wanted nor deserved to take.

Then a new fella showed up to run the bank. His face was gaunt and his accent corvine. According to my mama, that means "like a crow," and she went all the way to eighth grade, so you can believe it. It likewise tells you everything you need to know about Mr. Shepherd. On our front step (he refused to come inside), he cawed about interest and payments and wouldn't take any of Mama's good food home.

That was a bad sign, Mama said. She wasn't wrong.

Mr. Shepherd called in all the loans in Swan's Holler. All at once. The Cunninghams lost their house first. That didn't sit right with anybody, because Jesse Cunningham built that house with his two hands and owned it outright. I guess they'd used it against a loan for a new tractor, though. Least that's what I gathered from hushed conversations my parents had when they thought I was sleeping upstairs.

The Cunninghams had six boys, and they worked a piece of land right outside town. Always had. We thought they always would too. But we were wrong. The next thing we all knew, the Cunningham pew was empty at First Calvary, and the bank auctioned off the tractor and the house both.

After them come the Stricklands, who were sharecropping. They didn't own the land they farmed; they rented it. The problem was, the landowner got stripped to the skin in the stock market crash. He stopped paying his receipts, and Mr. Shepherd turned up with two police officers to run the Stricklands off their plot. They had beans and corn in, and the bank let those rot.

Plenty of us kids snuck over in the middle of the night and filled our shirts with what we could carry. There was only so much we could haul off in the dark, though. It made Daddy so mad he went hard silent every time we walked past that field full of ruined crops.

Pretty soon, Swan's Holler was more ruined than not. The couple stores we had closed up. The families I grew up with faded out one by one. Boys joined the army; girls run off to get married—everybody hoped there was something better somewhere else.

It was the same all over—our town in Indiana, yours wherever you are, all them ones out in dusty, dusty Kansas. The money dried up. The work did too.

Finally, so did the people. They turned into husks, blown away by bad fortune. It was hard times, and we all knew who to blame.

The bankers. The fancy money men up in New York who gambled when the rest of us knew gambling was a sin. Herbert damned Hoover too—at least him we run out of office. Roosevelt promised us a New Deal when he got elected, but so far all we had was a raw deal.

And Mr. Shepherd on our doorstep.

I stood behind Mama, one hand in the middle of her back. I was propping her up, because I could feel her shaking. It made me nervous too, but I was trying to be grown. So I glared over her shoulder while Mr. Shepherd handed over legal papers. I listened while he explained that what we had due was *due,* and we had two weeks to come up with it. Valiantly, I thought, I did not punch him in the face when Mama started to cry.

That's when I knew I had to do something. I had to fix this for my family. And since I knew who was to blame, I knew what I'd do. I wound a bandage around my new breasts, put on my daddy's pants and suspenders, and whittled a gun out of scrap wood. Then I hitched a ride to Boswell and robbed their bank at lunchtime. It wasn't fair, those bankers calling everything due and hoarding all our money.

By God, I was gonna set it right.

Now, here's a puzzle.

Is it better to jump a hundred feet into a river and hope you don't hit the rocks? Or is it wiser to turn yourself in when you're about caught?

Well, I don't know from wise, but I knew the banks of the Wabash were hungry. Sharp limestone jutted all around it, gnashing for a bite of somebody foolish enough to get close. Or damned fool enough to jump in blind.

Of the many things I cared to be, a fool wasn't one of them. Therefore, I did the next best thing and got as low as I could. Down in the weeds, covered in poison ivy, my nose pressed to the ground, I didn't dare breathe deep.

No matter what lying arithmetic I figured, I had no idea how many bullets Caleb had left. Since he was determined to chase me all over creation, I figured I'd better use the one advantage I had over him: I was a little bit smarter than a sack of hair.

Flattening out on the ground, I grabbed an exposed root. Then I dragged myself slowly forward.

Caleb crested the hill I'd slid down, then stopped. Gun raised, he looked all up and down, searching for me. I could tell from the way his eyes darted back and forth that he hadn't spotted me. Otherwise, I might have believed his bluff.

"Come on, Baby Boy," he called, tromping a few feet closer. "Nobody has to get hurt. Just come on out."

That's right, that's what they called me. Baby Boy Wabash.

Unlike some bank robbers, I went out of my way to keep my real name to myself.

Since I was knocking over banks in boys' clothes all up and down the western border of Indiana, the newspapers picked a name for me. Baby Boy because I was small, I imagine. Wabash because I didn't stray far from the river when I was working.

It didn't have much of a ring to it. But it wasn't too bad. It emphasized who he was, and who I wasn't.

Caleb tried again. "Please don't make me hurt you. I don't wanna make your mama cry."

Aww, that was sweet. Like hell was I coming out, but I had to give him credit for trying. Sweat pooled in the small of my back and in the backs of my knees. Already, I was itching. If I didn't get that poison ivy washed off soon, I'd be a sight at the church social. Even Caleb might manage some simple addition: *Yesterday, I was chasing a bank robber through the woods. Today, my girl's covered in bruises and blisters. Hmmm.*

Nah, I was giving him too much credit. That was the beauty of being a girl going around in boys' clothes. Nobody saw you. When I hitched rides, nobody warned me it was dangerous. Likewise, when I walked into a bank and ordered them to give me what was in the drawer, they did it. Now, fair enough, they probably did that in part because I jabbed the wood gun in my pocket at them.

Still, I knew what kind of attention a bandit got when she was a member of the fairer sex. Bonnie Parker looked real pretty sitting on the hood of that Ford Fordor, I had to admit. But she was shot dead on a lonely back road because everybody knew her too well and too many people wanted to take her and Clyde out.

Here's the thing: I didn't want to be famous. I just wanted to take care of my folks.

Mama thought I was off helping a lady doctor deliver babies. Daddy believed that too. Maybe it's because they wanted to.

When I went to the bank and paid off our loan, I warned Mr. Shepherd not to come back to our door ever again. We were done doing business with his like. From here on out, we'd be keeping our savings in our mattress. Where it was safe. Where sons of bitches like him couldn't *lose* it in one afternoon.

I was careful to never give Mama too much money. Sometimes I bought a live chicken or a canned ham and told her that was my payment. Quietly, I left ten-dollar bills in my neighbors' mailboxes and back porch doors.

The funny thing is, the rumor never got around. Even while I Robin Hooded it up, the people in Swan's Holler clamped down tight. It was like they were afraid if anyone knew they had money, it would melt away. Fool's gold, mayhaps.

Caleb got tired of staring and waiting. Without holstering his gun, he started sideways down the hill. His path put him on course to step on me if he kept going. I had to run. There was no way to drag myself out of the way fast enough. Excitement gave in to fear.

This was the first time in three years robbing banks that I was close to caught.

Blood rushing in my ears, mouth dry as a desert, I didn't have the luxury of weighing my options anymore. Closer and closer, Caleb stalked. So close, I smelled his cologne. My idiot stomach fluttered some. It needed to knock it off. This wasn't the time or place to be sweet on Caleb Newcastle, no matter how good his sweat and skin smelled.

I figured my best bet was to scare the socks off of him and then run as fast as I could. Pressing hands and knees into the soft forest floor, I hitched back. Taking a deep breath, I popped up like a jack-in-the-box. Only *my* jack-in-the-box screamed like a banshee. Caleb shouted too, and pumped off another shot. Something hot streaked over my shoulder.

The time for rumination was over. Money washed and dried just fine. So did I. I bolted for the edge of the river. It was dark and green, shaded by the trees. Guarded by sharp stones all the way down.

With one held breath, I jumped.

It turns out that after you jump, you wanna change your mind.

Unfortunately, by then, gravity has done made up your mind for you. There was no backing up on this one. It was me and empty air. Plummeting. Falling. The river slapped me hard when I hit it. My ribs hurt, like I'd run too far. The strength drained from my arms and legs. They were weights, pulling me down.

I sank deep, swallowed by cold water the color of a patent medicine bottle. It tasted like medicine too, herbs and mud and all manner of things dying and living and doing what all ever in it.

At first, I didn't even try to swim. My hips hurt like I'd yanked off both legs at the joint. Skin burning from hitting the water so hard, head dizzy and blank from terror, I floated down below. Beneath the surface.

Raising my face, I saw sunlight. At least I knew which way was up. Not a damned bit of good that would do me if I didn't get some air. The thing was, it was kinda pleasant down below. I wasn't hot or itchy anymore. My body was a limp thing, buoyed lazily on a current. It would have been real easy to give in. Give up. Sink all the way down and anchor myself in the mud for all time.

My parents would think I'd run off. Got a wild hair and never looked back. That was a cruel thing to do to a body. Seeing as I was Mama and Daddy's only, twice as cruel in my case. I started robbing banks to save them. I couldn't let it ruin them.

I suppose disappearing would have been better than getting arrested by Caleb Newcastle. Or anybody, for that matter.

A beacon of pain pulsed in my shoulder. That boy *shot* me. My lungs burned, and spangles flashed in front of my eyes. Swim or die, I told myself. Swim right now and run on home. Put some money in the neighbors' mailboxes. Tell Mama we delivered twins to some rich city people and they gave us a hundred dollars because they were burning them for warmth.

Up, up, and out of the water and back to Swan's Holler. Into the Pings' barn, trade out my robbing clothes for my good-girl dress, and get back to life. Get to the church social. Eat pound cake, talk with Maisie, let Caleb put his hand on my hip.

He wasn't so bad. Mostly he was pretty good. Emphasis on the pretty, and sweet to me too. He brought Mama flowers and talked to Daddy about the weather. He didn't blush when people joked we'd be married before twenty.

Up!

My head pounded, but I finally connected it back to my arms and legs. Scrambling and clawing at the water, I fought to the surface. Once I did, I hit a big old branch hanging low. It knocked the stars right into my eyes. I sunk under again, then remembered that I had planned to survive today.

Up!

It was so sweet, breathing. I had river in my nose, and my shoes were lost in the current, but I was alive. If there wasn't a chance of Caleb sighting me from the shore and shooting me for good, I woulda whooped.

Instead, I took a mouthful of water, then spat it. I breathed, and I swam. When the water went shallow, I hauled myself up. Bandy-legged, I staggered along the rocky bank.

It was a good thing I only ever asked for what was in the drawer. If I'd been greedy, carrying as much money as I could manage, I woulda lost it all, or drowned saving it. Pulling the powder sack from around my neck, I loosened the leather strings. Coiled up like baby snakes, greenbacks nestled down in the dark.

They were wet, but they were still mine.

Mama didn't believe me when I said that a rich lady with twins gave me a hundred dollars.

Lips tight, eyes narrow, she grabbed my chin between her fingers. Turning my head back and forth, she scoured me with suspicion.

In the end, she said to go wash the stink off and come help with supper. She looked me up and down, then folded the damp bills into the box where she kept her pin money.

Tucked up in some privacy, I washed myself best as I could from a pitcher. Studying myself in the mirror, I said, "You look a fright." Because I did, bedraggled and scratched, but whole.

Mostly whole, actually. There was a little half-moon taken right out of my shoulder. My first gunshot wound and, God willing, my last. It looked almost like a burn and didn't smell a thing like gunpowder. That kind of disappointed me, to be frank.

Dinner was biscuits and gravy. Sleep that night was good and hard and deep. And in the morning, I put on my patchwork dress and let Mama braid and twist my hair into a chignon. Baby Boy Wabash was sitting in the Pings' barn, filthy shirt and suspenders stuffed behind a bale of hay. Marjorie May Johnson was putting on a touch of her mama's rose water and striking poses in the front room.

The knock at the door startled me. I was still jumpy from my close call, but I had to slough that off. Daddy opened the door. With a big, booming voice, he invited Caleb inside and asked after his granny. She'd been sick with a fever, but according to Caleb, she was all better now. Once he finished yammering with my daddy, Caleb finally turned to look at me.

When he did, his blue eyes widened. He clutched his hat against his chest, his blond hair falling in messy waves across his brow. Not one inch of him looked worse for the wear. If anything, his golden tan made him glow. It deepened the pink of his lips. It reminded me why I let him be forward with me. Why I liked it when he clasped his hands against my waist and pulled me tight.

In fact, that's exactly what I let him do as soon as he got me out the door and down the street a little. Wrapping my arms around his neck, I drank him up — sweet, sweet lemonade. When he picked me up, I laughed in surprise as he spun me around. Then, like I was delicate, he put me back on my feet.

"You gonna dance with me at this social?" he asked, slipping my arm through the loop of his.

With a champagne bubble laugh, I said, "I just might."

We walked on, side by side, and I was happy. I robbed banks, I ran from the law — and then I ran right into his arms, once I turned from boy to girl again.

The way I saw it, that was the real mistake the Barrow gang had made.

It seemed to me that they'd have been a lot less likely to get gunned down if Bonnie had just had the sense to *be* Clyde.

❧ *Author's Note* ❧

When I was invited to write a story for *A Tyranny of Petticoats,*
I had two ideas. One was a murder mystery—I've written that
kind of thing before. The other was a cross-dressing, bank-
robbing teen bandit on the run. I've never written that kind of
thing before. How to choose, how to choose? As Mae West once
said, I went with the evil I'd never tried before.

There's a fine tradition of cross-dressing girls in fiction,
from Alanna in Tamora Pierce's Song of the Lioness novels
to Mary Faber in L. A. Meyer's Bloody Jack series. I love the
twists and turns, the constant tension, and the total subversion
of expectations these stories offer. I hope that you find my
story "Bonnie *and* Clyde" a worthy addition to the world of
adventurous historical girls in pants!

Hard Times

Katherine Longshore

WHEN THERE'S FOOD AROUND, A hobo jungle is like a high-school wiener roast—everybody huddled into groups, laughing and eating and talking about each other. Pretending the real world isn't out there, just beyond the tree line and across the tracks.

This world feels as small as my little Nebraska town did, but in this ragged piece of shade on the banks of the Columbia River, I am a misfit.

I'm not the youngest—there's a handful of teenage boys by the fire, and I've got Billy waiting for me way back near a thicket of huckleberries—but I am the only girl. To look at me, none would call me feminine, but I can feel the men watch as I pass.

I saw two of them at the orchard this morning. They got into a dustup because only ten pickers were hired and there were thirty of us. They're all friends now, though, bolstered by alcohol squeezed from Sterno cooking gel.

There's no work here and I've got nothing to add to the pot of mulligan stew—not even an onion—so I need to get Billy and get out. I don't want to be around when the canned heat fuels more than just loud voices and swagger.

I don't see Billy or his bindle, and worry rises in my throat, dry as the dust bowl winds. Billy's just a kid and as annoying as all get-out, but we stick together.

There's someone else back by the huckleberry thicket, though. I know him for a hoaxter as soon as I spot him, sitting on a fallen tree with his legs stretched out, deliberately nonchalant. His pants are pressed, and though his shirt's unbuttoned at the collar, it's clean. He's got a hat pulled low on his forehead and the thinnest mistake of a mustache I've ever seen.

He thinks he's Clark Gable in *It Happened One Night*.

A flash of blue and brown catches my eye before Billy catches me right in my midsection and knocks me to the dirt.

"Where've you been?" he cries. "I've been waiting!"

I bite back an uncharitable reply and hug him quick till I see Gable watching. Then I push Billy off. He's little, but he's twelve. When I was twelve, I was already taking care of my three sisters, before they got scattered to relatives.

He can't replace them.

"I got something," he says, his dirty, blond hair flopping right into his eyes.

"You need a haircut."

He pulls it back with one hand so I can see his baby blues and the smear of dirt across his forehead. "I like it this way." He sets his chin like Celia used to at home.

I shrug and stagger to my feet, bone weary from hard traveling.

Billy coughs but grins around it. He's the reason we're heading west, toward the ocean. Toward Seattle. Hopefully toward work. Away from the dust that brings on his asthma.

Billy unwraps his bindle carefully, like what he's got there is precious.

And it is. It's a feast. Bread and apples and cheese and something that looks suspiciously like—

"Roast beef," Billy says proudly.

My mouth waters.

We can't eat it here. Much as I'd like to add to the mulligan, this beef would cause a riot. I glance over my shoulder. No one's looking—not even Gable. I wrap the food quickly and stuff it back into the bindle.

"How did you ever do it?" I whisper. The men at the orchard said times were hard. No work. No money. No food.

"I went into town just like you said," he rattles. I try to quiet him, but there's no hushing Billy once he starts talking. "I stood on a street corner. There's folks everywhere. And just like you said, when I saw a lady wearing gloves, I sat down on the curb and I put my head in my hands and I told her the story you said to tell."

"It's your story, Billy." I look over at Gable again. He's studying his fingernails.

"The way you tell it is better." Billy puts on a sad, mewling voice that makes him sound younger. *"We lost our farm in . . ."*—he hesitates—*"foreclosure, and my pop just up and left. He fought in the War and thought he could get his bonus and find some work and feed us all, but he never came back from Washington."*

I nod. He's doing pretty good. Laying it on a little thick.

"So I came out to find work!" he crows.

I rub his head, making the hair flop back into his eyes, and he grins up at me like I'm better than roast beef, and for a second things don't seem so hard. Then someone starts clapping.

I spin around, keeping Billy and his treasure behind me.

Gable stands up, all knobs and limbs, one side of his mouth turned up and his hat still riding low, and he's slapping his hands together like he's not applauding but condemning.

"Excellent performance." He touches his fingers to his hat but doesn't tip it. Doesn't remove it.

He watches me to see if it stings that he didn't acknowledge me as a lady. I don't let him see that it does.

I left home in skirts and saddle oxfords but quickly learned that you can't jump a moving train with all that fabric flapping about or keep your feet warm in handsome shoes. Now I wear pilfered dungarees and a dead boy's boots.

Billy huddles behind me, hands on my waist, forehead dug deep into the center of my back. He tries to hide it, but Billy cries at night, trying to cuddle close because I'm quiet and soft and have never once given him a backhand smack like some of the men do. Like he's some rangy cur trying to snatch food from under their noses.

I can't let him get close and I can't let him cuddle, so I step away. Just because I've got soft curves doesn't mean I can get soft.

"It wasn't a show." I don't let my gaze waver from Gable's.

"Oh, yes, it was," he says with a foxy smile.

I feel utterly exposed. I don't look to see if the drunks with the greasy beards and hands stained pink with Sterno are watching us.

"It's the truth!" Billy says. "My pop was in the army. He fought in the War. And old Hoover would've just let him starve."

When Billy sticks up for himself, he sounds like me. Like he's sixteen and already weary of the world. Shame he can't keep his presidents straight.

"Roosevelt's president now," I remind him.

"I know that." Billy frowns at me. "*Hoover* would have let us starve. It's why we lived in a *Hooverville*."

I knew that Billy'd had it rough, but I hadn't realized his family had lived in one of those cardboard shantytowns. It makes me wonder what else I don't know about him.

Gable stoops to look Billy in the eye. "Telling a true story in a way that pulls heartstrings is a fair talent." He turns to me. "I should know. I'm a journalist."

The way he says it makes me laugh. All serious, like he really believes it.

"You're a newsboy?"

His mouth twists. "I'm a reporter."

That makes me laugh harder.

"I work for the *Wenatchee World*." He steps too close, his jaw clenched like he's ready to fight.

I'm not afraid of this showboat, but I take a step back anyway. "There's grown men in this jungle can't find work breaking their backs to build a dam. And you're telling me you earn a living with your words?"

He bites his lip. Only for a second, but long enough to tell me I've caught him in a lie.

"I have an article due next week," he says. I don't know if it's me he's trying to convince or himself.

"Bully for you." I raise an eyebrow to let him know I'm not impressed.

He stills. Suddenly, like a thought just struck him. He cocks his head to one side, looking more like Clark Gable than ever, and looks at me appraisingly.

"I'm investigating the migrant workers," he says.

Investigating doesn't sound good. I can already see the slander-ridden story he'll write for his rag, all about how we get fat and lazy on roast beef earned by sob stories while the rest of the country is hard at work.

"Migrant workers." I snort, trying to sound like I don't care. "You mean hobos."

"My dad—" He curses under his breath. "My *boss* wants to know what they're doing here."

There's the lie. He doesn't have to earn a living. But I can't begrudge anyone getting a job from his father. I'd be washing towels and sweeping hair in my dad's barbershop if he hadn't lost it in this damned depression. My dad, with his badger hair shaving brush and straight razor, covering his customer's face with sandalwood foam.

"Better get on with it, then," I mutter.

"There was an article about . . . about hobos in the *New York Times*."

"And you think you can do better?"

"It says there's a million men out on the rails in America." He's nothing if not persistent.

"A million men, eh?" I turn away. "Well, you've no need to talk to me."

"I want a different angle. You could tell me what it's like for a girl."

I could. I could tell him exactly what it's like for a girl. The lewd propositions and surreptitious pinches. The skepticism and mistrust. But that would just give him what he wants—a sordid headline with me as the poor featherheaded victim.

"I'd like to get a quote from this little man too." Gable ruffles Billy's hair.

I thought Billy was shielded behind me, but here he is, grinning up at this swindler like he's God's own mouthpiece. My throat pinches up tight.

"You want to pull your readers' heartstrings," I say to Gable.

He nods and shrugs, copping the blame.

"We were just on our way out." I push the parcel of food into Billy's chest and keep going, clutching his elbow when he stumbles a little.

"Don't you want the whole world to know your story?" Gable calls. He hasn't moved. He thinks we'll sell our souls for a few lines of print.

"You mean the *Wenatchee World*?" I turn to look him right in the eye.

This time he colors. I'd taken him for twenty, but he can't be more than eighteen. That little mustache is just a few well-tended hairs.

He clears his throat. "Pull on the right heartstrings and you might change your circumstances."

I'd leap at the chance if it were possible. But bad luck is as much a part of chance as good. Just like a freight train, you have to trust before you leap.

I shrug. "I have my own ways of changing my circumstances."

His gray eyes narrow, and the skin around them crinkles like he's smiling—or judging. "And what are those?"

The train answers for me—a lingering, forthright blast of the whistle.

I nod my head in the direction of the tracks and grin. "There's my summons."

I grab Billy's hand and walk away.

"Just let me ask you a couple of questions."

I'll be John Browned if he's not following us. "Ask away," I toss over my shoulder.

"Can you at least hold still?"

"No, sir, mister!" Billy shouts, catching on to my game. "We've got a train to catch!"

The westbound freight idles in the yard. The men at the orchard said it was due, and for once, luck is with me. There's even a boxcar with its door wide open in welcome, waiting right in front of us.

And there's no one inside.

Billy scrambles in and I follow, turning around to catch Gable staring, open-mouthed. "You want me to hop a train?" he asks.

"If you want this story, *you* want to hop a train." I pull a hammered spike out of my pocket and wedge it under the runners of the door.

Gable watches me, his hands on the boxcar floor, his feet still firmly on the ground.

"The spike keeps it from closing," I tell him. "You never know when it will open again. Besides, a moving door could take a man's arm off."

He plucks his hands back like he's been burned and tucks his chin.

Good.

Though it would have been nice to talk to someone besides Billy for a change.

I tell myself Gable's just like the boys back home. All swagger and charm, pitying my stupidity and innocence because I'm a girl with nothing in my curly-haired head but fashion and romance. But I know more than this so-called reporter. I'm more worldly-wise. More brave.

He doesn't walk away. He takes a breath—I see his chest rise—and looks at me.

"If I do this, if I take this train with you, I need you to agree to answer my questions." He's so serious. "My job depends on it."

But not his life. "Even if it's your father's paper?"

He presses his lips together. Looks away. "He can't afford a reporter who doesn't pull his weight." His chest rises again and his gaze meets mine. "He says it's time I make my own way. I don't get this story, I might as well stick with riding the rails."

I don't know if it's truth or if he's spinning a tale, but two toots of the train's whistle tell me we're about to move, so impulsively I stick out my hand. He stares at it for a thin slice of a second, and I can read on his face the backwardness of it all. Then he takes it, warm and sure, and neatly makes the leap into my domain.

We settle back into the dark corner of the boxcar as the engine starts to roar. I met one old hobo who said he loved the sound of the engine picking up every car, the shudder that runs the length of the train with each one. I've always felt like it was the footsteps of an approaching giant, thunderous and threatening.

When the train's under way, Gable takes out a little notepad and pen. "So what do they call you?"

No one asks that. They ask what kind of work I do. Why such a pretty little thing is out here. Wonder in their minds if I sell myself in pieces.

None of them ask my name.

It's been so long since I've said my own name, I can't find the sound of it on my tongue.

"What do they call *you*?" I retort.

"Lloyd."

I don't tell him he looks like Clark Gable.

"Curls."

My hated hobo moniker. It calls to mind soft things. Sickly-sweet things. Like Shirley Temple and velvet ribbons. Who I was then, not who I am now.

"It suits you."

I glare at him. "Unlike your mustache."

He lays the tips of his fingers along his upper lip, and I feel something almost like conscience.

"I'm Billy!" He pushes himself between us. "Billy the Kid." He stares at Lloyd's pen and paper, waiting for his name to be written down in all its glory. Lloyd looks over Billy's head at me and winks.

"And why are you out here?" When Lloyd smiles, it's like Billy's the only person he's ever wanted to talk to. Like he's been waiting his whole life for it. He's suited to his profession—his smile could make folks confess any manner of secrets.

"Hard times, mister!" Billy says. "Hard times!"

It's what all of us say. Why else would you risk life and limb, blowing across the country and back? Risking railroad bulls who would throw you headfirst off a moving train and sheriffs who'd sling you in jail till even your mother forgets your name? There's some out here who seek adventure, I suppose, though I can't find sense in that.

"Why are you here?" I ask. I could spend all night just tossing Gable's questions back at him. "You're not looking for any old story, are you?"

"My father thinks the migrants are a menace," Lloyd says. "That they'll bring fighting and robbery, that the . . . the women of Wenatchee won't be safe to walk the streets. He wants me to write a story to convince the city council to raze the campsite where you all stay."

"The jungle," I correct him, fearful for the men celebrating food, unaware the town will destroy them, leaving behind nothing but a chalk-drawn symbol warning others it's yet another place where it's not safe to stay.

"What do *you* think?" I look at him directly. His gray eyes turn blue just at the center. I find myself holding my breath.

"I asked for the job."

My breath comes out in a rush. "Did you talk to the men?"

Lloyd looks away. "No," he says. "I was afraid of them."

This unvarnished truth makes me squirm. Part of me wants to reach out to comfort him, like I would with Billy. The other part knows fear is like fire. It only takes a spark—like a newspaper article—to create a conflagration.

"They're desperate," I say finally. "No work. No food."

His pen is poised. Ready. "Are you scared?"

All the time.

But I can't say it, even in the wake of his confession, because it would mean admitting that the men are dangerous, deserving of fear, when all they want is a chance.

"No. We're all the same."

Lloyd studies me and I stare back. The longer he looks, though, the softer his face gets, until suddenly his eyebrows pinch forward and he looks down at Billy.

"I've heard that most ride the rails for six months," Lloyd says. "Then they go home. How long have you been out here?"

Billy looks up at me. Time isn't his strongest suit.

"I met Billy seven weeks ago," I say. "I've been out here eight. I think your information is wrong. Nobody can go back to how it was. The dust bowl dried us all up bitter as seeds and spat us out all over the land, and none of us yet has taken root."

Lloyd looks up from his pen, eyes wide.

"Can I use that?" he asks. "What you just said?" He clears his throat. "As a quote, of course."

"Why?"

"Because it's good. The way you said it. That'll grab their attention. Make them care."

I shrug, but warmth grows in my chest at his praise.

"And what is a girl doing out here?" he asks, looking up at me quick and then back down at his pen.

I wonder if he means *what kind of girl?*

I look back on the one I was — carefully modulated hair skin skirt shoes voice — and it's like she's not even me. The one who dreamed of being a teacher right up to the day the school ran out of money and closed its doors. There was nothing left to teach because hardship took it all.

I want to tell him that the bank took Dad's shop and his will to live. That Mama needed more money and fewer mouths to feed and that my leaving has only achieved one of those things. But I say nothing, because I don't want pity.

Out here on the rails, I've learned to keep my secrets close and my tongue still.

Lloyd glances around the boxcar, and his eyebrows pinch again. He must take my silence for refusal, because his questions change direction. "Where are you going?"

"There's no work here, so we're heading west."

"Seattle?"

"Maybe there's more in the city."

"Maybe there's just Skid Road."

That's a chance I have to take. "What do you care, as long as you get your story?"

"What about the New Deal programs? The CCC? Building dams and bridges and national parks?"

I snort. "It's for young *men*. There's many of us that don't qualify."

Billy shifts between us. It'll be five years before he can work for the Civilian Conservation Corps, and by then things will be better.

We hope.

Billy shifts again. Tugs my sleeve. "I'm hungry."

If we eat, we'd have to share. If not, I could spin a story, tug on Lloyd's heartstrings. Billy's used to hunger, but I bet Lloyd isn't. He could take that back to his readers.

But Billy dives into his bindle, pulling out meat and bread with a flourish, like he's a tuxedoed waiter in a Busby Berkeley movie instead of a scruffy kid in too-short pants. He tears off a hunk of meat and stuffs it in his mouth.

Inside, I cringe, but I keep my voice steady when I turn to Lloyd. "Join us. Hobos share when they can."

"You didn't back there." He jerks his head at the open door. At the men we left behind. To him, we're nothing but a couple of grifters, little better than thieves.

"Sorry, Rosie," Billy mumbles. "Forgot to share."

I close my eyes. Billy revealed our treasure and my real name in one fell swoop.

"It's all right," I tell him, and then mutter in Lloyd's direction, "We haven't eaten since yesterday."

Billy swallows. "No, *I* ate, remember? There was a potato left in the fire at the jungle before this one. You gave it to me this morning."

Now Lloyd'll think I'm soft. Why can't he just tell the *truth* in his blasted paper?

I divide the food into threes, but Lloyd puts a hand on my arm. It's warm, his touch gentle. "I've eaten."

I don't look at his gray-blue eyes when I force a piece of bread at him. "You don't know when you will again."

Darkness envelops us as we climb higher into the night. Billy answers all of Lloyd's questions, elaborating on the old stories. I only correct him when he fibs outright. Lloyd must know some kind of reporter shorthand so he can scrawl in the dark. He just lets Billy talk.

No one just lets Billy talk.

I turn my smile to the open door. The cold October wind gets colder, biting through the thick knit of my sweater—the one Mama made for Dad last Christmas. The din of the wheels on the tracks has the rhythm of a rope-skipping rhyme.

It builds the same kind of anticipation in me—that I'll make it to the end. That maybe something magical will happen if I do. Perhaps it's Lloyd's suggestion that talking to him could change my circumstances, but I'm starting to hope we'll find a place where I can stop moving.

"My aunt runs a boardinghouse in Ballard," Lloyd says. It takes me a second to realize he's talking to me.

"That near Seattle?" I ask. I try to sound casual. Like maybe I'll get a job. Like maybe I can afford a boardinghouse.

"It's *in* Seattle." Lloyd chuckles and I want to smack him. Like a girl from Nebraska would know that. "It's a neighborhood. She rents out mostly to fishermen. Scandinavians. She says it's . . . it's a hard life."

"Sounds like the jungle."

"She's getting overworked," he says. "Arthritis. She asked my father last time they spoke if he knew of someone who might help her run the place. Keep it clean, do the shopping and the cooking. It's not much, only room and board."

The thoughts stagger into my mind and I grasp at them. *His aunt. Boardinghouse. Looking to hire help.* It breathes life into that little spark of hope.

I lean toward him. "What are you saying?"

With a hollow *whoosh,* we're sucked into a profound darkness. The noise of the train is magnified, ringing back at us from all directions, like living inside the engine itself.

Billy wraps himself around me.

"It's a tunnel!" I shout, trying to disentangle him. He's been through tunnels before. They terrify him. I lean farther over, hoping Lloyd can hear me too. "We'll be out soon!"

But we're not. The train slows, still going up the mountain, but we're inside it. The air thickens with smoke and soot.

I reach into my back pocket for my bandanna. "Cover your face!" I shout to Lloyd. He scrambles beside us. I'm sure he has a handkerchief. He's just the type. I wonder if it's monogrammed. "Breathe through your bandanna!" I call into Billy's ear.

He lets go of me long enough to search for it, his movements getting more and more frantic. It's like a tunnel in a nightmare, deceitful and never-ending.

"I don't know where it is!" Billy screams. He's panicking, his little lungs like bellows beneath my hand.

I pat him down, searching his pockets, feeling through his bindle, fingers stumbling.

"Here!" I shove my bandanna over his nose as I crawl around him, finding dirt and sawdust, the paper-thin skins of onions that must have filled the boxcar before, the slick leather of Lloyd's shoe.

Lloyd's hand wraps around my wrist and drags me toward him. I pull back, but I'm off balance and I fall into his lap, a tangle of limbs and humiliation. I sit up quick and haul off to punch him when he covers my mouth with his handkerchief.

It smells like sandalwood. Like home.

"I'll be fine!" I push it back at him. "We'll be out before we know it."

He pulls me closer so he can talk in my ear without Billy hearing. "We're in the Cascade Tunnel." His voice is tight—no arrogance or judgment—and there's no smile in it at all. "It's the longest rail tunnel in North America."

A chill wraps around me.

"How long?"

He doesn't answer.

"Tell me!"

"Eight miles."

At the rate we're going, that could take a lifetime.

"Keep that over your face, Billy!" I shout, and pull him into me, as if my body will protect him. He's still coughing. Not wheezing yet.

Lloyd thrusts his handkerchief at me again, and this time I take it. I can't see him in the dark, but he's jostling, all elbows and quick movements. It's only when his shirt flaps against my face that I realize he's taken it off.

I'm reminded of *It Happened One Night*. Billy and I sneaked into the cinema somewhere in Idaho to see it. The real Clark Gable takes off his shirt, and the crowd was shocked into raucous outrage, which made me and Billy laugh like loons. We'd seen that and more in the jungles.

This is different.

Intimate.

Lloyd leans into me, his bare arm kissing my cheek.

"Use this instead!" he shouts. "It's thicker!"

He presses his shirt to my nose. It's warm and smells like coffee and Oxydol laundry soap—like radio serials and better times. I want to bury myself in it.

I cradle Billy between my knees, pressing the shirt to his face as well. Each breath he takes is a struggle I feel in my own chest. They come in time with the chug of the train, like the effort it takes is what's pulling us up the mountain. I count them, hoping to tick away the miles, feeling more helpless than I did the day the bank came knocking. More helpless than when I found my dad with the straight razor at his own throat.

Billy starts to wheeze.

"What's the matter with him?" Lloyd shouts.

"Asthma."

"Oh, God," Lloyd curses. "He's going to die in here."

He drops his forehead to my knee. Just another scared kid.

"He is *not!*" I shout.

I wrap my arms around both of them. Billy chokes on each teaspoon of air. The train shudders, howling with the effort to crawl its way out of this hole.

I think of the kids who came into Dad's shop for their first haircuts, screaming bloody murder in his cracked leather chair.

My dad talked to them the way you would a wild animal. Sat them still. Made them trust him.

That's the voice I find inside me.

"Breathe."

And we do.

"Breathe."

Even Billy.

The train launches from the mouth of the tunnel with a gasp like a drowning man, and the air freshens between gusts of soot and brimstone.

In the light of the fresh-risen moon, I can see Billy's face, the dark hollows of his eyes.

"Am I going to die?" He gasps.

"Not if I can help it."

And he believes me. He believes me enough to keep breathing.

I hold him close until the tension fades and he takes a long draft without it catching. I swipe at my eyes, my fingers gritty with soot and cinders.

"Well." I look at Lloyd. "I guess you've got the perfect string to pull for your story."

"It's your story."

"Yeah." I take a deep breath, my lungs no longer scalded by ash. "But you're the one getting paid to write it."

I give him back his shirt—smudged and blackened—and try not to watch as he puts it on. Try not to think about the clean, familiar scent of him pressed against me.

That's another thing these hard times have taken from me. The chance to have a beau.

"I won't get paid."

That snaps my attention back to his face. The corner of his mouth lifts in not-quite-a-smile.

"This is just a trial. To see if I can do it." Lloyd looks down at the notepad in his lap. "To see if I can write the story he wants."

"He wants you to write that the jungle is dangerous," I say. "That we're all criminals."

"I can't do that now." He flips over a page of notes, a long scrawl of Billy's words—and mine—across the paper. "I don't want to tell untruths because it's convenient or expected. I want to dig deep into the truth and aerate it so roots can take hold."

I try to believe in a world where the truth is fertile soil and not hot, dry dust spread fine by the winds.

He smiles again. "I've been looking for a chance to get out of Wenatchee, and I guess you gave it to me."

I start cramming things back into my bindle. Bandanna. A

crust of bread. My enameled tin cup. I look over at Billy, sound asleep and snoring, still a wheeze in his chest.

"You don't want to leave a good thing, Lloyd. This isn't any kind of life." I glare at him. "Don't you dare romanticize it."

He holds up both hands like I'm Public Enemy Number One, waving a pistol.

"I may be leaving bed and board," he says, "but I'm not leaving a good thing."

"Bed and board *are* a good thing!" I get up, unsteady in the sway of the train. "Don't you get that? A place to sleep and a guaranteed meal are all those million 'migrant workers' ask for. That and the satisfaction of a job well done—and the respect hard work deserves."

Lloyd looks up at me from where he sits against the wall, forearms resting on his knees. His eyes look black in the darkness.

"What if that respect and satisfaction are withheld?" he asks. "Are bed and board still worth it? Are times so hard we have to give up our dreams of making a better life?"

I thought I had. I thought the Depression had stolen the dreams I never knew existed because I had always taken them for granted—a warm bed, good food, friends, trust. Something to run toward instead of always running away.

A gust blows into the boxcar, thick with fog and a rich, humid, salty perfume. I walk shakily to the door and look out. Far in the distance, the earth flattens onto the horizon, the moon's glow doubled.

The ocean.

The end of the line.

That hope is still stuck tight in my chest, like a gasp of air swallowed hard.

I glance behind me, and Lloyd stands too. A hard rock of the boxcar throws him sideways, but he catches himself. Keeps his gaze on me.

He moves to stand beside me. Not touching.

"What are you looking for, Rosie?"

He says my name—my real name—and it cracks my chest open. For the first time in what seems like a lifetime, I feel like the girl I once was. Rose Marie Weaver. Book-smart and world-scared. Soft, maybe, but also optimistic.

Back then I believed that hard work moves you forward. Now I know you also have to grab luck before it passes you by.

I muster a deep breath because it takes a lungful to ask a favor.

"Would you introduce me to your aunt?"

"Yes," he says quickly, without even thinking. He ducks his chin to his chest. Embarrassed. "You trusted me, and I want . . . I'd like to know where to find you."

My heart stills.

He lifts his head. "I'd like to see you again."

"What about me?" Billy murmurs from the corner.

The quaver in my chest is like the flicker of a flame, and I laugh.

"Of course I'd want to see you, Billy," Lloyd says, but he's looking right at me. "If you think you can trust me too."

I can't speak. There are too many negatives. Too many questions. I've only just met this boy. I have to think of Billy. And Mama. And all the things these hard times have taken from me. All the things I've had to give up.

Except, perhaps, my dreams.

❦ *Author's Note* ❦

I was obsessed with movies and film history when I was young—spending hours in front of the television, watching classics like *It Happened One Night*, *The Thin Man*, and *The Gay Divorcee*. To me, it seemed the world of the thirties was populated by quick-witted detectives, rich heiresses, and honorable journalists. It was only after reading John Steinbeck's *The Grapes of Wrath* that I pictured a completely different scenario.

Two years ago, I came across a documentary film and accompanying book titled *Riding the Rails: Teenagers on the Move During the Great Depression* by Errol Lincoln Uys. I was captivated by the idea of the nearly quarter million teens who for many reasons left home and braved the dangers of the freight trains during the 1930s. The men and women who shared their stories decades later inspired me with their courage and resilience.

It seemed a natural progression to create a train-jumping teenager influenced by the very same movies I had watched and immerse her in a world of deprivation and danger. But I wanted to make sure it was a world still lit by hope, because that was something Hollywood offered during those dark times.

City of Angels

Lindsay Smith

I SHOULD HAVE KNOWN FRANKIE WAS a liar from the day I met her. She turned up at the Douglas airplane factory with pearls in her ears and a mouth that wouldn't quit running, even when she jammed up her rivet gun and cost me my lunch break having to redo the panel she'd messed up. "This is just a temporary assignment," she told me, leaning against the B-17's half-built hull and smoking a cigarette while I corrected her work. "I'm actually a spy for the OSS. They're going to drop me into France soon to rescue my fella."

She looked so tiny propped up against that beast, not at all like a weapon to be tossed out behind enemy lines. I wouldn't have minded tossing her out of a plane myself after that first day. But I knew how it was. She sounded as confident as all the rest of us once sounded, fresh from the Los Angeles bus terminal, face not yet scalded by the endless sunshine, still clinging to a drawl and a by-golly or two. Most girls learned to file their words and nails and teeth to sharp points after a few rounds at central casting, to shed the confidence for cutthroat common sense. Frankie, though, still hadn't lost the conviction that the world was going to bend her way.

Well, I was in no mood to bend.

I went to the shift mother first thing the next morning, asked her for a new assignment. Said Frankie would just slow me down. "Nonsense, Evie, you're our best riveter," she said, never meeting my eyes—no one ever met my eyes, like I was just some ghost. "Just work with her. Show her how it's done."

I tried. I showed her how to make a straight line, how to set her jaw to keep her teeth from rattling. But her attention was like a moth, always in search of a new light source: gossip with the other girls, each day's newspaper (which she skimmed for news from the European front), or the battered book of plays she pored over like a holy text.

Too often, she flitted toward me too. Endless questions, like I was some jigsaw puzzle someone had left out that she was determined to finish. Frankie was relieved, the way people always are, when I told her I hadn't come west to be a movie star. Was it my uneven gait from a too-short leg? ("Breech birth," Mama always said, like when she diagnosed cattle on the Steadmans' ranch.) Maybe just my family tree, ensuring I'd only ever be cast whooping around a stagecoach in feathers and hides. No, I wasn't here to be in front of the lens. I wanted to be the puppet master, pulling the starlets' strings. Hearing my words from their mouths.

"I've already done a few radio gigs," Frankie'd say to anyone who'd listen. "My Danny's assistant to one of the big directors down at Warner Brothers—I can't tell you his name. Soon as Danny's back from the war, he's promised to get me a screen test."

She had the looks, I'd give her that—glossy chestnut curls, lips quick to smirk. But like all the girls in this town, she knew it, and it soured everything about it. The great playwright Anton Chekhov said if you've got a gun onstage in act one, you better fire it by act three. That was how Frankie wielded her beauty in those early days, and I was just waiting for the recoil.

"I've got a fella too," I found myself saying. Like my James was a golden frame I've put around myself—*Look at me, I may not be a starlet, but I'm worthy. Someone thinks I'm worthy.* I never gossiped with the other girls, but I had to shut Frankie up somehow. "He's a petty officer in the Pacific fleet. We're gonna get married when he comes back home."

Frankie's eyebrows raised at that, and for once she looked at her work. But a few minutes later, she was chatting away again— recounting all the directors she dreamed of working with, the roles she wanted to play, the exhilarating life she led. But I knew it couldn't be as exciting as all that. She was here for the same reason all the rest of us were here, turning victory scraps into airplanes and spending ten percent of our earnings on war bonds so we'd earn our Minuteman flags. Hollywood didn't want us, and without a studio paycheck, without our boys to win the bread for us, we had to feed ourselves somehow.

Didn't stop Frankie from spinning her yarns all over the plant. Once I'd heard her stories, she stopped trying to impress me—or maybe the shift mother said something to her, I don't know—but every time I passed her and another cluster of girls, I heard the lies fluttering from her mouth, weightless as butterflies. "Well, as I was just saying to Vivien Leigh . . ." "I gotta leave early today, gonna read for the boys down at Paramount . . ." I'd hurry past, grateful for a few moments' work without her at my shoulder, and I'd let my rivet gun sing.

For a few blessed minutes, it was like it was before Frankie came. I'd clutch that rivet gun and pretend I was Kitty Cohen, the main character in my screenplay, *City of Angels*. Kitty was a gun moll who fought her way up to being the mob boss while all the men were off at war. Kitty was all curves and sweet poison; she never missed a beat, a word, a whisper, a frown. No one put anything over on Kitty, not even Detective Perry, though Lord knows he tried. Kitty wove a wondrous web around him and snared him so close he couldn't see the forest of her machinations for her silk-stockinged trees.

It was easier than thinking about James, across that stretch of glassy blue sea. About how our life would be when he returned. I loved him — of course I did. He believed in my writing and he worked hard and made me smile. But it wasn't like — well, like the movies, as foolish as that seemed.

I should have known better than to believe a scripted love story, but it's what I craved. True, James wasn't how I'd feared California boys would be, wanting too much and giving too little, hands grabbing and taking and trading this for that. We'd barely done more than kiss, just the occasional necking in a dark matinee. But I was nervous all the same. I knew marriage would bring more — expectations. My skin was supposed to crackle with his touch. I didn't feel it yet.

But I could do it. It was worth it, for the security he would bring. "Better find a man," Mama said, just before I left. "I ain't carin' for you no more."

I didn't like dwelling on that — and when Frankie returned from her sixth cigarette break of the morning, I took it out on her.

"You seem awfully chipper for someone whose boy's missing in action." I tossed her thick welder's mitts right at her gut; she flinched before catching them.

"He's—he's safe." She peered around the B-17's frame. "He's in a hospital in France."

"Is that so? Then why were you telling Maude you're goin' on some rescue mission with the Office of Strategic Services?" In my hands, the rivet gun spat out a perfect line. "Spy work, screen tests, cast parties with Bogie and Bacall . . . you're one busy girl."

Frankie paused in the middle of pulling on her mitts. I'd never seen her without her smile before, that big mess of lips smeared on thick as butter on toast. She looked so much smaller without it. Her whole face was soft and fragile. That's when I knew it wasn't just her natural good looks that made her who she was. She was always working, always performing, always forcing herself to shine like a spotlight. And I'd just burned it out.

She dropped the mitts on the floor and ran from the hangar, the dull thud of her worn-out oxfords ringing on concrete.

I swore to myself, went through the safety checks to shut down the rivet gun, replaced it safely, pulled off my goggles and mitts, and scrubbed at the grease I could feel smeared on my cheek. I took a deep breath and waited. I'd wanted to be cold like Kitty Cohen, like a scalpel peeling back Frankie's skin of lies so I could find out who she really was beneath. Instead I'd gone about it like a sledgehammer.

What did I care how she coped with the war, with her boy's unknown fate, with the failure every single one of us felt like a splinter we couldn't pull free? What did it matter to me if I had to assemble a few more panels than she did and let her take the credit? *Welcome to Hollywood, Evelyn.* If James were here, he'd tell me to be grateful to have any work at all.

I stormed from the hangar and headed for the bathroom, where I knew I'd find Frankie.

She was trying hard not to let anyone hear her cry, I'd give her that. From the other side of the stall door, I could barely tell she was there, save for the occasional muffled sob. We all had an unspoken agreement about crying in the bathroom — no one acknowledged it, and no one intruded. I should have done my business, washed my hands, and left as quietly as I could. Instead, I hovered in front of the sink, picking at a loose thread on my coveralls and remembering how I had felt those first days when James had shipped out. Like I was the one whose anchor had been pulled up; like I was adrift, invisible once more, lost in the sea of Los Angeles. Much as I hated to admit it, I knew how she felt — that fishhook pulling inside me, that need to be snared on something, connected to someone, to prove that I had worth. Wasn't it why I spent night after night hunched over my Underwood, making up stories in the hopes that someday they'd be immortalized on cellulose film? Why should I begrudge her for wanting the same?

"Frankie — listen." My voice was about as subtle as a nail head in the barren bathroom. The faint sounds of crying stopped. "I'm sorry. I know it's hard when your fella's gone and you've gotta fend for yourself."

"What do *you* know about it?" she snapped.

I looked down at my shoes, my baggy leggings hiding thick ankles. "I mean, all our lives we've been raised to take care of men and let them take care of us. Now they're all gone, y'know? No one told us that we could fend for ourselves, or taught us how. We're bound to struggle."

"I'm not *struggling*," Frankie cried. "I'm just . . ."

"Lonely," I said. In the silence that followed, I imagined her nodding. I traced the dented door with my fingernail. "Tell you what. Let me make it up to you, okay? Why don't you come for dinner at my landlady's house with me? We'd both love the company."

I don't know where the idea came from, but it felt right—two lonely souls should comfort each other, shouldn't they?

Even more shocking, Frankie agreed.

If I'd thought Frankie was a loaded gun before, well, it was nothing compared to the pistol she was at dinner with Mrs. Moskowitz. She could have charmed the mustache off Joe Stalin, the way she complimented Mrs. M's stewed cabbage from her victory garden—which, let's be frank, tasted about as appetizing as could be expected from something that came out of L.A. dirt. She didn't quite lie to Mrs. M the way I'd heard her lie to the other girls at the plant, but she wasn't the vulnerable, scrubbed-raw girl I'd heard in the bathroom that day either. No tall tales, but plenty of big dreams without the slightest hint of doubt weighing them down. For Frankie, fame was a one-way trip.

"It must be hard," Mrs. M said, "to be a girl on your own in these troubled times. When Evelyn first asked about renting a room from me, I was worried she'd never leave! What if she never found a man to marry her? How would she pay her rent? But she's a strong girl." She patted my hand but continued speaking like I wasn't in the room. "She's got a good man and she's always found work, even if it's not the work she wants."

"I think all women should be able to make it on their own," Frankie said. "It's not about needing a man or not—it just means she knows she can do whatever she sets out to do."

I dropped my napkin to the floor as an excuse to duck my head under the table; my cheeks were burning hot red.

"C'mon," Frankie said, after she helped me clean up Mrs. M's kitchen and rinse out the tin cans to take to the war scrap collection. "You got a radio in your room? Let's go listen to the news."

And so we crammed into my rented bedroom, Frankie perched on the edge of my narrow bed and me at my writing desk, listening to the latest broadcast from the front. I expected Frankie to really ham it up, lots of dramatic gasps and gestures like an amateur theater class, but she curled in on herself like a seashell and barely moved through the whole broadcast. Our boys were moving on Berlin. Hitler's defeat was imminent. More POWs liberated in western Germany, new horrors uncovered in the concentration camps . . . My stomach churned and churned. What use was I against the tragedies of the world? Men like James were out there taking the fight to the brutes, while I fretted over a make-believe story in my head.

Frankie, though, saw it differently. As soon as the news ended, she unfurled from her ball and smiled. "Just think, Evie. Those planes we built — they could've been the ones to drop the bombs on the Nazis. We helped set those prisoners free."

Well, I did a heck of a lot more of the building than Frankie did — but I smiled anyway, let her optimism thaw away some of my unease. The radio switched over to a music hour, and the sweet strains of the Glenn Miller Orchestra wove through my room.

Frankie leaped off the mattress and held her hand out to me. "C'mon, we deserve to celebrate. Let's dance."

I took her hand without even thinking about it. Frankie made everything seem natural with her easy smile. As much as I didn't trust Frankie, I wanted to feel that ease too; I wanted to go along with her for the ride. We stumbled around at first, both of us trying to take the follower's steps, but Frankie quickly jumped into the leader's role and adjusted to account for my limp, threading us deftly through the narrow space between my bed and desk and wall. We were both laughing, knowing what buffoons we must have seemed, but everything else just melted away. My irritation with Frankie at the factory; my stubbornly unfinished script; James, far across the sea; and the fear of what my life would become when he returned . . . No. There was nothing in the world right then but me and Frankie and the silky chords of "In the Mood."

I hadn't been wrong about Frankie, I thought, but I wasn't wholly right about her either. She was a liar and a show-off and a terrible factory girl, but she was determined and confident and generous too. Of course her looks made it easy to like her, but it was more than just that—I liked the way her soft hands cupped mine and her soapy scent trailed through the air. I liked her gentle steps to Glenn Miller and the way she spun into a snappy dance the moment "Yankee Doodle Dandy" started up, belting in her best James Cagney impression. Frankie was born to be a star, the kind that burns herself into your mind and refuses to be forgotten, and she made me want to bask in her starlight.

But the Andrews Sisters chimed in, crooning away about apple blossom time, and the rest of the world came crowding back. Before he shipped out, James promised to return to me, just like those song lyrics said, and make me his bride. Now that memory tied a double knot of nervousness and relief in me, and my hands fell away from Frankie's. There'd been nothing on the news about James's ship, or any news from the Pacific front. Was the war drawing to a close there too?

Frankie kept slow-dancing by herself for a few seconds, then stopped and studied the look on my face. She caught her plump lower lip in her teeth and looked around my room, then spotted my typewriter in its case, and her flashbulb grin returned. "Hey, you got any of your movie scripts here? Maybe I can read from them!"

I bashed my hip against the drawer where I kept *City of Angels.* "It's—it's not ready for a dramatic reading yet." When her smile faltered, I said, "But why don't you run through your monologues for me? The ones you're practicing for the screen test. I can give you notes on them."

Frankie shrugged, plopped down onto the mattress. "It's gettin' late. I should head back." But she made no move to stand.

I glanced out the window; Friday night in Los Angeles was always a dicey affair. What men were still left weren't the sort you wanted to run into in a darkened alleyway—zoot-suiters and draft dodgers and alcoholics and worse. "Maybe I should walk you home. And then—oh."

"And then walk back alone?" Frankie rolled her eyes and flopped back onto the bed. "I know. How about we have a slumber party? Like in grade school. Then I can run my lines for you in the morning."

I suspected then that I'd been snared in another Frankie trap. From what I'd pieced together at the factory, Frankie's roommate had a zoot-suit-wearing boyfriend who liked to invite himself over to their place, especially after he'd been hitting the sauce. Sometimes he hit the roommate too. "You take the bed. I'll get some spare blankets and pillows and sleep on the floor."

Frankie smiled at me like I'd pulled the moon down for her, and that made it even harder for me to mind being had.

She was out cold by the time I set up my pallet—pins still in her hair, even—so I tucked myself in and pulled out James's photo to whisper good night. I tried to imagine him whispering back, but I couldn't remember his voice, exactly—sticky and drawling, I thought, but maybe the navy had tightened it up. Maybe I remembered it all wrong

Two years now he'd been gone, and I'd only known him for

four months before that—I was fresh off the bus at sixteen, completely clueless when it came to men. "Complications," Mama said of them, though I never had trouble keeping away from them, and they kept away from me. James was undemanding, easygoing; sure, his letters all sounded the same after a while, but he was safe. Wasn't it enough? Why should a girl like me think she ever deserved more?

I must have drifted into sleep, into dreams of roaring planes and frantic Morse code beeps, then I slammed back into myself with a jolt and sat up. Moonlight trickled through my chintz curtains, highlighting the empty space in my bed where Frankie should have been. I frowned, pulled on a robe, and stepped out into the living room.

A halo of lamplight wreathed Frankie, curled up in Mrs. M's armchair, lips moving along with the stack of papers she was reading. My *City of Angels* script. I stood there for a moment, too shocked at her gall to say anything, but as I watched her, I realized she wasn't just mouthing the lines to herself—she was becoming Kitty Cohen. Her eyebrows drew down and her shoulders rolled back and she transformed into something . . . magnificent.

But—that script was private. It was *mine*. I stormed toward her and snatched it out of her hands, then headed back into my room.

"Evie, wait!" she cried, following me into the bedroom and shutting the door behind her. "Don't be mad!"

"It's not ready for anyone to see it yet. It's not even finished." I shoved it back into its drawer and sank back down onto my pallet, fists at my side like stones weighing me down. "You have no right to take my belongings—"

"But Evie, it's good." Frankie's eyes rounded; she leaned toward me with a dramatic flair. "I love it. A woman gangster—it's fabulous. And she's more than just a gangster. She's vicious, and wonderful, and she knows what she wants . . ."

I let my fists unfold. That's what I wanted Kitty Cohen to be—tough and cunning and determined, a woman for whom beauty, if she had it, was only one of her many tools.

"But the romance stinks," Frankie said.

I jerked my head up. "What are you talking about?"

"The detective who's investigating her? There's no passion there. It's like she's flirting with a saltine cracker." Frankie smiled. "You've gotta draw from what you know. Maybe from—from you and your James?"

I glanced toward the nightstand, where I kept James's letters. "Um, well . . . Why don't you tell me about you and your fella?"

Frankie reached for my hands then and gripped them in her own. She sat down across from me and stared right through me. My anger stilled at her touch. "They have to crackle off each other like a match and flint. Like when you look in his eyes and feel that fire in your gut, that hunger that could eat you from the inside out."

I nodded, but I had no idea what she was talking about. Not really. I imagined it, when I watched Lauren Bacall on screen; I tried to imagine it now, staring back at Frankie and her eyes like tarnished bronze. A current ran between us as she was consumed in her words; her hands tightened around mine, and I didn't want her to let go.

"You want nothing more than skin on skin, every inch of you burning and open to the other person's touch . . ."

The first tear sliced down my cheek, hot as a welding torch. "We've barely even kissed." More tears came, but I couldn't stop myself now. "I care for James, but I don't feel any of what you're— I mean, I just don't get that from him, or from any man, and I—"

"Shhhh." Frankie squeezed my hands. "I know. I know how it is."

Then she leaned toward me and kissed my right eyelid. I clenched my eyes shut, not knowing what to do, unable to move as she kissed my left eyelid as well. It was a motherly kiss, a patient kiss—nothing like the slobbery mess I'd made kissing James, but somehow it felt more right to me than all of those combined. I opened my eyes, shaking, to find Frankie's face looming in front of mine. She let go of my hands and pressed one quick, gentle kiss to my lips.

Before I could react, she stood up. "Get some rest, Evie," she said.

But it sounded like a greeting, not a good-bye.

Though she was gone when I woke up that morning, I couldn't push Frankie from my thoughts. Not only the way she'd looked at me, as if she knew a secret about me that I didn't know, but the rest of her too. Her confidence, her silky way of moving and flowing to embody whatever she needed to be. I dreaded seeing her at the factory—had it all been a foolish moment, the sort she'd flit away from like she did everything else? But she was waiting for me with her rivet gun cocked in one hand, and tossed out a Kitty Cohen line—"Looks to me like we're gonna have to share this town, Detective"—and I knew I had no reason to fear.

I corrected her grip on the rivet gun, and she actually followed my instructions for once.

After that, she wound up at Mrs. M's more evenings than not, sharing her meat ration when she was lucky enough to snag one, entertaining us with monologues after dinner before the evening news broadcast. When she acted, she was electrified. I listened to the passion in her voice and saw the sharpness in her eyes and I felt that fire spreading through me. The passion she'd spoken of.

And we'd go into my room, and she'd seize my cheeks and kiss me.

Slow, fast, didn't matter; it set my head spinning with hunger. For soft skin and her hardened stare. For the swell of her hips and the dip of her waist, all feminine, all beauty, all weaponized girl. Our fingers tangled together and then parted, and we'd sleep knotted up together, her scent filling my nostrils and my dreams.

But when I awoke, I'd remember — James. My duties, my promise to be a wife if not a homemaker, though I'd always wondered if he thought one would follow the other. I'd imagine him looking down on us and wondering why he'd never awakened that fire in me, why I'd never craved him like I craved Frankie and her starlight.

"I love you," Frankie would murmur, usually in her sleep, but one day she slipped it in between our struggle with a massive sheet of metal. No one was around to hear — I barely heard her through the din — but I was certain she'd said it.

The words weighed like rope around my neck. Were we allowed to love each other? Was I in love with her? What did it mean for us to love; where could it even go?

"What about Danny?" I asked her.

She just shrugged and held the sheet still while I worked the edges into place. "Oh, he doesn't care. He understands."

Understands what? I wanted to scream, but I was too afraid. I didn't know what we were — laughing and kissing and dreaming together, but never looking more than a day into our future. Our future together, that was; Frankie dreamed of her *own* future, name in lights and face on posters.

But maybe Danny understood. Maybe this was something that could be understood. Maybe James would understand too.

Dear James, I typed on my Underwood. *My dearest James.* No, cross that out.

I'm not sure how to tell you this. What was I telling him, exactly? Even I didn't know. I left the letter unsent.

"Come on, Evie," Frankie said. "We're going out tonight." She'd arrived at Mrs. M's in a stunning V-neck dress, tight down to her waist, then swirling into a perfect dancing skirt that hit her calves just so. She'd painted her lips bright red and set her hair in flawless liberty curls. She helped me take in my finest floral dress so it flattered me more, then she drew black lines up the backs of our bare legs with a steady hand. "Just because stockings are rationed doesn't mean we can't *look* like a million bucks," she said.

I didn't want to go out—into the seas of girls clustered around a few shore-bound sailors or, more often, exempted men pretending to be sailors, and angry zoot-suiters and the like. But Frankie said not to worry—there'd be no one like that where we were headed.

As soon as we ducked into the nightclub, I saw just what she meant.

In many ways, it looked like the stylish nightclub I went to with James and his friends just before he shipped out—sleek black glass and mirrors and a forty-piece brass orchestra on the main stage. Cigarette girls walked among the tables, wearing not much more than heels and red lipstick, while girls in an explosion of feathery costumes danced up front. But the crowd was all women—not a single Tom or Jerry to be seen.

"Welcome to the Shrinking Violet," Frankie said, looping her arm through mine. "A place for girls looking for some fun. Girls like . . ." She trailed off, but I knew what she meant.

Like us. The words thrummed inside me, strong as a siren's call. We weren't alone.

We crammed into a booth with a trio of well-dressed girls a few years older than us who peppered us with questions between performances. Frankie did most of the answering, her starlight dazzling them the same as it had dazzled me; even the waitress, Madge, seemed locked under her spell, and slipped us a drink on the house. No one was immune to Frankie, I thought; but as her hand rested on my knee, my heart swelled to know that she'd chosen me.

The Shrinking Violet rang with bright brass musical numbers and comedy skits and even a one-act play, a fun twist on *Romeo and Juliet* where Juliet, upon awakening to find Romeo supposedly dead, sought comfort from her scandalously dressed nurse and decided to run off with the nurse instead. Romeo awoke to an empty crypt and aw-shucksed his way off the stage to the cheers of the crowd.

After an impressive set of croony songs usually sung by men, the singer, Luisa, joined us in our booth and traded kisses on the cheek with Frankie. "Who's your girl?" Luisa asked Frankie, before tossing me a grin.

As usual, Frankie spoke before I could. "Evie's a writer. She's gonna work for Metro-Goldwyn one of these days, mark my words."

"Yeah? She write about girls like us?" Luisa laughed. "Good luck gettin' that past the censors. Maybe you could write a new act for me here. The Romeo and Juliet number's getting a little stale, y'know? Talk to Violet. She'd love to get some new talent in the club."

Luisa gestured behind us to a private box at the top of the hall. A dark figure stood silent, leaning against the railing, watching over the club with what looked to me like a satisfied smirk.

"Violet runs the club?" I asked.

"Runs it? She owns it, books the performers, oversees all the productions, does about everything but pour the drinks and wait the tables—aw, thanks, Madge," Luisa said, as the waitress brought her some water. "A self-made woman. And she's always happy to help out our own, y'know what I mean?" Luisa winked. "Seriously, if you're any good, Violet'd pay you well, I'm sure."

A self-made woman. Like my Kitty Cohen. Maybe they didn't just exist in my shoddy scripts. I smiled up at Violet and thanked Luisa before she headed back to the stage for the next show.

"That was incredible," I said to Frankie as we headed home. "I had no idea there was—that anything like that existed." *That we're not alone.*

Frankie grinned and tucked a loose strand of hair behind my ear. "You can find anything in this town, Evie. Just a bit of fun, right?"

I was too enchanted by our evening to let her words sting. "And they need writers. And probably performers too! Why haven't you auditioned for Violet?" I asked.

Frankie's gaze darkened; she shrugged and glanced off down the street, where servicemen waited in line for another dance hall. "Oh, I dunno, it's not really what I want. I might as well swing for the fences, y'know? Land a real studio gig. Then I'll know I've made it for real." She snorted. "If I can."

I clutched both her hands in mine. "Frankie. You're incredible. Of course you can. You can win an Oscar, I know it. Soon the studios'll be beating down your door. I just thought it might be nice for you to start out among girls like us, and—"

"You really think I'll make it?" She squeezed my hands tighter, urgency punctuating her words. "You aren't just saying that?"

"Of course I think so. I—" I swallowed. I knew she'd said

it before, but Frankie said a lot of things. "I love you, Frankie. I know you can do anything you aim for, and I—"

She kissed me before I could finish, a toe-curling kiss that melted away the rest of the world. Frankie loved me back—she had to, didn't she, to kiss me that way? That's why she'd brought me to the Shrinking Violet. I wasn't alone in loving her, in loving girls, in finding my true self—

"Hey, would you look at that!" exclaimed some wise Joe as he passed us on the sidewalk. "Sorry, ladies, but I bet your guys'll be wantin' *that* job back when they get home too!"

I yanked away from Frankie, but I knew just how I looked—lips ripe and swollen, panting for breath, my every skin cell crackling and alive. The man chuckled to himself and continued down the boulevard, but his words rattled around inside me like loose rocks in my shoe as we headed back to Mrs. M's. There was no more hiding who I was.

I was in love with another girl.

"Don't be silly," Frankie said that night, in the silvery dark of my room. "We're just havin' fun, you and me. No need to put a label on it or nothin'."

"It's not just fun for me." My heart was throbbing, sore and worn out. "This is who I am—who I've always been. I just never admitted it before." And I *wanted* it to be more. The way she looked at me sometimes, like I was the only one who knew the roles she wanted to play—that's the way she made me feel all the time. "I don't want to be someone I'm not anymore."

Her laugh was like metal shearing in two. "You think you can just declare it, and no one's gonna mind?" She turned away from me. "That Mrs. M would keep renting to you? That the studios would hire you? Ain't it tough enough, just being a gal? Why do you want to make it even harder for yourself?"

"Because it's the right thing to do." I cupped my hand around hers. "All those girls at the Shrinking Violet—they aren't afraid. I shouldn't be either."

"Those girls at the Shrinking Violet can't get work anywhere else. Even in this day and age, with no menfolk around. You think they're there because it's so lucrative?" She pulled her hand away. "Get some sleep, Evie. I think the champagne's gone to your head."

After she'd left that morning, I was back at my typewriter. If she didn't think I should declare myself to the whole world, well, there was at least one person to whom I owed the truth.

I'm coming to understand something about myself that I hadn't known before. I care deeply for you, but I'm not sure I'm able to be a wife—to you or any man.

Once the words stared back at me, black ink on white, I realized they were the words I'd been searching for all along.

I'd come to Los Angeles to find myself—the work and life that I wanted. Now, for the first time, I felt that I actually knew who I was. Behind the scenes, writing the script, not acting out someone else's story. Loving a girl who inspired passion in me, instead of a man I was expected to look to for security. It was terrifying, to throw away the script I'd been working from my whole life—but now I felt certain that I could write my own.

"I told him. I told James the truth about me." I gazed into Frankie's eyes that night, aching to drown in their depths.

"What truth?" She turned away from me and buried herself in her script. Another audition, this time for a supporting role. Frankie supported no one, but she was, I could tell, grateful the studio had given her a second chance.

"That I like girls. That I like you." I reached for her shoulder, but she shrugged me off.

"I don't see why you worry about defining it." She leaned back in her chair. "How should I say this line? 'Oh, Deborah, I don't know how you always land the right man!'" She rasped breathlessly. "Or is it a joke? 'Oh, Deborah, I don't know how you always land them . . .'"

I wanted to believe, though, that Frankie appreciated me telling James the truth. She just needed to get her big break—we both did. If we couldn't do it now, with the war on, then when would we get another chance?

As it turned out, my letter never reached James.

One afternoon, Mrs. M called me to the front door, and I bounded out of my room, thinking Frankie had rushed straight from her audition to tell me she'd landed the part.

But I didn't recognize the dark-haired man standing there, crow's-feet crinkling his damp eyes, hat crushed in his restless hands. And yet I knew him—his features lined up so well with James's.

"Listen. You're—you're Evelyn, right?" He took a deep breath, eyes wrenching shut. "I'm James's father. Ricky Falcone. I'm afraid I have some bad news."

I sank into the armchair, no longer able to feel my legs.

The explosion had ripped straight through the hull, he said. James had died trying to save his fellow sailors. Smoke inhalation, shrapnel wounds . . . An honorable death. But it didn't matter. I felt dishonorable—I'd never properly ended things with James. He died thinking I loved him, that I'd been true. He'd never heard my words. My declaration of me. Hot tears of shame and grief needled at my eyes, threatening to spill.

"James told me he wanted to make a wife of you when he returned," Ricky continued. His eyes never really found mine. "If you're in a—a *situation,* or you need money, or anything—"

"No. No, I couldn't, Mr. Falcone." James had been a good man and a good friend; I thought I'd loved him once. But I couldn't accept his father's help. "You're very kind, but I . . . I'm very sorry for your loss."

I was no one's responsibility. I was my own woman, for good and bad.

When Mr. Falcone left, I slumped against the door and allowed myself a few raw tears. James deserved to be mourned. He deserved someone better than me—but no, I told myself, that wasn't quite right. He'd deserved someone different from me. Someone who could have loved him fully. Didn't we all deserve that? I wanted to believe so.

Frankie didn't land the part, but we celebrated anyway. I'd set aside *City of Angels;* in truth, Frankie was all I could think of those days. I saw her in my mind when I awoke and tasted her on my lips when I fell asleep. That, and factory production had ramped up, and everyone said Berlin would fall to the Allies any day. Frankie and I worked double shifts, side by side, daydreaming of how we'd use the money from our war bonds when we cashed them in.

"A mink coat," she said with a swoon, "just like Marlene Dietrich."

"A house of our own," I said.

Frankie rolled her eyes, though she was smiling—that smile was like a hook where I always hung my coat. "A night at the Brown Derby."

That was Frankie—she was the comet blazing through the sky, and I wanted to be the tail. But it was dangerous to think anything was a guarantee with a girl like her. Every moment with her slipped too quickly from my grasp.

A commotion at the factory; gasps and squeals threading through the raucous din of the machines. *Frankie! Frankie!* They called her name like the legions of fans she dreamed of outside Grauman's Chinese Theatre. Frankie pushed her goggles up into her kerchief-wrapped hair and shut down her equipment.

A hardness formed in my gut, clenching like when I'd written my letter to James, like when his father had sat me down to tell me of his death.

A swarm of girls pressed around the corner, ushering a young man on crutches with them. "Francesca," he said, like she was the sweetest honey. And she was.

But I also knew, then, that she was no longer mine.

He'd been rescued with a dozen other army privates from a camp and spent weeks recovering in a hospital bed in England. He was feverish, too ill to write to her, but as soon as he was mended he received a medal and an honorable discharge and came straight for her. I overheard all this with the dozens of other girls crowded around, swooning and clutching their hands to their hearts. They'd been dazzled by Frankie and her lies and exaggerations and her starlight.

She never returned to the factory after that day. Soon more servicemen trickled in, claiming their girls or, more often, claiming our jobs. The shift mother called me to her office and asked me if I wouldn't mind stepping aside for another GI who'd come home and, she said delicately, needed the work more than I did. He'd served his country, after all. When I started to mind, though, I realized she wasn't really asking.

We declared victory in Europe, though the battles in the Pacific raged on, over the same stretch of sea where James had lost his life believing I was waiting for him back on shore. I wandered Los Angeles and all the places Frankie and I had been. The drugstore where we got milk shakes, now packed with soldiers and their gals. The place she shared with her roommate—twice

I tried to find the nerve to knock, to call, but the third time, as I paced the sidewalk, I saw a young family leaving the apartment, crossing the parking lot under the hot white gleam of California summer.

"You'll find work again," Mrs. M said, as I chewed on the night's meal (pork chop, no longer rationed) and stared out the window as the late-evening sun splashed across the new cars whizzing by on the avenue. "Maybe once I cash in my war bonds, I can hire you to do some cleaning for me. Or I can check with the other ladies in my bridge club. . . ." She stirred her Ovaltine. "What about Francesca? Did she finally land a role? Maybe she could get you work as an assistant at the studio. . . ."

"Francesca's not coming around anymore." I dropped my fork. "Listen, Mrs. M, there's something I have to tell you. It's none of your business, but if I don't tell someone, it's going to eat me up."

Her lips quavered. "Evie, dear, if you're in any sort of trouble —"

"I was in love with someone, but it didn't work out." I squeezed my eyes shut. "Another girl."

Mrs. M didn't say anything for a long time. Slowly, I opened my eyes to find her staring at me expectantly. "Well?" she asked. "Is that it?"

"You're not going to — to kick me out?" I asked.

"Is it going to keep you from paying rent?" She took a sip of Ovaltine, leaving a chocolate mustache on her upper lip. "Dear, we all came to California in search of ourselves. Herbert and I wanted better weather for his illness, though it turned out it didn't do him much good. You came here 'cause you have a story to tell. Might as well tell it."

I ended up having to cash out most of my war bonds when

a new job never materialized—no need to hire a dark-skinned girl like me when hundreds of vets needed work. I went to the movies—and walked right back out when one of the shorts in front of a Bogart show starred Francesca Miller in a Daniel Fiorelli production. I didn't need to see those eyes watching me, that smile scrawled across the screen.

More important, I had time to write, and the first thing I tackled was a new draft of *City of Angels*, this time as a one-act play. I'd sit in a corner booth at the Shrinking Violet and sip on soda water while I reworked the story. I'd chat with Luisa and Madge when they had breaks, and while I never felt the same spark with them that had flared in me with Frankie, it was nice to have a few friends in this world who didn't make me feel like I had to hide.

Plus, it was good to have their support for what I was about to do.

I climbed the stairs to Violet's office with legs like gelatin, hugging my brown folio tight to my chest. Violet's guard, the only man I'd seen in the whole club, ushered me inside. Violet lounged behind her desk, smoking a cigarette in a long holder, her creamy satin gown crisp against her dark skin. "Evelyn," she said, my name streaming from her mouth in a puff of smoke. "The girls tell me you have a play for me. Something a little more serious to be part of our revue here at the club."

"It's called *City of Angels*." I hesitated, then held the folio out to her. "In a city of women, all the men called off to war, a gun moll named Kitty Cohen decides to seize control of her old squeeze's gang for herself. But she's pursued by a clever young detective on the force, Mary O'Shea. Sparks and bullets both fly as they outwit each other, and fall for each other—"

"I get the idea." She tapped away the ash from her cigarette as she flipped through the script. "Ha. 'Looks like we'll have to share this town.' That's cute, I like that." She glanced up at me. "You got studios interested in this?"

"No, I didn't think—"

"What're you asking, a thousand? Two? I can give you two, but I can't go any higher. I gotta pay my girls. Six months exclusive, you can revise it, then you can take it to the studios—"

Two thousand dollars! I could live another year off of that. Enough time to write another script. Maybe two—one for the studios and another for the Shrinking Violet. "You've got yourself a deal."

❦ *Author's Note* ❦

Rosie the Riveter endures as the most instantly recognizable symbol of American women's contributions to World War II, though the munitions and aircraft assembly lines were far from the sole opportunities women found for employment on the home front. In fact, countless jobs traditionally reserved for men opened to them—transcription, logistical support, translation, scientific research, engineering and industrial design, transportation, and much more. Government-sponsored propaganda posters like "We Can Do It!" glorified these jobs while at the same time reassured any doubtful (or, okay, sexist) husbands that it was their wives' patriotic duty to work. While women were barred from serving in the United States armed forces until 1948, thousands joined civil defense groups like the Women's Army Auxiliary Corps or served as nurses in the field.

Hollywood, too, served an important function in the Allied forces' efforts to unite public opinion and discourage the Axis powers of Nazi Germany, Italy, and Japan. Movies produced during World War II often featured critical comedic portrayals of the Axis leadership, rousing patriotic musical numbers, and sweeping dramas like *Casablanca* (whose epic ending Evie could surely sympathize with). While censorship in this period focused on preventing the leaking of information that could compromise military action, the Hays Code restricted studios from portraying anything that might "lower the moral standards of those who see it," which unfortunately included homosexuality, as far as the code's authors were concerned.

❦ 1967: California ❧

Pulse of the Panthers

Kekla Magoon

I.

I'D ALWAYS BEEN A GOOD GIRL. ALWAYS followed the rules. Kept my nose clean, as Granny liked to say.

Our farm was a whopping twenty-seven acres, and I had the run of the place. The garden, the orchard, the barn, the fields. When a hot breeze blew, I would follow it. Hike up my skirt, run off the porch and down our long grassy drive to the dirt lane that led to the rest of the world. Most times I could run straight out into the road and just stand there. Let the wind swirl around me as it tunneled between the fields on either side. Two cars a day passed by, maybe, headed to or from other farms down the lane. You could tell when they'd gone past, because those tires stirred up dirt and left a silt-brown cloud hanging above the avocado trees lining the drive. You could tell when they were coming too. The dust would rise, a long way off, and billow closer.

I'd never wondered much about life past the end of the lane.

We had a television set, out in the barn. Daddy liked to keep up with the news, but Granny wouldn't allow such newfangled contraptions into her house. *It took me my whole adult life to get used to having that radio in the living room,* she always said. *Then they go on and invent something new. No call for it.* She had this scratchy-throat voice, from years of breathing in Granddad's tobacco smoke. 'Course, he went on into the sky a few years before I came along into the world.

Daddy might have been the man of the house, but Granny sure enough ran the place. So the TV went into the barn. Daddy always did things how Granny wanted. "Get that girl some books," she'd say. And sure enough, Daddy'd come home with some for me. I had quite a collection by that summer. Twenty-two books in all. That was more than anyone I knew, including the girls who still went to school. They had books, but they had to give them back at the end of the year. I'd gone to school over in town up until eighth grade, and then Daddy pulled me out. Needed help around the farm, he said, with Granny getting on in years.

"Let her learn," Granny said. "I can manage." But she couldn't. Her back didn't want to bend low enough to weed anymore. Her fingers shook trying to grip the handle of a broom or a rake. Sometimes she didn't even see all the eggs that our hens laid, right in plain view in their nests.

We had a television set, out in the barn, I was saying. And I had all these books too. So I knew about the world. Daddy had a rocking chair out there that he'd pulled off the porch. Come evening, after supper, he'd go sit out there. Watching. Rocking. Muttering from time to time about the state of things. I watched with him, most nights. He only brought in the one chair, so I sat on the floor by his knee, far enough away not to get rocked on, sifting scraps of straw through my fingers.

The world came into our barn every night. And most nights, I was glad enough to be safe in that barn, and not out there in the rest of it. It sounded bad out there. On television some nights they pulled numbers out of a machine, and if your birthday matched, you had to go and fight in the war in Vietnam. If you were a boy, that is, and over eighteen.

Black people didn't need to go all the way to Vietnam to find a war, Daddy said once while we were watching the draft. Sometimes the newspaper showed pictures of civil rights demonstrations. People protesting a system that said black people should live separate; black people should stay in their place, and that place should always be small. If you were black and you lived in the South, you had to fight. If you were black and you lived in a city, you had to fight. Didn't have to go anywhere, even. That fight came right to you.

Nothing like that ever came close to our farm. I could walk through the field and get to town. There was a general store there, and a post office, and a restaurant, and a bar I couldn't go into. Everyone knew me. Everyone was black.

The worst thing I'd ever had to fight was a jackrabbit, dead set on digging up my string bean plants. I was a good girl. The edge of my world was the end of that lane.

2.

I wandered through my garden picking rhubarb and blackberries. The berries along the fence were plentiful this time of year. They were full and ripe, and you had to pluck them just so or you'd have nothing but berry mash and stained fingertips for your effort.

Rhubarb-and-blackberry crumble sounded delicious to me. I could make a right good crumble, Granny always said.

Daddy came out of the house, over the yard. I thought he was making for the fields, but he headed straight for me. He stepped right over my rabbit fence and stood between the string bean stalks, as if tall and lanky things should stick together. He was chawing on the end of a long stalk of grass, like he did when he had things on his mind.

"Sandy," he said. "Listen up a minute, baby girl."

I'm sixteen now, I wanted to tell him, hating the way he still called me that. But this was one of a lot of things I wanted to say that Daddy wouldn't want to hear. I would always be his baby girl, and I think he liked to remind me. So I hugged my berry bowl and said nothing.

"The Panthers are coming," Daddy said. "Be here tomorrow, sometime after first light."

My fingers fumbled. The berries bled. "The Panthers?"

"The Black Panthers," he said. As if I didn't know.

The whole wide world closed around me. "The Panthers," I repeated. We'd seen them on TV, a few months ago. They stormed into the California state legislature in Sacramento, openly carrying shotguns, rifles, and other legal weapons, in protest of a bill that would strip rights from black citizens. It made the national news. *Those boys are gonna get themselves killed,* Daddy'd said that night. Not the kind of thing I'd forget.

"What are they coming here for?" I asked.

Daddy moved the stalk of grass from one side of his mouth to the other. "Take the cart to the store and stock up," he said. He moved like he was going to walk away and then he didn't. "Don't need to say nothing to Jake about the reason for the excess."

"How many people?" I asked.

"'Bout a dozen."

I'd never cooked for that many. "For lunch tomorrow?"

Daddy nodded, short. "And on through the weekend."

Saturday lunch, Saturday dinner. Sunday breakfast, lunch, and dinner. I didn't want to say it, but I had to. "It's going to take more than the cart," I blurted.

Daddy shifted the grass. "You reckon?"

"Yeah, 'cause they'll eat like you. Not like Granny."

I was being a little impudent, maybe. But then Daddy got that sliver of a smile on his face. The one that means he's thinking *How'd I get a kid so smart?* That's according to Granny.

"Can you get enough for lunch tomorrow?"

"Sure."

Daddy chawed on the grass for a moment. "Write the rest on a list," he said. "I'll call it over. They'll stop in town on the way and pick up what you need."

"What are they coming here for?" I dared ask the question a second time. My heart was beating like a crazy drum.

"It's none of your concern." His brows darkened and gathered, like a quiet storm. "You'll cook for them, as our guests. Otherwise you're to have nothing to do with them. You hear?"

I could read between the lines. The Panthers would be dangerous. Exciting.

"You hear?" he said, louder.

"Yes, sir."

Daddy strode away, hands jammed in the pockets of his overalls, grass head dancing past the side of his cheek. Hands in his pockets meant he wasn't sure about something.

We'd had guests for dinner lots of times. I always made chicken or roast beef. Fresh vegetables from the garden. I specialized in potatoes. Not growing them—cooking them. Baked, mashed, fried, home-fried, gratin. I did a nice corn casserole too, when we could get fresh corn. We could get some this time of year.

My ribs began to ache from the ceramic lip of the berry bowl digging into my side. I relaxed my grip, though my heart still quaked in this brand-new rhythm, a fresh pulse from somewhere outside of me.

I'd need to pick a lot more blackberries.

3.

"He thinks I don't know what he's up to," Granny said, smacking a wooden spoon against her palm. "I always know."

I had my eye on the kitchen window. Watching for the telltale dust cloud to rise over the trees.

I could see on the map that we were fifty miles from Oakland. That's where they'd have started out. But who knew when? Or how fast they would drive? Or how much traffic there might be on the blacktopped roads? Or if they'd stop for gas, or breakfast in a restaurant in another town like ours?

"I always know," Granny muttered.

"What's he up to?"

"Sneaking around with those friends of his," she said. "Them wild boys." Her eyes grew all big and she waved the spoon. "My boy, he's too smart for the likes of them. Fools," she insisted.

Dust blurred the sky, low in the distance. "They're here," I said.

"Uh-uh, uh-uh," Granny said, and hefted herself off toward her room.

I'd spent the morning frying chicken. It waited on the table, on a platter, under cloth. When I saw the dust cloud, I pulled the potato salad from the icebox and started slicing the bread. I fired up the oven to warm the crumble.

The cars slithered through the avocado trees like a slick black snake. Three cars.

Engines cut. Doors popped open like the snake had grown legs. Fourteen men emerged, stretching their limbs.

I'd expected them to be men, I guess, but they were boys, mostly. Not much older than me. A couple looked downright scrawny.

They carried sacks of things, loose totes stuffed with perhaps a few clothes each. Some cradled armfuls of worn-looking books. I counted five canvas duffel bags bulging with guns. One guy bent into the trunk and came up with an armload of paper grocery sacks. I opened the kitchen screen door.

"I've brought the groceries," he said, with a spreading, tilted grin. He was taller than me, but not by much. He wore a jaunty, rough-sewn cap of olive green. His eyes were dark and alive with energy. They seemed to smile even more than his mouth did. "Where would you like them, miss?"

My cheeks warmed. "I'm Sandy."

"Where would you like them, Miss Sandy?" He was teasing me now.

My mouth twitched open 'cause it couldn't help itself. I hoped my teeth looked as clean and strong as his.

"Right here on the counter is fine."

He hefted the sacks into place. "All right, then." He brushed his hands off on his pants. "I'm Bobby."

"Pleased to meet you," I said. That's what you were supposed to say, I thought. It had been a right long while since I'd met anyone for the first time. Everyone around town had been here for years.

It was strange to be alone with a boy in the kitchen. He looked around like he was seeing something special. I guess it was all new to him, the way he was new to me. He glanced at the stove, then me. The icebox, then me. The sink and counter and the bags he'd laid down, and me.

Finally he said, "Uh, well, those are the groceries, then."

"Where?" I said, 'cause I felt like being funny. I'm not usually funny, at least outside of my head.

He smiled again. Teeth and lips and a tongue that darted out for a quick teasing second.

"Yo, Bobby," someone called. "We're going out back."

"See you," he said.

"Tell them there's lunch. When you want it." I wanted him to turn around. And he did.

"Sure thing." He pounded the door frame as he slid away. "Smells right good in here too."

As I moved to unpack the groceries, I felt wide awake and sort of tingly. Across my chest and down my legs, a blush over my whole body. I waited for it to go away, but it didn't.

4.

The Panthers gathered around our dining table. Laughing and chattering, clinking silverware against dishes, lip-smacking and groaning about my home cooking.

We didn't have fifteen chairs, so some of them stood. Others sat along the baseboards, balancing plates on their knees. I guess I should have dusted down there. Daddy sat at the head of the table. I lingered in the doorway. Granny stayed in the living room, rocking in her chair, arms crossed in a huff. You could hear it in the rhythm of the runners on the floor: *These young'uns. They don't know.*

The guys fell into companionable silence, finger-licking the chicken from its bones. The calm became something almost spiritual. When they were done, one by one, they resumed laughing and chatting and the room came alive again.

For the first time, I noticed how quiet our house is, most of the time. Dinner is usually a quiet, grunting affair, where Daddy swiftly shovels food into his mouth before retreating to the barn for the evening. And there is always something left over, which is what Granny and I eat for lunch the next day.

The Panthers scraped the plates clean.

5.

Watching through the hinges on the open barn door, I could stand in shadows and no one would see me. Oil lamplight washed over their faces, drawing them glowing then dark.

Torry read pages out loud from a book called *The Wretched of the Earth*. He folded the book and asked the group, "So what does Fanon mean when he talks about exploitation?"

"He's talking about how we used to be slaves, and even though people say we got free, we're still trapped."

"Things are supposed to be different now, but the system's still stacked against us."

"How so?" Torry asked. He had a certain kind of voice on, like a teacher in the classroom. He knew the answer, but he wanted someone else to say.

"Guys like us do all the work but get paid very little," said El. "Meanwhile those rich white guys sit back and reap most of the profits."

"We can work full-time, or two jobs, even, and still barely be able to make rent, or keep the heat on, or keep the pantry full."

"Say more about why."

"Same type of guys that own the businesses own our apartment buildings. They set the wages and the rent, just so. They want to keep us jiving and checking, keep us poor and struggling day to day."

"So we don't have time to think," Bobby said.

"So we don't have time to get together and rise up."

Out the corner of my eye, something went creeping. A rabbit or a fox, most likely. Something I couldn't turn my head fast enough to see.

But I did turn my head, away from the hinge gap into the darkness. I became aware then of the stark black air behind me. The new moon cast blankness over everything.

The house loomed up as a shadow in the foreground, miles of fields beyond. Miles of road beyond that, I supposed, and on into the cities.

What must it be like? I wondered. And in the breath behind that: *Why have I never wondered before?* I had seen so much of the city in the newspapers and on television, but I had never really wanted to go.

"What'chu doing?" said Bobby's voice behind me.

I jumped about a mile.

He laughed as I turned to face him. "We're even now. You about scared me into tomorrow. Hiding here in the dark like that." His silhouette against the light from inside the barn made it hard to see his face.

"Oh, uh—" I stammered. "I was just coming to, I mean—" Sighing, I gave up the ruse. "I kind of just wanted to listen."

"Sure, sure," Bobby said. "I just had to . . . you know." He shuffled. "Step out to the field for a second. I'll be right back."

I lingered behind the open doorway, out of sight of the rest of the Panthers. Bobby came back a minute later. I could hear the scratch of him zipping up his pants. He stopped a few yards short of me and flung his arms out in the country air. He tossed his head back and gazed at the sky.

"Whew," he said. "How'd you hook up all these stars?"

I stepped out into the grass to join him.

"Don't you have stars in Oakland?"

"Barely," he answered. "Too much light from the buildings. I've never been in a place this dark. With so much open space. It's amazing."

"You don't get outside of Oakland so much?" I asked. Maybe we had that in common.

"I've never been out of Oakland," he said.

We stared at the stars together. Bobby nudged his foot toward mine and ended up stepping on my bare toe. "Ow," I said.

"Sorry!" He put his hand out, as if to soothe something, and came up holding mine. "I didn't know you don't have shoes on."

I always went barefoot. I couldn't imagine not touching the earth. On TV, the cities looked dirty and crowded, but not the kind of dirt you wanted to let touch your feet.

But never mind my feet. Bobby was holding my hand. He slid his fingers between mine. The places where we were touching felt warmer than anything in the world.

"What's it like in Oakland?" I asked him. "I've never been to a place where you have no space and it doesn't get dark and you can't see any stars."

"You can go into the park at night," he said. "You just gotta watch out for pigs and whatnot."

"You have pigs in the city?"

Bobby's shoulders pitched forward, following his laugh. "Not those kind of pigs. It's what we call the police." He snorted three times quick. "Swine. The lowest of the low. Filthy. Greedy. Getting fat off the scraps of everyone's table. Politicians. Businessmen. Government. The Man."

I got a little offended on behalf of my pigs. "That's just mean," I said. "They're real sweet animals."

Bobby laughed again. "I never seen a real pig before," he said. "So I guess I can't rightly judge."

He was still holding my hand. Warmth radiated up my arm. He pulled lightly, moving toward the barn again. "I gotta get back. You coming in?" he asked.

"No," I said. "I'll get in trouble." Right away I wished I hadn't said it that way. I would have preferred for Bobby to think I was my own person. But Daddy was the one I had to live with.

"Your dad?" Bobby said.

I nodded. "He doesn't want me to talk to any of you."

Bobby nodded too. "My mom took a lot of convincing. But in the end, she knew it was right, what the Panthers are doing. Protecting the community. Educating and empowering people." He tilted his head. "Your dad's already involved, though, so what's the holdup?"

Bobby was talking like I was going to join the Black Panthers or something. "I just wanted to listen, that's all."

He smirked. It was dark, but I could feel it. "That's how it starts."

"There's no Black Panthers out here anyway," I said.

Bobby waved his arm. "You got a barn full of them right now."

"Ha-ha."

"I'm serious," he said, his hand warming mine in the night-time breeze. "Come to Oakland. We've got plenty of friends you can stay with."

"No," I said. "There's no way I could do that." But the thought burrowed right into my mind, deep into the place of dreams and visions.

6.

Panthers sprawled, asleep, on our couches. Our rugs. Panthers in our barn, huddled around a blaze of sticks in a bucket.

All the things on TV felt closer now. I could feel their presence, sleeping beneath me.

I was not afraid of the guys themselves, but of everything they represented. The world, and all the shadow things about it.

I got out of bed and stood at the window, looking out over the fields and the trees and the lane.

Why don't I go past the end of that lane? I never really gave it any thought before.

Maybe because it's not safe out there.

7.

Gunshots ringing through the fields startled me awake. I scrambled out of bed and flew into the hallway. I made it half-way down the stairs before I remembered we had houseguests. Couldn't go running outside in only my nightie.

I dressed quickly and ran out back. The Panthers were gathered in formation, doing target practice in the middle of our field. Tin cans were lined up on the rail fence. Bull's-eyes were buttoned to trees.

Daddy was out there, talking them through it. He had his coveralls on, but no chaw grass in his mouth, which was unusual. Apparently he had a lot to say to the Panthers, which was also unusual. I crept closer to try to hear, but in the open field, I couldn't get too close without him seeing.

This is why they had come, I realized. You couldn't go around playing target practice in downtown Oakland. The Panthers needed guns to protect people in their community, and we had the space to learn to use them. Daddy moved along the line, helping some of them with their stance and hand position. Torry helped the others. He had served, I got the feeling, like Daddy, long ago.

I got closer than I thought I might. Daddy was absorbed in talking through the proper function of a rifle. About half the guys had rifles. The guys holding shotguns and pistols were waiting their turn to try. Bobby pulled away from the pack and came toward me. "Hey, Sandy." He had a shotgun in his hand.

Daddy looked up over the rifle, through the crowd of boys, and met my eye. He didn't say anything. Didn't have to. I took two steps back, and I was grateful he didn't call me out in front of the guys.

"I can't stay," I told Bobby. "I'll get in trouble."

He shrugged. "Can't help trouble. When you're a Panther, trouble finds you." His voice contained so much right then. Sadness, resignation, excitement, terror, hope. I hugged my arms against my chest and tried to smile.

"You wanna hold it?" he said, flipping the rifle around vertical and holding the barrel out to me. "It ain't loaded yet."

"No, no," I stammered, choking my way toward a reason. I already knew how to hold and fire a rifle, but that was beside the point. I settled for the basic truth. "Then I'll really get in trouble."

8.

I moved through the kitchen to a sound track of guns being fired. After an hour or so, it cooled from constant discharge to occasional. I fired up the griddle.

Bobby came in while I was stirring pancake batter. I'd just cracked the eggs, so my hands were a mess. He saw me working the faucet with the edge of my palm and he reached around me. The water flowed cold. I scrubbed quickly, but not too quickly, seeing as his arm was still around my back.

"Thanks."

"You got something I can eat?" he said.

"I'm making breakfast."

He peered into my bowl and frowned. The batter looked, at the moment, like a lumpy white soup. "That's gonna be a thing?" he asked.

I gave him the look he deserved for that comment. "Haven't you ever been in a kitchen before?"

He scratched his head. "I brung in some groceries for a girl one time."

I couldn't help but smile at that one.

9.

Bobby held the platter while I stacked up pancakes. He ran his mouth about a mile a minute, talking up the Panthers and all the things he was learning. Every other sentence was "Huey says *this,*" or "Bobby says *that.*"

"You've got the same name as one of the founders?" I asked. Huey Newton and Bobby Seale were the founders of the Black Panther Party. Since the movement had started in Oakland, this Bobby knew them personally.

"Yeah, but I'm way cooler," he said. Then he laughed. The sound splashed through the air like a ripe berry bursts on your tongue, with something sharp as rhubarb behind it. "Nah, I'm not. Bobby and Huey, man—" He shook his head. "Doesn't get cooler than them."

"Why are you in the Panthers?" I wondered if he would think me stupid for asking. We were black. There were enough reasons.

He shook his head. "A hundred reasons, you know?"

"What's one?"

It was strange. I could ask these things and he'd answer.

"My best friend got beat down," he said. "Oakland pigs."

"Is he okay now?"

Bobby's gentle eyes flamed for a second. "Okay as you get after a thing like that."

I think of the guys our age out in the yard. Imagine one of

them falling. Bleeding. Cowering under the beat of a baton. "Is he here?"

"Naw. He comes to Panther class with me sometimes." Maybe Bobby read the question in my eyes, because he added, "Political education class. That's mostly what we do. Learn about history and politics. Economics. The way the world works."

I thought back to the things Torry had talked about in the barn. "Like last night?"

"Pretty much."

"So why isn't he here with you?"

"He's still got scars, ya know?" Bobby said. "Walks with his head down. I try to tell him chin up, but it ain't that easy, right? That shit takes a toll."

I nodded like I understood.

"He's down with the Panther cause and all, though. Empowerment. Helping people around the neighborhood. Bringing people together, ya know?" He thumbed toward the backyard. "But now I'm at the next level." Bobby juggled the pancake platter. "It takes some stones, ya know? To arm up and everything."

"Stones?"

He looked embarrassed. "Like, courage, right?"

"Sure."

"Yeah, you know what I mean." He glanced me over. "You look like the courageous type of girl."

"You think?" I wasn't sure I'd ever done anything courageous. I always did what I was supposed to. Courage, I thought, meant breaking the rules. Putting yourself on the line. There was a line somewhere, I knew. I'd just never come up on it.

10.

"These boys," Granny said. "These boys." She sat at the kitchen table, wrapping and unwrapping a fistful of twine, rocking her shoulders in a slow, sad rhythm.

"It's okay," I told her. "They won't be here much longer." I would have tried to keep the strange sorrow out of my voice, but it crept in there without me knowing.

"They strung him up by the neck, you know," Granny said.

"Who?" I said.

"My Petey."

She was confused again. "Granddad?" I confirmed. "He died of pneumonia, remember?"

"No, baby," she said softly. "He didn't."

The oven was hot. I slid in the pan with the roasts—fat and juicy. They were going to be good.

"What are you talking about, Granny?" The *fump* of the oven door punctuated my question.

"They strung him up," she whispered. "Uppity, they called him. He wrote articles, you know. He riled people up something fierce in his day, my Petey. When he talked, people stood up and listened. Came from miles around."

"Granddad was an activist?" I said. That didn't sound like anything I'd heard before.

"The neighbors cut him down. Brung him home to me," Granny said. "Ada and I, we wrapped him for the ground ourselves."

Her voice was like fingers, snaking back in time. She got confused sometimes, but other times she rose above her own mind and found clarity. Here and now, I believed her.

"That's when I moved my boys out west. You can carve your own stake out here, Petey always said. That was his dream. So we went on and lived it." She murmured to herself, to the string. "It's been a good life. Quiet. So quiet."

"Not so quiet now," I said. "But it's only one more day."

"And the day after that, and the day after that," Granny said. "The tomorrows keep on coming."

I sliced the tips off the string beans, two by two. Daddy entered the frame of the kitchen window, leading Ember out of her pen toward the barn.

How did Granddad really die? I wanted to run out to the field and ask him, but I couldn't. I knew I couldn't. Daddy had a wall around him, and questions like that stood no chance of getting through.

He patted Ember's neck, whispered something in her ear. He once told me the cow was named Ember "because I always wanted something to burn." Him saying that lit a thousand questions in me—all, to this day, unspoken.

"I wanted him to be like me," Granny said. "But he more like his daddy."

II.

"You'll want to get going," Daddy told the Panthers over dinner. "Sun's setting in an hour or two."

"We drive after dark," El said.

Daddy's leg twitched, uncomfortable. "Thought you didn't go looking for trouble."

"We're citizens, abiding the law," El said. "No curfew on the books for white America. We ought to impose one on ourselves?"

"It's just good sense," Daddy mumbled.

"Depends on your kinda sense," El said. "I gotta change my life around so I don't get wrongfully shot? What kinda sense is that? That's the mentality we're in this to change."

Daddy got quiet then. We never rode in the truck at night. Never went into town at night. Why would we? You did your business in the daytime.

I went out to the porch and looked down the lane. Crows flew low above the avocado trees, silhouettes against the sunset sky. I knew they were crows, same way I knew it was avocado trees. This was my land. My lane.

I didn't have to fight. Might never have to.

But what if I wanted to?

12.

Bobby looked good, standing there on my porch, even though I knew it meant he was leaving.

"I'll see you in Oakland," he said, and I leaned forward then, because I thought he might throw his arms around me or something. But he didn't. He smiled, though. That broad, lazy spread of lips and teeth. Familiar now.

He bounded down the stairs, out to the procession of waiting cars. He joined the good-natured scuffling over who got to ride shotgun. Maybe "riding shotgun" meant something different in the Panthers. Like in the Old Wild West. I pictured Bobby hanging out the window, rifle loaded and cocked.

My veins thrummed, straining out of my skin. The cars were not so full. I could fit there, in the middle, between Bobby and El.

Doors slammed. Engines roared.

They drove off into the wide empty sky. No clouds. No birds. Just restless laughter through the open car windows and the sound of tires on dirt.

Arms came out the windows. The cars honked and the passengers waved. I threw both arms over my head. My feet itched to run. I took the two steps down to the dirt road and chased after as the procession snaked away beneath the arms of the avocado trees.

I ran until I could no longer see them, until the cars took the turn at the end of the drive.

The walk back to the house took ages that day. I stood on the porch, looked down the lane. Waited for the churned-up dirt to settle back over the fields. I stayed and watched until the sun went down—all the way down, till the air was black and Granny started calling for her supper. I stayed out there till I couldn't anymore, and that dust cloud never faded.

🎭 Author's Note 🎭

I have researched and written about the Black Panther Party for about ten years. My novels *The Rock and the River* and *Fire in the Streets* feature teens who explore the Panther movement in 1968 Chicago. The Black Panther Party was founded in Oakland, California, in October 1966 by Huey Newton and Bobby Seale, two black college students who had grown frustrated with the slow progress of civil rights change throughout the United States. They believed that the civil rights movement's efforts to overturn segregation laws did not fully address the needs of struggling people in urban communities. Huey and Bobby developed a plan for addressing the core problems in their community, issues such as economic injustice, insufficient education, hunger, underemployment, and police brutality. They brought together a group of like-minded young men and women to organize, educate, and empower people in Oakland to defend their civil and human rights. The Black Panther

Party's Ten-Point Platform and Program outlined their specific goals and demands for equal treatment and opportunity for all. Each point articulated one concrete point of action within the Panthers' overarching vision for "land, bread, housing, education, clothing, justice, and peace."

The Panthers quickly became controversial because their strategy involved armed self-defense against police brutality and white-supremacist aggression. They monitored police activity in their neighborhoods and sought to ensure that the law was being properly upheld, rather than abused by people with power. The Panthers' values and tactics energized thousands of young people around the country who had become disillusioned by the passive-resistance approach of the traditional civil rights movement. Within a few years, the Panthers had chapters in more than forty cities around the country. They operated schools, community centers, food programs, health clinics, and more — all free of charge to people in need. Their energy changed the course of the civil rights movement significantly. My next book project, *PANTHERS! The History and Legacy of the Black Panther Party in America,* explores the Panther movement in depth. The issues they raised and the forces they fought against still trouble our society today, and as we continue to address these struggles in our midst, there is much we can learn from those who have gone before.

The Whole World Is Watching

Robin Talley

W E'RE RUNNING. ALL OF US. THE hippies in their dirty clothes. The protesters with handkerchiefs tied around their faces. The marshals with their bullhorns. Everybody's running.

"Come on!" my boyfriend, Floyd, yells beside me. "The pigs are still after us!"

I pump my legs, grass and gravel pounding through the thin soles of my loafers. I'm gasping for breath. I can't run any faster than I already am.

"We've got to keep moving, Jill!" Diane shouts as she catches up to us. Even in this madness she manages to look down and roll her eyes at where my hand is linked with Floyd's.

"Yeah, those pigs move faster than you'd think with those stumpy little legs of theirs!" I yell.

Floyd laughs. Behind us, Tom chortles as he pants to keep up.

I glance back over my shoulder. All I see behind my friends is chaos. Everyone's scrambling to get away from the police, tripping over roots and rocks.

Now that we've reached the trees, there are only a handful of officers left in the pack. The rest must have stayed back by the rally at the band shell. There were still plenty of people to club there.

It's been like this all week. My friends and I drove in from New York on Friday, and ever since, we've been running. Thousands of us are in Chicago protesting at the Democratic National Convention—it was the one real chance we might have had to stop the war in Vietnam—but to the police, "protest" means "time to beat people over the head."

"Look out!" Tom shouts. Diane, Floyd, and I duck just in time. A rock sails over my head.

"What the hell?" Diane yells, looking behind us. A hippie wearing an Indian headband sees us and shrugs.

"Shit, sorry, sister," the hippie calls. "I was aiming for the pigs."

"What pigs?" I look ahead to where the hippie is pointing. Two cops are running, dodging through the trees toward a group of boys who look like they might still be in junior high school. The boys are yelling insults at the cops and holding handkerchiefs over their faces.

"Hey!" I shout to the police. "Don't you have anything better to do than beat up on little kids?"

The officers ignore me, but the boys look my way. The cops see that they're distracted and move faster, lifting their clubs to strike. The boys turn to run, the police hard on their heels.

I had to open my big mouth.

"Shit," Floyd says. The boys and the officers run behind

a cluster of trees and out of sight. We all slow to a stop except Diane. She takes off for the edge of the trees, her light-brown braid bouncing. For a second I think she's going after them, but then she trots back toward us.

"The kids got away," she reports. "The pigs moved on to somebody else."

"Well, isn't this just swell." Floyd drops my hand and runs his fingers through his long blond hair, his eyes sweeping across the crowded park. The officers who were chasing us must have gone off after someone else too. The only police I can see now are walking toward the outskirts of the park or back to the rally site.

Grant Park is huge, sprawling along the shore of Lake Michigan. The band shell where our rally just ended is at the north end of the park, but the cops chased us south, toward the bridges that connect the park to the rest of the city. I wonder how many people are still at the band shell now that the afternoon sun is starting to get low. The protest leaders said we were at least five thousand strong today.

"What the hell was that about?" Floyd says. "I know the pigs don't need an excuse, but come on, it was a damn *peace* rally."

"Something happened at the flagpole." Tom tries to put his arm around Diane's shoulders, but she shakes him off. "Some dude tried to take down the flag, or burn it, or something, so the bastards came down on all of us."

"And then they went ape," Diane says. She's talking to Tom but looking at me. She's watched me like an obsessive hawk ever since I took up with Floyd. I knew she would, but I didn't know how guilty it would make me feel.

"Are they still having the march?" I ask Tom. He's an officer in Students for a Democratic Society, so he's plugged in with the marshals who are organizing the protests. "Or did the pigs make them cancel?"

"People are still lining up on Columbus, but they don't have a permit yet," Tom says. "They say they're going all the way to the Amphitheatre to protest the peace plank getting voted down."

We all look down. We'd been so sure the plank would pass. I didn't want to believe there are people who don't want the war to end, but I guess there are, and I guess a lot of them are Democratic delegates.

They've been voting all day at the Amphitheatre, five miles south of the park. That's where the actual convention is happening. The delegates are shuttling back and forth from the Amphitheatre to the glittering hotels lined up on the other side of Michigan Avenue. Hiding in their sky-high penthouse suites, it's easy for them to pretend we don't matter. Even though we're shouting right under their feet.

"Let's go," Floyd says. "I'll show those pigs at the Amphitheatre where they can stick their peace plank."

Diane rolls her eyes, but Floyd doesn't see her. She's never thought much of Floyd. To be honest, neither had I. Not until a few weeks ago.

A group of hippies passes us. One of the men knocks me with his elbow by accident. He turns, sees me, and nods, his lip twitching with surprise. "Sorry about that, sister."

"It's all right." I resist the urge to roll my eyes too. No one calls Diane "sister," but I've gotten it a dozen times a day since we've been here. I think it's because there are hardly any other Negro girls around.

No, not *Negro girls*. I'm supposed to say *black women*. It's been nearly a year since I left Tennessee, but I'm still getting used to how people talk up north.

I learned most of it from Diane. She's white, and from Ohio instead of the South, but she showed up on our first day at Barnard College just as green as me. She figured out how to fit in faster, though. Her dorm room was right next to mine on our freshman corridor, and we became best friends the day we moved in. There was something about the warm look in her green eyes that made it impossible not to trust her.

I was so nervous those first few weeks of college. I'd never seen that many white girls in cashmere in all my life. But by our second day there, Diane already knew everyone. She introduced me around, and soon after that she introduced me to the men she'd met at Columbia too.

Later on, as Diane and I spent more time together, there were other introductions. It turned out there were things more startling than a dormitory full of white girls in cashmere.

"Are we really supposed to march all the way to the Amphitheatre, though?" Floyd says as we trudge through the trees. "That'll take for daggone ever. The convention will be over before we get there."

"Doesn't matter," Diane says. "The pigs will never let us out of the park to begin with."

"When did you get to be such a negative chick?" Floyd asks her as he loops his arm around my waist. Diane waits until his back is turned, then sticks out her tongue. I glance from side to side to make sure no one saw, even though I can't help giggling.

Maybe I shouldn't have linked up with Floyd as quickly as I did. I wouldn't have done it at all if my father hadn't decided to visit. He called me on the hall phone three weeks ago and said he hadn't seen me since Christmas and he wasn't going to wait any longer. He was driving all the way from Tennessee that very day, in his ancient Dodge with the brake lights taped up and the front bumper sagging. I knew he wouldn't be happy to see me with a long-haired white man, but that day, all I could think was that he'd never forgive me if he knew I was with a girl. Even with my fancy New York clothes and my natural hair and my white boyfriend, he'd still see me as his baby girl. If he thought I was going against the word of the Lord God Himself, though, that would be another thing altogether.

My father raised me to stay away from the police but to be polite if there was no avoiding them. *"Yes, sir." "As you say, sir." "Of course, Officer."* Daddy grew up in the height of Jim Crow, shuffling along in the street. In the world he knew, only whites walked on the sidewalk. If my father ever saw me running from a blue-helmeted police officer with his club held out to strike, he'd lock me in my old pink-ruffled bedroom until I was ninety.

I close my eyes and give my head a tiny shake. If Daddy knew where I was right now, he'd drive that old Dodge back up north again, charging straight over the curb and into the park. He'd throw open the passenger door, haul me into the car, and tear out of Chicago with the tires squealing.

The sun is fading fast. We're near Columbus Drive, so we can see the protesters lined up in the street. There have got to be thousands of them there already, filling the street as far as we can see in both directions, but it doesn't look like anyone's actually marching. They're all standing in rows, chanting.

"PEACE NOW!" most of them shout, holding up their fingers in the *V* sign. A new refrain is working its way back from the front of the line too: "DUMP THE HUMP! DUMP THE HUMP!"

The convention delegates are supposed to vote tonight on the Democratic nominee for president. Everyone knows it's going to be Humphrey. President Johnson has already kept us in Vietnam for four years, but Vice President Humphrey will keep us there another ten if he gets his way. And he will, now that the delegates have voted down the peace plank.

The Democrats had a chance to stop the war today, but they decided to be cowards instead. Now they're going to nominate a president who thinks peace is the same thing as weakness. We might as well just vote Republican.

I graduated high school last year in a class of fifty. Twenty-six girls and twenty-four boys. Since then, we've already lost three of those twenty-four boys to the war.

All three enlisted the first chance they got. Even before the war started, most of the boys in our town went straight into the military out of school; getting a scholarship to a faraway college was nothing but a crazy dream for most of us.

Two of those boys from my class died the first chance they got too.

The third boy simply disappeared. The best his parents can figure, he was taken prisoner. Reverend Taylor still prays with the congregation every Sunday that this will be the week Jesse comes home safe.

I don't pray anymore. I stopped last spring after I saw a photo in the paper of wounded soldiers being dragged through the jungle. One of them was writhing on the ground in pain. At the edge of the photo, one soldier had his arms raised to the sky. The newspaper said he was signaling for a helicopter to come get the wounded men, but to me it looked like he was shouting at God for leaving them behind. I wanted to shout at God too.

A new chant rises up from the crowd. "HEY, HEY, LBJ! HOW MANY KIDS DID YOU KILL TODAY?"

"Why isn't anybody moving?" Floyd says.

Tom shrugs. "Still waiting on the march permit, I guess."

"PEACE NOW!" The shouting from the crowd has changed back. "PEACE NOW! PEACE NOW!"

I nod along with them. There's something hypnotic about a good protest. Standing with dozens or hundreds or thousands of people who all want the same thing you do. Calling out for it together from the depths of your soul.

"I'm getting in line," I say. "Who else is coming?"

"I want to go talk to the marshals first," Tom says. "I can't believe they're serious about marching all the way to the Amphitheatre. They've lost their damn minds."

"Okay," Diane says. "You guys go and we'll wait here. We can meet up afterward."

It's a relief when Floyd unloops his arm from my waist and heads south with Tom. It's always a relief. At first being with him feels just fine, but then once he's gone I realize how much better things are without him.

It's starting to get dark as Diane and I wade into the crowd. She smiles big at me now that the men are gone. I check to make sure no one's watching us. Then I smile back.

I didn't even know women could be with women until I got to New York. I was in government class the first time I heard about it. We were having a discussion about feminism and what it meant for society. A bunch of the girls—women—in the class, mostly the ones wearing the cashmere sweaters, were saying feminism would destroy the family as we knew it. Another woman, who had long hair and wore sunglasses even though we were inside, kept saying, "No, no, feminism is the future, man, get it?" One of the women in cashmere—the one with the blondest, curliest hair—said, "So why don't you go try being one of those radical lesbian feminists, then, if you're so keen on it?" and the girl with the sunglasses said, "Yeah, I tried out the lesbian trip. I don't know if it's for me, but if you're curious, man, you should definitely give it a go." Everyone laughed nervously, and the teaching assistant dismissed us early.

That night I asked Diane if she knew what it meant to be a "radical lesbian feminist." We were smoking and listening to music in my dorm room, lying on the rug, staring up at the stained white ceiling.

Diane had already told me she was a feminist by then. This was our first semester, when the idea of being a feminist still seemed scary. It sounded almost as bad as being a communist.

"Yeah, I've heard people talk about it down at the women's collective," Diane told me. "They call it *existential lesbian feminism*. It's about teaching men a lesson. The only way they'll learn we don't need them is if we really don't need them for *anything*. Get it?"

I nodded slowly. *Existential lesbian feminism*. A political philosophy based around women having sex with other women. And I'd thought regular feminism was extreme.

I wondered how women *did* have sex with other women. Maybe they'd . . . oh. *Oh.*

I blushed harder with every passing minute. The political philosophy sounded crazy, but the women-being-with-other-women part didn't sound like such a terrible thing.

"I think I get it," I told Diane.

Two weeks later, Diane came over to listen to music again, and this time I definitely got it. We both did. It was amazing, actually.

I'd never felt about anyone the way I felt about Diane. I'd had boyfriends in high school, and I'd flirted with men at college parties, but what she and I had after just those first few weeks was something else altogether.

The problem was, by the time the spring semester started, Diane wanted to tell other people about it.

"The whole point of being a lesbian feminist is to prove a point to the man," she said.

"Is this seriously just about politics to you?" I asked.

"Well, no. I mean, I also like you. A lot. But the personal is political, get it?"

"Not this time, it isn't."

Diane and I had started hanging out more with Floyd and the rest of the Students for a Democratic Society crowd by then. The men in SDS were cool, but, well, they were men. One night after a meeting we stayed up late writing a Students' Bill of Rights. It started off serious, with things like "Ban the draft" and "Freedom of assembly" and "Respect all people." Then everyone started trying to be funny. The longer the night went on, the longer the list got. By the end Floyd and Tom had added "Free booze for all," "Free dope for all," and "Free women for all." Diane and I told them to cross the last one out, but they just laughed and said, "Girls never get jokes, man."

After that, Diane wanted to tell them about us more than ever, but I wouldn't let her. If men thought those sorts of things were funny, I figured that only proved they'd never understand about Diane and me. They'd never look at me the same. And their "jokes" would only get worse.

Diane and I slide into line with the other marchers gathered on Columbus Drive. A woman at the end of a row with dirty hair and a stoned-out expression smiles and makes the *V* sign at me. "Right on, sister."

"Right on," I reply, linking arms with her. Usually I stay away from the serious hippies—the ones who've been living on the streets so long they smell—but there are so few women here we've got to stick together.

Diane links onto my other arm. "Thank God we got rid of them. Floyd is driving me batty."

I stop smiling. "Take it easy on him, would you?"

"Oh, give it a rest. If you seriously like him, you should at least tell him the truth. Unless you want me to do it for you."

My heart thuds. "You wouldn't really. Would you?"

"No." Diane sticks her lower lip out in a pout. "Not unless you said it was all right. I need to know, though. Are you serious about him, or was this just a short-term thing while your dad was visiting? Because you know it isn't right to string him along like that. Any more than it is me."

The hippie woman next to me leans over. She's watching our conversation, her lip quirked.

"I don't know," I say, trying to ignore the hippie's breath on my neck. "It's complicated."

"You should've just lied to your dad," Diane says. "Did you think he'd somehow suspect you were a lesbian unless you proved otherwise?"

The hippie's jaw drops. I wish we'd found a different place to stand.

"You act like it's so easy." I try to keep my voice down so only Diane can hear. It's hard in the crowd, though. "You know it's not that simple. I care about Floyd, okay?"

Diane sighs. "Jill, I'm not asking you to break up with him. Just be honest. Tell him you're a lesbian."

I glance from side to side again. I wish she'd stop using that word. "Look, I don't even know if I *am* a lesbian. I don't believe in this whole philosophy the way you do. I don't think being with a woman proves anything except that it can be fun to be with a woman."

The hippie is gaping at us openly. Oh, well. It's not like *she's* going to tell anyone. Certainly not my dad.

"All right, then tell him *that*." Diane pulls her arm free from mine and throws her hands up in the air. "You act as if it's something to be ashamed of."

"Well it *is*, kind of," I say.

Diane turns to me, her forehead creased. "You're ashamed of me?"

"Not *of* you, just—" I shake my head. "You don't want your parents to know either. That's because they'd think it's wrong, isn't it?"

She shrugs and looks away.

"Even in New York, even *here*, lots of people think it's wrong," I say. "You really want to shout it out to the whole world?"

"No," she says. "Just to your boyfriend."

I sigh. "You really think he'd keep it to himself? The whole school will hear about it the next time he gets stoned at a party."

"And that would be so terrible?"

I shake my head. I don't know what to say.

"I just hate lying to our friends," Diane says. "Especially your so-called *boyfriend*. God, even that word, *boyfriend*. It sounds like such a lie. It's so *conventional*, and you're so *not*."

I want to argue with her. I was as conventional as they came before I left home.

Everything about life in New York felt so radical compared to what I'd known before. In New York, you can hear three or four different languages just walking down the block. Women wear pants every day. Black people and white people sit next to each other on the subway like it's nothing. There are student demonstrations every week for peace, for poverty, for civil rights.

I've only been there for a year, but that's enough to know it's where I belong. After Christmas break, I swore I'd never go back to Tennessee. I stuck around at Barnard for the summer session even though my father sent three letters pleading for me to come back. He's been terribly lonely since my mother died three years ago.

But I couldn't face that house again. My little brother, counting down the days until he's old enough to enlist. My grandmother, nagging me to get my hair done and to hurry up and find a husband so I can come back home.

The sky is so dim it's nearly dark. A new chant starts up at the front of the line. It echoes to the back so slowly we can't even tell what they're saying at first.

"Having a boyfriend isn't automatically *conventional*," I tell Diane. "I like Floyd."

"Do you really?" Diane says. "Do you love him?"

I laugh. "Now who's the conventional one?"

That's one of the things that's always frustrated me about Diane. She takes this all so seriously. Everything has to be a profound statement on something. If it isn't politics, it's love.

Floyd is a lot of things, but profound isn't one of them. Floyd's feet are flat on the ground. *Flat* is a good word for Floyd, generally. He's been pretty good about taking me out on dates and being nice to me at parties, but I can't shake the feeling that he likes the idea of dating the black freshman girl with the natural hair more than he likes the actual me.

I thought Daddy would be glad to see I had a boyfriend. A man to take care of me in the big city. It turned out I was wrong.

My father found some cheap hotel in Harlem, but he could only stay for two days before he had to get back to work at the factory. We went on the Staten Island Ferry and baked in the heat while my father looked at the city skyline and shook his head as though he didn't see what all the fuss was about. I ordered takeout from my favorite Chinese restaurant and we ate it on the floor of my dorm room, my father fumbling with unfamiliar chopsticks. His eyes darted across the rows of thick textbooks with complicated titles, the ashtrays scattered around the room, the stacks of albums with long-haired white men on their covers. He was trying, I knew, but he didn't understand why I'd chosen this world over the only one he'd ever known.

When I introduced them, Floyd was polite, respectful, friendly. He went to prep school in Massachusetts, so he knew to wear a tie and call my father "sir." But he didn't know not to put his hand on the small of my back as we crossed the street to the fancy restaurant he'd picked out for dinner. When he touched me, I swear I saw Daddy's heart break right in front of me.

"STREETS BELONG TO THE PEOPLE!" The new chant has finally reached us. "STREETS BELONG TO THE PEOPLE!"

I join in, shouting along with the others. The hippie girl does too, her voice low and gravelly.

Diane leans in to talk into my ear. I wish I couldn't hear her over the chanting, but I can. I could probably pick out Diane's voice in the middle of the Ho Chi Minh Trail.

"Tell me the truth," she says. "Tell me the real reason you picked him instead of me."

I sigh again, trying come up with some explanation about how much I like Floyd. Then I see Diane's face out of the corner of my eye. Her eyes are wide and pleading.

She wants the truth. She *deserves* the truth.

"Everyone would look at us," I say slowly. Diane blinks. For a second I think she didn't understand me, but then she starts to draw back, pulling her arm away from where it's linked with mine, and I know she heard. "If we were together for real. They'd stare at me everywhere I went. I'd know they were talking about me, and I'd know what they were saying."

Diane looks straight into my eyes for a long moment.

"That's what matters to you?" she finally says. "What people you don't even know say behind your back? What about what *I* think? Don't I count more than whoever walks by you on Riverside Drive?"

"Of course." I don't know what she wants me to say. I gaze down, which only reminds me of how disheveled I look. The sleeves of my blue button-down are wrinkled and stained. I fell in the dirt back at the band shell when the cops first charged. Diane stayed behind to help me up and got kicked in the leg by a cop for her trouble. "It's just—I don't know. It's complicated."

Diane pulls back again, like she's about to leave. I want to reach out and take her hand. I don't.

"WHOSE STREET? OUR STREET! WHOSE STREET? OUR STREET!"

The chant is getting louder. Angrier. Fists are waving in the air above us.

"They didn't get the permit for the march!" the hippie girl shouts next to us. "It's over!"

It looks like she's right. There's fury roiling in the front of the line, filtering its way to the back along with the chant. One of the marshals shouts into his bullhorn for people to stay calm.

"We should go!" I shout to Diane. At first she ignores me, but then she glances my way and nods.

I let go of the hippie's arm. Diane and I slip out of the line and into the trees with some of the other marchers.

"Let's try to find the others," Diane says. "I think they're up at—"

Behind her comes what sounds like a bomb going off. Then the screaming starts.

"Shit!" Diane yells. We both scrabble into the back pockets of our jeans for our bandannas. "Damn pigs! Nobody's even doing anything!"

This has happened at least a dozen times this week, but it's always just as scary as it was the first night. And it always, always hurts.

I tie my bandanna around my nose and mouth and swivel my head from one end of the park to the other. A white cloud of tear gas wafts toward us from the north. We can already smell the thick chemical odor. That means the pain is only a few seconds away. Behind the cloud there's a row of National Guardsmen wearing gas masks. They're advancing toward us. Gas spews into the air in long streams.

A man near us picks up a gas canister that's fallen to the ground and chucks it back toward the Guardsmen. Then a coughing fit overtakes him and he collapses to his knees.

Diane grabs my arm. We run together through the park, trying to outrace the white cloud, even though we both know that never works. Where there's one cloud of gas, more will follow.

Around us people are shouting, running, clutching cloths to their faces. The gas creeps into my eyes, my nostrils, down my throat. My lungs twist in on themselves. My cheeks burn. Tears roll down my face, leaving streaks behind them that scald my skin.

This isn't the same gas I've been breathing all week in Lincoln Park. This has to be stronger. Military-grade.

We run south, deeper into the park, but the gas only gets thicker. Diane is coughing so hard I don't know if she can run much farther. I blink against the pain in my eyes and scan the park for a safe place to wait it out, but the Guardsmen keep moving, their faces invisible behind their gas masks as they get closer and closer to us.

Whenever there are too many of us in one place, even if all we're doing is standing around, the pigs spray tear gas. They have their masks, but all we have are bandannas and handkerchiefs and Vaseline to spread on our cheeks, and even that barely makes a dent against the pain.

Diane stops running. She bends at her waist, coughing harder. Her eyes are squeezed shut. Her hand is pounding against her chest.

Oh, no. She's panicking.

"Move!" I yell, grabbing her arm and pulling her forward so hard she has no choice but to follow. She stumbles at first, but then we're running together, back toward what's left of the line of marchers. I cough harder, resisting the urge to wipe my eyes. I learned the hard way that it only heightens the pain.

The whole park is covered in the white haze. Our only choice is to take one of the bridges across Michigan Avenue toward the hotels.

My cheeks are on fire. I shift my bandanna higher and grab Diane's hand. She takes mine, still bent over, coughing, as I lead her to the closest bridge.

We're almost there when I see the rifles. No, machine guns. There are rows and rows of National Guardsmen lined up in front of the bridge with *machine guns.*

I think again about my little brother, so eager to run off to war. Machine guns are for soldiers fighting in the jungle. Not cops in the park here at home.

They've got the bridge blocked off. I guess we're supposed to stay here and breathe in the tear gas until we collapse.

"The Jackson bridge is open, man!" someone shouts behind

us. The crowd surges north. I scan the crowd for Floyd and Tom, but if they're here, I can't see them.

We shuffle toward the bridge with the rest of the crowd, the gas still rolling over us in waves. Diane hasn't let go of my hand. I squeeze hers without thinking.

It's chaos as everyone charges across the bridge. The gas thins out as we get away from the heart of the park, but it's still in the air, coating our skin, burning our throats. Diane's eyes are red and puffy. Her face is streaked with tears. I want to help her, to wipe her face clean and hold her until she feels better, but there are too many people around, and besides, we've got to keep moving.

It's getting dark as we approach the end of the bridge. Ahead of us, Michigan Avenue is full of people. The mood is different here than it was in the park. Protesters are milling around, talking. I even see a few smiles. There are cops in the crowd and the lingering memory of gas in the air, but the police on this side of the bridge aren't wearing masks. Maybe they're used to the smell.

Down the block, toward the Conrad Hilton hotel, where most of the delegates are staying, there are carts with mules pulling them. I thought I'd seen everything there was to see this week, but I never thought I'd see mules walking through the streets of Chicago. Diane is standing up straight now, looking recovered from the gas, and I'm about to point out the mules when I see Floyd and Tom. They're far down the block, close to the hotel. They've taken off their handkerchiefs. I take off my bandanna and shove it in my pocket.

There are a few hundred people between us, but we can catch up if we walk fast. The cops are moving out of the street and forming into rows on the side streets, so it's easier to make our way forward now. Diane is walking fast already, moving ahead of me through the crowd.

I raise my voice so she can hear me. "There's Floyd and Tom! Come on, let's catch up with them!"

Diane looks back over her shoulder at me. It's hard to tell from her face what she's thinking. She turns back, weaving her way through a group of hippies with peace signs painted on their faces, and shouts, "I don't think I can."

"What?" I don't think I heard her right.

She slows down enough to let me keep up with her, but this time she doesn't look at me.

"Jill." Diane shakes her head. "I like you, okay? You're funny and you're smart and you helped me get through the gas just now and you're one cool chick, but I don't think I can keep doing this. Not after what you said before. I get that it's complicated for you, but for me, it just hurts too much. When we leave here, you're going to have to find a new best friend."

"Oh, come on." I try to grab Diane's arm, but she pulls out of my grasp, darting through the hippies too fast for me to follow. "Diane! Wait!"

It's no use. Her light-brown braid is already vanishing behind a group of cops. It feels like I'm losing something I'll never be able to find again.

I start moving south toward the hotel, but I'm not eager to meet up with the others anymore. Is Diane going to tell them? No, she wouldn't do that. But what will the rest of the summer be like if we aren't even friends anymore? What about next year, and the year after that?

I'm still staring off at the spot where Diane disappeared when something sails over my head. Another rock. I turn to see who threw it so I can tell him to give it a rest, but the man behind me is standing with his arms folded. The sharp look on his face is enough to make me shut my mouth. This man doesn't look like a protester. He's wearing a sport shirt and slacks, and he's at least ten years older than most of the men here.

I wonder if he's a plainclothes officer. Tom said there were some mixed in with the crowd. But a police officer wouldn't have thrown a rock, would he?

Chants are rising around us. The murmurs and laughter in the crowd are fading. The cops Diane passed have moved out of the street and into a lineup. There are more cops here than there were before. It looks like there are more of them than there are of us.

"PEACE NOW!" a group near me starts shouting. They're holding up their fingers in the peace sign. "PEACE NOW! PEACE NOW!"

"PIGS ARE WHORES!" the man in the sport shirt shouts.

It's completely dark by now. Even with the streetlights it's difficult to see. I push through the crowd toward the hotel, but everyone is jostling, and it's harder to move than it was before.

"PIGS ARE WHORES! PIGS ARE WHORES!" More men have joined in the shout. I glance over at the cops. They're staring out into the crowd underneath their blue riot helmets and clear plastic visors. Their hands are locked on their clubs.

This doesn't feel right.

I'm only half a block from the hotel now. I try to move faster, but the crowd is making it impossible. The chants are changing again.

"DUMP THE HUMP!" one group shouts. Across from them, another group is trying to drown them out with "HELL, NO, WE WON'T GO! HELL, NO, WE WON'T GO!"

In front of me, a long line of protesters is standing with elbows linked. I duck under a pair of arms, holding up the peace sign as I go so they'll know I'm one of them and not a plainclothes cop. Not that there are any black woman cops in Chicago.

I'm almost at the hotel when I catch a glimpse of Tom and Floyd fifty feet ahead. I look around for Diane, but she's not with them. Floyd is arguing with a man wearing a vest. The man is holding something over his head. A bottle, maybe.

"Floyd!" I shout. Floyd looks around for me. When his back is turned, the man in the vest throws the bottle. It shatters on the pavement in front of the row of cops. Oh, God.

Floyd shouts at the man in the vest. The cops aren't looking at where the bottle fell, though. They're looking at something to their right, like someone's giving them a signal.

"SIT DOWN!" the protest marshals yell into their bullhorns. The other chants die out. "SIT DOWN! SIT DOWN!"

No one knows what to do. The people nearest the cops start to sit down on the pavement. I do too. So do Floyd and Tom. Some men stay standing, though, like the man in the vest. The man in the sport shirt stays up too. He's looking right at the cops, and he doesn't look afraid at all. He's got to be one of them. The man in the vest isn't, though. He's trembling, his eyes wide.

All at once, the cops are walking toward us, fast, like they have a purpose. They're all in neat rows. Hundreds of them.

They're getting closer. They aren't stopping. Are they seriously going to march right over us?

I scramble to my feet when the cops are nearly on us. Around me, everyone else is doing the same thing.

The cops don't slow down. I don't understand what's happening.

A vehicle barrels down the road. A paddy wagon. I'm staring at it, my mouth gaping, when a cop charges at me.

I scream. Everyone's screaming. The cop is coming straight at me, his club pulled back, ready to strike. All around him, the rest of the cops are running too.

I bend down, covering my head with my arms, and feel a rush of air as the officer runs past me. He brings his club down on the head of the parade marshal behind me, the one who was shouting for us to sit down.

They're everywhere. Every direction I turn. Cops, shouting. Cops, swinging their clubs. The marshal behind me is lying on the ground, blood pouring from his head. The cop swings his club down on him again and again, striking his chest, his back, his head.

Diane. I've got to find Diane. I dart my head from side to side, frantic, but it's impossible to see who's who in the darkened chaos. I've lost sight of Floyd too.

A man sprints past me, four cops on his heels. One of them strikes the man across his head. He collapses onto the ground. The cop charges toward someone else. Other people come running by, trampling the man on the ground. He cries out, but no one seems to hear him.

"Hey!" I shout. "This man needs help!"

No one seems to hear me either.

Everywhere I turn it's more of the same. People shout. Clubs wave in the air, then crash down onto heads and shoulders. Protesters are dragged through the streets by their arms or legs and then stuffed into the backs of the paddy wagons. Blood pours from their wounds.

Between the screams, people are shouting, "THE WHOLE WORLD IS WATCHING! THE WHOLE WORLD IS WATCHING!"

I look up. It's true. There are TV cameras pointed at us from the Hilton. I wonder if we're on live right now. If the delegates are watching us from the convention floor. Chanting might not change anyone's minds, but this—seeing this on their TV screens — *this* should make them see things differently. No one could watch what's happening here and say this is right.

Then I see Diane. I think it's Diane, anyway. From the back, it looks like her light-brown hair has come loose from its braid and is spilling over the collar of her denim shirt. A cop is running at her, but she's looking the other way.

"Diane!" I scream. I run toward her, ready to knock her to the ground to get her out of the cop's path.

I'm about to grab her when she turns. Only it isn't her. It's a boy, his eyes wide with fear.

I'm staring at him, my eyes just as wide, when a hand clamps down on my shoulder and yanks me back with a strong grip.

The cop swings me around to face him. He's tall and fat, his face spread into a grimace behind his clear plastic visor. His eyes are blue and beady. He looks straight into my face as he slams the club down onto my shoulder with all his strength.

I collapse to the ground, sprawled on my back. The pain shoots into my neck, my head, my arm. It feels like I'm on fire. A heavy boot crushes my hand, someone running past me without looking where he's going. I barely feel it.

My father was right about the police. I should have listened.

Above me, the cop lifts his club to swing again. I try to cover my body with my arms, but I can hardly move. I close my eyes and wait for the blow.

"Hey!" someone shouts above me. The club doesn't come down.

I open my eyes.

It's Diane. She throws herself in front of the cop, both her arms in the air.

"She didn't do anything!" Diane shouts. "Leave her alone! You already hit her!"

"She's with those longhairs!" the cop shouts.

"No she's not!" Diane shouts. She's standing ramrod straight. It would take a bulldozer to get her out of the cop's path. "She's with me!"

Maybe the cop realizes she's right, that I didn't do anything. Maybe he doesn't want to keep arguing over some black girl. Maybe he gets what Diane really means—that I'm *with* her, with her. Whatever it is, he shakes his head at Diane, like he's disgusted, and turns away. His club is still raised, ready to strike someone else.

"Come on!" Diane bends down and grabs my hand, the one the man's boot didn't crush. "We've got to get out of here!"

There's no way I can move. I'm certain of it. But when Diane pulls me up, somehow my muscles respond, peeling me off the pavement. I stare at her hand, at her face. She's the only thing in the world that makes sense right now.

"THE WHOLE WORLD IS WATCHING! THE WHOLE WORLD IS WATCHING!"

When I'm on my feet, Diane starts running, pulling me after her. Everyone around us is running east, back into the park, but Diane pulls me west, dodging protesters and cops and clubs. I have no choice but to trust her. I don't even know how my legs have the power to carry me. Around us, people are on the ground, moaning, bleeding. Cops are dragging more and more people through the streets.

Diane pulls me under an awning.

"Floyd," I mutter. "Tom. We've got to find them."

"I saw them when I was looking for you," Diane says. "They were running back into the park, but there weren't any cops after them. They'll be all right."

Oh. Floyd didn't wait for me.

All right, then. I guess I know where that leaves us.

Diane looks back over her shoulder. The pain is shooting down my side now that we've stopped moving. Diane loops her arm under my shoulders to prop me up. Her grip hurts, but I don't tell her that. It feels good to have her holding me, even with the pain.

"I can't believe it." I close my eyes and lean my head into her shoulder. The movement makes me wince. "You shouldn't have come back for me."

"I was going to come back anyway." Diane runs her hand over my hair. "I didn't know there was going to be a riot, though."

"I can't believe you tried to reason with that cop." I laugh. "And it actually *worked*."

She smiles. "I can't believe it either."

"You saved me," I say.

"Yeah, well. I wanted to keep you around." Her smile gets wider.

"Even after what I said?"

Diane shrugs, the light in her eyes fading slightly.

"I'll tell them," I say.

I think about Floyd, running off into the trees. I think about Diane, standing in front of that cop who would have been just as happy to bring his club down on her as on me.

"You don't have to do that." She looks away. "This doesn't have to be a trade."

"It's not about that." I shake my head and lay my hand on her chin. "It's about this."

I kiss her.

I kiss her right there, on the street, in front of the other protesters. In front of the cops. In front of everyone.

She kisses me back. We're both laughing, our faces filthy with dirt and tear gas, but it's the sweetest kiss of my life.

My body still aches, and the world around us is still nothing but chaos, but for that second, it doesn't seem to matter. It took something awful to make me realize it, but Diane means more to me than I ever wanted to admit.

And this isn't just about Diane. It's about me. It's about not always looking over my shoulder to see who might be watching. Not always thinking about who everyone else expects me to be. What *I* think of myself is what matters.

I don't know what's going to happen tomorrow. All I know is, in this moment, it feels like the whole world is watching me. And that's exactly what I want it to do.

❧ *Author's Note* ❧

The summer of 1968 was a tense period even before the Democratic National Convention got under way in Chicago. The Reverend Martin Luther King Jr. had been assassinated just a few months earlier. So had presidential candidate Robert F. Kennedy. In Chicago, the riots following Dr. King's murder had resulted in numerous deaths. When protesters announced their plans to hold demonstrations against the Vietnam War during the convention that August, Chicago mayor Richard Daley and other leaders called in extra police officers and the National Guard, trained them in riot-control techniques, and equipped them with Mace and tear gas in addition to their standard guns and billy clubs. The ten thousand protesters who gathered in the city were met with more than twenty thousand police officers and National Guardsmen.

Clashes between police and demonstrators were common throughout the weeklong convention. More than a thousand demonstrators and about two hundred police officers were reported injured, and nearly seven hundred protesters were arrested. Some plainclothes officers were later accused of inciting violence while disguised as protesters. Although police attacks against protesters took place throughout the convention week, the violence on the night of August 28 was broadcast on network TV, and it was that night's brutality that incited a national outcry. It became known as the "Battle of Michigan Avenue," and a government report later called it a "police riot."

Chilling video of what happened that night is available on YouTube. For a firsthand account of the entire week of protests, read John Schultz's book *No One Was Killed: The Democratic National Convention, August 1968.*

About the Contributors

J. ANDERSON COATS is the author of *The Wicked and the Just*, a 2013 YALSA Best Fiction for Young Adults pick and the winner of the 2013 Washington State Book Award for Young Adults, as well as a novel for younger readers, *The Many Reflections of Miss Jane Deming*. She lives near Puget Sound.

ANDREA CREMER is the *New York Times* and international best-selling author of the Nightshade series and the Inventor's Secret series. Andrea has always loved writing, but it took a horse and a broken foot to prompt her to finally write the novel she'd always dreamed of writing. Before becoming a full-time novelist, Andrea resided in the academic world, where she taught early modern history.

Y. S. LEE is the author of the award-winning Agency novels, a quartet of mysteries featuring a mixed-race girl detective in Victorian London. After earning a PhD in English literature, Ying realized that her true love was gritty historical detail—something she tries to make the most of in her fiction. She lives with her family in Kingston, Ontario.

KATHERINE LONGSHORE is the author of several historical novels for young adults, including *Gilt*, a story of friendship and betrayal in the court of Henry VIII, and the "*Downton*-esque" *Manor of Secrets*. Writing allows her to indulge her twin passions for history and travel while remaining at home with her husband and kids.

MARIE LU is the *New York Times* best-selling author of the Legend trilogy, the Young Elites trilogy, and *Warcross*. Before writing full-time, she worked as an art director in the game industry. She lives with her husband and dogs in Los Angeles, where she spends her time writing and getting stuck in traffic.

KEKLA MAGOON is the Coretta Scott King–John Steptoe Award–winning author of more than a dozen novels and nonfiction books for young readers, including *How It Went Down; The Rock and the River;* and *X: A Novel* (with Ilyasah Shabazz). Her books have been selected as ALA Notables, YALSA Best Books for Young Adults, *Kirkus Reviews* Best Books of the Year, and more. Kekla conducts school and library visits nationwide and teaches writing at Vermont College of Fine Arts.

MARISSA MEYER is the *New York Times* best-selling author of the Lunar Chronicles, a series of classic fairy-tale retellings set in the distant future (a long, long time after the Black Hills gold rush), and the novel *Heartless*.

SAUNDRA MITCHELL is a great lover of history. She enjoys manipulating it in fiction like *The Vespertine* and celebrating it in nonfiction like her new series, They Did What!? She lives in Indiana and thinks more people should write stories set there.

BETH REVIS is the *New York Times* best-selling author of the Across the Universe trilogy, *Star Wars: Rebel Rising*, and other YA books. She credits her father with fostering her knowledge and love of the Wild West and thanks him for fact-checking this story.

CAROLINE TUNG RICHMOND is the author of *The Only Thing to Fear* and *The Darkest Hour*, a YA novel set in Occupied France during World War II. A self-proclaimed history nerd, Caroline lives with her husband and daughter in the Washington, D.C., area—not far from several Civil War battlefields.

LINDSAY SMITH is the author of the Sekret series of paranormal spy thrillers set in Soviet Russia; *Dreamstrider*, a high-fantasy adventure; and *A Darkly Beating Heart*, a time-travel novel. She grew up watching far too many movies from the 1940s—from Abbott and Costello comedies to musicals to anything dazzling with old Hollywood glamour. Not one for California weather, however, she lives in Washington, D.C., with her husband and dog, and writes on foreign affairs.

JESSICA SPOTSWOOD is the author of the Cahill Witch Chronicles, a historical-fantasy trilogy, as well as the contemporary novel *Wild Swans*. She grew up near the Gettysburg battlefield but now lives in Washington, D.C., where she works for the D.C. Public Library system as a children's library associate.

ROBIN TALLEY is the author of *Lies We Tell Ourselves*, a finalist for the 2015 Lambda Literary Award for LGBT Children's/Young Adult, as well as the contemporary novels *What We Left*

Behind and *Our Own Private Universe* and the thriller *As I Descended.* Robin lives in Washington, D.C., where she enjoys being surrounded by history, though she's glad to be living in the twenty-first century.

LESLYE WALTON is the author of *The Strange and Beautiful Sorrows of Ava Lavender*, which was a 2015 Pacific Northwest Book Award winner and a 2015 YALSA William C. Morris YA Debut Award finalist, and *The Price Guide to the Occult.* She lives in the Pacific Northwest but has recently been finding her dreams filled with vast desert skies and the gorgeous pink flowers of the prickly pear cactus. Her short story is the result of those dreams.

ELIZABETH WEIN is the *New York Times* best-selling author of *Code Name Verity, Rose Under Fire,* and *Black Dove, White Raven.* All three feature women as pilots in the early twentieth century—such rare birds in their own right that a black woman among them is a veritable phoenix. "The Color of the Sky" is a closer look at one of the real pilots whose life inspired a character in *Black Dove, White Raven.*

Acknowledgments

———

Putting a book out into the world is always a team effort, but even more so with an anthology. I am enormously grateful to the following people:

Hilary Van Dusen, for her wonderful enthusiasm and guidance throughout this process. Miriam Newman, for her insightful line edits. Betsy Uhrig, for her brilliant copyediting. Nathan Pyritz, for the lovely interior design. James Weinberg, for the stunning cover design. Jamie Tan, for helping the book to find its readers. Jim McCarthy, for his stalwart support and excellent editorial matchmaking. April Genevieve Tucholke, for suggesting that I should try editing an anthology in the first place. Andrea, Beth, and Marie, for immediately saying yes, for title brainstorming, and for believing in me. Dhonielle Clayton, for her helpful notes on my story. Jill, for answering my random midnight copyediting questions and the occasional flailmail. Jenn, for being the best friend a girl could ask for. Steve, for fielding countless "Come read this— which sounds better?" editorial questions and for loving me even when I'm on multiple deadlines. My parents and grandparents, for instilling in me a love of history and for buying me all the books I wanted.

And especially: Jillian, Marie, Leslye, Andrea, Caroline, Beth, Marissa, Ying, Elizabeth, Saundra, Katy, Lindsay, Kekla, and Robin, for writing me such wonderful stories and then trusting me to edit them. It's been such a pleasure to work with all of you.

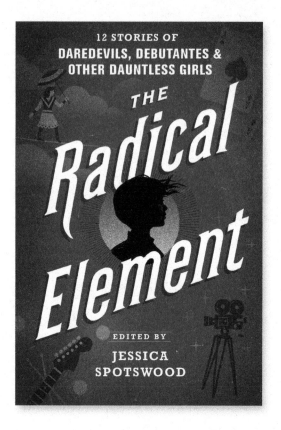